"No matter how intently
he searched her eyes,
he couldn't be sure
she wasn't lying.
Her fanciful
tale might be the
unvarnished truth..."
W9-CCM-575

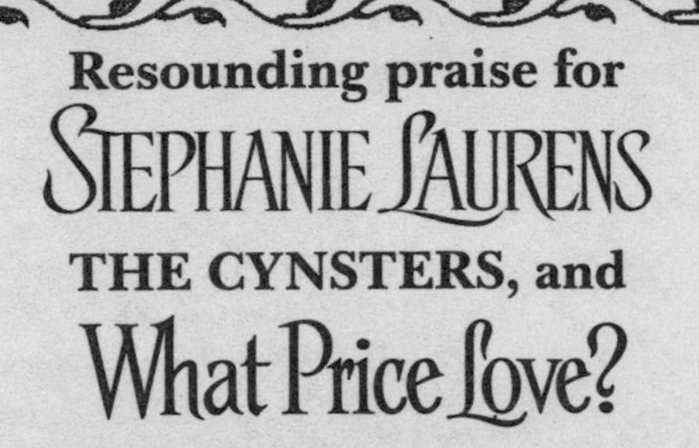

"Laurens's writing shines. . . .
[An] exceptional series."
Publishers Weekly

"A love scene written by Stephanie Laurens
is like an elaborate wedding cake: rich, decadent,
and covered in layers of intricate and
sumptuous treats. . . . Her stories are
well crafted, honest, and fast-paced. . . .
This book is particularly good. . . . Don't miss."
Columbus Dispatch

"Fascinating . . . lusciously sensual . . . Deftly laced
with passion and danger, *What Price Love?* is sexy,
suspenseful, and splendidly satisfying."
Booklist

"Once again, Stephanie Laurens has gifted readers
with a Cynster novel. . . . The book is vintage
Laurens: extra heavy on steam, with large doses
of romance and intrigue. . . . If you've liked other
Cynster books, you will really enjoy this one.
If you've never read a Cynster book,
you'll still enjoy it. . . . Irresistible."
Columbia State

"I'll buy anything with
Stephanie Laurens's name on it."
Linda Howard

By Stephanie Laurens

Cynster Novels

What Price Love?
The Truth About Love
The Ideal Bride
The Perfect Lover
On a Wicked Dawn
On a Wild Night
The Promise in a Kiss
All About Passion
All About Love
A Secret Love
A Rogue's Proposal
Scandal's Bride
A Rake's Vow
Devil's Bride

Bastion Club Novels

A Fine Passion
A Lady of His Own
A Gentleman's Honor
The Lady Chosen
Captain Jack's Woman

And in Hardcover

The Taste of Innocence

STEPHANIE LAURENS

What Price Love?

A CYNSTER NOVEL

AVON BOOKS
An Imprint of HarperCollins*Publishers*

This is a work of fiction. Names, characters, places, and incidents are products of the author's imagination or are used fictitiously and are not to be construed as real. Any resemblance to actual events, locales, organizations, or persons, living or dead, is entirely coincidental.

AVON BOOKS
An Imprint of HarperCollins*Publishers*
10 East 53rd Street
New York, New York 10022-5299

ISBN: 978-0-06-084085-3
ISBN-10: 0-06-084085-4
www.avonromance.com

First Avon Books paperback printing: February 2007
First William Morrow hardcover printing: March 2006

Printed in the U.S.A.

10 9 8 7 6 5 4 3 2 1

What Price Love?

The Cynster Family Tree

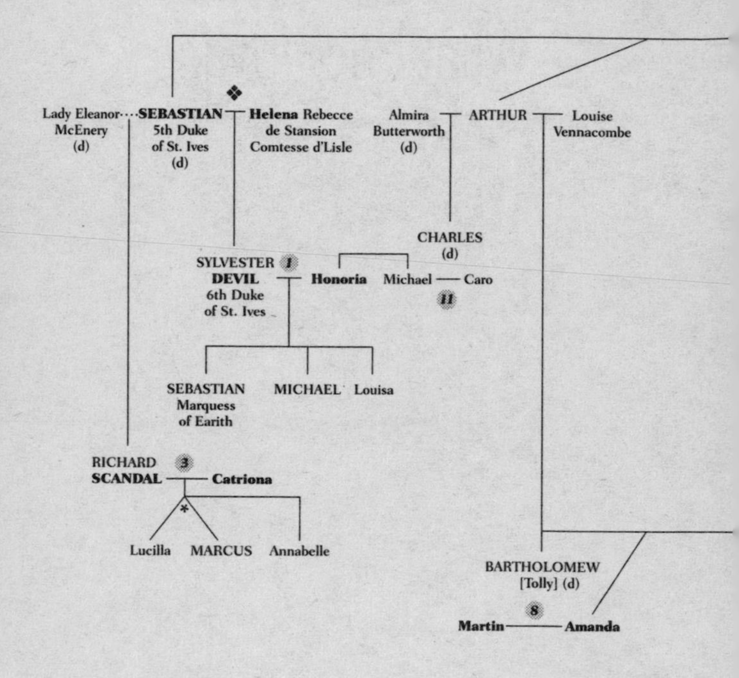

THE CYNSTER NOVELS

1. *Devil's Bride*
2. *A Rake's Vow*
3. *Scandal's Bride*
4. *A Rogue's Proposal*
5. *A Secret Love*
6. *All About Love*
7. *All About Passion*
8. *On a Wild Night*
9. *On a Wicked Dawn*

❖ *Special—The Promise in a Kiss*

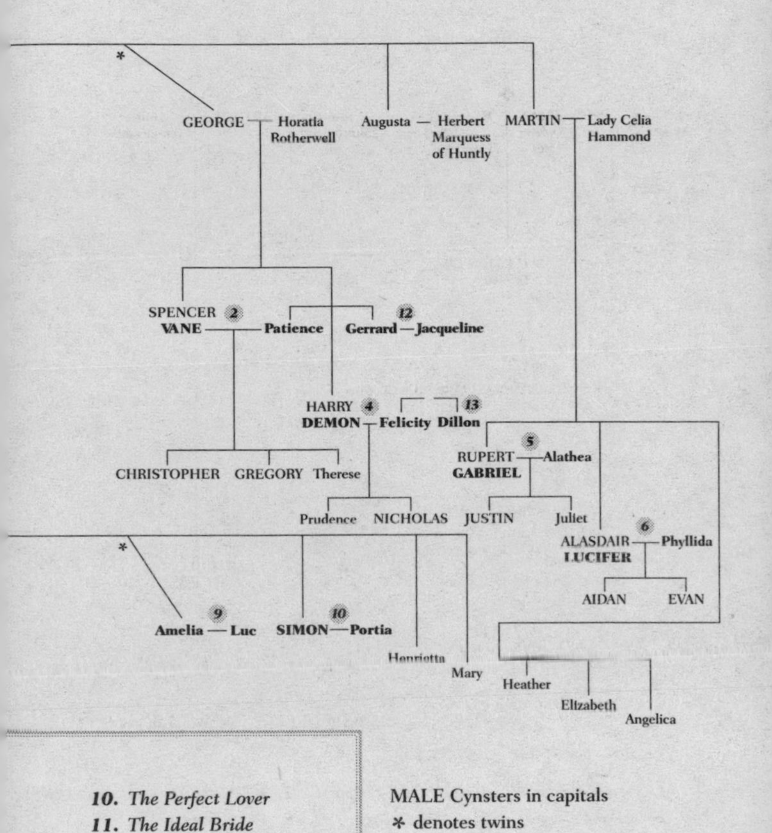

10. *The Perfect Lover*
11. *The Ideal Bride*
12. *The Truth About Love*
13. *This Volume*

MALE Cynsters in capitals
* denotes twins
Children born after 1825 not shown

Prologue

August 1831
Ballyranna, County Kilkenny, Ireland

"I'm looking for Paddy O'Loughlin."

Fronting the bar counter in the Pipe & Drum, Lady Priscilla Dalloway met the tavern keeper's arrested gaze and wished she'd thought to disguise her diction. But then she watched recognition flare in Miller's eyes and realized there would have been no point. She'd worn an old riding habit and a wide-brimmed hat, but there was nothing she could do to disguise her face; a veil wouldn't help gain Paddy O'Loughlin's confidence.

Miller, a beefy man with a round, bald head, continued to study her as if she might pose some exotic threat. Inwardly sighing, she leaned confidingly on the counter. "He's not in any trouble—I just want to talk to him." She'd softened her already soft brogue, but Miller didn't budge or blink; she infused a touch more persuasiveness into her tone. "It's just that my brother's now filling the position from which Paddy recently retired, and I wanted to know what Paddy could tell me about the work and the place."

That was all she was willing to reveal. She wanted reassurance as to Rus's well-being, but she wasn't prepared to air the Dalloways' dirty linen before Miller, no doubt as big a gossip as his peers.

Miller frowned, and glanced around.

It was two o'clock; there were three workmen farther along the bar, and a few scattered at tables, all glancing surreptitiously at the Quality miss who'd walked into their den. The barroom windows were small, their glass thick and wavy, admitting little light; the room was a medley of browns and greens, dingy and drab, with only the gleam of glasses and bottles on the wall behind the counter to fix the eye.

Miller eyed his other customers, then set aside the glass he'd been drying, stepped closer and lowered his voice. "You're saying young Lord Russell's up and taken Paddy's old job?"

Pris managed not to hiss through her teeth. "Yes. I thought perhaps Paddy could tell me about Lord Cromarty's stables." She shrugged as if it were perfectly normal for an earl's son to become an assistant stableman, and equally mundane for his sister to ride for two hours cross-country to inquire of the previous incumbent as to the conditions of his erstwhile employment. "I'm just curious."

And concerned over why a man like Paddy O'Loughlin would leave what should have been an excellent position. He was a local legend when it came to horses and horseflesh; he'd helped train a number of exceptional racehorses over the years. She hadn't met him, but had known he lived outside this village, known, therefore, where best to inquire for him.

Miller studied her, then angled his head at a large man in workman's garb nursing a pint at a table in the dimmest corner. "You'd best ask Seamus O'Malley. He and Paddy were best mates."

Pris's brows flew up at Miller's use of the past tense.

He nodded portentously. "Anyone can help you, it's Seamus." He stepped back, adding, "And if it were my brother in Paddy's old shoes, I'd ask."

Concern transformed to outright anxiety. Pris straightened. "Thank you."

Turning, she regarded Seamus O'Malley. She knew nothing of him. Quitting the bar, she walked across the room.

O'Malley sat hunched over a table, nursing a pint pot between work-roughened hands. Pausing beside him, she waited until his gaze rose to meet hers. He blinked owlishly at her, clearly recognizing her but at a loss as to why she was standing there.

Quietly, she stated, "I'm looking for Paddy O'Loughlin—Miller suggested I speak with you."

"He did?" Seamus shifted to peer at the bar.

Pris didn't turn to see. When, presumably reassured by Miller's nod, Seamus looked back at her uncertainly, she pulled out the second chair at the table and sat. "Miller said you knew Paddy well."

Seamus eyed her warily. "Aye."

"So—where is he?"

He blinked, then went back to staring into his almost full pot. "Don't know." Before Pris could prod, he went on, "None of us do. He was here one night, a sennight gone it was, and he ambled off home come closing time, like he always did. But he never reached home." Seamus glanced at her, briefly met her eyes. "The path to his cottage runs through the bogs."

Pris tamped down a sharp surge of panic, tried to think of some other interpretation, and couldn't. "You're saying he was murdered?"

Returning his gaze to his glass, Seamus shrugged. "Don't know, do we? But Paddy'd walked that path ten thousand times, man and boy, and he weren't even drunk—barely tipsy. Hard to swallow that he'd lose his way and die like that, but no one's seen hide nor hair of him since."

Cold dread welled in Pris's stomach. "My brother, Lord

Russell, has taken Paddy's old job." She heard her voice, steady but distant, was aware of Seamus's instant concern. "I wanted to ask Paddy about Cromarty's stables. Did he say anything about the place—about the people, the work?"

The expression on Seamus's face was a disturbing mix of worry and sympathy. He sipped, then in a low voice offered, "He'd worked there for three years. Liked the place well enough at first, said the horses were fine, but recently . . . he said there was something going on that he didn't hold with. That's why he left."

"Something going on?" Pris leaned forward. "Did he say anything more? Give any hint as to what the something was?"

Seamus grimaced. "All he said was that that devil Harkness—he who's head stableman at Cromarty's—was in it up to his ears, and that it, whatever it was, involved some register."

She frowned. "Register?"

"Paddy never said what register nor how it mattered." Seamus contemplated his beer, then looked at Pris. "I've heard tell your brother's a great one with the horses, but I ain't never heard him spoken of as one who'd tip a man the wink, nor be likely to nobble a horse, nor be involved in any other shady dealing. Lord knows Paddy weren't no saint, but if there were something going on at Cromarty's stables he couldn't stomach, then seems likely your brother might have difficulties with it, too."

Pris stared at him. "And now Paddy's gone."

"Aye. I'm thinking it might be wise to let your brother know." Seamus hesitated, then more gently asked, "He's your twin, ain't he?"

Pris nodded. "Yes." She had to work to strengthen her voice. "And thank you. I'll tell him about Paddy."

She started to rise, then paused and fished in her pocket. Standing, she slipped a silver sixpence onto the table. "Have another pint—for Paddy."

Seamus looked at the sixpence, then grunted softly. "Thank ye. And you tell that brother o' yours to watch himself."

Pris turned and strode out of the tavern.

Two hours later, she swept into the back parlor of Dalloway Hall.

Her paternal aunt Eugenia, a widow who had come to live with the family on Pris's mother's death seven years before, sat on the chaise calmly tatting. Curled on the window seat, Adelaide, Eugenia's orphaned goddaughter, now her ward, had been idly perusing a novel.

A pretty girl with glossy brown hair, two years younger than Pris's twenty-four, Adelaide looked up and set aside her book. "Did you learn anything?"

Grimly stripping off her gloves, Pris headed for the ladies' desk by the windows. "I have to write to Rus immediately."

Eugenia lowered her needles. "From which I take it you discovered something disturbing. What?"

Pris dropped her gloves on the desk, swung the heavy skirts of her habit around, and sat in the chair angled before the desk. Both Eugenia and Adelaide knew where she'd gone, and why. "I'd expected to hear that Paddy had had a fight with the head stableman, or something of the sort. I'd hoped his reason for leaving Cromarty's would be simple and innocuous. Unfortunately, it's not."

Across the faded splendor of the Aubusson rug, Pris met Eugenia's wise eyes. "Paddy spoke of something going on at Cromarty's that he couldn't stomach—that's why he left. And now he's disappeared—his friends think he's been done away with."

Eugenia's brown eyes widened. "Great heavens!"

"Oh, dear!" Hand rising to her throat, Adelaide stared.

Turning to the desk, Pris opened the drawer. "I'm going

to write to Rus and tell him he has to leave Cromarty's employ at once. If there's something bad happening with the horses—well, you know Rus. He'll get involved trying to put it right. But I don't want him in any danger, not if it's the sort where people disappear, never to be heard of again. If he can't bear to come home and deal with Papa, then he'll have to look for work training horses for someone else."

To her horror, her voice threatened to quaver; she paused to draw a steadying breath.

Rus had always been horse-mad. His one burning ambition was to train an Irish Derby champion. While she didn't share his enthusiasm, Pris fully understood the fervor of his dreams. Unfortunately, their father, Denham Dalloway, Earl of Kentland, had rigid views on what constituted an appropriate occupation for his son and heir, namely the care and management of the family estates. Breeding and training horses was all very well for others, the implication being others of lesser degree, but was an unacceptable occupation for the next Earl of Kentland.

Of the earl's three sons, Rus was the least likely to be satisfied with the role of county landowner as his sole focus in life. Like Pris, he took after their mother, more Celt than English, wild and dramatic and mercurially alive. Both twins could see the benefit in the estate being well managed, but estate management lacked allure. Luckily, their nearest brother, Albert, now twenty-one, took after their father—solid, dependable, stoic; Albert delighted in and would unquestionably excel at all aspects of estate management.

Pris, Rus, and Albert had always been close, as indeed all the Dalloway children were, but the other three, Margaret, Rupert, and Aileen, were much younger—twelve, ten, and seven years old, respectively—more to be protected than viewed as coconspirators. Even before their mother had died, the three eldest siblings had made a pact: Rus would do as their father wished and look after the estate until Albert returned from university in Dublin, then they would put their plan to their sire, that Albert should manage the estate in Rus's name while Rus devoted himself to establishing and running a racing stud.

It was a prescription for the future the three of them could happily follow and make work.

Two months ago, Albert had returned from Dublin, his studies at an end. Once he'd reacquainted himself with the estate, the three had duly put their plan to the earl—who had rejected it out of hand.

Rus would continue to manage the estate. If he had a mind to it, Albert could assist him. Regardless, however, no Dalloway would ever stoop to indulging in horse breeding on a commercial scale.

So declared the earl.

Rus had exploded. Pris and Albert quite saw his point; he'd curbed his driving desire and done everything their father had asked of him for seven years, and now felt he was owed a chance to live the life he yearned to live.

The earl had curled his lip and refused point-blank to even consider their scheme.

Words had been exchanged, things said, wounds dealt on both sides. Pushed beyond bearing, Rus had stormed out of Dalloway Hall in a wild fury. He'd taken nothing more than what he could cram in his saddlebags, and ridden away.

Seven days later, just over three weeks ago, Pris had received a letter to say he'd found work at Lord Cromarty's stables, one of the major racing establishments in neighboring County Wexford.

The schism between her father and brother was now deeper than it had ever been. Pris was determined to repair the rupture in her family, but the wounds would take time to heal. She accepted that. But with Rus gone, out of her world for the first time in her life, she felt truly alone, truly bereft, as if some part of her had been excised, cut away. The feeling was much more intense than when her mother had died; then she'd had Rus beside her.

She'd gone looking for Paddy seeking reassurance, something to soothe her growing uneasiness over Rus's safety. Instead, she'd learned Rus was in a situation where his life might come under threat.

Pulling a sheet of paper from the drawer, she laid it on the blotter. "If I write a note immediately, Patrick can ride over and deliver it this evening."

"Actually, my dear, before you write I daresay you should read this."

Pris turned to see Eugenia extracting a letter from beneath the endless fall of her tatting.

Eugenia held out the missive. "From Rus. It was delivered with the post after lunch. When he couldn't find you, Bradley gave it to me rather than leave it on the salver in the hall."

Where their father might see it. Bradley was their butler; like most of the household, his sympathies lay with Rus.

Rising, Pris took the letter. Returning to the desk, she broke her brother's seal, then, sinking onto the chair, unfolded the sheets, smoothed them, and read.

The only sounds in the room were the repetitive clack of Eugenia's needles, counterpointed by the tick of the mantelpiece clock.

"Oh, no! What is it? What's happened?"

Adelaide's agitated questions snapped Pris back to the present. Glancing at Adelaide, then at Eugenia, taking in their worried expressions, she realized her own must reflect her mounting horror.

"Rus has gone to England—to Newmarket—with the Cromarty racing string." She licked her suddenly dry lips and looked again at the pages in her hand. "He says . . ." She paused to steady her voice. "He says he thinks Harkness, the head stableman, is planning to run some racket that somehow revolves about horse breeding while in Newmarket. He overheard Harkness explaining to the head lad—Rus says he's a villainous sort—about how the illicit undertaking worked, and that it involves some register. He, Rus, didn't hear enough to understand the scheme, but he thinks the register Harkness was referring to is the register of all horses entitled by their breeding to race on English tracks."

She flipped over a page, scanned, then reported, "Rus says he knows nothing of the details in the register, but if he's ever going to become a breeder of racehorses, he should obviously learn more about it regardless, and he'll be able to follow it up as that register is kept at the Jockey Club in Newmarket."

She turned the last page, then made a disgusted sound. "The rest is full of platitudes assuring me he'll be safe, that it'll all be perfectly fine, that even if there *is* anything wrong, all he has to do is tell Lord Cromarty, and it'll all be right as rain, don't worry . . . and then he signs himself 'your loving brother off on an adventure'!"

Tossing the letter on the desk, she faced Eugenia and Adelaide. "I'll have to go to Newmarket."

Adelaide's chin firmed. "*We'll* go to Newmarket—you can't go alone."

Pris sent her a fleeting smile, then looked at Eugenia.

Her aunt studied her, then nodded, and calmly folded her tatting. "Indeed, dear. I see no alternative. Much as I love Rus, we cannot leave him to deal with whatever this is alone, and if there is some illicit scheme being hatched, you cannot, to my mind, risk even a letter to warn him, in case it falls into the wrong hands. You will need to speak with him. So!"

Folding her hands on the pile of tatting in her lap, Eugenia looked inquiringly at Pris. "What tale are we going to tell your father to explain our sudden need for a sojourn in England?"

One

September 1831
Newmarket, Suffolk

"I had hoped we'd have longer in reasonable privacy." Letting the door of the Twig & Bough coffee shop on Newmarket High Street swing shut behind him, Dillon Caxton stepped down to the pavement beside Barnaby Adair. "Unfortunately, the sunshine has brought the ladies and their daughters out in force."

Scanning the conveyances thronging the High Street, Dillon was forced to smile and acknowledge two matrons, each with beaming daughters. Tapping Barnaby's arm, he started strolling. "If we stand still, we'll invite attack."

Chuckling, Barnaby fell in beside him. "You sound even more disenchanted with the sweet young things than Gerrard was."

"Living in London, you're doubtless accustomed to far worse, but spare a thought for us who value our bucolic existence. To us, even the Little Season is an unwanted reminder of that which we fervently wish to avoid."

"At least with this latest mystery you have something to

distract you. An excellent excuse to be elsewhere, doing other things."

Seeing a matron instructing her coachman to draw her landau to the curb ten paces farther on, Dillon swore beneath his breath. "Unfortunately, as our mystery must remain a strict secret, I fear Lady Kershaw is going to draw first blood."

Her ladyship, a local high stickler, beckoned imperiously. There was no help for it; Dillon strolled on to her now-stationary carriage. He exchanged greetings with her ladyship and her daughter, Margot, then introduced Barnaby. They stood chatting for five minutes. From the corner of his eye, Dillon noted how many arrested glances they drew, how many other matrons were now jockeying for position farther along the curb.

Glancing at Barnaby, doing his best to live up to Miss Kershaw's expectations, Dillon inwardly grimaced. He could imagine the picture they made, he with his dark, dramatic looks most commonly described as Byronic, with Barnaby, a golden Adonis with curly hair and bright blue eyes, by his side, the perfect foil. They were both tall, well set up, and elegantly and fashionably turned out. In the restricted society of Newmarket, it was no wonder the ladies were lining up to accost them. Unfortunately, their destination—the Jockey Club—lay some hundred yards distant; they had to run the gauntlet.

They proceeded to do so with the glib assurance that came from untold hours spent in ton ballrooms. Despite his preference for the bucolic, courtesy of his cousin Flick—Felicity Cynster—over the last decade Dillon had spent his fair share of time in the whirl of the ton, in London and elsewhere, as Flick put it, keeping in practice.

In practice for what was a question to which he was no longer sure he knew the answer. Before his fall from grace and the scandal that had shaken his life, he'd always assumed he would marry, have a family, and all the rest. Yet while spending the last decade putting his life to rights, repaying his debts of social and moral obligation, and reestablishing himself, his honor, in the eyes of all those who mattered to him, he'd grown accustomed to his solitary existence, to the life of an unencumbered gentleman.

Smiling at Lady Kennedy, the third matron to detain them, he extricated himself and Barnaby and strolled on, casting his eye along the line of waiting carriages and their fair burdens. Not one stirred the remotest interest in him. Not one sweet face even moved him to curiosity.

Unfortunately, becoming known as a gentleman with a hardened heart, one unsusceptible to feminine enticements, had piled additional fuel on the bonfire of the ladies' aspirations. Too many now viewed him as a challenge, a recalcitrant male they were determined to bring to heel. As for their mothers, with every year that passed he was forced to exercise greater care, to keep his eyes ever open for social snares, those traps certain matrons set for the unwary.

Even those select ladies with whom he occasionally dallied discreetly in the capital weren't above hatching schemes. His last inamorata had tried to convince him of the manifold benefits that would accrue to him should he marry her niece. Said benefits had, of course, included her fair self.

He was beyond being outraged, beyond even being surprised; he was close to turning his back on the entire subject of marriage.

"Mrs. Cartwell, a pleasure to see you, ma'am." Taking the hand the haughty matron extended, he shook it, bowed to the vision of loveliness sitting beside Mrs. Cartwell, then stepped back and introduced Barnaby. Always interested in people, Barnaby exchanged platitudes with the lovely Miss Cartwell; cravenly grateful, Dillon stood back and let him have the stage.

Mrs. Cartwell was monitoring the exchange between her daughter and Barnaby, the third son of an earl and every bit as eligible as Dillon himself, with absolute concentration.

Reduced to the redundant, Dillon's mind returned to the matter he and Barnaby had retreated to the Twig & Bough to discuss, until they'd been ousted by the invading ladies. They'd chosen the quieter shop catering to the genteel element rather than the club coffeehouse favored by the racing fraternity for the simple reason that the subject of their discussion would set ears flapping and tongues wagging among the racing set.

Another racing scandal was precisely what he was working to avoid.

This time, he wasn't engaged on the wrong side of the ledger; this time, he'd been recruited by the angels, to wit the all-powerful Committee of the Jockey Club, to investigate the rumors of race fixing that had started to circulate after the recent spring racing season.

That request was a deliberate and meaningful vote of confidence—a declaration that the Committee viewed his youthful indiscretion as fully paid for, the slate wiped clean. More, it was a clear statement that the Committee had complete faith in his integrity, in his discretion, and in his devotion to the breeding and racing industry that the Committee oversaw, and that he and his father before him had for so long served.

His father, General Caxton, was long retired, and Dillon was now the Keeper of the Breeding Register and the Stud Book, the two official tomes that together ruled the breeding and racing of horses in England. It was in that capacity that he'd been asked to look into the rumors.

Rumors being rumors, and in this case issuing from London, he'd recruited the Honorable Barnaby Adair, a good friend of Gerrard Debbington, to help. Dillon knew Gerrard well, had for years, through their connections to the powerful Cynster family; Barnaby had recently assisted Gerrard in solving a troublesome matter of murder. When Dillon had mentioned the possibility of a racing swindle, Barnaby's eyes had lit.

That had been in late July. Barnaby had duly investigated, and in August had reported that while the rumors were there, all were vague, very much of the strain that horses people had expected to win had instead lost. Hardly a novel happening in the racing game. There'd seemed little substance, and no real fact behind the rumors. Nothing to warrant further action.

Now, however, with the first races of the autumn season behind them, something rather odd had occurred. Odd enough for Dillon to summon Barnaby back.

In the peace of the Twig & Bough, he'd related the details of three separate attempts to break into the Jockey Club, along with reports of some man asking about "the register" in local alehouses, rough taverns catering to the dregs of the town.

They'd just finished discussing what was known of the inquisitive man—an Irishman by his accent—when the influx of ladies had rousted them. Dillon's office in the Jockey Club was their current goal, the only place they might conclude their sensitive discussion in some degree of privacy.

But it was slow going. Escaping Mrs. Cartwell, they fell victim to Lady Hemmings. As they left her ladyship, Dillon seized the chance created by two groups of ladies becoming distracted by their own gossip to quickly steer Barnaby between two carriages and across the street. They lengthened their strides; by the time the ladies noticed they'd slipped sideways and escaped, they were turning into the long avenue flanked by tall trees that led to the front door of the Jockey Club.

"Phew!" Barnaby shot him a glance. "I see what you mean. It's worse than in London—there are few others about to draw their fire."

Dillon nodded. "Luckily, we're now safe. The only females ever glimpsed within these hallowed precincts are of the horse-mad sorority, not the husband-hunting packs."

There were no others, male or female, presently on the

path leading to the front door; easing his pace, he returned to their interrupted discussion. "These break-ins—if someone's asking about 'a register,' odds are they mean the Breeding Register, presumably the target of our would-be thief. Nothing else within the Jockey Club has any real value."

Slowing to an amble, Barnaby looked at the red brick building standing squarely at the end of the shady avenue. "Surely there are cups, plates, medallions—things that would be worth something if melted down? Isn't it more likely a thief would be after those?"

"Most of the trophies are plated. Their value lies more in what they represent, not in their commercial worth. And this thief's not a professional, but he is determined. Besides, it's too coincidental—someone asking about 'the register,' and shortly after, someone tries to break into the club where the one item referred to in Newmarket as 'the register' resides."

"True," Barnaby conceded. "So how is the Breeding Register valuable? Ransom?"

Dillon raised his brows. "I hadn't thought of that, but such a tack would be dangerous. Loss of the Breeding Register would stop all racing, so using it in such a way, essentially holding the entire racing fraternity to ransom, would very likely prove an unhealthy experiment. If the Breeding Register disappeared, I would expect to see it magically reappear within three days." He glanced at Barnaby. "This industry isn't short of those prepared to take the law into their own hands, especially over a matter like that."

Barnaby frowned. "But I thought you said it was the Breeding Register our would-be thief was after?"

"Not the register itself—the set of books—but the information it contains. That's where the gold lies."

"How so?"

"That," Dillon admitted, "is something I'm not *precisely* sure of—it's a function of what the information is to be used for. However, in light of our earlier rumors, one possible use leaps to mind."

He met Barnaby's blue eyes. "Horse substitution. It used to be prevalent decades ago, before they implemented the present system. One horse would gain a reputation for winning, then, in one race, the owners would substitute another horse, passing it off as the previous winner, and the punters would lose. The owners would be in league with certain bookmakers, and would pocket a nice cut from the lost bets, as well as pocketing even more from bets they or their friends laid *against* their 'champion' winning."

"Aha!" Barnaby's eyes narrowed. "Unexpected losses—as have been rumored to have occurred over the spring season."

"Just so. And that's where the Breeding Register comes in. It's an obligatory listing of a horse's bloodlines confirming its right to race on English tracks under Jockey Club rules. Bloodlines are fully documented in the Stud Book, while the register is essentially a licensing listing—every horse has to be approved and entered before being allowed in any race at any track operating under the auspices of the Jockey Club. *However,* along with the horse's name and general details, each register entry contains a physical description supposedly sufficient to ensure that a given horse, with given name, age, bloodlines, and racing clearance, can be distinguished from any other horse."

Dillon snorted. "Impossible to be a hundred percent certain always, yet armed with those descriptions, the race stewards at the tracks monitor all the starters before every race, and reexamine and verify all the placegetters after the race has been run. That's why horses have to be entered for races weeks in advance, so the stewards can be issued with copies of the descriptions each starter should match."

"And those descriptions come from the Breeding Register held here in Newmarket?"

"Making the stewards' copies is what my register clerks do, at least during the racing seasons."

"So why would our would-be thief be interested in the descriptions contained in this register? How would it benefit him?"

"I can think of two ways." Dillon looked ahead; they were nearly at the Jockey Club's door. "First, if his master was planning to substitute for a champion he owned, he'd need to be sure what points feature most highly in the register description, because the substitute horse would absolutely have to possess those points to make the substitution work."

Halting before the pair of shallow stone steps leading up to the club's double doors, he faced Barnaby. "The second possibility is that whoever has sent our thief is planning a new substitution, but hasn't yet located a suitable substitute horse. Scanning the descriptions in the register would take time, but would unquestionably identify the best possible match for a substitution."

He paused, then added, "Bear in mind that in a substitution racket, the substitute only has to pass the prerace check, which is the least detailed. Because the substitute finishes out of the places, it's not subjected to the more stringent check conducted after the race."

Barnaby frowned. "So what we might have here is an already established racket that ran certain substitutions last spring and escaped detection, plus an Irishman, presumably acting for some owner, looking to gain access to the Breeding Register to facilitate further substitutions."

Dillon nodded. "And as to whether the former is directly linked to the latter, logically there's no reason it has to be. But I'd lay odds they're connected."

Barnaby softly snorted. "It certainly has that feeling."

They turned to the club's front door. Both paused as through the central glass pane they glimpsed the club's doorman, inside, hurrying to reach for the latch.

Sweeping the doors wide, the doorman bowed obsequiously, almost tripping over his toes as he stepped aside to allow a lady to pass through.

Not just any lady. A vibrant vision in emerald green, she halted on the top step, taken aback at finding herself facing a masculine wall.

Her head, crowned with a silky tumble of blue-black curls, instinctively rose. Eyes, an even more intense emerald than her elegant gown, rose, too; widening, they locked with Dillon's.

Barnaby murmured an apology and stepped back.

Dillon didn't move.

For one incalculable moment, all he could see—all he knew of the world—was that face.

Those eyes.

Brilliant green, glinting gold, they lured and promised.

She was of average height; standing two steps up, her glorious eyes were level with his. He was dimly aware of the classical symmetry of her heart-shaped face, of perfect, very white skin, fine, almost translucent, of delicately arched brows, lush black lashes, a straight little nose, and a mouth a touch too wide. Her lips were full and blatantly sensual, yet instead of disrupting the perfection of her beauty, those distracting lips brought her face alive.

Like a callow youth, he stood and stared.

Wide-eyed, Pris stared back and tried to catch her breath. She felt like one of her brothers had punched her in the stomach; every muscle had contracted and locked, and she couldn't get them to relax.

Beside her, the helpful doorman beamed. "Why, here's Mr. Caxton, miss."

Her mind whirled.

To the gentlemen, he said, "This lady was asking after the register, sir. We explained she had to speak with you."

Which one was Caxton? Please don't let it be *him*.

Tearing her gaze from the dark eyes into which she'd somehow fallen, she looked hopefully at the Greek god, but fickle fate wasn't that kind. The Greek god was looking at his sinfully dark companion. Reluctantly, she did the same.

His dark, very dark brown eyes that before had appeared as startled as she felt—she doubted he often met ladies as dramatically beautiful as he—had now hardened. As she watched, they fractionally narrowed.

"Indeed?"

The precise diction, the arrogantly superior tone, told her all she needed to know of his social rank and background. The flick of inherent power brought her head up, brought the earl's daughter to the fore. She smiled, assured. "I was hoping to view the register, if that's possible?"

Instantly, she sensed a dramatic heightening of their interest—a focusing that owed nothing to the quality of her smile. Her gaze locked on Caxton, on the dark eyes in which, unless she was sorely mistaken, suspicion was now blooming, she mentally replayed her words, but could see nothing to explain their reaction. Glancing at the Greek god, she saw the alert look he sent Caxton . . . it was her accent that had triggered their response.

Like all the Anglo-Irish aristocracy, she spoke perfect English, but no amount of elocution lessons would ever remove the soft burr of her brogue, the stamp of Ireland on her tongue.

And Rus, naturally, was the same.

Tamping down the sudden surge of emotion—trepidation and expectation combined—she looked again at Caxton. Meeting his eyes, she arched a brow. "Perhaps, now you've returned, sir, you could help me with my inquiries?"

She wasn't going to let his beauty, or her unprecedented reaction to it, get in her way.

More to the point, his reaction to her gave her a weapon

she was perfectly prepared to wield. She would do anything, absolutely anything without reservation, to help Rus; running rings around an Englishman and tying him in knots barely rated.

Dillon inclined his head in acquiescence and gestured for her to reenter the building—his domain. Her distracting smile still flirting about her even more distracting lips, she swung around, waiting for the doorman to step back before passing through the portal and into the foyer.

Climbing the steps, Dillon followed her in. He'd noted the calculation that had flashed through those brilliant eyes, was duly warned. An Irish lady asking to see the register? Oh, yes, he definitely would speak with her.

Pausing in the foyer, she glanced back at him, an innately haughty glance over her shoulder. Despite the dictates of his intellect, he felt his body react, yet as he met those direct and challenging eyes, he had to wonder if she, her actions, her glances, were truly calculated or simply instinctive.

And which of those options posed the bigger danger to him.

With a distant, noncommittal smile, he gestured down the corridor to the left. "My office is this way."

She held his gaze for a heartbeat, apparently oblivious of Barnaby at his shoulder. "And the register?"

The suggestion in her tone had him fighting a grin. She wasn't just fabulously beautiful; she had wit and a tongue to match. "The latest volume is there."

She consented to walk down the corridor. He followed by her shoulder, half a stride behind. Far enough to be able to appreciate her figure, her tiny waist and the curvaceous hips the prevailing fashion for slightly raised waistlines did nothing to disguise, to imagine the length of leg necessary to run from those evocatively swaying hips to the surprisingly dainty half boots he'd glimpsed beneath the hems of her emerald green skirts.

A small flat hat sporting a dyed feather sat amid the

thick curls at the back of her head. From the front, only the tip of the feather was visible, curling above her right ear.

He knew enough of feminine fashion to identify both gown and hat as of recent vintage, almost certainly from London. Whoever the lady was, she was neither penniless nor, he suspected, his social inferior.

"The next door to the right." He was looking forward to having her in his office, in the chair before his desk, where he could examine and interrogate her.

She halted before the door; he reached past her and set it swinging wide. With a regal dip of her head, she moved into the room. He followed, waving her to the chair facing his desk. Rounding the wide desk set between two tall windows, he took the chair behind it.

Barnaby quietly closed the door, then retreated to an armchair set to one side, opposite the bookcase in which the latest volume of the Breeding Register resided. Briefly meeting Barnaby's eyes, Dillon understood he intended being the proverbial fly on the wall, leaving the questions to him, concentrating instead on watching Miss . . .

Returning his gaze to her, he smiled. "Your name, Miss . . . ?"

Apparently at ease in the straight-backed chair, comfortably padded with arms on which she'd rested hers, she smiled back. "Dalling. Miss Dalling. I confess I've no real idea of, nor interest in, racing or racehorses, but I was hoping to view this register one hears so much about. The doorman gave me to understand that you are the guardian of this famous tome. I'd imagined it was on public display, like the Births and Deaths Register, but apparently that's not the case."

She had a melodic, almost hypnotic voice, not so much sirenlike as that of a storyteller, luring you to believe, to accept, and to respond.

Dillon fought the compulsion, forced himself to listen dispassionately, sought, found, and clung to his usual aloof distance. Although uttered as statements, he sensed her sentences were questions. "The register you're referring to is known as the Breeding Register, and no, it's not a public document. It's an archive of the Jockey Club. In effect, it's a listing of the horses approved to run on those racetracks overseen by the club."

She was drinking in his every word. "I see. So . . . if one wished to verify that a particular horse was approved to race on such tracks, one would consult the Breeding Register."

Another question parading as a statement. "Yes."

"So it *is* possible to view the Breeding Register."

"No." He smiled, deliberately a touch patronizingly, when she frowned. "If you wish to know if a particular horse is approved to race, you need to apply for the information."

"Apply?"

At last a straight, unadorned question; he let his smile grow more intent. "You fill out a form, and one of the register clerks will provide you with the required information."

She looked disgusted. "A form." She flicked the fingers of one hand. "I suppose this is England, after all."

He made no reply. When it became clear he wasn't going to rise to that bait, she tried another tack.

She leaned forward, just a little. Confidingly fixed her big green eyes on his face, simultaneously drawing attention to her really quite impressive breasts, not overly large, yet on her slight frame deliciously tempting.

Having already taken stock, he managed to keep his gaze steady on her face.

She smiled slightly, invitingly. "Surely you could allow me to view the register—just a glance."

Her emerald eyes held his; he fell under her spell. Again. That voice, not sultry but something even more deeply stirring, threatened, again, to draw him under; he had to fight to shake free of the mesmerizing effect.

Suppressing his frown took yet more effort. "No." He shifted, and softened the edict. "That's not possible, I'm afraid."

She frowned, the expression entirely genuine. "Why not? I just want to look."

"Why? What's the nature of your interest in the Breeding Register, Miss Dalling? No, wait." He let his eyes harden, let his deepening suspicions show. "You've already told us you have no real interest in such things. Why, then, is viewing the register so important to you?"

She held his gaze unwaveringly. A moment ticked by, then she sighed and, still entirely relaxed, leaned back in the chair. "It's for my aunt."

When he looked his surprise, she airily waved. "She's eccentric. Her latest passion is racehorses—that's why we're here. She's curious about every little thing to do with horse racing. She stumbled on mention of this register somewhere, and now nothing will do but for her to know all about it."

She heaved an artistic sigh. "I didn't think those here would appreciate a fluttery, dotty old dear haunting your foyer, so I came." Fixing her disturbing green eyes on him, she went on, "And that's why I would like to take a look at this Breeding Register. Just a peek."

That last was said almost tauntingly. Dillon considered how to reply.

He could walk over to the bookcase, retrieve the current volume of the register, and lay it on the desk before her. Caution argued against showing her where the register was, even what it looked like. He could tell her what information was included in each register entry, but even that might be tempting fate in the guise of someone allied with those planning substitutions. That risk was too serious to ignore.

Perhaps he should call her bluff and suggest she bring her aunt into his office, but no matter how intently he searched her eyes, he couldn't be sure she was lying about her aunt. It was possible her tale, fanciful though it was, was the unvarnished truth. That might result in him breaking the until-now-inviolate rule that no one but he and the register clerks were ever allowed to view the Breeding Register for some fussy old dear.

Who could *not* be counted on not to spread the word.

"I'm afraid, Miss Dalling, that all I can tell you is that the entries in the register comprise a listing of licenses granted to individual horses to race under Jockey Club rules." He spread his hands in commiseration. "That's really all I'm at liberty to divulge."

Her green eyes had grown crystalline, hard. "How very mysterious."

He smiled faintly. "You have to allow us our secrets."

The distance between them was too great for him to be sure, but he thought her eyes snapped. For an instant, the outcome hung in the balance—whether she would retreat, or try some other, possibly more high-handed means of persuasion—but then she sighed again, lifted her reticule from her lap, and smoothly rose.

Dillon rose, too, surprised by a very real impulse to do something to prolong her visit. But then rounding the desk, he drew close enough to see the expression in her eyes. There was temper there—an Irish temper to match her accent. It was presently leashed, but she was definitely irritated and annoyed with him.

Because she hadn't been able to bend him to her will.

He felt his lips curve, saw annoyance coalesce and intensify in her eyes. She really ought to have known just by looking that he wasn't likely to fall victim to her charms.

Manifold and very real though they were.

"Thank you for your time, Mr. Caxton." Her tone was cold, a shivery coolness, the most her soft brogue would allow. "I'll inform my aunt that she'll have to live with her questions unanswered."

"I'm sorry to have to disappoint an old lady, however . . ."

He shrugged lightly. "Rules are rules, and there for a good reason."

He watched for her reaction, for some sign, however slight, of comprehension, but she merely raised her brows in patent disbelief and, with every indication of miffed disappointment, turned away.

"I'll see you to the front door." He went with her to the door of his room, opened it.

"No need." Briefly, she met his eyes as she swept past him. "I'm sure I can find my way."

"Nevertheless." He followed her into the corridor.

The rigidity of her spine declared she was offended he hadn't trusted her to go straight back to the front foyer if left to herself. But they both knew she wouldn't have, that if he'd set her free she'd have roamed, trusting her beauty to extract her from any difficulty should she be caught where she shouldn't be.

She didn't look back when she reached the foyer and sailed on toward the front doors. "Good-bye, Mr. Caxton."

The cool words drifted over her shoulder. Halting in the mouth of the corridor, he watched the doorman, still bedazzled, leap to swing open the door. She stepped through, disappearing into the bright sunshine; the doors swung shut, and he could see her no more.

He returned to his office to find Barnaby peering out of the corner window.

"Sweeping away in a regal snit." Turning from the window, Barnaby took the chair she'd vacated. "What did you make of that?"

Dillon resumed his seat. "A very interesting performance. Or rather, a performance of great interest to me."

"Indeed. But how did you read it? Do you think the Irishman sent her?"

Slumping back, his long legs stretched before him, fingers

lightly drumming his desk, he considered it. "I don't think so. For a start, she's gentry at least, more likely aristocracy. That indefinable confidence was there. So I doubt she's directly involved with the Irishman asking questions in hedge taverns. However, were you to ask me if the Irishman's *master* sent her, that, I think, is a real possibility."

"But why ask just to *look* at the register? Just a peek, she said."

Dillon met Barnaby's gaze. "When she first encountered us and the doorman said one of us was Mr. Caxton, she hoped it was you. You saw her. How many males do you think would have remained immune to her persuasions, the persuasions she might have brought to bear?"

"I wasn't swayed."

"No, but you were on guard the instant you heard she was interested in the register, and even more once she'd spoken. But she, and whoever sent her, wouldn't have expected that."

Barnaby humphed; he regarded Dillon. "But you're immune, impervious, and unimpressionable in that regard." His lips quirked. "Having set eyes on you, hearing that you were Caxton, guardian of the register, must have been a most unwelcome shock."

Dillon recalled the moment; a shock, yes, but unwelcome? In one respect, perhaps, but otherwise?

What he had detected in that first moment of strange and unexpected recognition had been an element of flaring curiosity. One that had affected him in precisely the same degree.

"But I take your point," Barnaby went on. "After one peek, why not two? And after two, well, why not let the darling girl pore over the register for an hour or two. No harm if it's in your office—and no great misery to have to watch her while she pores."

"Indeed." Dillon's tone was dry. "I imagine that's more or less how matters would have transpired had I been more susceptible."

"Regardless, her advent now gives us two immediate avenues to pursue. The Irishman and the attempts to break in here, and the startlingly beautiful Miss Dalling."

Energized, Barnaby looked at Dillon, then grimaced. "In light of the tendencies Miss Dalling has already displayed, I'd better play safe and leave you to investigate her. I'll focus on the unknown Irishman and anyone who can tell me anything about people loitering after dark in this vicinity."

Dillon nodded. "We can meet tomorrow afternoon and share what we've learned."

Barnaby rose. Meeting his eyes, Dillon smiled wryly. "While trawling through the hedge taverns, you can console yourself with the thought that following Miss Dalling will almost certainly result in my attending precisely those social events I would prefer to avoid like the plague."

Barnaby grinned. "Each to our own sacrifices." He snapped off a jaunty salute, and left.

Seated behind his desk, his gaze on the now-empty chair, Dillon thought again of Miss Dalling, and all he now wanted to know.

Two

"I can't see Rus anywhere." Pris scanned the throng of horses and jockeys, trainers, strappers, and lads engaged in a practice session on Newmarket racetrack. A minor race meet was approaching; many stables took the opportunity of a practice session to trial their runners on the track itself, or so the ostler at the Crown & Quirt had informed her. Such practice sessions also helped whip up enthusiasm for the various runners.

That, Pris thought, explained the large number of the racing public who, like Adelaide and she, were standing behind the rails on the opposite side of the track, studying the horses. At least the milling crowd provided camouflage.

Adelaide squinted across the track. "Can you see anyone from Lord Cromarty's stables?"

"No." Pris examined the motley crew, jockeys circling on mounts eager to be off, raucous comments flying between them and the trainers and lads on the ground. "But I'm not sure I would recognize anyone other than Cromarty himself. He's short, and as round as he's tall—he's definitely not there. I've seen his head stableman, Harkness, once. He's big and dark, rather fearsome-looking. There are one or two similar over there, but I don't think they're him. Not dark enough—or fierce enough, come to that."

She looked around. "Let's walk. Perhaps Rus or Cromarty are on this side of the track, talking to others."

Unfurling their parasols, deploying them to deflect the morning sun, they paraded along the sward, attracting not a little attention.

Pris was aware of the appraising glances thrown their way, but she'd long grown inured to such awestruck looks. Indeed, she tended to view those who stared, stunned and occasionally slavering, with dismissive contempt.

She and Adelaide tacked through the crowd, surreptitiously searching. Then, rounding a large group of genial gentlemen comparing notes on the various runners, she saw, standing some yards directly ahead, a tall, lean, dramatically dark figure.

Caxton's dark gaze was fixed on her.

She quelled an impulse to take Adelaide's arm, turn around, and head in the opposite direction. She wished she could do so, but the move would inflame Caxton's unwelcome suspicions, quite aside from smacking of cowardice.

That he could and did affect her to the extent that beating a retreat was her preferred option irritated enough to have her elevating her nose as she and Adelaide approached him.

He waited until she halted before him, before allowing a slight smile to show. A smile that made her want to kick him—and herself. She should have halted some paces away and made him come to her.

At least he bowed and spoke first. "Good morning, Miss Dalling. Out surveying the field?"

"Indeed." She refused to react to the subtle emphasis that

suggested he wasn't sure which field she was eyeing. It had been years since she'd played such games; she was rusty. Better she stick to the shockingly direct. "This is Miss Blake, a close friend."

Dillon bowed over Miss Blake's hand and exchanged the usual greetings. Miss Blake was a pretty young lady with burnished blond-brown hair and bright hazel eyes; in most company she would shine, yet beside Miss Dalling, Miss Blake appeared washed-out, faded, so much less alive. "Is this your first visit to Newmarket?"

He glanced at Miss Dalling, including her in the question. She hadn't offered him her hand; indeed, she'd kept both hands wrapped about her parasol's handle.

It was the Irish princess who answered. "Yes." With a swish of her skirts, today a vivid blue, she turned to the track as a bevy of horses thundered past. "And when in Newmarket . . ." She gestured to the track, then glanced at him. "Tell me, do all the stables trial their runners? Is it obligatory?"

He wondered why she wanted to know. "No. Trainers can prepare their horses in whatever way they wish. That said, most take advantage of the days the track is made available, if nothing else to give their runners a feel for the course. Each track is different. Different length, different shape—different in the running."

Her brows rose. "I must tell Aunt Eugenia."

"I thought she was racing-mad—surely she would know."

"Oh, her passion for racing is a recent thing, which is why she's so keen to learn more." She surveyed him as if deciding how useful he might be.

He met her gaze, knew she was gauging how best to manipulate him, if she could . . . he let his knowledge show.

She read his eyes, understood his message; to his surprise, she considered it—as if debating whether to challenge him to withstand her wiles—before opting to ask, perfectly directly, "As you wouldn't let me see the register, perhaps you can tell me what exactly the entries in it contain, so I may tell my aunt and fill in at least that part of the puzzle for her."

He held her gaze, then, aware of Miss Blake standing beside them, her gaze flicking from one face to the other, he turned to address her. "Is the lady your aunt, too?"

Miss Blake smiled ingenuously. "Oh, no. She's Pris's aunt. I'm Lady Fowles's goddaughter."

Dillon glanced back at Pris—Priscilla?—in time to catch the frown she directed at Miss Blake, but when she lifted her eyes to his, they were merely mildly interested.

She arched a brow. "The register entries?"

How much to divulge—anything, or enough to tempt her further? Further to where she might reveal why she was asking, and who she was really asking for. "Each entry carries the name of the horse, the sex, color, date, and place of its foaling, its sire and dam, and their bloodlines—a horse must be a Thoroughbred to race in Jockey Club races."

They were standing not far from the rails; as more stables sent their horses out onto the track, the would-be punters, the touts, betting agents, and the usual hangers-on crowded closer to get a better view. One man jostled Miss Blake—because he'd gone wide-eyed staring at Miss Dalling.

Gripping Miss Blake's elbow, steadying her, Dillon caught Miss Dalling's eye. Releasing Miss Blake, who mumbled a breathless thank-you, he waved to the area farther from the track. "Unless you're keen to view the horses, perhaps we should retreat to more comfortable surrounds?"

Miss Dalling nodded. "Aunt Eugenia has yet to become fixated on individual animals."

Dillon felt his lips twitch; he was aching to ask if Aunt Eugenia truly existed. Instead, he strolled between the two ladies across the well-tended lawns, angling away from the track.

Miss Dalling glanced at him. "So what else is included in the register?"

How best to whet her appetite? "There are certain other details included with each entry, but they, I'm afraid, are confidential."

She looked ahead. "So someone wanting to race a horse on a Jockey Club track must register the horse, providing the details you mentioned, plus others, and then they receive a license?"

"Yes."

"Is this license a physical thing, or simply in the form of a permission?"

He wished he knew why she wanted to know. "It's a piece of paper carrying the Jockey Club crest. The owner has to produce it in order to enter his horse in a race."

Silence followed. Glancing at her face, he saw a line etched between her brows; whatever was driving her interest in the register, it was, to her, serious.

"This piece of paper—does it carry the same information as the entry in the register?"

"No. The license simply states that the horse of that name, sex, color, and date of foaling is accepted to run in races held under the auspices of the Jockey Club."

"So the 'confidential details' aren't on the license?"

"No."

She sighed. "I have no idea what that means, but I'm sure Aunt Eugenia will find it fascinating. She will, of course, be avidly eager to learn what the confidential details are."

The glance she threw him plainly stated that the "confidential details" would be her next target, but then she smiled. "But who knows? Perhaps once I tell her what you've said, she'll be ready to go off on some other tack."

Dillon inwardly frowned. Her light, faintly secretive smile still playing about her distracting lips, she looked away, leaving him wondering what to make of her last statement. She'd uttered it as if reassuring him she probably wouldn't be back to try to drag more details from him . . . but he wanted her to return, wanted her to try—wanted her to grow increasingly more determined, and therefore more reckless.

She was the sort to get reckless, to lose her Irish temper and toss caution to the winds—he intended to goad her to it, and then he'd learn all he wanted and needed to know.

But he wouldn't learn anything unless she came back.

Turning to Miss Blake, he smoothly engaged her in conversation, asking what she thought of the horses, of Newmarket itself, had she tried the Twig & Bough. Anything to prolong his time in Miss Dalling's company—anything to learn more of her and her entourage.

In that respect, saddling herself with an innocent, sweet young thing like Miss Blake wasn't what one would expect of a clever and intelligent *femme fatale*. Yet Miss Dalling qualified as clever and intelligent, and her type of beauty was the epitome of *fatale*—the sort men died for.

Presumably Miss Blake was truly a connection, which suggested Miss Dalling was, at least in part, as she appeared—a gently bred young lady.

He glanced at her, strolling by his side, head up, scanning the stable crews on the other side of the track. Being a gently bred young lady didn't preclude her also being an adventuress.

With his eyes, he traced her perfect profile, then realized she, and Miss Blake, too, were not idly scanning. They were searching.

"Are you looking for someone in particular?"

Pris slowly turned her head, using the moment before she met his eyes to decide how to answer. "As you know, we're from Ireland. Aunt Eugenia said there should be a number of Irish stables here—she asked us to look and see if we noticed anyone."

"Anyone who looked Irish," Adelaide helpfully piped up. "Or sounded Irish."

Pris hurried to reclaim Caxton's attention. "Do you know

which Irish stables will be running horses here over the next weeks?"

He met her eyes, then glanced across the turf. "There are Irish stables who bring horses over to compete, but most rent stables out on the Heath and bring their runners in to local stables only on the day they run. They generally use local jockeys, ones who know the course well." He nodded toward the congregation of stable hands. "The only crew from Irish stables you're likely to come across today are the owners and trainers, maybe a head stableman."

"I see." Pris was keen to close that avenue of conversation before it revealed too much.

Caxton halted. "If you wish, I could escort you that way. I wouldn't recommend that ladies venture into that area alone, but you'll be safe with me."

Halting, too, she met his eyes, and wished she dared take up his offer; she was desperate to locate Rus. Failing him, she'd be happy to find any member of the Cromarty crew. But . . . she forced an easy smile. "Perhaps some other time. I fear we've dallied long enough. Aunt Eugenia will start to worry over where we are."

She held out her hand. "Thank you for your company, sir. Aunt Eugenia will be grateful for the information you imparted."

He grasped her hand. She was immediately conscious of warmth, of heat, of a prickling awareness that spread from where his fingers closed firmly about hers. Keeping her gaze level and unwavering, she made a mental note to avoid giving him her hand again.

"Restricted though it was?" His eyes held hers. More, he studied her, watched her.

"Indeed." She drew back on her fingers. He held them for an instant, then let them slide from his . . .

She sensed the implicit warning, but was uncertain precisely what he was warning her not to do, which line he was warning her not to cross.

Neither her face nor his hinted of deeper meaning. Adelaide glowed as he turned to her; she gaily bade him farewell.

Before Pris could execute a clean parting, he asked, and Adelaide blithely volunteered that they'd driven into town, and that their gig was stabled at the Crown & Quirt on the High Street.

Pris watched him like a hawk, but he gave no indication that the information was of any particular interest to him. Smiling easily, he bowed and wished them a safe journey home.

With a regal inclination of her head, she linked her arm in Adelaide's and resolutely drew her away. It took effort, but she refused to look back, even though she felt his dark gaze lingering on her, literally, until they passed out of his sight.

"I have to find some way to locate Rus." Pris sat at the luncheon table in the neat manor house Eugenia had rented and absentmindedly picked at a bunch of grapes. "It must be as Caxton said—Cromarty's rented a stable out on the Heath."

"How big is this Heath?" Eugenia had pushed back from the table and lifted her tatting into her lap.

Pris wrinkled her nose. "As far as I can tell, it's enormous, and has no finite boundary. It's an area spreading out from the town, big enough for all the strings of horses to be exercised there twice a day."

"So finding one stable isn't going to be easy."

"No. But if we ride around during the training sessions—early morning and late afternoon—we might sight Cromarty's string. Rus said he assisted with the training sessions, or at least he did in Ireland."

Adelaide spoke from across the table. "Should we go this afternoon?"

Pris wanted to, but shook her head. "Caxton's suspicious, although I'm sure he doesn't know what to be suspicious about. We told him we were looking for Irish stables to sate your"—she inclined her head to Eugenia—"avid curiosity. If he sees us out hunting this afternoon, we'll appear too eager, too urgent to locate the Irish stables. I don't want to invite his attention any more than I already have."

Looking up from her tatting, Eugenia bent a very direct look on Pris. "You fear him. Why?"

Pris swallowed the denial that rose to her tongue; Eugenia, she'd learned, was exceedingly clear-sighted. Eventually, she offered, "I think it's because he's so very handsome—just like me." She met Eugenia's gaze. "And just like me, people look no further than his face and figure, and forget that there's a very good brain at work behind the mouthwatering façade."

"He's certainly handsome," Adelaide averred, "but he's rather overwhelming. He's very dark and hard and sharp. He may be beautiful, but he's not comfortable."

Pris found nothing to argue with in that. Drumming her fingers on the tablecloth, she thought over all she'd learned, trying to find some way forward.

"So what are you planning to do next?" Eugenia asked.

Pris looked up and met her eyes. "We can ride out early tomorrow morning and start searching through the strings exercising on the Heath. The ostler at the inn said all strings exercise there every morning, and Caxton won't expect us to be out at such an hour. If he's suspicious enough to think to look for us, he'll look at the afternoon sessions. Meanwhile . . ."

She frowned, then pushed back her chair. "If I could just get a look at that blasted register, I'd have a better idea what sort of scheme Harkness might be hatching. A better idea of what Rus will think to do."

Eugenia's lips curved. "One benefit of being twins."

Rising to her feet, Pris managed a smile. "Indeed. If you'll both excuse me, I'm going to take a turn about the gardens."

"I found her at the track midmorning, walking with a friend—a Miss Blake." Sprawled in the chair behind his office desk, Dillon laced his fingers across his waistcoat. "Miss Dalling tried to learn more about the register, but that wasn't why she was there. They were searching for someone. She said she was looking for the Irish crews, but I'm not sure if that was the truth or simply the most obvious answer to my question."

"Did you learn where they were staying?" Barnaby sat slumped in the armchair opposite the bookcase, long legs stretched out before him, ready to share the results of his day's sleuthing.

Dillon nodded. "I followed them home—she'd driven them into town in a gig. They're staying at the old Carisbrook place. I asked around. There really is an aunt—a Lady Fowles—and she's rented the house for several weeks."

"Hmm." Barnaby frowned at his boots. "How do you read her—Miss Dalling? Is her interest in the register really because of her eccentric aunt?"

Dillon glanced out of the window at the gathering dusk. "I think she's a consummate liar, sticking to the truth as far as possible, inventing only where necessary."

Barnaby's lips twisted. "The hardest sort to catch."

"Indeed. So what did you learn about the man interested in the register?"

"An Irishman with dark hair, tallish, lean, and younger than I'd supposed—midtwenties by all accounts. Not much more anyone could tell me, although one ancient described him as 'gentry down on his luck.' "

Dillon frowned. "I know all the Irish owners and trainers

here this season, at least by sight, and that description rings no bells."

Barnaby waved. "In the same vein as for the lovely Miss Dalling, there's no need for him to be associated with any stable—his connection to this might be quite otherwise."

"True. Did you learn anything more about the break-ins?"

"Only that this place is a burglar's delight. It sits so far back from the road with that avenue of huge trees, and"—Barnaby pointed through the window, beyond the rear of the building—"there's a nice stand of woodland out there. It's ridiculously easy to approach this place at night, and no one's the wiser."

Leaning back, he looked up at the ceiling. "The first time he came, he didn't come prepared—he tried the windows, but couldn't spring the locks, then had to retreat when the night watchman came around. The second time, he gained entry through the kitchen window, but the door into the building proper was bolted, so again he had to retreat. The last time, he forced a window and got into the offices down the corridor. He started searching, going through the shelves, but then knocked over a box, bringing the night watchman running, and had to flee."

Barnaby looked at Dillon. "Incidentally, the watchman's description, while hardly detailed, just an impression of height, build, and coloring, and age in how easily he fled, suggests the young Irishman with the questions could indeed be our burglar."

"That suggests we have only one group we need pursue . . ." A minute passed, then Dillon met Barnaby's eyes. "There's something afoot. You, me, the Committee, we all know it, but all we have are conjecture and suspicion. We need to catch this Irishman—he's the only person we know of who can shed light on whatever's going on."

Barnaby nodded. "I agree—but how?"

"You said this place was a burglar's delight—now he's

got so close, presumably he'll come back. What if we make it extra tempting for him to do so, wait until he makes his move . . . and then step in?"

"What are you suggesting?"

"Last time he got into the offices, so, assuming he is indeed after the Breeding Register, he knows this wing is where he needs to concentrate." With his head, Dillon indicated the side window. "As you pointed out, the woods are close. He'll use them for cover, to circle the building and learn where the night watchman is, to check whether anyone is working late. This room's at the corner—that window stands out. What if, assuming he comes tonight, he sees it left just a little open?"

Barnaby grinned. "Like a moth to a flame, he'll come up and look in, see it's an office, and . . ."

Dillon smiled grimly. "Like a moth to a flame, he'll get his wings burned."

Late that night, Pris slid from her saddle at the edge of the woods onto which the Jockey Club backed. The moon was half-full, obscured by fitful clouds; beneath the trees, it was dark, not still so much as suspenseful—as if the trees were holding their breaths, waiting to see what would come . . .

Quelling a shiver, she sternly shook aside her fanciful thoughts and tethered her mare to a low-hanging branch. There were bushes and shrubs scattered beneath the trees, but they weren't so thick she would miss seeing any man-sized shape skulking in the shadows.

She slid into the undergrowth. In breeches, boots, and jacket, with a kerchief about her neck, her hair up and severely confined, and a soft, wide-brimmed hat pulled low on her head, she could at a distance pass for a stable lad. The Lord knew there were plenty of those about Newmarket.

Carefully forging deeper into the dark wood, she scanned

ahead, searching for any sign of any other person creeping up on the Jockey Club. She could see the building through the trees, the red brick dull but with glimmers from the pale mortar and pointing, the white-painted window frames gleaming in the occasional shaft of moonlight.

Her words to Eugenia over the luncheon table had reminded her; she did, indeed, know how Rus thought. When he'd written his last letter to her, he hadn't known what the register was, not in detail, nor how it related to whatever illicit scheme Harkness was planning. Rus had intended to learn about the register. He'd known it was kept at the Jockey Club; presumably, he'd gone there and asked, as she had.

Perhaps that was where Caxton and his friend had last heard an Irish accent.

It would certainly seem odd to have two people with precisely the same accent—even the same inflections and tones—inquire about the register in a short space of time. No wonder they'd been suspicious.

Doubly so if they had reason to suspect some scam was being planned.

They might already suspect Rus.

She knew Caxton suspected her, at least of being peripherally involved. Regardless, she had to get a look at the register. Once she had, she would know as much as Rus did—perhaps more if he hadn't yet seen it.

Given how tight-lipped Caxton was, given her sense of his character—potentially hard and unforgiving of errors—she wasn't going to waste time charming his clerks. Not until she'd exhausted more direct avenues.

And entrenched in her mind was the knowledge—not a guess but a certainty—that if Rus hadn't yet learned what the register contained, then he would pursue the same direct avenue as she.

Fingers and toes mentally crossed, she prayed Rus would come there that night. Getting a look at the register and finding her twin, reassuring herself that regardless of all else, he was hale and whole, and safe . . . right now, that was all she asked of the deity.

Reaching the edge of the wood, she hunkered down beside a tree; slowly, she scanned the back of the building from left to right, paying attention to the layout, aligning it with what she'd seen from inside the previous day. Caxton had referred to the register as an archive. There would be more than one tome, stored who knew where, but she felt sure at least one, the one currently in use, would be in his office, sitting in the bookshelves there.

All she needed was one glance, just enough to see what those "confidential details" were.

A window to the right of the building, at the corner closest to her, had been left a tantalizing few inches open. Her eyes fixed on the darker gap; a second later her mind caught up. She'd been gauging the distance from the center of the building where the foyer was, along the corridor she'd traveled to Caxton's office . . . that's where the open window was.

She eyed the sight with burgeoning suspicion. Her words to Eugenia rang in her mind. She knew better than to underestimate a man with a beautiful face.

She stared at the window; her unease only grew. She simply could not imagine Caxton leaving that window open *accidentally.*

Furtive movement at the far end of the building caught her eye—a flitting shadow that instantly merged into the dim wood. She glanced again at the open window and remained where she was, stilling, breathing evenly, becoming one with the night.

The open window was a trap. But was the shadow she'd seen Rus, or Caxton keeping watch? Despite his sophisticated elegance, she wouldn't put it past him to skulk among the bushes at midnight, ready and very willing to tangle with an intruder; his civilizing veneer wasn't thick.

She reached with every sense, straining to hear any telltale sound, any crackle, any snap, squinting through the darkness to try to distinguish any movement, any shifting shape.

And detected a figure quietly, stealthily, making its—his—way in her direction.

Wits racing, she held her position. If it was Rus, would he realize the open window was a trap?

Even if he did, was he desperate enough, reckless enough, to chance it regardless?

Silence, complete and absolute, fell. Her heartbeat sounded loud in her ears. She could no longer hear nor see any sign of the man. The minutes stretched. Her eyes started watering; she blinked.

A figure rose from the bushes fifteen yards away. The man strode quickly out into the cleared space directly behind the building.

Pris cursed. The moon was playing hide-and-seek in the clouds; there wasn't enough light to see the man's face, and his clothes were too loose for her to be sure . . .

Slowing, the man glanced around, slipping both hands into his pockets.

And Pris knew.

Starting up, she opened her mouth to hail her twin—

Another man—one with golden hair—burst from hiding and charged toward Rus.

Pris gasped, but Rus had heard the man's footsteps, was already pivoting to meet him.

Rus lashed out with a boot and caught Caxton's friend in the ribs. He staggered, but then gamely flung himself on Rus.

Pris knew Rus, judged he'd win the fight, so she held still in the shadows, waiting for him to break away.

A curse and a sudden movement to her right had her swinging that way. Her heart leapt to her throat.

Another man had been hiding in the wood farther along. *Caxton*. Pris watched him rush to help his friend subdue Rus.

Without thought, she whirled, leapt, and crashed around in the shadows. A quick glance showed her the distraction had worked; Caxton had stopped midway between the wood and the pair wrestling before the open window. He stared into the wood.

She had a split second in which to decide whether to yell something—anything, Rus would recognize her voice—to let her twin know she was there, in Newmarket, not Ireland. But Rus was fully engaged with Caxton's friend. Hearing her voice would distract him; knowing she was close, pursued by Caxton . . . Rus might do something stupid and get caught.

Caxton was still staring, unsure what he'd seen. Lips firmly shut, Pris darted back and forth, then saw his clenched hands relax. He started after her.

She turned and fled.

She knew where she was going. She told herself that was advantage enough. She was quick and nimble; she would be faster than he was darting through the trees. Once she reached her horse, she'd be safe.

He gained on her steadily.

Her heart was in her mouth, her breath sawing in and out, her lungs burning by the time she saw the faint light ahead where the trees ended and the sward began. Where her horse was tethered.

Caxton's heavy footfalls hit the ground, it seemed mere yards behind her; she could feel the reverberations through her soles.

Desperate, she burst from the shadow of the trees and raced, gasping, flat out toward the mare—

A huge weight struck her in the middle of her back.

She went down.

Dillon knew the instant he locked his arms about the figure who it was. He'd played rugger in his school days; he'd launched the flying tackle without real thought.

But as his weight bore her down she struggled furiously

and managed to half turn in his instinctively loosening hold.

He cursed and tightened his grip, but then they hit the ground, him on top with her on her back stretched full length beneath him.

The impact jarred them; they both lost their breaths. For one instant, all was still, then she transformed into a wildcat, twisting sinuously beneath him, hands rising, claws extended for his face.

He wrenched his arms free, caught her hands half a second before she made contact.

She swore at him in Gaelic, bucked, kicked, fought him like a heathen. He had to shift, twist; he only just managed to avoid her rising knee, to block it and press it back with his thigh.

"Hold still, *damn it*!"

She didn't listen. He could hear her ragged breaths, almost sobs, but she seemed beyond the reach of his voice.

Ruthlessly, he exerted his strength, pressing her hands to the ground on either side of her head, relentlessly using his full weight to subdue her.

It wasn't—definitely wasn't—his idea of a wise move. He could feel every undulation of her supple body beneath his, every caress of her remarkably feminine, sinfully suggestive curves as she writhed beneath him.

His body had reacted instantly—painfully—to the feel of hers. Now . . .

"For God's *sake*!" He bit off a curse. "Unless you want me to take you here and now, *be still*!"

That got through to her; she froze—totally and utterly.

He waited; when she remained quiet, rigid beneath him, he dragged in a breath, braced his arms, and eased his weight onto his elbows, enough to look down at her face—not enough for her to have any hope of dislodging him.

They lay in the open, their faces inches apart, but her

features were shaded by his head above hers; looking up, she wouldn't be able to see his expression any more than he could see hers.

He had to fight not to glance down at her lips, and farther, at her breasts, still heaving, repeatedly brushing his chest. He forced himself to concentrate on her eyes, wide and framed by the dark curve of her lashes. "What are you doing here?"

For one instant, she stared up at him, then she flung another Gaelic epithet at him and tensed—but she didn't try to buck him off. Possibly because he now lay between her slender thighs. Then she spoke. "Is this how you entertain yourself, then? Accosting ladies in the woods?"

She'd poured scorn and more into her sultry voice, but there was a hint of panic edging it . . .

The accusation seemed singularly inapt.

Dillon frowned. He stared into her wide eyes. Despite not being able to see their expression, he suddenly understood. Suddenly realized on a wash of sensual heat just what was causing her to lose her grip on her wits.

Realized what it was keeping her lovely eyes doe-wide.

Keeping her breathing skittish and panicky.

Beneath him, he felt her quiver, recognized the response as involuntary, something she would die rather than admit to—something she couldn't suppress or prevent.

He could feel his heartbeat heavy in his loins, could feel the heat of hers trapped beneath him, pressed against him. He felt the telltale tension thrumming through her, resistance combined with a reaction she couldn't control.

One that left her weak.

He would never have a better chance of getting her to tell him all she knew. Deliberately, he let his hips settle more definitely between her thighs.

Her breath caught; alarm flashed through her. "Get off me."

The last word hitched, caught.

He froze. Inwardly swore. She was one step away from outright panic. *Damn*—he couldn't do this.

He was about to tense and lift from her when a crashing in the wood captured both their attentions.

Turning his head, he watched Barnaby stagger from the trees. He was holding his side and had clearly failed to capture the Irishman.

Very much the worse for wear, Barnaby slumped against the bole of a tree. "Thank God." He dragged in a painful breath. "You caught him."

Dillon sighed. Without releasing his captive's hands, he pushed up, got his feet under him, and rose, hauling her unceremoniously up before him.

He looked over her head at Barnaby. "No. I caught *her*."

Three

By the time Caxton steered her into his office, Pris had her wits firmly back under control. It helped that, in marching her back to the Jockey Club, he'd done no more than grip her elbow. Even that much contact was more than she would have wished, but it was a great improvement over what had gone before.

Those moments when she'd lain beneath him welled again in her mind. Resolutely, she jammed them down, buried them deep. She couldn't afford the distraction.

He thrust her into the room, in the direction of the chair before his desk, the one she'd previously occupied.

After hauling her to her feet, with a detachment that, to her in her highly charged, overwrought state, had somehow smacked of insult, he'd tugged loose her kerchief, pulled her arms behind her, and bound them. Not tightly, but too well for her to slip her wrists free.

She'd borne the indignity only because her wits had still

been reeling, her traitorous senses still whirling, leaving her weak—too weak to break away.

But their plodding journey through the wood had given her time to catch her breath; she was feeling considerably more capable now.

Halting beside the chair, she narrowed her eyes at Caxton as he came up beside her. "You'll need to untie my hands."

It was the earl's daughter who spoke. Caxton met her eyes, considered, then reached behind her and tugged the knot free.

Leaving her to untangle her hands, he walked on; rounding his desk, he dropped into the chair behind it.

Behind her, Pris heard the door shut and the latch click home. As she sat—noting that Caxton hadn't waited for her to do so before sitting himself—she glanced at his friend. He limped to the armchair and slowly let himself down into it.

She managed not to wince. Her confidence in Rus hadn't been misplaced; there was a bruise on the man's cheekbone, another on his jaw, and from the way he moved, his ribs hadn't escaped punishment. He looked thoroughly roughed up, yet she detected a shrewdness, an incisiveness in his gaze; he was still very much mentally alert.

Shaking out her kerchief, she rolled it, then calmly knotted it once more about her neck. She looked at Caxton, noted he was frowning, then realized his gaze had lowered to her breasts, rising under the fine shirt as she reached to the back of her neck.

Thanking the saints that she didn't blush easily, she lowered her arms. "Now that we're here, what can I do for you, gentlemen?"

She had every intention of making this interview more painful for them than for her.

Dillon blinked, then locked his gaze on her face, on her fascinating eyes. "You can start by telling us what you were doing skulking about the wood."

Her emerald eyes opened wide. "Why, skulking about the wood, of course. Is that a crime?"

He didn't try to stop his jaw, his whole face from hardening. "The man in the wood—who was he?"

She considered asking what man. Instead, she shrugged. "I have no idea."

"You were there to meet him."

"So you say."

"He's a felon who's been trying to burgle the Jockey Club."

"Really?"

Dillon could almost believe the arrested look that went with that, as if he'd told her something she hadn't known. "You know him, because you deliberately distracted me from helping Barnaby—Mr. Adair—apprehend him. You knew he'd overcome one man, but not two. You're his accomplice—you helped him get away. Presumably you were his lookout."

She sat back in the chair, outwardly as at ease, as comfortable and assured as she'd been in her emerald gown. Arms resting on the chair's cushions, she met his gaze directly. "That's a fascinating hypothesis."

"It's the truth, or something close to it."

"You have an excellent imagination."

"My dear Miss Dalling, what do you imagine will happen if we deliver you to the constable and tell him we discovered you, dressed as you are, hiding in the wood behind the Jockey Club, just as a man seeking to break into the club fled the scene?"

Once again, she opened her eyes wide; this time, a gentle, subtly mocking smile played about her mobile, thoroughly distracting lips. "Why, that the poor constable will curse his luck and be made to feel terribly uncomfortable, for as we've already established, skulking about in the woods is no crime, your assertion that I know the man is pure conjecture, conjecture I absolutely deny, and as for being dressed as I am, I believe you'll discover that, too, is not against the law."

The poor constable would be mesmerized by her voice. If she spoke more than two phrases, it required a conscious exercise of will not to fall under her spell. And, of course, in this case, she spoke the unvarnished truth. Sitting back in his chair, Dillon studied her, deliberately let the moment stretch.

She met his gaze; her lips curved, just a little—enough for him to know she knew what he was attempting, that she wasn't susceptible, wasn't going to feel compelled to fill the silence.

Despite his intention not to shift his gaze, he found himself glancing at her attire. In a town like Newmarket, the sight of ladies in breeches, while not socially acceptable, was hardly rare. An increasing number of females—Flick being one—were involved in one way or another with preparing racehorses, and riding such animals in skirts was simply too dangerous. When he called on Flick, he was as likely to find her in breeches as in skirts.

It was his familiarity with ladies' breeches that prodded his mind. Miss Dalling's weren't made for her; they didn't fit well enough, being a touch too big, the legs a trifle long. Likewise the jacket; the shoulders were too wide, and the cuffs fell across the backs of her hands.

Her boots were her own—her feet were small and dainty—but the clothes hadn't been hers originally. Most likely a brother's . . .

Lifting his gaze, he captured hers. "Miss Dalling, can you tell me you *don't* know this man—the man Mr. Adair attempted to apprehend?"

Her fine brows arched haughtily. "My dear Mr. Caxton, I have no intention of telling you anything at all."

"Is he your brother?"

Her lashes flickered, but she held his gaze, direct and unflinching. "My brothers are in Ireland."

Her tone had gone flat. He knew he'd hit a nerve, but he'd also hit a wall. She would tell him nothing more, at all. Inwardly sighing, he rose, with a wave gestured to the door. "I would thank you for assisting us, Miss Dalling, however . . ."

With a look of cool contempt, she rose. Turning, she paused, studying Barnaby. "I'm sorry you were injured, Mr. Adair. Might I suggest ice packs would help with those bruises?"

She accorded him a regal nod, then, lifting her head, walked to the door.

Dillon watched her, noting the swaying hips, the supreme confidence in her walk, then he rounded the desk and went after her.

Even now, especially now, he wasn't about to let her wander the corridors of the Jockey Club alone.

"Damn it, Rus, where *are* you?"

Holding her frisky bay mare on a tight rein, Pris scanned the gently undulating grassland that formed Newmarket Heath. Here and there between the scattered trees and copses, strings of horses were being put through the daily round of exercises that kept them in peak condition. Horsey breaths fogged in the crisp morning air. Dawn had just broken; it was cold and misty. Beyond the practicing strings, wholly absorbed with their activities, the Heath was largely empty; other than herself, there were few observers about.

More would gather as the sun rose higher; she intended to be gone before too many gentlemen rode out to view the runners for the race meet tomorrow.

The string she'd been observing from a safe distance wasn't Irish. Straining her ears, she could just pick up the orders and comments tossed back and forth. This group was English, definitely not Lord Cromarty's string.

Suppressing her disappointment, doing her best to ignore her mounting anxiety, she set the mare cantering on to the next string.

It was the second morning she'd ridden out. Yesterday, Adelaide had accompanied her, but Adelaide wasn't a confident rider; Pris had spent as much time watching over her as she had scanning the sward. This morning, she'd risen earlier, donned her emerald velvet riding habit, and slipped out of the house in the dark, leaving Adelaide dreaming.

Of Rus, no doubt. In their unwavering devotion, Adelaide and she were alike, albeit for different reasons.

Two nights before, she'd truthfully told Caxton her brothers were in Ireland. Rus wasn't her brother—he was her *twin*. He all but shared her soul. Not knowing where he was, simultaneously knowing he was facing some as-yet-nebulous danger, set fear like a net about her heart.

With every day that passed, the net drew tighter.

She had to find Rus, had to help him break free of whatever it was that threatened him. Nothing else mattered, not until that was done.

Catching sight of another string, she turned the mare in that direction. The horse was still fresh; Pris let her stretch out in an easy gallop, but given that she was riding sidesaddle over unfamiliar ground, she kept the reins taut.

The sting of cold air burned her cheeks. Exhilarated, she pulled up on a slight rise and looked down on the exercising string.

Settling the mare, she squinted at the distant horsemen. She couldn't get too close; she might not recognize Harkness, but given he'd been working with Rus, he would almost certainly recognize her.

She needed to locate Lord Cromarty's string, but until she knew more, she didn't want anyone from his lordship's stables other than Rus knowing she was in Newmarket.

Straining her ears, she listened, but was too far away.

Twitching the mare's reins, she trotted around to a knoll closer to the string but more directly downwind.

Again she sat and listened. This time, she heard. Closing her eyes, she concentrated.

Familiar lilting accents, a gently burred brogue, rolled across her senses.

Breath catching, she opened her eyes and eagerly scanned the men before her. She fixed on the large man directing the exercises. Harkness. Big, dark, and fearsome. Her mind wasn't playing tricks on her—she'd found Lord Cromarty's string!

Her heart lifting, she studied the two men beside Harkness; neither was Rus. She was about to shift her focus to the circling riders—so much harder to study as they rose and fell with their horses' gaits—when a shifting shadow in the clump of trees to her right drew her eye.

A horseman sat on a powerful black standing in the lee of the trees. He wasn't watching the exercising horses; his attention was fixed on her.

Pris cursed. Even before she took in the lean build and broad shoulders, and the dramatically dark, wind-ruffled hair, she knew who he was.

Abruptly, she wheeled the mare, tapped her heel to the glossy flank and took off. She raced down the knoll, gave the mare her head, and flew, hooves pounding, away across the Heath.

He would follow, she felt sure. The damn man had doubtless been following her all morning, perhaps even all yesterday morning. By now he would know she was searching for one particular string. Thank the saints she'd noticed him before she'd done anything to distinguish Cromarty's string from all the others she'd observed.

A quick glance over her shoulder confirmed the big black was thundering in her wake.

The mare was fleet of foot, and she rode a great deal

lighter than he, but the black was like its rider—relentless. It came on, heavy hooves steadily eating up her lead.

Leaning low over the mare's neck, she urged the horse on, streaking across the lush green. The wind tugged at her curls, sent them rippling over her shoulders. Shifting her weight as she swung around a stand of trees, she tried to think of what she should say when he caught up with her.

Would he wonder why she'd fled? Would he guess her real reason—that she wanted him far from the string she'd been watching? But no—their last clash, especially those moments behind the wood, were reason enough for her to flee him. And he knew that, damn him! She recalled all too well that instant before his friend had arrived when he'd decided to try a certain method of persuasion that, to her immense shock, had had her heart standing still.

With a peculiar, never-before-felt fear, and an unholy anticipation.

No. She had a good reason not to want to fall into his hands again.

But she didn't want him thinking about that last string. Remembering it enough to go back later and check. She had to convince him it was just another string like all the others she'd viewed, not the one she was searching for.

She glanced behind her. He was even closer than she'd guessed. Stifling a curse, she looked ahead—she was rapidly running out of Heath. The stands of trees were getting larger; she was heading into more wooded terrain.

He was going to catch up with her soon, but she would rather any catching was done on her terms. As for making sure he didn't focus on that last string . . . she might not want to fall into his arms, but there was one weapon she possessed that, in her experience, was all but guaranteed to rattle his brain, to fog his mind and cloud his memories.

She wasn't keen—wielding that weapon was neither smart nor safe—but desperation beckoned.

The last thing she wanted, the very last thing Rus needed,

was Mr. Caxton, Keeper of the Breeding Register, calling at Lord Cromarty's stables.

Dragging in a breath, she gathered the mare in, let Caxton bring his mount up on her right flank.

She picked her moment, swerved hard and sharp, swinging around a clump of trees large enough to qualify as a wood. The black was less maneuverable; the rapid shift in direction left him careening on.

Curses erupted behind her as Caxton wrestled the beast around, but then she whipped around the wood, streaked along its rear, rounded it again, returning to where she'd started; by then he'd followed and was on the other side.

Hauling the mare to a halt, she slid from the saddle, snagged the reins on a branch, grabbed her skirts, and pelted into the wood.

She raced through the cool shadows, grateful it was reasonably clear under the trees. She found what she was looking for roughly in the wood's center, a huge old tree with a wide, thick bole. Panting, she whisked around behind it, drew her skirts in, and leaned back against the trunk.

She closed her eyes, fought to catch her breath. Caxton would either find her, or he wouldn't.

The minutes stretched. She couldn't hear anything over the pounding of her heart. There was light enough to see, sunbeams lancing through the canopy to dapple the ground; the air was cool, sweet with the scent of wood and leaves.

Her heart slowed, steadied. She strained to hear. All about seemed still. Unthreatening.

A twig snapped, close, on the other side of the tree.

A second later he loomed at her shoulder. Real, larger than life, twice as handsome. Sinfully beautiful and darkly dangerous.

He looked down at her, leaning against the tree, her hands gripping her skirts, then arched his brows, arrogantly unimpressed.

She didn't stop to think. Straightening, she raised one

hand, reached for his nape, came up on her toes, and drew his lips to hers.

And kissed him.

Dillon's thoughts stopped the instant her lips met his. It was as if he mentally blinked, and when he opened his mental eyes there was nothing there . . . except for the beguiling sweetness of her lips shifting seductively against his. Delicately tasting, subtly yet evocatively tempting.

His eyes were open, but he couldn't see. He tried to bring his vision into focus, couldn't. Instead, he let his lids fall, surrendered, and accepted he was caught, somehow trapped in the moment, that her bold and totally unexpected attack had caught him unawares and snared him.

His lips gave under hers, eased, shifted; he started to respond to her blatant invitation, his arms rising to hold her, then instinct reared and he caught himself. Tried to pull back, free—tried to find the will to do so.

The clasp of her small hand at his nape tightened; she stepped closer, her lips taunting. Her body brushed his, sinuous, sirenlike. Her other hand rose, came to rest splayed against his chest, then she slid it slowly upward, over his shoulder to twine about his neck as she moved closer yet.

He felt the change in him, the sudden surge of driving need he recognized, yet didn't. This was desire grown unusually strong, unusually forceful, born of lust heightened by her beauty, colored by a primal need to dominate, to subjugate, lashed to life by her cool contempt—a medley of deeper passions she'd effortlessly stirred, and seemed determined to unleash.

More fool she.

But if she wanted . . . so did he.

He played out his inner reins, lifted his arms, and closed them about her. Gathering her more definitely against him, he felt the hitch in her breathing, was even more aware of the unadulterated need that seared him. A need to conquer, to possess. To meet her challenge head-on, and triumph.

To put her in her place, beneath him once again.

He did as he wished, and kissed her back. For long moments, he toyed with her, a give-and-take that remained at the level she'd initiated, neither light nor unmeaningful, yet not threatening, more promise than action. A superficial sensual landscape, one where sexual taunts and responses belonged.

She was comfortable enough there, sufficiently in control. Able to duel with him.

He mentally smiled and ruthlessly took control, backed her against the tree, parted her lips, surged into her mouth, and laid claim. Crashed through her outer defenses and engaged her, tasted her, not the sweet but the sensual, the more intimate self she'd until then kept guarded.

Shocked, Pris tried to draw back only to feel his arms lock about her. Like steel, they caged her, trapping her, the tree a solid wall at her back, his body an even more intimidating barrier before her. A threatening barrier. As if to demonstrate, his hands, palms and fingers strong, spread over her back, then he drew her even more definitely into him, against a body far harder, far stronger than her own. One mind-numbingly masculine.

He surrounded her, alien and powerful—and intent.

Her body responded, but not as she wished. Instead of fighting to break free, her limbs melted, her muscles turned to jelly. Clamping her hands on his shoulders, fingers sinking into heavy muscle, she struggled to hang on, to cling to control, or at least to her wits, but he wouldn't allow her even that much—angling his head over hers, he mercilessly plundered her mouth and sent her wits careening.

Some part of her continued to struggle, to frantically look for some way out even while her senses reeled, even while her mind was overwhelmed, all thought submerged by the waves of sensuality he sent pouring through her.

She tried to draw a line and hold to it, tried to dig in her sensual heels, but he ruthlessly, relentlessly undermined her, and drove her back—into deeper waters. Waters into which she'd never before stuck a toe.

His lips were commanding, demanding, forcing her to scramble to appease, to placate. His tongue dueled with hers, and he constantly won, seizing as his reward the right to caress, explicit and knowing, until shudders of pleasure racked her spine.

She was breathing all but entirely through him, helpless in his arms, unable to retreat. To call a halt, to step back from the engagement she'd started, to break away from what it had become.

There was heat and fire in him; with him wrapped about her she couldn't mistake it. Couldn't miss the rigid evidence of his desire so flagrantly impressed against her belly. Yet there was a coolness behind all he did—that aloof control that despite her best efforts, her fond hopes, she hadn't rattled or rocked in the least.

Even while he engaged with her, even while he set her wits spinning, her senses whirling, he was watching her. Steering her.

He wasn't lost in this unfamiliar world. He wasn't out of control—he was dictating.

This, she suddenly realized, was a lesson—a warning.

As if he sensed her realization, his hands, until then splayed firmly across her back, shifted. One rose slightly, holding her pressed to him while his other hand slid slowly down, over her hips, then lower.

Even through the velvet of her habit, she felt the sensual assessment in his touch, the blatant possession.

Far from reacting with contemptuous fury, her traitorous body and even more traitorous senses all but swooned. Heat raced over her skin, prickled beneath his palm as he fondled, then more explicitly caressed.

His head angled over hers, his lips pressing hers farther apart; the ruthless yet languid thrust of his tongue became even more openly intimate, more devastatingly erotic.

She couldn't stand against him—couldn't stand against herself, the self he connected with, that he could command. That he'd called forth and turned against her.

Her defenses crumbled; all resistance—in her mind, in her bones and sinews—simply faded away. On a shattered sigh, half-tortured moan, she surrendered.

Dillon knew it; he had to wage a war with himself not to react. Not to brace her against the tree, lift her skirts, and sheathe himself in her wanton heat.

He closed his eyes tight, sank into her mouth, and fought to leash his demons, his almost overpowering need to have her, here and now. Fought to convince himself that what he'd already taken, what he'd already enjoyed, was enough. For now.

He'd won, triumphed, but he hadn't expected the battle to rage so far. Recognizing her tack, he'd responded in the only way that, in the heat of the moment, he'd deemed possible—in kind. But he hadn't expected her to meet him and match him on field after field, hadn't expected her to defend so recklessly, to hold against him until they'd come to this—this critical point in passion's dance; he'd expected her to yield long since. He hadn't expected to have to press her so hard, to have to wield his own sensual weapons so strongly, not to this extent.

To the extent where he was inwardly shaking, racked with volcanic yet unslaked desire, raked by passion's claws.

A self he didn't recognize, one driven by hot desire, reminded him she'd started this. He'd called her bet—shouldn't she pay his price?

With her locked against him, her slender body and lush mouth fully yielded, all his, the temptation to ravish her—to deal with what she'd started in the most appropriate way—whispered darkly through his mind.

Yet now she'd surrendered and was no longer fighting him, there was a subtle innocence in her responses; no longer screened by her determination to counter him, she—the woman within—seemed so very vulnerable.

He might wish—that harder, darker side of him might want—but he didn't have it in him to harm her.

Drawing back from the kiss required effort; they'd traveled too far along passion's road to simply stop and step away. He needed to draw her back to the world, needed to force himself step by step back from a precipice he'd never before faced.

The realization that that last was indeed true helped.

Eventually he lifted his head. He looked down at her lips, swollen, slightly bruised; he hadn't been gentle. He shifted his gaze to her eyes, watched as she drew in a breath, then her lashes fluttered, and rose.

Revealing eyes brilliant and dark, deeper than emerald, the veil of ebbing passion slowly fading.

He studied those eyes, tried to ignore the compulsive beat in his blood, still painfully attuned to her, aware to his throbbing fingertips of the rise and fall of her breasts beneath her velvet jacket as she fought to catch her breath.

There was comprehension in the eyes that stared back at him, eyes that, like his, would never be distracted by superficial beauty, that would look past it, search deeper, and see.

They both knew what had happened, what had just occurred, what question had been decided. She'd thought to challenge him, had risked doing so knowing that at the least she'd learn which of them was the stronger on this plane.

She'd hoped she'd be able to manage him, bedazzle and hypnotize him with her not-inconsiderable charms. She'd wantonly rolled the dice—and lost; he saw the knowledge in her eyes.

He couldn't stop a cynical, arrogant smile from curving his lips. "I believe that answers that."

Her eyes flashed, temper flaring, but, still recovering, she made no reply.

He looked into her eyes for a moment longer, then, very slowly, released her. "Might I suggest we'd be wise to return to the horses?"

It would definitely be wise to get some distance between them.

She looked away, toward the horses.

He forced himself to step back, let her slip from between him and the tree; silent and, he judged, slightly dazed, she started back to the edge of the wood.

Without a word, he fell in beside her.

Pris struggled to get her limbs to work, to get her mind to function, struggled to assimilate all that had happened and all that hadn't. There'd been a moment there . . . she slammed a mental door on those thoughts. If she dwelled on what she'd sensed, she'd never be able to deal with him—and deal with him she must.

He was striding beside her; she didn't dare glance at him—she was still much too quiveringly aware of him, of the impression of his body against hers, of the insidiously dangerous thrill of being trapped in his arms, his lips on hers, his tongue dueling with hers . . .

Thrill? What was the matter with her? Being kissed by him had obviously warped her mind.

She frowned as they neared the edge of the trees, frowned even more definitely when, glancing about, she realized there was no convenient fallen log, no stump she could use to regain her saddle.

He'd noticed. With a curt wave, he gestured her to her horse. He followed, still close. Steeling herself, she halted by the mare's side and swung to face him.

Finding herself looking at his neatly tied cravat, she forced her gaze up to his eyes, just as his hands slid about her waist and gripped.

And it happened again. Heat flared, then spread from where he touched; desire and more rose like a wave and surged through her. And him. His eyes locked on hers; the expression in his face, all hard angles and austere planes, perfectly sculpted, classically beautiful, stated very plainly that he wanted her. But . . .

Although desire flared in his mink-dark eyes, it was harnessed, controlled. He studied her for a moment, then evenly, rather coldly, said, "I would suggest, Miss Dalling, that if you have the slightest sense of self-preservation, you will not again attempt to sway me using yourself as bait."

Her temper flared. Haughtily, she raised her brows.

His features resembled cold stone. "Regardless of what men you've previously bent to your will, be under no illusion. If you offer yourself to me again, I'll take."

It took considerable effort to meet his gaze and stare him down, considerable effort to stop herself from reacting to the unsubtle threat. She hadn't needed to hear it; if she'd learned anything in the last minutes, it was that he was one gentleman she'd be wise to avoid.

She had every intention of doing so, as far as she was able. She pointedly glanced at her horse.

Lips set, he hoisted her up. He sat her in the saddle, held the stirrup for her—as if he were accustomed to assisting ladies in that way.

She wondered who . . . then resolutely turned her mind from such unnecessary questions. "Thank you." With a chilly nod, she gathered the reins and wheeled the mare.

And promptly gave the horse her head. Anything to get out of Caxton's sight as soon as humanly—equinely—possible.

Pris rode like the wind, letting the physical exhilaration soothe her mind and settle her still-shaky senses. She was approaching the rented manor house before she felt calm enough to think.

"Hardly surprising," she muttered, reining the mare to a walk. "It's not every morning I'm nearly ravished."

She knew Caxton had considered it. Considered it, then deliberately backed away and spared her.

Recalling the moment, recalling how she'd felt—been reduced to feeling—she hissed through her teeth. "He should be outlawed. If he can do that to me, inured as I am to physical charms, what effect does he have on more susceptible young ladies?"

The mare snorted and walked on.

Pris humphed. Regardless, Caxton had given her a reprieve. Like the gentleman he was, he'd declined to take advantage of her sadly misjudged attempt to manipulate him. She should have known he would prove immune, the more cautious part of her had known he might be, but she'd had to try . . . the reason why returned to her.

Brows rising, she considered; if she hadn't recalled why she'd kissed him until that moment, the chances were good that he'd forgotten entirely the string she'd been watching before she'd led him on their merry chase.

Good. Indeed, *excellent*! That was precisely what she'd set out to do, and she'd succeeded.

But she'd lost Cromarty's string; she hadn't even had time to see if Rus had been on one of the horses. Caxton's fault; it was intensely annoying, especially given her increasing anxiety—blind but even more troubling for that—over Rus's safety.

At least she now knew the area in which Cromarty's string worked. She'd go out and locate them again, find Rus, and all would be, if not well, then a great deal better.

As for what came next, she sincerely hoped she'd be able to avoid Caxton, arrogant rake that he was. His warning irked; worse, her temper being what it was, her nature as it was, warning her not to do something invariably left her even more tempted to take the risk, regardless.

Reaching the manor, she turned the mare's head toward the stable. There was something about Caxton's warning that didn't ring true. Replaying his words, his inflections, she tried to read the emotions beneath. His reined desire she recalled clearly.

She'd dismounted in the stable yard, absentmindedly handed over the mare and was striding to the manor's side door when the discrepancy hit her.

He'd had no real reason to utter any warning.

He'd known she'd seen the danger. If he were as truly in command as she'd thought—as he'd pretended to be . . . as he'd allowed her to believe him to be?—if he were half as clever as she suspected he was, he should simply have let her go.

She halted.

If she *couldn't* sway him sensually, why bother warning her off?

He wanted her to tell him what she knew; if he was impervious to her, why not let her try again and simply hold her off again, using the moment to get her to tell him what he wanted to know? Manipulation of that sort worked both ways, something he, of all men, beyond question knew.

She stood in the strengthening sunshine, turning over all the possibilities in her mind. Only one fitted.

He wasn't nearly as impervious as he'd seemed.

He didn't want her testing him again because, next time, she might succeed in holding him to a line that wasn't so close to the edge of the sensual cliff, might succeed in gaining enough control to have the upper hand.

Or at least have some bargaining power.

"Well, well, well." Eyes narrowing, she considered, then mentally nodded and walked on. That was certainly something to note and remember, especially if, as she greatly feared, avoiding him proved impossible.

She'd found Cromarty's string, and had learned of one possible chink in Caxton's otherwise formidable armor. All in all, her morning hadn't been a complete waste.

Four

"This morning, she was obviously searching for one particular string." Sprawled in an armchair in the family parlor of Demon and Flick's home, Dillon described all he'd learned about Miss Dalling to Demon and Flick, attended by their two eldest children.

He and Barnaby, seated on the window seat, had met midmorning; after discussing their findings, they'd decided to seek Demon's advice. Few knew the inner workings of the racing industry better, and there was no one whose judgment Dillon trusted more when it came to racing swindles.

"When she noticed me watching her, she rode off. I followed. Once she realized she couldn't shake me, she returned to the Carisbrook house."

An abbreviated account, but accurate in the essentials. Dillon glanced at Flick, perched on the arm of Demon's chair. She wasn't wearing breeches today; she'd been spending time with her offspring rather than her husband's Thoroughbreds. The older two children, Prudence and Nicholas, had joined their elders in the parlor as if they had the right; Nicholas, eight years old, a miniature Demon in looks and sharp as a tack, was lolling on the window seat beside Barnaby, listening for all he was worth, while Prudence, known to all as Prue, the eldest at ten years old, in looks a Cynster although the stubborn set of her chin reminded Dillon forcibly of Flick, had claimed her place on Demon's other side. Like her mother, she deemed anything that went on in her vicinity as much her interest as anyone else's; she was fascinated by the tale Dillon had come to share.

"I seriously doubt Miss Dalling is directly involved in whatever's going on," he concluded, "but she definitely knows something, something more than we do. I think she's protecting someone, very possibly her brother."

"She certainly reacted when you suggested it was he I'd been wrestling with," Barnaby put in, "and what you don't know, because I forgot to mention it, is that the bounder did indeed look like her."

Dillon blinked. Barnaby amended, "Well, a scruffy male version of her, at any rate. In fact, he looked like a down-on-his-luck cross between her and you."

Flick had been avidly following their exchange. She opened her mouth to ask the obvious question.

Prue beat her to it. "What does she look like? Is she pretty?"

They all looked at Dillon.

He hesitated, then admitted, "She's not *pretty*. She's the most stunningly, startlingly, strikingly beautiful young lady I've ever set eyes on. If she goes to town without a ring on her finger and doesn't accept an offer inside a week, the matchmaking mamas will be sharpening their knives."

Flick's brows rose high. "Good gracious! And this goddess is haunting Newmarket?"

A speculative gleam lit Flick's blue eyes. Dillon studied it, then glanced at Demon, wondering what tack his powerful brother-in-law would take. Demon had very firm views on Flick getting involved in anything dangerous. Against that, he allowed her to ride his horses, so his definition of dangerous was flexible. Flexible enough for him and Flick to have remained happily married for over ten years.

Demon hadn't even had to look at Flick to know what she was thinking. He glanced at her. "Do you think you might be able to learn more from Miss Dalling by pursuing an acquaintance socially?"

Flick grinned. "Meeting her socially will pose no problem whatsoever. However"—her gaze returned to Dillon—"extracting the necessary information might require persuasion of a sort I'm not qualified to give." Her smile grew. "We'll see."

Dillon didn't appreciate the calculation he glimpsed in Flick's cerulean blue eyes. "Her aunt has rented the Carisbrook place. She says the aunt's an eccentric, presently fascinated by racing, thus excusing her interest in the register."

"Hmm." Flick looked thoughtful. "You met her out riding—how well does she ride?"

He smiled. "Not as well as you."

That earned him long-suffering looks from Flick, Demon, Nicholas, and Prue. Flick was the best female rider in the land. She could give Demon a run for his money, and he, unquestionably, was the best there was. Saying Miss Dalling didn't ride as well as Flick was saying nothing at all.

"She's actually quite good." He thought back, then raised his brows. "In fact, she was damned good, far better than the average lady rider."

"So she does know horses?" Demon asked.

Dillon understood what he was suggesting. "Yes, but not as you mean. She understands horses as I do, not as the two of you do."

Demon grimaced. "So there's no reason to think her family owns a stud, or similar enterprise. However, there is some connection with horses."

Dillon inclined his head.

"So"—Demon glanced at Flick—"we'll leave Miss Dalling to you, my dear, at least until we know more on that front. Meanwhile"—he looked at Dillon and Barnaby—"we need to decide how best to probe the possibility a substitution scam has been operating and is set to continue during this season's races."

Barnaby sat forward, all nonchalance falling from him. "So you agree there's something going on? That it's not us overextrapolating from disconnected pieces of information that happen to have fallen into our laps?"

Dillon searched Demon's face. The severely handsome, angular planes held a certain grimness.

"I don't believe your concerns arise from overactive imaginations." Demon's lips twisted. "Indeed, much as I wish I could brush your evidence aside and assure us all that there's really nothing in it, you've gathered too many pieces for them to be coincidental. And if they're not coincidental, then there's only one other explanation—there's another organized racing scam under way."

Dillon and Barnaby exchanged a glance, then Dillon looked at Demon. "So how should we proceed?"

They revisited all they'd learned. Prue and Nicholas grew restive. With a maternal smile, Flick stood; waving the men back to their seats, she herded the children to the door. "It's time for our ride." She nodded a farewell to Barnaby, then Dillon, and exchanged a glance with Demon. "You can tell me all later."

Demon raised his brows, but when he turned back, there was a smile in his eyes.

After establishing all they knew, they settled on the questions they most wanted answered, then evaluated their options. One source they urgently needed to reassess was the rumors of unexpected losses over the spring season.

"If we could establish which races and which horses were involved, that would give us a place to start."

Barnaby grimaced. "When I poked around earlier, the

rumors turned to smoke and mist—no one would name names."

Demon snorted. "Too many gentlemen think too much of how others will see them. They'll grumble and groan, but when it comes to making specific complaints, heaven forbid! There may even be more recent losses we haven't yet heard about. The greatest losses from such a scam occur not at the racetrack, but through the offtrack betting centered in London. That's where the big wagers will be laid, and 'unexpected losses' felt most keenly. With the right encouragement, we should be able to persuade at least some of those who've been grumbling to be more specific."

Clearly someone had to follow up the London rumors. However, with the autumn racing season under way, neither Dillon nor Demon could leave Newmarket. Demon could, however, alert Vane, his brother, and his cousins Devil and Gabriel Cynster, all of whom were presently in town. "If we explain and identify the grumblers, they'll know how to get those disgruntled punters to name names."

Demon looked at Barnaby. "Are you willing to return to London and, with the others, see what you can turn up?"

Barnaby was eager. "I'll drop a word in the pater's ear, too." His father was involved with the new police force. "Some of the inspectors might have heard something. I'll head down this afternoon."

"Meanwhile, I'll keep my ear to the ground here." Demon turned to Dillon. "As for you . . ." His predatory grin flashed. "Apropos of Flick's direction, I doubt she'll make any headway with Miss Dalling. A social connection, however, should give *you* more opportunity to persuade the lady to our cause."

Dillon pulled a face. "If she would only tell me what she wants to know about the register—or better yet, why—" He broke off, then shook his head. "I'm convinced she knows something, but—"

"*But,*" Demon cut in, "she's frightened to reveal what she

knows, first because she doesn't understand what it means, and second because she's protecting someone." He held Dillon's gaze. "What you have to do is gain Miss Dalling's trust. Without that, you'll get nothing out of her—with that, she'll tell you all."

Demon smiled, but there was no lightness in the gesture, only a fell intent. "Simple."

Dillon held his gaze, unimpressed. "Simple?" He allowed his skepticism full rein. "We'll see."

Pris chafed and swore, but forced herself to wait, to let the rest of the day, then another go by before she once again rose with the dawn and slipped out to find Lord Cromarty's string.

She kept her eyes peeled as she streaked through the misty landscape, but detected no pursuit. If Caxton was waiting out on the Heath, with any luck he wouldn't recognize her. Mounted on a solid but unremarkable bay gelding, she was riding astride, dressed in breeches, boots, and jacket, with her wide-brimmed hat pulled low and a muffler wound about her chin. Once she found Cromarty's string, she intended to follow them to Rus; much easier to amble in a stable's wake if she looked like any other stable lad.

To her relief, Cromarty's string was exercising close to where she'd last seen them. She watched from the cover of a stand of trees, scanning the riders; Rus was not among them.

She didn't know precisely what Rus did as assistant stableman; his duties in Newmarket might not include the morning exercises.

While Harkness put his racers through an exacting series of gallops, she thought of Rus, let his face fill her mind, remembered shared exploits that made her smile. At last Harkness called a halt. The string formed up in a long line and headed off.

She fell in, not directly behind but as far back as she dared, and to the right, always at an angle to the string's line of travel; if anyone glanced back, she wouldn't be obviously following them.

The string walked, jogged, then walked again. Eventually they crossed a road and turned up a lane. Pris stopped to read the signpost; SWAFFAM PRIOR was lettered on it. If she was seen, she would appear to be heading for the village; entering the lane, she ambled on.

She kept her distance from the stragglers of the string. Finally the string turned right down a narrower lane; buildings lay grouped at its end.

They appeared to be substantial. Leaving the lanes, Pris cut through the fields; circling, she found a low, wooded rise beyond the buildings and pulled up. Screened by the trees, she looked down on the establishment; it was clear this was where Lord Cromarty was stabling his horses.

Her heart lifting with anticipation, she watched the horses being unsaddled, walked, brushed down, watered. She squinted, studying every man who walked through the yard.

Not one of them was Rus.

Lord Cromarty came out of the house to speak with Harkness. After considerable discussion, Harkness sent a lad for a horse—a high-spirited black mare. The lad paraded her before Harkness and Cromarty, then at Cromarty's nod, returned the horse to her stall.

Pris remained mounted in the shadow of the trees, anticipation fading, anxiety burgeoning as a sense of unease rose and whispered through her. Cold, chill fingers trailed her nape.

Rus wasn't there.

She knew it in her heart, even without the evidence of her eyes.

After another futile hour, she drew away. Returning to the lane to Swaffam Prior, she debated, then turned the gelding's nose toward the village.

She had to learn if Rus was still somewhere, somehow, in Cromarty's domain.

Patrick Dooley, Eugenia's devoted and trusted factotum, spent the evening in the tavern at Swaffam Prior. He returned late, with disquieting news.

Pris hadn't even considered retiring, too strung up to relax; Eugenia had settled on the chaise in the drawing room to keep her company, and Adelaide had remained, too.

Patrick joined them. He reported that, as Pris had guessed, the stable hands from Cromarty's stable did indeed spend their evenings at the tiny tavern. He hadn't even had to ask after Rus; his disappearance had been the main topic of conversation. According to the stable hands, "the toff," as they affectionately called him, had been going about his business as usual until about ten days ago. Then one morning, he simply hadn't been there.

Their description of Rus rang true—pernickity manners but a great one with horses. None of Cromarty's crew knew anything of any falling-out with Cromarty or Harkness; to a man they were mystified by Rus's abrupt departure.

But what had excited their interest and kept it on the boil was Harkness's reaction; when he'd discovered Rus gone, he'd flown into a towering rage. Cromarty, too, had been furious. The upshot was Cromarty had offered a reward for any news of Rus, saying he knew too much about the stable's runners, their quirks, and what made them run poorly, and they wanted to make sure he didn't sell such secrets to their competitors.

"So he's gone," Patrick concluded, "but no one knows where to."

Patrick was Irish, a stalwart of Eugenia's small household. Although only six years older than Pris, his devotion to her aunt was beyond question.

She studied his impassive countenance. "Rus has to be

alive. If he wasn't, Harkness and Cromarty wouldn't have posted a reward. Rus realized something was amiss and escaped before they could stop him. He got free and went into hiding."

Patrick nodded. "That would be my guess."

"Where would he hide?"

Patrick's gaze turned rueful. "As to that, you'd have the best idea."

Pris grimaced. Through the years Eugenia had spent at Dalloway Hall, Patrick had come to know Rus and her well; beyond herself and Albert, she would have said Patrick had the greatest understanding of her twin.

"I don't know much about the racing business, but . . ." Patrick met her eyes. "Would he have stayed around here or gone to London?"

She blinked. "I don't know. He was here three nights ago, but now? Hiding in London would be easier, and he has acquaintances there, friends from Eton and Oxford. He might think to get help with whatever he's discovered in town."

"I'll check the coaches, see if he caught one to London or anywhere else." Patrick glanced at Eugenia. "I'll need to go to Cambridge and check there, too, in case he went across country and caught a coach from there."

Eugenia nodded. "Go tomorrow. You concentrate on that avenue. Meanwhile, we'll see what we can do closer to home." She looked at Pris. Her soft voice took on a steely note. "This is clearly no lark, not a matter of your outrageous brother kicking up his heels, but something truly serious. We must do all we can to assist Rus with whatever matter he's embroiled in. So—what can we do?"

Pris thought, then uttered a sound of frustration. "It all comes back to that *bloody* register!" She glanced at Eugenia. "Sorry, but without knowing what that damned register contains, we have no clue as to what Rus might have stumbled on. We know he's after the register, or was.

Learning what's in it should give us some idea of the sort of illicit doings he might have uncovered."

"Is there no other copy?" Patrick asked.

Pris shook her head. "And it's closely guarded—even more so now." She colored faintly. "I slipped back last night and looked around—searched the woods in case Rus had come back. He hadn't, but I saw two extra guards patrolling around the building. Caxton knows Rus and I are both after the register, and he's determined we're not going to see it."

Eugenia's brows rose. "Perhaps we ought to consider ways of swaying Mr. Caxton." She glanced at Pris. "You said he was highly eligible."

"I also said he was more beautiful than I am, and similarly immune to 'gentle persuasion.' "

She saw Patrick's slashing smile flash; she directed a frown his way, but he, too, was immune.

"I don't suppose," he said, "that you'd consider swaying Caxton as a challenge?"

Crossing her arms, she humphed. "Perhaps, but . . ."

That was one challenge she might not win.

"I was wondering . . ."

They all turned to look at Adelaide. A soft frown was creasing her brow. "I saw a lending library in the town. This is Newmarket, after all—perhaps they have a book that will tell us something about this register?"

Pris blinked. "That's an excellent idea." She smiled. "Well done, Adelaide! We'll go tomorrow, and while we're there, we'll also search for a map. I want to find where all the common land is and whether there are any derelict cottages or abandoned stables hidden away out on the Heath."

Patrick nodded. "Another excellent idea."

"Well, then!" Eugenia gathered up her tatting. "We all have something to get on with tomorrow. I suggest we go to bed—there, it's midnight."

They stood as the clocks throughout the house chimed.

Climbing the stairs behind Eugenia, conscious of the

comfort of the familiar sounds about her, Pris wondered where Rus was, whether he had any comforts at all, what the sounds surrounding him now were.

She needed to learn where he was. And whether the cold lump of fear congealing in her stomach was justified.

"As it happens we do have a map showing the stables and studs." The lady behind the counter of the lending library smiled at Pris. "I'm afraid you can't borrow it, but you're very welcome to study it." She nodded across the foyer of the lending library. "It's hanging over there."

Pris swung around, eyes widening as she saw a very large, very detailed map covering a considerable section of the opposite wall.

Behind her, the helpful lady continued, "We get so many gentlemen calling in, trying to find their way to this stud or that stable, that we had the aldermen make that up for us."

"Is it up-to-date?"

"Oh, yes. The town clerk drops by every year to make adjustments. He was here in July, so the details are very recent."

"Thank you." Pris flashed the lady a brilliant smile. Leaving the counter, she crossed the foyer that ran across the street end of bookcases stretching back into the dimness of the building. There were chairs and low tables grouped in the area, more or less in the library window. Two old ladies were sitting in armchairs, comparing novels. Pris halted before the large map mounted on the wall.

It was huge and wonderfully informative. It even showed some of the bigger stands of trees out on the Heath. She located the wood in which she and Caxton had kissed; backtracking, she found the area where Cromarty's string exercised, then traced the route back to the stable southeast of Swaffam Prior. Even the tavern in the village was carefully marked.

Elsewhere, somewhere between the bookcases, Eugenia and Adelaide were pursuing books on the Breeding Register.

Locating the Carisbrook house, Pris scanned the major estates, the studs and famous stables ringing the town. She memorized the names and outlines of the larger properties, searching for distant sheds or disused buildings, any places Rus might be using as a refuge.

She knew he was close, still in the vicinity. While the possibility of his having gone to London had to be examined, she didn't believe he had.

Next to a large stud labeled Cynster, she found a smaller property, an old manor with a house called Hillgate End. The name carefully lettered beneath was CAXTON. Pris took note of the surrounding lanes and woods, her mind—if not her enthusiasm—preparing for the inevitable, that she would have to approach Caxton again.

After their interlude in the wood, she absolutely definitely didn't want to think of having to do so. Of having to risk it. Turning her mind from the prospect, she set about quartering the Heath, searching for old or disused dwellings.

Behind her, the bell above the library door jingled. An instant later, one of the assistants exclaimed, "Why, Mrs. Cynster! You're just the person we need. I have a lady here terribly keen to learn about the register—I assume that's the Breeding Register Mr. Caxton keeps—but we've no books about it, which I must say seems strange. Perhaps you could speak with her?"

Pris looked around, and beheld a vision in soft summer blue. Mrs. Cynster was a youthful matron, extremely stylish, elegantly gowned with a wealth of guinea gold curls exquisitely cropped. By her side, a young girl, perhaps ten or so, stood patiently waiting.

The young girl saw Pris. The girl's eyes grew wide, then wider. Staring unabashedly, she blindly reached up and tugged her mother's sleeve.

Pris turned back to the map. She was often the recipient of such stunned fascination, but in this case, given her mother, the girl had an unusually high standard for comparison.

Regarding the map, Pris considered the Cynster stud, with the smaller Hillgate End estate nestled above it. Mrs. Cynster, assuming she was *the* Mrs. Cynster, was Caxton's neighbor.

Behind her, Mrs. Cynster agreed to speak with Eugenia; the assistant led her away between the rows of bookshelves. Pris heard the young girl hushed when she tried to tell her mother about Pris, heard her scuffling footsteps as she reluctantly followed the ladies.

She had a few minutes at most to decide what to do. To decide how best to use the opportunity fate had sent their way. Mrs. Cynster might be Caxton's neighbor, yet Pris couldn't see the man who had interrogated her in his office sharing his problems—she was fairly certain he thought of her as a problem—with his neighbors, particularly not the ladies.

There was no reason Mrs. Cynster would know anything about her, let alone the motives behind her and Eugenia's quest to see the register. But if Mrs. Cynster knew anything about that blasted register, or even something useful about Caxton . . .

Turning from the map, Pris walked down the corridor between two bookshelves, using Eugenia's voice to guide her.

"I have to confess," Mrs. Cynster was saying, "that although I've lived in Newmarket almost all my life, and have an interest in breeding and training horses, I really have no clue as to what, precisely, is in the Breeding Register. I know all racehorses are registered, but as to why, and with what details, I've never thought to ask."

Eugenia saw Pris and smiled. "There you are, my dear." She glanced at the golden-haired beauty. "Mrs. Cynster—my niece,

Miss Dalling. She's been so helpful trying to find answers to my questions."

Mrs. Cynster turned. Pris met pure blue eyes, open and innocent, yet there was a quick and observant mind behind them.

Smiling, she bobbed a curtsy, then took the hand Mrs. Cynster extended. "I'm very pleased to meet you, ma'am."

Mrs. Cynster's smile widened; she was a small woman, several inches shorter than Pris. "Not nearly as pleased as I am to meet you, Miss Dalling. I hate being behindhand with the latest, especially in Newmarket, and you're obviously the lady I've recently heard described as 'stunningly, startlingly, strikingly beautiful.' I had thought the description a trifle overblown, but I see I was being too cynical."

Her dancing eyes assured Pris the compliment was genuine.

"I wonder . . ." Turning her blue eyes on Eugenia, and Adelaide standing quietly beside her, then glancing again at Pris, Mrs. Cynster raised her brows. "I would love to introduce you to local society—I understand you've recently come to stay at the Carisbrook house, but it will never do to hide yourselves away. Besides, although it's never the first topic of conversation with the local ladies, many of us know a great deal about horse racing." She looked at Eugenia. "You will certainly be able to learn more."

A smiling glance included Pris and Adelaide. "I'm hosting a tea this afternoon. I'd be delighted if you could attend. I'm sure some of us would be able to learn more details for you from our husbands if we knew what most interested you. Do say you'll come."

Eugenia looked at Pris. She had only a heartbeat in which to decide; smiling, she nodded fractionally.

Eugenia returned her attention to Mrs. Cynster. "We would be honored to accept, my dear. I must say, all research and no play is rather wearying."

"Excellent!" Beaming, Mrs. Cynster gave them directions, confirming she was indeed the chatelaine of the Cynster racing stud.

Which meant her husband would most likely know what details had to be supplied to enter a horse in the Breeding Register.

Pris's smile was quite genuine; anticipation rose, hope welled.

Mrs. Cynster took her leave of them, then summoned her daughter. "Come, Prue."

Pris glanced at the young girl, an easy smile on her lips.

And met a pair of blue eyes—not the same as her mother's but harder and sharper; the expression on the girl's face was one of delighted expectation.

Pris blinked; Prue only smiled even more, turned, and followed her mother away between the bookcases. Pris caught the final, delighted glance Prue threw her before the shelves cut her off from sight.

"Well!" Eugenia straightened her shawl, then turned to leave, too. "The social avenue sounds a great deal more promising than these books. Such a lucky meeting."

Following Eugenia and Adelaide, Pris murmured her agreement, her mind elsewhere. Why had Prudence Cynster looked so expectant?

Pris had younger sisters, had been at that stage herself not so long ago. She could remember what topics most excited girls of that age.

Stepping out into the sunshine in Eugenia and Adelaide's wake, she decided that, while attending Mrs. Cynster's afternoon tea was the obvious way forward, a degree of caution might be wise.

Five

Four hours later, Pris was reasonably satisfied with her entrance into Newmarket society. She'd adopted a "severe bluestocking" persona; garbed in a simple gown of gray-and-white-striped twill with her hair restrained in a tight chignon, she worked to project a quiet if not studious appearance.

The Cynster gathering had proved larger than she'd expected; a host of young ladies and a surprising number of eligible gentlemen strolled the lawn beside the house under the watchful eyes of a gaggle of matrons and older ladies, seated comfortably beneath the encircling trees.

"Thank you, Lady Kershaw." Pris bobbed a curtsy. "I'll look forward to seeing you tomorrow evening." With a light smile, she parted from the haughty matron.

Invitations to dinners and parties were an inevitable consequence of attending such an event, but having discovered most here had some connection to the racing industry, she was at one with Eugenia in accepting whatever invitations came their way. Who knew from whom they might learn the crucial fact? Until they found it, they would press forward on every front. She and Eugenia were earls' daughters, and Adelaide had moved all her life in similar circles; dealing with Newmarket society posed no great challenge.

Once the introductions had been made they'd gone their separate ways. Adelaide had joined the younger young ladies; charged with seeing if she could discover any word of derelict stables or the like from her peers, she was happily applying herself to the task.

Eugenia, meanwhile, was pursuing the register with duly eccentric zeal. Unfortunately, it wasn't possible to talk solely of that; when Pris had last drifted past, Eugenia had been exchanging views on the latest London scandal.

Pausing by the side of the lawn, Pris scanned the guests. Her task had been to engage the not-quite-so-young ladies as well as the gentlemen, to see what she could learn. She'd steadfastly adhered to her role of bluestocking, responding to the usual sallies her beauty provoked with blank if not openly depressing stares. Her attire hadn't helped as much as she'd hoped, but her attitude had carried the day. Her reputation was now going before her; the sallies were becoming less common, and more young ladies viewed her with interest rather than incipient jealousy.

That was rather refreshing; she was enjoying the greater freedom the role allowed her to interact with others on a plane beyond the superficial. She'd always found people interesting, but over the last eight and more years, her beauty had become a wall, prohibiting easy, unstilted discourse.

Now, however, completing her scan of the gathered multitude and confirming she'd chatted to them all, she felt her real self stir, felt the prick of rising impatience.

A movement within the drawing room caught her eye. The doors to the lawn stood open; with the bright sunlight streaming down, the interior was full of shadows. As she watched, one moved—with a predatory grace that set mental alarms ringing.

She'd remained on guard until she'd assured herself neither Caxton nor his friend Adair were lurking among the guests. Now, senses focused, watching the shadow resolve into the shape of a man, watching him stroll out onto the sunlit steps—seeing his dark locks and sinfully dark elegance revealed—she swore.

His gaze had already fixed on her.

Pris turned and rejoined a group of guests.

Dillon watched her merge with the crowd. He hesitated at the edge of the lawn, debating his best avenue of attack.

He'd spent the last three days thinking of little else but the lovely Miss Dalling, and while many of those thoughts had revolved about her potential role in any racing scam, some had been a great deal more private. While he understood, even agreed in principle with Demon's suggestion that given the seriousness of the situation, the potential damage to the racing industry, then using more personal persuasions to gain her trust and learn all they needed was justified, he felt strangely reluctant to pursue her in that way . . . or, at least, for those reasons.

After their last meeting, he was not at all sure he wished to reengage with her personally at all.

He'd warned her off. Never before had he even thought of such a thing, yet with her he'd been moved to it, for one compelling reason. No other woman had ever tempted him as she had. She'd cut through his control effortlessly, as if it hadn't been forged in the steamy hothouse of ton affairs, tested by the most experienced and never before found wanting, and left him facing a side of himself he hadn't, until that fraught moment in the wood, known he possessed.

No matter how he'd made it sound, his warning had been driven by self-preservation. His, not hers.

He'd always regarded himself as sensually aloof, passionate maybe yet always in control, never at the mercy of his appetites, never driven by a need that raked and clawed. She'd shown him he'd been wrong, that with the right female, the right temptation, he could be just as driven as others—as Demon, as Gerrard, as the other Cynster males he'd spent most of the last decade around.

That was not a comforting thought, especially as it seemed he needed to "persuade" her to tell him her secrets. Getting that close to her, tempting her, dallying as far as he needed to, was going to severely strain his until-now-vaunted control, already, with her, seriously weakened.

Given his body's instant reaction to the sight of her, a delectable vision in a gown of vertical gray-and-white stripes highlighted by fine stripes of gold, standing momentarily alone, surveying the crowd—an outsider who, courtesy of her beauty, stood apart, as he often did—he seriously doubted that, in this case, familiarity would breed contempt. More likely insanity if he was constantly forced to battle his newfound demons.

Nevertheless . . . her equally instant reaction to him, her instinctive move to seek refuge with others, had set the ends of his lips curving. The predator in him recognized her flight for what it was. Perhaps there was hope? Perhaps "persuading" her wouldn't demand more than he could safely risk?

"There you are!"

He turned to see Flick bustling toward him. Stretching up, she planted a kiss on his cheek, and whispered, "She's over there with the Elcotts—did you see?"

"Yes." Flick had sent word that Miss Dalling and her aunt would be attending her afternoon tea. "How long have they been here?"

"A little over an hour, so you've plenty of time. Now"—turning, Flick surveyed her guests—"would you like to meet the aunt?"

"Indeed. And after that, you can try to clear my path." Dillon pretended not to notice the avid looks cast his way.

"I have absolutely no interest in any sweet young lady—just Miss Dalling."

Flick chuckled as she took his arm. "I agree she's not sweet, but at least she's interesting. However, my good lad, I greatly fear that regardless of *your* lack of interest, there are too many here whose interest you cannot ignore."

He groaned, but surrendered, allowing her to lead him into the waiting throng. He exchanged greetings with various matrons, bowed over their daughters' hands, effortlessly maintaining his usual aloof distance; even while he was looking at each sweet young miss, his senses were tracking his true prey. She was circling, keeping more or less behind him as he moved through the crowd.

She'd taken his warning to heart. How to tempt her close enough to rescind it was a novel challenge.

Then Flick steered him to an older lady sitting alongside Lady Kershaw. "And this is Lady Fowles. She and her niece and goddaughter are spending some weeks at the Carisbrook place. Allow me to present my cousin, Mr. Dillon Caxton. Dillon's in charge of the famous Breeding Register."

"Really?" Lady Fowles smiled up at him, an eagle sighting prey.

Bowing over her hand, Dillon met a pair of shrewd gray eyes.

"I've heard a great deal about you, young man. From my niece. So disobliging of you not to tell her all I wanted to know."

Her ladyship's smile robbed the words of all offense. Dillon responded with a smile as he straightened. "I'm afraid the details of the Breeding Register are something of an industry secret."

He wondered if her ladyship knew of her niece's late-night exploits. It seemed unlikely; for all her purported eccentricity, Lady Fowles appeared perfectly sane.

She did, however, proceed to grill him about the register. He slid around her questions, imparting instead various

Jockey Club rules, ones that were public knowledge. Given his long association with the club, he could hold forth at length without any real thought.

That left his mind free to dwell on Miss Dalling, to consider how to lure her close . . . all he had to do was continue talking animatedly with her aunt. Miss Dalling had more than her fair share of curiosity.

Even as his senses pricked, telling him she was near, Lady Fowles looked past him, and beamed. "There you are, my dear. I've been attempting to wring information about the register from Mr. Caxton here." Her ladyship threw him a sharp look. "Producing water from stone would be easier."

She looked again at Miss Dalling as she joined them. Dillon turned to face her; she remained a wary few feet away.

"Mr. Caxton." Her tone was cool. She curtsied; Dillon bowed.

Eyes widening, her ladyship suggested, "Why don't you see if you can weaken his resolve, my dear? Perhaps he'll be more amenable to sharing such details with you."

Hiding his satisfaction, Dillon looked at his prey. Her eyes, startled, lifted to his. He could almost feel for her—thrown to the lion by her aunt.

"I don't think that's at all likely, aunt." Primly correct, she waited, expecting him to make some comment declining her company and withdraw.

He smiled charmingly, as if taken by her beauty; she wasn't fooled—sudden suspicion bloomed in her emerald eyes. "I know how devoted you are to satisfying your aunt's thirst for knowledge, Miss Dalling." Smoothly he offered his arm. "Perhaps we should stroll, and you can test your wiles? Who knows what, in such congenial surrounds, I might let fall?"

She stared at him, then looked at his arm as if it were something that might bite.

"Ah . . ." Tentatively, she reached out. "Yes. Very well."

Lifting her head, eyes narrowing, she met his gaze. "A stroll would be . . . pleasant."

He felt the hesitant pressure of her fingers on his sleeve keenly; he suppressed a strong urge to cover them with his, to trap them.

They took their leave of her aunt and Lady Kershaw. Dillon turned toward the end of the lawn. "Let's go this way."

She assented with a nod.

There were fewer guests farther down the lawn. He guided her through the groups, avoiding meeting the eyes of those who sought to engage them. "Tell me, Miss Dalling, what drives your aunt's interest in the register?"

She glanced at him, wary yet direct. "I realize you might not comprehend how it might be, but my aunt is obsessive. When she decides she must know something, she simply won't rest until her curiosity is appeased."

"In that case, in this instance, she'll wear herself to the bone. The details of the register are not for public consumption."

"She's hardly 'public.' I cannot see why—" She broke off.

He glanced at her face; her expression told him little, but her eyes had widened—something had just occurred to her.

He sensed when she jettisoned all attempt at a façade; the tension in the lithe body beside his subtly altered, becoming more relaxed, more fluid, yet more focused as she shifted to attack.

"Tell me this, then." She met his eyes, her gaze direct, challenge in the green. "*Why* are those details such a secret?"

He held her gaze, then looked ahead. They'd left the other guests behind; focused on him, she didn't notice when he turned into the yew-lined walk that led to the stable.

How far should he go? "Those details can be used to falsify races in various ways. The Jockey Club prefers not to draw attention to those ways, hence the secrecy surrounding the register's information and how it's used."

She frowned, pacing alongside him. "So the information is used in some way to . . . validate racehorses?"

When she looked up, he caught her gaze. Dropped all pretense, too. "I'll make a deal with you. If you tell me why you need to know what's in the register, I'll tell you what you want to know."

She studied his eyes for a pregnant instant, then looked ahead. "I've already told you why—more than once. My aunt wishes to know—you've spoken with her, you know that's true."

A hint of truculent impatience roughened her brogue.

Dillon inwardly sighed. Demon was right. Gaining her trust was the only way he was going to learn her secrets.

And the only quick and certain way to get close was to seduce her.

He didn't let himself think, just acted. Halting, he faced her. Lowering his arm, he caught her hand and smoothly backed her until the thick, fine-leaved hedge stopped her.

Then he stepped closer, the movement so practiced, so polished, it shrieked of his experience.

Her eyes had widened. She stared at him—incredulous—for one fraught instant, then she glanced right and left, and realized where they were. Out of sight, alone.

Her gaze whipped back to him. "What the devil do you think you're doing?"

An irritated demand; there was not the slightest hint of panic in her tone.

Her recalcitrance acted like a spur. Bending his head, he leaned in. Raising one hand, he twined a finger in a lush, black curl that had slipped loose from her too-severe chignon and now bobbed by her ear.

The sensation of warm silk wrapping about his finger momentarily distracted him. Gently, he tugged his finger free, then realized she'd stopped breathing. He glanced at her eyes, caught her stunned stare, hesitated, then gently, languidly, with the pad of his finger traced the fine skin of her jaw.

For one instant, desire swirled in those fabulous emerald eyes; she fought to quell a shiver—he sensed the flare of response, watched her lids flutter half-closed.

Only a saint wouldn't have shifted closer still, until their bodies were a scant inch apart, until he could feel the heat of her, the beckoning delight of her, all along his body. He was definitely no saint; he reveled in the sensation.

He whispered his next words over her cheek. "I thought perhaps, obsessed as *you* are with the details of the register, you might like to persuade me to your cause?"

Her lids flew up. The eyes that locked with his weren't hazy with desire; it was temper, steel-bright, that flashed at him. "What happened to"—her voice altered; she couldn't match his tone, but she succeeded with his inflection—" 'I would suggest, Miss Dalling, that if you have the slightest sense of self-preservation, you will not again attempt to sway me using yourself as bait'?"

He held her irate gaze for two heartbeats, then shrugged. "I changed my mind." He lowered his gaze to the delectable twin mounds showing above her scooped neckline. "I reconsidered in light of your charms. Obviously I spoke too hastily, in the heat of the moment." Lifting his gaze, he met her eyes. "As it were."

Her eyes narrowed to slits; she studied him for a long moment, then crisply stated, "Nonsense." Raising both hands, she pushed at his shoulders.

Sheer bemusement had him stepping back. She whisked around and started back up the walk. Then she stopped, unsure, and glanced around. "Where are we?"

Feeling very like shaking his head, he strolled up to her, waving back at the buildings filling the end of the walk. "My brother-in-law's stable. Given your aunt's great interest in horse racing, I assumed the stable of the premier racehorse breeder in England might be of some interest to you."

She stared at the stable long enough for him to wonder if she might take him up on his offer, giving him more time with her in a more private, more enclosed space . . . but then she shook her head. "My aunt has only one highly specific obsession at present. I need to concentrate on satisfying that."

Whirling, she marched back up the path.

Inwardly sighing, he fell in beside her. "I had thought that's what I was suggesting."

The look she threw him was scorching. "Do you seriously expect me to believe I have any chance of 'persuading' you—regardless of what time and energy I might devote to the task?"

They stepped back onto the lawn. He halted, caught her gaze as she paused beside him. He raised a brow, deliberately taunting. "How will you know unless you try?"

She held his gaze, her expression dismissive . . . but she thought about it. He remained unmoved, unaffected, challenging yet not threatening.

Eventually, she lifted her chin. "I'll bid you a good day, Mr. Caxton."

Her tone suggested she hoped he fell in a bog on the way home. He smiled and elegantly inclined his head. "Miss Dalling." He waited until, head high, she turned away, before quietly adding, "Until next we meet."

She froze, spine rigid, then, without acknowledging his words in any way, she walked away across the lawn.

Dillon watched her until she rejoined her aunt, saw her bend to speak into her ear. Before any other lady could capture him, he stepped back into the yew walk and beat a strategic retreat.

He didn't take any chances. The next morning, he spoke with his clerks and race stewards, making it plain that their continued employment depended on them resisting any blandishments or temptations of any kind to divulge details of the Breeding Register, or the Stud Book.

Later, he reported to the Committee, the three gentlemen elected as stewards by the members of the club, modifying his warning accordingly, describing it as a precaution arising out of his ongoing investigations.

He didn't mention Miss Dalling.

She was involved, but he didn't yet know how, nor why she was after the register's details. He was having increasing difficulty envisaging her, much less her aunt, as lending themselves in any way to any illicit enterprise.

His day passed in meetings with owners, trainers, and jockeys, with the town's aldermen and various denizens of the turf.

He wondered when Barnaby would return, whether he and the Cynsters would be able to turn up firm information.

Time and again, his mind returned to Miss Dalling, to that brief and rather surprising interview in the yew walk. Although the thought made him sound like a coxcomb, experience had taught him few ladies could have broken from his spell, not at such close quarters, let alone snap into perfectly genuine ire.

Ire shouldn't have been within her range of responses, not at that moment.

When he touched her, she responded, if anything more ardently, more acutely than others, yet if there were no direct contact, her mind remained incisive, her temper determined, her will strong—and she saw straight through him.

He found her unbelievably refreshing.

He caught himself wondering what waltzing with her would be like, how she might react . . .

Flick had been right. Miss Dalling might not be sweet, but she was definitely interesting. Having dangled his bait, he was looking forward to crossing her path again that night.

* * *

Surveying Lady Kershaw's ballroom, Pris felt relief seep through her, felt oddly tense muscles ease as she detected no elegantly ruffled dark locks, no sinfully handsome gentleman waiting to waylay her.

Other gentlemen eyed her speculatively, but they barely registered; she didn't fear them. She wasn't even sure she feared Caxton so much as what he might tempt her to do. To risk. Especially given her increasing anxiety over Rus.

She'd returned to the lending library that morning; the woman behind the counter had confirmed that their wonderful map showed only buildings currently in use. She'd suspected as much, yet still it was a blow.

Patrick had confirmed that Rus hadn't caught any coach, nor hired one. Her twin was as striking as she; no ostler would have forgotten him. So Rus was, as she'd thought, still in the vicinity, hiding and in danger not just from Harkness himself but from all who might think to secure the offered reward.

Someone in Newmarket, among the many they would meet socially, had to know what she needed to learn. Moving through the guests, she exchanged greetings with those she remembered from Mrs. Cynster's afternoon tea, allowing them to introduce her to others.

She'd built on her image of a serious if beautiful bluestocking, disguising her dashing gown of dark green silk by draping a black knitted silk shawl over her bare shoulders and tying it between her breasts. The long fringe hid much of her figure; the dark mesh dimmed the jewel hue of the gown. Long dark gloves added to the impression of repressive severity; her bountiful hair was once again restrained in a tight chignon.

Her social experience combined with her years allowed her the status of still-eligible yet independent spinster, one who no longer needed to remain under her chaperone's eye.

Smiling, chatting, she circulated, paying most attention

to the gentlemen; she was a dab hand at using her looks to prompt older men into trying to impress her, in this case with their understanding of the racetrack.

Although the ladies who'd heard of her aunt's obsession steered the conversation to the register, she'd realized it might behoove her to widen her inquiries. Caxton's comments on the subject had been brief, but he had revealed one pertinent point; she encouraged any who could to describe what occurred at the end of races, how the winning horses were treated, what the rules were, what checks were made.

After an hour of steady application, with a delighted smile she turned from two portly gentlemen who had finally told her of the race stewards and their role in verifying winning horses.

"The stewards won't tell you anything—don't bother to ask."

With a squeak, barely stifled, she very nearly jumped back—away from *him.* He loomed over her. Her heart had leapt to her throat; she had to wait a moment before it subsided and her lungs started working again.

All because of the waft of his breath over the edge of her ear.

Dragging in a breath, she lifted her chin and fixed him with a look designed to slay.

He met her eyes and smiled.

She felt like blinking, managed not to, but that smile . . . it wasn't one of his practiced gestures, but genuine and sincere.

For some ungodly reason, she amused him.

She elevated her nose farther. "You were eavesdropping."

His smile deepened; he reached out and took her arm.

Why she didn't twist free and storm off she had no idea.

Twining her arm in his, he met her gaze. "I told you more than I should have yesterday. You had that far too easily. If you want to know more, you'll have to work harder."

"Yesterday I wasn't even—" She broke off. Glanced at him.

He caught the glance, returned it with a knowing, faintly arrogant smile.

She blinked and looked ahead. Last afternoon she might not have been trying to extract—seduce—information from him, yet he'd told her something. Apparently deliberately.

Was he really willing to divulge the register's secrets in return for . . . ?

Was she in any position to ignore the possibility that he might?

Was Rus?

She was about to turn to him—how did one embark on such an "exchange"?—when his hold on her arm tightened. He steered her to the dance floor as the musicians at the end of the room started playing.

"Come and dance."

She inwardly shrugged, happy enough to put off the uncertain moment. They were playing the introduction to a waltz; she turned into his arms before she'd thought.

His fingers closed about hers; his palm settled, warm, hard, and shockingly strong in the middle of her back. She sucked in a breath, felt her senses quake, determinedly forced them to behave and not betray her sudden sensitivity. Fixing her gaze beyond his shoulder, she fought to concentrate on the revolutions of the dance, then realized that wasn't helping at all.

He was sweeping her effortlessly, powerfully around the room, her traitorous senses happily caught in his spell. In the shift and sway, in the seductive shush of her skirts against his trousers, in the sudden heat that flared as his hard thigh parted hers and he spun her into the turn.

Her lungs seized. She shifted her gaze to his face.

He met her eyes, read them, then smiled. That seductive, wholly genuine smile that sent her wits careening.

She couldn't drag her gaze from his, couldn't free her senses from his hold, from the sensual web the dance had become.

His dark eyes slowly heated. The hard planes of his face subtly shifted, as if he, too, felt it, as if he, too, were conscious of the tightening grip of sensation, the burgeoning craving the dance evoked.

Not the dance. Them dancing.

Never before had she considered the waltz a sensual experience, yet when the music faded and he whirled her to a halt, she felt exhilarated. Keyed up, nerves on edge, as she'd felt only once before.

When he'd kissed her in the wood and nearly ravished her.

Something must have shown in her face. His dark eyes raced over her features; when his gaze fixed on her lips, they throbbed.

He muttered something, his tone low, harsh. Instead of releasing her, his hand closed more tightly about hers; his arm fell away reluctantly as, head rising, he scanned the room.

She moistened her lips. Her wits seemed to be working unusually slowly.

She had a strong suspicion that if they'd been functioning normally, they'd be urging her to flee. Something else was keeping her rooted to the spot, wholly focused on a man who was the personification of danger.

"This way." Dillon looped her arm in his, with his other hand trapped her fingers on his sleeve. Lady Fowles had noticed them dancing; smiling benignly, she'd returned to her conversation. It was helpful that Miss Dalling had established herself as independent; no brows would be raised if he escorted her beyond the ballroom's walls.

Rather than head for the terrace, as a number of other couples were, he steered her to a door that gave onto a corridor, presently deserted.

He'd been visiting the Kershaws since he was in short coats; he knew the house and all its nooks well. The rarely used conservatory, down the corridor and out of sight of the ballroom, was the perfect place in which to pursue Miss Dalling—in which to encourage her to pursue him.

Guiding her down the corridor, ignoring her weak, "What . . . ? Where are we going?" he halted before the glassed conservatory doors, set one swinging wide, and whisked her through.

"Mr. Caxton—"

"Dillon. If we're going to be engaging in personal persuasions, it seems only reasonable to be on first-name terms." Tacking down a narrow corridor between masses of leafy shrubs, towing her behind him, he halted and turned to look at her. "What's your first name?"

She frowned, narrowed her eyes. "Priscilla."

His lips twitched. "What does your brother call you?" When she didn't immediately answer, he guessed. "Pris?"

She didn't deny it. She looked around, then back, realizing they were out of sight of the corridor or anyone coming through the door. There were no lamps burning, but the moonlight poured through the glassed roof, providing steady illumination, enough to see by. She glanced toward the gardens beyond the glassed walls, but dense foliage screened them from that direction, too.

Her frown grew more definite. "Mr. Caxton, I don't know what 'persuasions' you think to employ, but regardless, I'll thank you to escort me back to the ballroom."

Clearly holding her hand was insufficient contact. Dillon sighed, let her hand fall, reached for her, and neatly jerked her into his arms.

Six

She gasped as she landed against him. He didn't need to see her wide emerald eyes hazing to know she was instantly swamped with desire. As was he. Closing his arms, locking her against him, he bent his head and covered her lips—already parted on that evocative gasp.

He surged into her mouth, laid claim, then settled to plunder, to taste her, to provocatively taunt until she responded, until her fingers tangled in his hair, then gripped, until her lips firmed and her body tensed, until her tongue met his, all fire and passion.

Reminding himself that this time he was going to remain firmly in control—that it was imperative he do so, that there was a purpose behind the kiss, one beyond the welling, burgeoning, cascading pleasure—once she was fully engaged in the kiss, once he judged she'd lost any reservation she might have possessed over dallying with him in such a dangerous way, he mentally drew back sufficiently to gauge her state.

If he wanted answers, he would need to render her thoroughly witless, take her to that sensual point where experiencing the next touch, the next sensation was the only thing that mattered in life. She recognized the risks she courted with him, that he could indeed sweep her onto that plane of vulnerable, trembling need.

He prayed she didn't realize the same risk applied to him.

Pris sensed his retreat; she read it as a caution, as a belated recognition that this much heat, this much passion, wasn't wise.

Too late. Her fingers speared through his heavy locks; seduced by the silky texture, she held his head steady and pressed boldly nearer until his hard frame fully impinged against her curves. If he thought he could tease her—offer a mere glimpse of the pleasure she might have, and draw back and dangle more like a carrot before her—he could think again.

The tiny part of her mind still functioning knew that reacting so flagrantly was reckless. She didn't care. His arms tightened about her and she delighted; his hands spread over her back, hesitated.

She kissed him voraciously, tempted, beckoned; he tried to hold aloof, then the dam broke, and he responded.

With heat. With a fiery response that curled her toes.

His palms hardened, pressed, then slid low, evocatively molding her hips to his.

Her abandoned senses exulted. Nearly swooned when he ruthlessly took command of the kiss, took command of her senses, and recklessly spun them both into the eye of a passion-wracked storm.

He held her there, for long moments let the sensual winds buffet her, rake her nerves, her mind, let them tempt and promise.

When he lifted his head just enough so he could speak, his breath a warm flame over her sensitized lips, she was clinging to him, clinging to the remnants of her wits, still whirling in the vortex of welling, swelling need.

"Did you find the string you were searching for?"

The words made no sense, connected with nothing in her mind. She blinked, then realized, remembered. "Ah . . . no."

He kissed her again, waltzed her back into the waiting conflagration, until every nerve sizzled, until heat raced through her veins and pooled low. Until the world had disappeared behind a mist of desire, and only the two of them existed.

Lifting his head, he caught her lower lip between his teeth, gently tugged, then released it and murmured, "Is it your brother you're protecting?"

This time, it took longer to gather her wits, longer to find the strength to think. She tried to frown, but her features seemed unresponsive. Her lashes fluttered as she battled to assemble the right words . . . no? Yes?

It was only because she couldn't decide but had to think harder that she realized what he was doing. The effort required to snap her mind free of his sensual web left her weak; luckily, he was holding her. "I have no idea what you're talking about."

Her delivery lacked incisive strength but was enough to make him draw an exasperated breath.

She would have smiled, but he kissed her again. For one long moment she let him pull her, unresisting, back under the glorious wave, then she mentally jerked back. She drew her lips from his enough to whisper, "What's in the confidential section of the register?"

His only answer was a curse; she was smiling broadly when he kissed her again. But she now had his measure, and her own; she refused to let him submerge her wits. Reluctantly, she pulled back again, but tried another avenue of attack and leaned heavily into him. Let her stomach cradle his erection and sinuously moved against him.

He sucked in a breath, closed his eyes. He looked like he was in pain.

Another form of persuasion. Artfully she caressed, slowly, she hoped seductively. "How do the confidential details stop the falsifying of winners—is it some sort of description?"

She made the words as soft as she could, let her voice slide into the low, sultry tones she knew from experience rattled the cages of men's libidos. She'd never before used her body, her voice, to deliberately entice; she derived more feminine satisfaction than she'd thought possible when he answered, his tone a gravelly rumble, "Yes." He paused; to her delight, he was struggling to think. "I can't tell you more than that."

He could, if he would. She slid her hands from his nape to his shoulders, was about to run her palms down his chest when he glanced down.

"That's the ugliest shawl I've ever seen." With a tug, he unraveled the knot between her breasts.

Before she could catch the screening silk, it slithered over and off her shoulders and fell to the floor.

Leaving her—the real her—revealed, clad in her deep green silk gown with its daringly abbreviated bodice. It was a perfectly acceptable gown, yet her breath tangled in her throat; her nerves stretched. She glanced up, and her lungs seized.

He was looking at her—at her breasts mounding above the low, straight edge of her bodice, at the expanse of fine white skin now exposed—and there was heat in his eyes. His gaze caressed like flames, touching, brushing—threatening to consume.

Before she could do the sensible thing and step away, he raised both hands and, almost reverently, closed them about her breasts.

Sensation, sharp, indescribably shocking, lanced through her.

Her knees buckled.

He swept one arm around her, gathered her to him, held her against him, supported as his other hand eased, then caressed, fingers firm and seeking through the silk. Her pent-up breath hissed out, a sharp exhalation in the warm, earthy dark.

Forcing up her suddenly heavy lids, she looked into his face. Watched some expression move across the angular planes; in the weak light it was impossible to decipher it.

Easier to follow were his physical reactions, the tightening of the steely muscles that banded her back, the thin slash of his lips as they fractionally parted. His eyes as they tracked his fingers, as his gaze devoured and rising heat licked along her spine.

Even easier to sense was his fascination. With her body, with the firm flesh his palm sculpted, with the nipple his knowing fingers found and, to the sound of her desperate gasp, teased to furled attention.

With the delicate skin above her neckline that the pads of his fingers skimmed . . .

Then he bent his head and found her lips again, whirled her back into the spinning vortex of desire, into the conflagration that so temptingly threatened to consume her senses—just as long as she surrendered and let go of her wits.

Let him sweep them away and command her.

She wouldn't—knew that she couldn't, that she didn't dare. That she couldn't risk it.

The kiss evolved into a battle of wills, of wits, a flagrant duel of the senses. He pressed; she countered, fighting to keep her mind from the seductive play of his hand at her breast, from the evocative thrust of his hips against hers when, denied, he let his other hand slide down her back, over her hips to her bottom, to grip, then knead provocatively, then to mold her hips to his.

He was devilish, experienced—unused to being denied.

He had more weapons in his arsenal than she'd dreamed of, yet even while she realized he hadn't been anywhere as near losing control as he'd let her believe, she also sensed, and his reluctance to engage those more potent weapons he possessed confirmed, that he was walking as fine a line as she—the line between conquest and surrender, not to himself, or to her, but to passion.

She pressed her hands up, framed his face, clung as she kissed him, as she met the next thrust of his tongue and with reckless abandon drew him deep.

His control shook, wavered.

Abruptly she discovered she'd waltzed them to the edge of a sexual precipice, and they were suddenly teetering on the brink.

She didn't have strength enough left to haul them back.

Neither, it seemed, did he.

His hands, on her body, firmed, his grip suddenly more demanding.

"Yes, Mildred—I do assure you it's *quite* purple around the edges of the petals."

Lady Kershaw's haughty tones achieved what neither of them could. Jerked back to sanity, they both froze. Both rediscovered their reins and pulled back. Quietly, barely moving, they broke the kiss, hesitated for a moment, their breaths mingling, then they carefully lifted their heads and looked around.

"It's this way—right at the back near the windows."

Neither of them moved. They were in an aisle off the central walkway bisecting the conservatory. The brisk *tap-tap* of heels and a *swish* of skirts heralded Lady Kershaw and at least one other lady.

Pris held her breath, felt his hands tighten about her waist, tensing as if to whisk her behind him, but the ladies—Lady Kershaw and Mrs. Elcott—engaged in a heated argument about a particular bloom, swept past the open end of the aisle without noticing them.

She glanced at Caxton—Dillon. They were surely on first-name terms now. He caught her eye, held a finger across his lips.

Then he bent and retrieved her shawl.

She took it, bunched it in one hand as he pointed farther down the aisle. Taking her hand, he drew her with him; she tiptoed so her heels didn't clack on the tiles.

He turned right at the end of the aisle, into another that followed the outer glass wall back toward the house. Before they reached the front of the room, the glass changed to brick. He halted by a door in the wall. Easing it open, he looked through, then stepped out, whisking her with him, then turned and shut the door.

They were in a small foyer connecting an external door with the corridor to the ballroom; Pris told herself she was glad the door hadn't led into some other private room.

Her pulse was still racing, her skin still warm. Far safer to retreat, regardless of the compulsion of her traitorous desires.

Shaking out her shawl, she draped it over her shoulders and tied the ends once more between her breasts, concealing her dashingly dramatic bodice.

Glancing up, she surprised a disgusted look on Dillon Caxton's face.

Meeting her gaze, he held it for a moment, then shook his head. "Never mind."

He waved her back into the corridor. Without another word, they returned to the ballroom.

Just before they stepped across the threshold, he closed his hand about her elbow and halted her.

Brows rising, she looked back and up at him.

He trapped her gaze, quietly said, "Tell me why you need to know, and I'll answer every question you have."

She held his gaze for a corresponding moment, then equally quietly replied, "I'll think about it."

Facing forward, she stepped into the ballroom.

* * *

On her bay mare, crossing the Heath in the wispy fog of early morning, Pris skirted veiled riders from various strings out exercising in the chill. Disguised again as a lad, hat low, head down, her muffler about her chin, she cantered steadily toward the area favored by the Cromarty string.

The Heath, she'd learned, was the property of the Jockey Club and made available to the stables with racehorses registered to run at the Newmarket track. While watchers were discouraged from viewing any trials, the early-morning gallops were another matter; she glimpsed the odd figure cloaked in mist studying the horses as they were put through their paces.

She rode on, praying that Rus would take advantage of the cover of the filmy fog to spy on Harkness and Lord Cromarty's horses.

Her problems were compounding. When Dillon Caxton had offered to answer every question if she told him why she needed to know, while she'd known he'd been referring to the register, for one instant, she'd wished he'd been speaking of other things. Things of a more private nature.

"The last thing I need is to grow infatuated with a damned Englishman, especially one who's more handsome than I am."

Especially given he harbored the clear aim of interrogating her under the influence of passion.

People got others drunk in order to question them. He'd tried to make her drunk on desire, intoxicated with sensual pleasure. The bastard. He'd added significantly to her worries. She had no idea why she was so susceptible to his "persuasion"; his dramatic, overtly sensual good looks should have inured her to his charm—mere attractiveness invariably bored her. Instead . . .

She was increasingly anxious that if he sought to more definitely tempt her, she wouldn't be able to resist, to hold against him, or her own too-impulsive desires.

The next time . . .

Her nerves tightened. The longer she remained in Newmarket, the longer she took to locate Rus, made a "next time" increasingly inevitable. Then Caxton would press her further, and further, until she stopped resisting his questions. And him.

She wasn't so inexperienced she didn't know that the lust he wielded to fog her mind was perfectly real.

Her senses skittered, whether in fevered anticipation or anticipated fright, she didn't like to think. Muttering another curse, she shut her mind to such unproductive thoughts and peered ahead. She was nearing the right spot.

Through drifting mists, she detected the outline of another string exercising, the thud of hooves reverberating oddly through the damp air. Breathy snorts mingled with instructions and quick replies, distorted by the fog; reining in a sufficient distance away not to draw attention, she tuned her ears to the chatter, instantly distinguishing the soft burr of her mother tongue.

Instead of easing, her nerves coiled tighter. Lifting the mare's reins, she soundlessly urged the horse into a slow walk, traveling a wide circle around the area where Cromarty's horses trotted and galloped.

She rode slowly to avoid detection, the clop of the mare's hooves submerged beneath the racehorses' relentless pounding. The fog was both an aid and a disadvantage; at one point when it thinned she realized she'd ventured too close to the parading horses. Keeping her head down, she adjusted her route to arc around a large copse.

Rounding it, she looked ahead.

On the far side of the copse, wreathed in fog, a lone figure sat ahorse. Black hair, good seat. He was staring intently into the copse—perhaps through the copse at the horses?

He was too far away; she couldn't judge his height and build, yet . . .

In the instant her heart lifted in hope, the man turned his head and saw her.

Horror speared icelike through her veins.

The man cursed, lifted one arm.

Swallowing a yelp, she ducked, simultaneously clapping her heels to the mare's flanks. A ball whistled over her head, whining eerily through the fog; a split second later, the report of the pistol crashed over her.

Spooked by the sound, by her fear and her urging, the mare shot off, streaking across the green, parallel to the copse.

Past the man, but separated by sufficient distance for Pris to see him as nothing more than a blurred shape through the billowing fog. A blurred shape drawing forth another saddle pistol.

Her heart in her mouth, she swung the mare around the copse, forcing the man, cursing again, to wheel his horse before he could follow.

She headed straight for the exercising string, the horses trotting and galloping disrupted as, having heard the shot, the stable lads reined in.

Pressing low, clinging to the mare's neck, the black mane whipping her cheeks, Pris streaked through the milling horses—straight through and on across the Heath.

The man on his heavier horse thundered after her.

Harkness. He looked like the very devil and had a temper to match.

Pris felt her heart rising into her throat; swallowing, she rode with hands and knees, urging the little mare to fly.

The mare was nimble and had a good turn of speed. It had been years since Pris had ridden so fast, so recklessly, so desperately, but as the minutes elapsed she sensed the heavier horse falling behind. Easing the pace, she rose up and risked a quick glance back.

Harkness was still there, doggedly coming on. The heavier horse would outstay her mare, and the Heath was immense.

Facing forward, Pris held the mare one notch back from her previous headlong pace and forced her mind to function, to ignore her clamoring fear.

She couldn't outrun Harkness; she would have to lose him.

Somewhere in a landscape that was open grassland with no stand of trees large enough to hide her.

The map in the lending library took shape in her mind. She recalled the wooded estate bordering the Heath to the southeast—dense woodland, not paddocks. Hillgate End, Caxton's home.

It was the closest cover in which she might lose Harkness. Allowing him to catch up with her was out of the question.

The gallant mare responded as she veered southeast and picked up the pace. She eased the horse into a fluid gallop; quick glances behind showed Harkness closer, but he was once again falling behind.

She could almost hear his curses.

Facing forward, her own lungs tight, she urged the mare on.

Sooner than she'd expected, a line of trees rose before her. She headed for them, then swung along the line, searching for a bridle path.

A dip in the land, an area of worn turf, pointed to the entrance she sought. Her eyes locked on the spot.

She was fifty yards from it when a horseman appeared coming out of the woods, blocking the opening.

Pris recognized him instantly.

In the same instant he recognized her.

Her heart leapt again; cursing, she swerved away from the trees, swinging the mare back out onto the Heath.

The new direction took her closer to Harkness. She inwardly swore; she no longer had breath to spare for words. Desperately urging the mare on, she wondered how much longer her game little mount could last.

The thunder of hooves coming up hard on her right reminded her she had another pursuer.

One glance at him, at the black he once again had under him, and all thought of eluding him fled. Her brothers would have described the black as a good 'un, a sleek Thoroughbred, elegant and powerful, relentless and remorseless.

Much like his rider.

If he caught her and they stopped, would Harkness risk a shot? Worse, would he brazenly approach and accuse her—

She didn't get a chance to evaluate her options; the black drew level, then, ridden to an inch, surged ahead and headed the mare . . . toward Harkness.

Panic rose; Pris swore and reined in hard, bringing the mare, heaving and snorting, to a plunging halt.

Under exquisite control, the black slowed and circled her.

Pris glanced at Harkness, but he was temporarily hidden by a dip.

Dillon halted Solomon parallel to the mare, a foot apart. He frowned at Priscilla—Pris—not at all liking what he saw.

Her mare was one step from blown, and so was she. She was desperately sucking in air, her breasts rising and falling beneath the thin hacking jacket that was part of her disguise. Her eyes were wide, slightly wild; as he watched, her hair tumbled from beneath her hat and cascaded in a tangle of heavy curls down her back.

Fear hung like an aura about her, and that he didn't like at all.

"What the devil are you about?"

Her eyes, until then staring past his shoulder, shifted to his face. She swallowed. "Nothing."

When he looked his irritation, she drew in a breath, held it as if seeking strength, then amended, "I was out riding. Just"—she waved—"riding."

"Do you always ride as if the devil himself were after you?"

She lifted her hat, wiped her damp brow with her sleeve. "I . . . the mare needed a run. She likes to run."

A withering retort burned his tongue, then he saw . . . his blood turned to ice in his veins.

Reaching out, he plucked the hat from her fingers.

Pris looked up, lips thinning; reaction and more coursed through her as she reached out and tried to grab her hat back.

He anticipated her move and easily avoided her, leaning away, the black shifting back a step.

Dillon didn't look at her, but stared at her hat.

She frowned. "What . . . ?"

He raised the hat brim to his face and sniffed.

Then his gaze lifted and fixed on her face.

Pris's lungs seized. She couldn't breathe. The look on his face, stark, the classically perfect planes stripped bare of even the thinnest veneer of social glamor, the veil of civilization wrenched aside to reveal . . . something that hungered, that hunted, that trapped and devoured and possessed.

Something that burned in his dark, dark eyes, something primal and ruthless and haunting.

That look was focused entirely on her.

Slowly, without letting her free of his gaze, he lifted her hat, and tilted it so the brim was visible.

She dragged in a breath and glanced—at the deep scallop punched through the edge of the hat's brim, the partial hole ringed by a rusty burn.

Fear congealed in her veins. He touched the hat's crown

with one long finger, drawing her gaze in fascinated horror to the nick in the hat's crown.

Shock shivered through her. Harkness's shot hadn't gone all that wide . . .

Her world was suddenly edged in black.

She heard Dillon swear, felt him press the black closer, sensed him near.

The distant thud of hooves reached them. She blinked; they both looked.

The morning sun had burned off the mists; Harkness was clearly visible as he crested a rise a hundred yards away.

He saw them and pulled up, wheeling his mount in the same movement. With a glare Pris felt even across the distance, he rode back the way he'd come, immediately disappearing from sight.

Eyes narrowed, Dillon turned to her. "Who was he?"

Steely menace colored his tone.

She looked down. "I don't know."

The word he uttered was very far from polite.

After a fraught moment, he said, the words clipped and tight, "He shot at you. *Why?*"

The question had her looking up, realizing. "I . . . ah, don't know."

Harkness had mistaken her for Rus. He'd been waiting—following precisely the same logic she had.

From the look on Dillon's face he knew she knew the answers to both his questions. Turning her head, she stared after Harkness.

Had he realized his mistake? Her hair hadn't fallen until she'd stopped; Harkness wouldn't have seen it, and from a distance, on horseback, dressed as she was, it wouldn't be easy to distinguish her from Rus.

And Harkness wouldn't be expecting *her* to be there, for there to be someone about he could mistake for her striking brother.

Yet if he'd thought she was Rus . . . Pris looked at Dillon.

She knew Harkness's reputation; the man was bad and bold. Why had he so readily turned tail rather than come after Rus?

Dillon had been facing away from Harkness. Her gaze slid to Dillon's horse. The black was an exceptional specimen, tall, with long, elegant lines, and totally, completely black. "Do you often ride him?"

Dillon's eyes remained on her face. "Yes."

"So he's known about the town?"

He didn't answer, but after a moment said, "Are you saying that man recognized me because of Solomon?"

That was the only explanation for Harkness's abrupt retreat. She shrugged, leaned over, and grasped her hat, twitching to retrieve it.

Fingers instinctively tightening, Dillon held it for a moment, then let her tug it free. Through eyes still narrow, he watched her tuck up her hair, then cram the hat over it. The result was wobbly, but apparently satisfied, she gathered her reins, then looked at him, and inclined her head.

"Good day, Mr. Caxton."

He snorted. "Dillon. And I'll escort you home."

Her chin rose; she glanced sharply at him as he brought Solomon alongside the drooping mare. "That won't be necessary."

"Nevertheless." He couldn't stop himself from grimly adding, "You've had enough adventures for one day."

She looked ahead and made no reply.

He'd much rather she'd ripped up at him. He was tempted to say something to prick her Irish temper; the knowledge he wanted an excuse to rail at her—to release the gnawing, clamorous need to react, to act and seize and wield a right some part of him had already decided was his—held him back.

He'd never felt such a reaction before, had never been even vaguely susceptible to its like. Why she—who aroused so many emotions in him, and all so easily—should likewise trigger such a powerful, almost violent response simply by being reckless, by being in danger, by doing things—reckless things—that put her in danger . . .

The roiling tide rose, welling at his thoughts. He cut them off, slammed a door on his urges—primitive, he knew, and unlikely, in this instance, to be met with anything but haughty and contemptuous dismissal.

Jaw clenched, he glanced at her, riding easily by his side.

After a moment, he looked ahead. Trust—hers—that's what he was after. Time enough once he'd learned her secrets to introduce her to this other side of him that she and only she evoked.

Provoked.

Riding silently beside him, Pris was very aware of his leashed temper; it rubbed against hers like a hand ruffling fur the wrong way. There was heat there, too, lurking behind the anger, using it as a screen. It tempted her to engage, to let her temper flare and clash with his, but she was simply too weary, too exhausted, to risk such a foolhardy, reckless, and wild act just now.

No matter how tempted.

It was like riding beside a tiger, but . . .

Harkness had shot at her thinking she was Rus, and he'd been aiming to kill. The realization slid through her, solidifying and growing colder, more icy and sharp with every passing mile.

The mare plodded on. Dillon held his black to a walk; the horse was beautifully schooled. Despite wanting to run, he obliged, and like a gentleman paced neatly alongside the weary mare. Almost protectively.

Very like his master.

The understanding intensified the coldness spreading inside her. She couldn't afford to lean on Dillon Caxton, not now, not yet, perhaps not ever. She didn't know if she could trust him. The events of the morning had brought Rus's plight even more forcefully home. Her twin was in very deep trouble.

The cold had seeped to her bones, to her marrow. She was shivering inside, but fought to hide it. She hunched her shoulders, her arms tight against her body.

From beside her came a muffled curse. Dillon shifted in his saddle; before she could summon the energy to glance his way, warmth fell around her shoulders, then engulfed her.

She stiffened, lifted her head even as her fingers greedily gripped and held the heat to her, the coat about her.

"For God's sake, *don't* argue!"

She shot him a severe glance.

He returned it with interest. "Disobliging female that you are."

Her lips twitched. Looking ahead, she kept the coat close, savored its warmth, his body heat trapped in the silk lining. Without looking his way, she inclined her head. Stiffly said, "Thank you."

The horses walked on. The icy chill inside her thawed.

By unspoken accord, they'd taken a route circling the town; no need for any ladies or gentlemen out early to see her. By the time they neared the Carisbrook house and reined in fifty yards from the stable, she felt warmed through, restored to her customary health, her usual decisive temper.

Shrugging out of the coat, she handed it back. "Thank you."

He responded with a dark look. Taking the coat, he slung it about his shoulders and shrugged into it. She forced herself to look away from the enthralling sight of the muscles of his chest flexing beneath the fine lawn of his shirt.

He should come with a warning tattooed on his forehead.

He settled into his saddle and reached for his reins. She looked at him, calmly met his gaze. "I'll bid you a good day, Mr. . . ." Briefly, she smiled. "Dillon."

He didn't smile in return; large, lean, and relaxed in his saddle, he held her eyes with a steady gaze she found a touch unsettling. After a moment, he asked, his voice low, a hint of the sexual seeping through, "When are you going to tell me the truth?"

She didn't look away from that dark stare, heavy with unspoken implications. After a pause she allowed to grow fraught, she lightly raised her brows. "When are you going to tell me what I want to know?"

A minute ticked past as they eyed each other, an acknowledgment they still stood on opposing sides of a fence.

"Priscilla, you are playing a very dangerous game."

The words were low, precise, uttered with little inflection; they still set something inside her quivering.

Her temper stirred; haughty willfulness infused her as she lightly arched her brows, then, gathering her reins, she turned the mare and started her for the stables—glancing back at the last to say with sultry deliberation, "Until next time . . . Dillon."

Seven

"You're absolutely sure?" Seated in an armchair in Demon's study, Dillon stared at Barnaby; he didn't know what to think.

Earlier that afternoon, Barnaby had returned from London, found him in his office, and insisted on dragging him out to the Cynster stud to share his discoveries simultaneously with Demon and Flick.

Perched on the window seat, Barnaby nodded. "No question at all—Vane and I had the same story from different sources. The spring races the rumors concerned were the New Plate at Goodwood, and the Cadbury Stakes at Doncaster, and *in both cases,* the losses were sustained on runners from the same stable—horses whose runs were completely inconsistent with their previous form. That stable is Collier's, near Grantham."

Seated behind his desk, Flick as usual perched on the arm of his chair, Demon looked at Dillon. "Collier's dead."

His gaze still on Barnaby, Dillon nodded. "Yes. I know."

Barnaby's face fell. "Dead?" He looked from Dillon to Demon.

"Definitely," Demon said. "It created quite a stir. Collier was well-known. He'd been in the business for decades and had some fine horses. Apparently he was riding by a local quarry, something spooked his horse, and he was thrown down the quarry cliff. His neck was broken." Demon looked at Dillon. "What happened to the stable? Who inherited?"

"His daughter. She had no interest in the stable or the horses—she sold them off. I saw the paperwork crossing my clerks' desks."

"Who bought them—any particular party?"

"Most went in singles or pairs to different stables."

Demon frowned. "No mention of a partner?"

Dillon studied Demon's face. "No. Why?"

"Collier got into difficulties at the end of the autumn season last year—he bet on some of his own runners and lost heavily. I'd wondered if he'd be racing again, but after the winter break he returned, not only with no cuts to his string, but with two very classy new runners."

"Not Catch-the-wind and Irritable?" Barnaby asked. "Those were the horses involved in the suspect races."

Demon described the two horses; Dillon agreed to check. He looked at Barnaby. "Was there any suggestion the horses were stopped—that the jockeys held them back?"

"No. All those complaining seemed certain the jockeys did their best—they didn't want to implicate them, but couldn't see how else it was done."

Demon and Dillon exchanged a look. "How it was done," Dillon said, "we can guess. Who benefited is the question."

"Actually," Demon said, "the first question might be: how did Collier die? Was it an accident, or . . ."

"Or given the rumors"—Dillon's voice hardened—"and the likelihood someone would eventually look into them, as we are, was Collier silenced?"

"Silenced? Why?" Barnaby asked.

"So he couldn't implicate whoever had funded the substitutions," Flick replied.

Barnaby looked puzzled. Flick explained, "The other way to fix a race and make a great deal of money is to run a particular horse that does well until it establishes a sound reputation—excellent form—and then, for one race, switch another horse for it. Your 'favorite' then loses. After the race, you switch the real horse back. By the time any inquiry is afoot and the stewards think to examine the horse that unexpectedly lost, it's the right horse, and there's no evidence of any wrongdoing."

Barnaby nodded. "But why couldn't it just have been Collier behind it, with his death an accident as presently thought?"

"Because," Dillon said, "finding substitute horses is expensive. They have to be specific matches, and Thoroughbreds as well."

"So," Flick said, "if Collier was hard-pressed, there must have been someone else involved."

"More"—Demon caught Barnaby's eye—"someone had to have bailed Collier out."

Barnaby's brows rose. "On condition he train and race—and arrange, however it's done—the substitutions?"

Dillon nodded. "That seems likely."

"I see." Barnaby looked at Demon, then Dillon. "It looks like a visit to Grantham should be my next jaunt."

Dillon rose. "I'll get the details of Collier's stable from the register, and we can check that the horses Demon remembers were the suspect runners. When are you thinking of leaving?"

"There's a ball at Lady Swalesdale's tonight." Standing, Flick shook out her skirts. "I'm sure her ladyship would be delighted to have you join us."

"Ah . . ." Barnaby looked at her, then Dillon. "I'll be off north at first light. I'll need to spell my horses. I rather think I'll give Lady Swalesdale's a miss."

Demon coughed to hide a laugh.

Flick leveled a severe glance at Barnaby.

Dillon scoffed, "Coward."

Barnaby grinned. "You're just sorry you can't escape, too."

In that, Barnaby had been wrong; Dillon hadn't been interested in escaping Lady Swalesdale's ball. Quite the opposite—he'd been looking forward to observing the lovely Miss Dalling coping with her smitten swains. If he was any judge of her temper, they'd soften her up nicely—for him.

Leaning against the wall of an alcove, concealed by the shadows cast by a large palm, he watched Priscilla Dalling captivate—and, whenever she noticed him watching, flirt with—a tribe of local gentlemen, one and all besotted by her bounteous charms.

While he appreciated the picture she made in her lavender silk gown with its keyhole neckline that, far from being decorous, drew attention even more provocatively to the deep valley between her breasts, while his eyes drank in the sleek yet curvaceous figure her well-cut gown so lovingly revealed, while his gaze was drawn to the exposed curve of her nape, to the vulnerable line highlighted by the black curls cascading from the knot on her head to bob seductively alongside one ear, it wasn't her physical beauty that held his interest.

She did. The animation in her face, the grace with which she moved, the laugh he occasionally heard over the rumble of voices, the life he sensed within her.

Beauty had never meant much to him—it was just the outer casing. What was inside mattered more. When he looked at her, he saw a fiery spirit, a feminine reflection of himself. It was that that lured him, that drew him to her.

He continued to watch cynically as she dealt with her admirers. The outcome of her flirting was already trying her temper—serve her right. The gentlemen were a boon in his eyes; they had her corralled; she couldn't slip from his sight without them giving warning.

Two days had passed since he'd encountered her racing for her very life over the Heath. Two days since he'd discovered some man had come far too close to ending her life.

The draining of all color from her face when he'd shown her the hole in her hat still haunted him. She hadn't known how close to death she'd come.

He'd ridden his own temper hard and kept away for the rest of the day, and the next, knowing he'd meet her tonight. He'd seen her at a distance in town; since he'd escorted her back to the Carisbrook house, she'd left it only in the company of her aunt and Miss Blake. No one had come to visit her, and she hadn't slipped away to any illicit meeting; he'd had four of his stable lads on special duty, watching the house day and night.

Through the palm fronds, he studied her face—the set of her chin, her eyes—and decided she hadn't yet softened enough for his purpose. It wasn't yet time to offer her an escape.

He'd left Barnaby armed with the direction of Collier's stable, east of Grantham. They'd confirmed Collier's classy new runners had been the horses involved in the suspect races. Over dinner, Barnaby had remembered to mention that Vane had stumbled on similar whispers about a race run at Newmarket a few weeks before, early in the autumn season.

That had been most unwelcome news. Vane and Gabriel were hunting for more details.

The earlier suspect races had been at Goodwood and Doncaster, under Jockey Club rules, true, but not the same as a race at Newmarket, run under the Club's collective nose. If it was part of the same scheme, the perpetrators were arrogant and cocksure. And there would almost certainly be more to come.

Dillon knew the scheme wasn't targeted at him personally, yet as the Keeper of the Breeding Register and Stud Book, the office responsible for the verification of horses' identities, the scheme was a direct challenge to his authority. More, the Committee had asked him to investigate and deal with the problem, setting said problem squarely in his lap. His past indiscretion, even if now history, only compounded the pressure.

The scheme might not have been conceived with a personal aspect, yet for him it had assumed one; he felt as if he were facing an as-yet-unsighted enemy who had a lethal arrow nocked and aimed at him—he had to cut the bowstring before the arrow could be loosed.

He refocused on Pris Dalling. Far from being on the side of his enemy, he was convinced she was presently standing somewhere in the mists between him and the opposition.

A moment passed, then he stirred, impatient to act, wishing she'd dismiss all the others and come his way.

She started edging from her admirers. He straightened. Watching more intently, he noted her sudden nervousness, the way she sidled to keep the shoulders of her attentive swains between her and someone farther up the ballroom.

Dillon scanned the guests. Lady Swalesdale had assembled a small multitude, all the locals of note as well as many owners who belonged to the ton. He glanced again at Pris; to his educated eye, panic was rising beneath her glib surface, but who was inciting it was impossible to guess.

He was about to quit his sanctuary when she acted. Brightly smiling, she dismissed two gentlemen; the instant they left, she excused herself to the remaining three—judging by the wilting hand she raised to her brow, unimaginatively claiming a sudden indisposition.

The three were disheartened, but in her hands so malleable. They bowed; with what Dillon knew would be perfectly sincere thanks, she left them and headed his way.

She walked purposefully, casting swift, sharp glances up

the room, taking good care to remain screened from that direction. She drew near the alcove, then to his surprise, stepped into the shadowed opening, simultaneously beckoning a nearby footman to attend her.

The footman came hurrying to bow before her. "Ma'am—miss?"

"I'm Miss Dalling. I wish you to take a message to my aunt, Lady Fowles. She's seated on a chaise at the top of the room. She's wearing a pale green gown and has ostrich feathers in her hair. Tell Lady Fowles that I've been called away and am returning home. I would rather she remain and enjoy the evening—she shouldn't return early on my account. Please convey that to her immediately."

Pris listened while the footman repeated the message, and nodded.

"Do you wish me to summon your carriage, miss?"

"No, thank you. Just deliver my message." She bestowed a brilliant smile on the footman; he bowed and all but charged off on his quest. She glanced up the room, drew in a breath, and slipped out of the shadows.

Quickly, as unobtrusively as she could, she tacked through the guests at this end of the room and slipped out through a secondary door. The corridor beyond was presently empty, but the ball was barely an hour old; guests were still trickling in through the main ballroom doors farther down the corridor, near the front hall.

Those main ballroom doors were propped wide; she couldn't risk walking past them—couldn't risk Lord Cromarty seeing her. The last glimpse she'd had of him he'd been standing with a group of similar gentlemen, unfortunately facing those doors.

Until he'd walked in, it hadn't occurred to her that in going about in Newmarket society she risked meeting him. Cromarty had met her, exchanged a few words with her; Rus had been with her at the time, less than a year ago.

There were drawbacks to being so physically notable; it

made her very recognizable. She couldn't risk Cromarty getting even a glimpse.

She hadn't forgotten a single word of Rus's letter; if he'd found anything untoward in what Harkness was doing, Rus would have gone to Cromarty. While she wasn't going to jump to conclusions regarding Cromarty, neither was she willing to endanger Rus by letting Cromarty know she was there.

If Cromarty was involved, he'd know she'd either find Rus, or he'd find her. All Cromarty needed to do was watch her, and eventually he'd have Rus.

Partly hidden by a tall lamp, she hovered in the hallway until another footman crossed to the ballroom. Stepping into plain sight, she beckoned imperiously. "My cape, if you please. It's lavender velvet, waist-length, with gold frogging."

The footman blushed, stammered, but quickly fetched the cape. She allowed him to set it about her shoulders, then dismissed him, giving the impression she was waiting for someone.

The instant the footman passed into the ballroom, she turned and hurried down the corridor, away from the ballroom and its lurking danger, deeper into the body of the house.

At the end of the corridor, she found a secondary staircase; descending to the ground floor, she peered out of a window and saw a side garden with paved paths leading away toward a band of trees.

Swalesdale Hall was only a mile or so from the Carisbrook house. She knew the direction; the moon was rising, shedding enough light for her to see her way.

Who knew? She might even bump into Rus; she knew her twin was out there somewhere. Alone.

The thought cut at her. Finding a door to the garden, she pushed it open and stepped outside.

She glanced around, but there was no one else about. Closing the door, she took her bearings. A cool breeze ruffled the creeper that grew on the walls. Selecting the most likely path from the five that led from the door, she set out, walking along the silvered flagstones toward the shelter of the trees.

In the open, less than halfway to the trees, a sudden premonition that there was someone behind her washed like an icy wave down her spine.

Even while her mind was reassuring her that she was imagining things, she was turning to look.

At the man who was sauntering silently in her wake.

A scream rose to her throat—she struggled to swallow it as the moonlight revealed who he was.

Her relief was so profound, she fleetingly closed her eyes—then snapped them open; she'd stopped walking—he hadn't.

He eventually halted with a single pace between them.

By then her temper had flown. "What the devil do you think you're doing, following me? *And,* what's more, in a manner guaranteed to scare me out of my wits!"

What wits were left to her; at least half were fully occupied drinking in his presence—the width of his shoulders, the lean tautness of his chest, the long, strong lines of his rider's legs, his brand of masculine grace even more pronounced when cloaked in the crisp black-and-white of evening dress. A lock of dark hair showed ink black against his forehead; in the sharp contrast created by the moonlight, he appeared a dark and dangerous creature, one conjured from her deepest fantasies and rendered in hot muscle and steel.

He was tempting enough in daylight; in the light of the moon, he was sin personified.

Her accusations had sounded shrill, even to her ears.

He'd tilted his head, studying her face. "I apologize. I didn't mean to scare you."

If she'd thought he was laughing at her, she'd have verbally flayed him, but there was sincerity in his tone, a touch of honesty she knew was real. She humphed and crossed her arms. With effort refrained from tapping her toe while she waited for him to say something, or better still, turn around and leave her.

When he simply stood there, looking down at her, she hauled in a breath, nodded regally, and swung around once more. "I'll bid you a good night, Mr. Caxton."

She started walking.

From behind her, she heard a sigh. "Dillon."

She didn't need to look to know he was following her.

"Where are you going?"

"Home. The Carisbrook place."

"Why?"

She didn't reply.

"Or"—the tenor of his voice subtly altered—"more to the point, who arrived in the ballroom that you didn't want to meet?"

"No one."

"Priscilla, allow me to inform you that you're a terrible liar."

She bit her lip, told herself he was deliberately goading her. "Whom I choose to meet is none of your damned business."

"Actually, in this case, I suspect it is."

They'd reached the trees. She didn't fear him, not in the sense that he wished her harm, but she, and her nerves, were not up to the strain of marching through a dark wood with him prowling at her heels. Tempting fate was one thing—that would be madness.

Halting, head high, she turned, and tried to stare him down—difficult given she had to look up to meet his shadowed eyes. "Good night, Dillon."

He looked down at her for a long moment—long enough for her to have to deliberately will her senses to behave—then he looked past her, toward the trees. "You do know it's more than a mile to the Carisbrook place?"

"Yes." She lifted her chin higher. "I might prefer to ride a horse, but I'm not unaccustomed to using shank's mare."

His lips twitched; he glanced at her. She got the impression he was about to say something, then thought better of it. Said instead, "More than a mile *cross-country*. Through the fields." He looked down all the way to her hem. "You're going to ruin that new gown, and your slippers."

She was, and was inwardly cursing the necessary sacrifice.

"I drove here in my curricle. Come to the stable, and I'll get my horses put to and drive you home."

He made the offer evenly, straightforwardly, as if it were simply the gentlemanly thing to do. She stared at his face, but couldn't read it; the light was too weak. Crossing the fields alone in the dark, or sitting beside him in his curricle for the few minutes required to travel a mere mile—which was the more dangerous?

Eyes on his face, she willed him to promise not to bite. When he simply waited, unmoved, she stifled a sigh and inclined her head. "Thank you."

He didn't gloat, but elegantly waved to another path following the tree line. "We can reach the stable that way."

She set out, and he fell in beside her, adjusting his long strides to her shorter ones. He made no attempt to take her arm, for which she was grateful. Their last meeting, and the manner of their parting, was high in her mind, combining with her memories of their encounter previous to that, when he'd tried to blind her with passion. Hardly surprising that her nerves had stretched taut, and her senses were jangling.

She felt it when he glanced at her.

"Are you enjoying your stay here?"

The words were diffident; he might have been making polite conversation, yet she sensed he wasn't.

"I'm enjoying the town well enough. It's an interesting place."

"And the occupants? You appear to have made quite a few conquests."

Something in his suave tone, a hint of steely displeasure, struck a nerve. She sniffed disparagingly. "But they're so easily conquered."

She heard the catty dismissiveness, the underlying rancor, and inwardly sighed. "I apologize, that wasn't fair. I daresay they're nice enough, but . . ." She shrugged, and kept her gaze fixed ahead.

"But you'd rather they didn't fall at your feet." Cynical empathy laced the words. "No need to apologize. I understand perfectly."

She glanced at him, but they were moving through the shadows; she couldn't read his expression. Yet she'd seen him in the ballroom, dodging the importunings of a small army of young ladies; later he'd disappeared, and she'd known a pang of envy that she hadn't been able to do the same.

He did understand.

That was such an odd situation, to meet a man who faced the same problem she routinely did, the same problem that drove Rus demented. As they walked through the shrouding dark, it seemed possible to ask, "Why do they do it? I've never understood."

He didn't immediately answer, but as the stable appeared before them, he softly said, "Because they don't see us clearly. They see the glamor, and not the person." They paused at the edge of the gravel court before the stable. Through the moonlight, he caught her gaze. "They don't see who we are, nor what we really are, and as we're not as inhumanly perfect as we appear, that's a very real problem."

A groom came out of the stable; Dillon turned his way. "Wait here. I'll get my curricle."

In a matter of minutes, he was handing her into a stylish equipage, drawn by a pair of blacks that took her breath away.

Oh, Rus—if only you could see . . .

Joining her on the box, he glanced at her; sitting beside her, he gathered the reins. "You appreciate horses."

Not a question. "Yes. I have a brother who's horse-mad—who lives and breathes and even dreams of horses."

"I see." There was a smile and real understanding in his tone. "You've met Flick—Felicity Cynster, my cousin. She was horse-mad from infancy, and her husband, Demon, who I've known as long, is even worse." They rattled down the drive. "I don't think you've met him yet."

"No." She hung on to the curricle's rail as he turned out into the lane in style. "It's a form of obsession, I think."

"I wouldn't argue with that."

The rattle of the wheels, counterpointed by the sharp clop of hooves, settled to a steady beat. The night about them was quiet and still, the breeze nothing more than a gentle caress.

"Are you going to tell me who you're running from to-night?"

"No."

"Why not?"

Because I can't. Because I don't dare. Because it isn't my secret to share. She shifted on the seat, very conscious of him close beside her, the warm solid reality of him. His sleek elegance disguised how large he was; he was taller, broader, much heavier than she, much stronger, much more powerful.

Seated side by side on the curricle's narrow seat, his presence surrounded her.

What she couldn't understand was why it made her feel safe, when she knew beyond doubt that he was the biggest threat to her—to herself, to her peace of mind—that she'd ever faced.

"The man who tried to break into the Jockey Club." She turned her head to view him as they rolled briskly along. "Have you found him yet?"

She needed to keep her mind on her goal and not allow him to distract her, to lure her to trust when it might prove too dangerous.

Dillon glanced briefly at her, then looked back at his horses. "No." He considered the opening, decided to offer more. "He's Irish—just like you."

"Is he?"

She didn't even bother to pretend she hadn't known. He glanced at her again. She caught his gaze, opened her eyes wide. "How difficult could it be to find one Irishman in Newmarket?"

Despite her attempt to make the question a taunt, he knew it was real—she actually wanted to know.

Lips curving cynically, he looked to his horses. "As you've no doubt discovered, Priscilla, finding an Irishman in Newmarket is no problem at all. But finding one *particular* Irishman? Given the number of Irish lads and jockeys working here, let alone those over for the racing, locating any particular one is like finding the proverbial needle in a haystack."

She didn't reply. He shot her a glance, and found her expression serious, almost brooding.

"Who is he?" The question was out before he'd thought. She looked at him; he added, "Perhaps I could help."

She held his gaze for an instant, then shook her head and faced forward. "I can't tell you."

He checked his blacks for the turn into the Carisbrook drive. At least she'd stopped pretending she wasn't looking for some Irishman. He'd suggested brother, and she'd denied it. If not brother, then . . . lover?

He didn't like the thought, but forced himself to examine it. She was gently bred, of that he was sure, but she wouldn't be the first gentleman's daughter to lose her heart to some charismatic horse fancier. Against that, however, stood her aunt's involvement. Lady Fowles was simply too familiar a type of lady for him to believe she would ever be a party to

Pris chasing after some dissolute, or even merely unsuitable, lover.

It came back to a brother.

Or a cousin. Flick, after all, had stood by him, had done things that even now gave him nightmares in order to help him break free.

"I was once involved in a race-fixing swindle."

Her head swung around so fast her ringlets flew. *"What?"*

He met her stunned gaze, then, glancing around, slowed his horses. The drive was a long one; they were only halfway to the house. If he was going to reveal even *that* to persuade her to trust him, they needed somewhere to talk. If he remembered aright . . .

He found the track a little way along, almost grassed over. Turning the horses onto it, he set them walking.

"Where . . . ?" She was peering ahead, over the lawn to where a line of trees crossed their path.

"Just wait."

Guiding the blacks through the trees, he drove them up to the summerhouse standing beyond the end of the elongated ornamental lake before the house.

Reining in, he stepped down. Playing out the reins, he tethered the pair so they could stand and graze. The curricle rocked as Pris clambered down; he glimpsed slender ankles amid a froth of skirts.

She walked to him, puzzlement in her face. "What did you say?"

He waved to the summerhouse. "Let's go inside."

She led the way, plainly familiar with the wide, open room tucked under the domed roof. Of painted white wood, the summerhouse was simply furnished with a wicker sofa and one matching armchair, both liberally padded, placed to look down the vista of the lake to the distant house.

Pris sat in one corner of the sofa. She was not just intrigued but captured, not just eager but urgent to hear what he'd meant. And what he intended—why he'd volunteered to speak of such a thing.

But she needed to see his face, so the safety of the armchair wasn't an option. Outside, the moonlight cast a pearly sheen, but within the summerhouse, it was considerably dimmer. At her wave, he sat beside her. She studied his face; she could discern his features, but not the emotions in his eyes.

"I can't believe you—the Keeper of the Breeding Register—were ever involved in anything illicit. At least not about racing."

He met her gaze. After a moment, asked, "Can't you?"

It was as if he'd deliberately let his glamor fall, completely and utterly, so that she was suddenly looking at the real man, without any protective screen at all. She looked, examined; gradually it came to her.

She blew out a breath. Curling her legs, she shifted so she could fix her gaze on his face. "All right. Perhaps I can imagine it. You were wild as a youth, and—"

"Not just wild. Reckless." He paused, his eyes steady on hers; after a moment, he asked, "Isn't that what it takes?"

She didn't reply.

A pregnant moment ticked by, then he faced forward, settling his shoulders against the sofa's back, stretching out his legs, crossing his ankles, sliding his hands into his trouser pockets. He looked across the smooth surface of the lake to the distant glimmer that was the house; his lips curved, not cynically but in self-deprecation.

"Wild, reckless, and game for any lark." His tone suggested he viewed his younger self from a considerable distance, a separation in time and place. "Hedonistic, conceited, and selfish, and, naturally, immature. I had everything—name, money, every comfort. But I wanted more. No—I *craved* more. I needed excitement and thrills. My father tried, as fathers do, to rein me in, but in those days neither of us understood what drove the other." He paused, then baldly stated, "I became involved in betting on cockfights, got deeply in debt, which then left me—as the only son of the wealthy Keeper of the Stud Book, a revered member of the Jockey Club—open to blackmail."

He paused, gazing unseeing down the lake, then went on, his voice even but with darker currents rippling beneath. "They wanted me to act as a runner, organizing jockeys to hold back their mounts—a common enough scam in those days. I was just . . . cowardly enough to convince myself that falling in with their plan was my only choice."

This time, his pause lasted longer, the emotions ran deeper; Pris could find no adequate words to break it, so she waited.

Eventually, he stirred and glanced briefly at her. "Flick stood by me. She got Demon to help, and together they pulled me free of it. They exposed the race-fixing racket and the gentleman behind it—and forced me to, gave me the opportunity to, grow up."

"What happened to the cowardly streak?" When he glanced at her, she pointed out, "You wouldn't have mentioned it if you weren't sure you'd grown out of it."

His teeth flashed in a brief, cynically acknowledging smile before he looked back at the lake. "The coward in me died the instant the blackguard behind the scheme pointed a pistol at Flick." His gaze shifted over the silent water. A moment passed before he said, "It was strange—a moment when my life truly changed, when I suddenly saw what was important and what wasn't. To have someone I loved suffer because of something I'd foolishly done . . . I couldn't—absolutely and beyond question could not—face that."

"What happened? Was she shot?"

He shook his head. "No."

He said nothing more. She frowned, analyzing, then it came to her, like a premonition, only more certain. "You got shot instead."

Without looking at her, he shrugged. "Only reasonable in the circumstances. I survived."

A penance, a payment he didn't want to discuss. She had a good idea why he'd told her what he had, and where he was steering their conversation—in a direction she didn't want it to go. "The wild and reckless."

She waited until he looked at her, met her eyes. "Being wild and reckless is part of your soul." She knew that as well as she knew her own. "You can't lose characteristics like that, so where are they now? What do you do to satisfy the craving for excitement and thrills?"

She was curious; his eyes traveled her face, and she suspected he understood. That he saw that that was a question to which she'd yet to find an answer herself.

The smile that curled the ends of his lips suggested a certain sympathy. "Back then, I wondered—feared—that I'd become addicted to gambling, but to my relief, I found that wasn't so. I am"—he tilted his head her way in wry acknowledgment—"addicted, but to the rush of excitement, the thrill that comes with . . . success, I suppose. In winning, in succeeding, in beating the odds." He glanced briefly at her. "Luckily, my addiction didn't care in which endeavor I succeeded—it was the achievement that counted."

"So which endeavors have you been succeeding in?" She opened her eyes wide. "I can't imagine tending the Breeding Register for the Jockey Club qualifies."

Dillon grinned. "Not on its best day. My position there is more a long-term interest, almost a hereditary one. No, through Demon and the rest of his family, the Cynsters, I became involved in investing."

"Not the Funds, I take it?"

The dryness of her comment made him smile. "Having been educated by the best in the field, some of my wealth is of course deposited in the Funds, but you're right—the excitement and thrills come from the rest. The ferreting out of new opportunities, the evaluating, the projections, the possibilities—it's a wager of sorts, but on a much grander scale, with many more factors to take into account, but if you learn the right skills and use them well, the chances of success are immeasurably greater than in gaming—and the thrills and excitement commensurately more intense."

She looked at the lake and sighed. "And therefore more satisfying."

He eyed her profile. He wasn't entirely certain why he'd told her so much, but the telling had only reinforced his sense of obligation. He owed so much to so many—to Flick most of all, but also to Demon and the Cynsters in general. When he'd been in trouble, they'd freely and openly given him the aid he'd needed to reclaim his life. Through them, he'd made friends, acquaintances, and connections that he valued immensely, that were fundamentally important to who he now was.

Others had given him a great deal when he'd been in need.

Now Pris Dalling, and whoever she was protecting, needed help; he couldn't walk away, couldn't not offer his aid in turn.

"I told you about my past so you'd understand that, if you or whoever you're protecting has become embroiled in any illicit scheme and are finding it difficult to break free, then I, of all people, will understand." He waited until she turned her head and faced him, he sensed reluctantly. "If they're in trouble and need help, I'm prepared to give it, but in order to do so, you'll have to tell me who they are and what's going on."

Holding his gaze, Pris found herself facing the crux of her problem. She knew in her heart Rus would never willingly have become embroiled in any illicit scheme, but why hadn't he come forward and reported whatever it was he'd learned? Why was he hiding?

She didn't know; until she did . . . grimacing, she looked back at the lake. "I can't tell you."

Despite her best efforts, the words rang with real reluctance; despite her loyalty to Rus, the urge to grasp the hand Dillon held out was surprisingly strong—especially after that incident with Harkness, compounded by Cromarty's appearance that evening.

Since sighting Rus on the night he'd tried to break into the Jockey Club, she'd learned nothing more of his whereabouts. And with Harkness stalking the Heath and Cromarty swaggering about the ballrooms, her ability to search was becoming restricted.

She needed help, *but* . . .

Dillon moved, drawing his hands from his pockets and shifting to face her.

He was regrouping to press her further; she struck before he could, offense being infinitely preferable to defense, especially where he was concerned. She looked at him, let their gazes clash and lock—suddenly very aware of him, large, dark and dangerous, one muscled arm draped along the sofa's back. "I need to know the implications of what I'm telling you before I do. If you'll tell me what's in the register . . . ?"

He held her gaze for a heartbeat, then inflexibly replied, "I can't."

Where the compulsion came from she didn't know—part aggression, part rising fear, and partly that wild and reckless craving for excitement and thrills that was as intrinsic a part of her as it was of him.

"Perhaps I can persuade you . . . ?" The words fell from her lips, sultry and low.

Before he could react, raising her hands to frame his face, she leaned forward and kissed him.

Eight

Pris wanted nothing more than to distract him, and herself. To set aside her escalating troubles and for just a few minutes be herself. To soothe her restless soul with just a taste of the wild and reckless.

He tasted of both, of a dark flaring need that tempted and taunted, that teased her with a promise of illicit and dangerous pleasures, of atavistic delights beyond her ken.

His lips met hers without hesitation, returning the pressure, but no more; he took what she offered, but made no demands, left her to make the running as if aloofly sitting back to see how far she would go—how serious she was about persuading him.

Not in her wildest imaginings did she think she could, certainly not like this. Her wish to see the register wasn't the reason she leaned into him, traced his lower lip with the tip of her tongue, boldly entered his mouth when he parted his lips, and tempted him more.

Asked for more. All but pleaded.

He moved; his arm left the back of the sofa and slowly encircled her, then tightened, urging her to him. His other hand rose, fingers splaying to cradle her head as he smoothly slid the reins from her grasp, drew her nearer yet, all but into his lap as he angled his head and took control.

Of the kiss, and all else she would cede to him, but passivity wasn't her style; she drew a line and held to it, letting him kiss her as he would, show her what he would, but reserving the right to redirect their play if she wished. If she wanted.

Now, this minute, she wanted him. Wanted to feel his tongue stroking hers, wanted to experience again the hot tide of wanton desire he so readily called forth. His lips moved on hers, demanding, definitely commanding, yet still unurgent, still effortlessly, arrogantly, controlled.

She met each questing stroke of his tongue, dueled, retreated, allowed him to explore, then grasping his head tightly between her hands, boldly returned the pleasure.

Sensed, then, just for an instant—a second of hesitation when she felt his control momentarily crack, and she saw past it—what he hid behind his sophisticated façade.

Something not sophisticated at all. Something primal, powerful, and predatory, something with teeth and claws and burning eyes, a desire so wild, so reckless and passionate that, if let free, unrestrained, it possessed power enough to shake both their worlds.

The ultimate temptation for the wild and reckless.

The ultimate sin for those who couldn't resist the lure.

She saw, craved. Hungered. She reached for it, without hesitation sank into him, drew him deep into her mouth, and with lips and tongue invited.

Dillon inwardly cursed, and resisted. He'd intended calling her bluff, nothing more. Intended letting her masquerade as the *femme fatale* she pretended to be—he knew it was a pose—to let her play out her hand and learn she couldn't win . . .

He'd forgotten how susceptible he was. Not to her,

herself—the simple appreciation for a female body he could and would have easily controlled—but to the passion she evoked and sent racing down his veins, to the sheer unadulterated lust that, with her in his arms, fogged his brain.

He tried to ignore it, battled to block it out—and failed. Heat swirled through him, rose like a tidal wave he couldn't hope to hold back. In desperation, he gripped her waist and tried to ease her back, to create space between their heating bodies, preferably to break the kiss—an engagement that was rushing down an increasingly slippery slope to raging, mindless need.

She wouldn't have it, simply wouldn't be denied; she came up on her knees, clamped her hands on his shoulders, and used her leveraged weight to wedge him into the sofa's corner. The angled sides restricted him; she compounded his problems by sinking more definitely, more enticingly against him, and letting her hands roam.

Under his coat, over his chest, opening and brushing aside his waistcoat, sweeping wide, then down to grip his sides while her tongue played havoc with his senses, and the soft weight of her firm feminine curves, supple and giving, beckoned and lured . . . that prowling, predatory side of him he barely recognized, yet knew to be him. That facet of him she so effortlessly provoked into being.

He fought to catch his mental breath, to get a firm grip on his wits if not his senses. Metaphorically girding his loins, he gathered his will and tried his level best to sit up and move her back—

She felt his muscles bunching, countered his move.

He raised his shoulders free of the corner, only to have her determinedly bear him down, fractionally to the side and around so that his back hit the raised arm of the sofa. The shuffle of female limbs screened by fine silk over and between his thighs, the shushing shift of her skirts as she twitched them and wriggled, totally distracted him.

Then somehow he was leaning back against the sofa's

padded arm, his legs angled across the seat, with her poised over him, in his arms, straddling him, her warmth seeping through the cloth of his trousers as she settled over his hips.

His mind, his wits, his senses reeled, struggling to assimilate every aspect, every contact.

Her lips had never left his; now they firmed, and she brazenly engaged him, flagrantly incited, sirenlike, sinuously shifting over him . . .

Was she really as innocent as he'd thought?

Before he could accumulate sufficient wit to attempt an answer, she blew all chance of rational thought from his brain.

At his waist, her small hands gripped his shirt, tugged it free of his waistband, then slid beneath.

Her touch—the feel of her small, warm, intensely feminine hands pressing avidly, greedily to his already heated skin—seared like a brand.

And incinerated every civilized safeguard he possessed, shredded his vaunted control, and blew the tattered remnants away.

He reacted. Caught her head, palmed her nape, and ravenously kissed her back, but it was no longer the he who usually was, but a merged entity, a seamless melding of the dangerous predatory male and the cool, clever, experienced gentleman.

The primitive and possessive, and the arrogant and demanding.

He was lost, and so was she. Some distant, disconnected part of his mind knew it, but was helpless to act, to access sufficient will or strength to pull them both free.

Of the completely ungovernable, totally irresistible tide of passion that roared into being and captured them both.

Swept them into a sea of desire and hot, urgent yearning. Onto a plane where for both of them nothing mattered beyond the next heated touch, the next explicit caress.

Her desperate fingers fumbled with his cravat; he groped

blindly with one hand, trapped the swinging end of the braid that anchored her cape at her neck, and wrenched it free.

The cape slid from her shoulders, down and away with a sibilant *shush.* His palm touched the silk of her gown, rose, and found her breast, cupped, then he closed his hand and kneaded. He was incapable of disguising the need in his touch, the possessiveness that drove him. Releasing the firm mound, he sought and found her laces, and quickly, expertly undid them.

The instant her bodice loosened, he drew it down, slid his hand beneath, pressed the material farther away as his palm caressed hot silken skin. She shuddered. A prickling tide of sensual relief swept through him at the contact, not easing but flagrantly arousing, heightening his need, deepening his lust. The kiss turned incendiary; he held her head immobile as he plundered her mouth, soft, giving, intensely feminine. Intoxicating. His hand surrounded and seized; his fingers closed, possessed, then captured the tightly furled peak and tweaked, squeezed.

On a gasp, she broke from the kiss. Desperate for air, she tilted her head back.

Inwardly he smiled, and seized the moment. He released her nape, let that hand trace down the line of her spine to settle at the back of her waist, simultaneously took advantage of her instinctive offering; leaning forward, he set his lips to her vulnerable throat, pressed a heated knowing caress to the sensitive spot beneath her ear, then skated hot kisses down that tempting line.

He paused to lave the pulse that beat wildly at the base of her throat, paused to taste, to savor the galloping desire that held her in its grip. Satisfied, he moved on, down, with his lips tracing a path over the swell of her breast to the tightly ruched bud his fingers had teased to aching, throbbing hardness.

He closed his lips about it. She jerked in his arms.

He soothed it with a wet lick, and she trembled.

His mind took note, but the beast within him, aroused and needy, saw no reason to stop and consider. Instead, he bent to the task of teaching her all he could make her feel, all she could experience if she gave herself to him.

With expertise aplenty on which to call, he quickly reduced her to a state of sobbing need. Fractured and ragged, her breathing rang with a sensual desperation that was music to his ears.

His own need clawed and roared; anticipation wielded a sharpened spur. He drew back, leaning back against the sofa arm, surprised to find he needed to catch his own sensual breath, that he was breathing rapidly, too . . .

Her gown had fallen to her waist, her chemise crushed with it. With his eyes he devoured the lush mounds revealed, the swollen, heated female flesh to which his hands and lips had already laid claim.

The sight more than pleased, it delighted, sent a hot rush of passion surging through his loins, increasingly urgent, increasingly insistent. The sexual compulsion was beyond anything he'd felt before, stronger, more powerful, more real.

Somehow more aligned with who he really was, with what he really was. Reckless and wild.

One glance at her face, at the slivers of emerald bright with desire that glowed beneath her heavy lids, told him beyond doubt that she felt it, too—the ungovernable, irresistible craving, the desire that was simply impossible to deny.

He could have her now. She was straddling him, her knees sunk in the cushions on either side of his hips. He could simply lift her skirts, release his staff, and sheathe himself in her softness, but the beast within wanted much more. Demanded much more, from her, of her.

Nothing but complete surrender. Nothing less than sensual submission.

The world had already fallen away. Only the two of them

remained, cocooned in the moon-glimmered dark in the silence of the summerhouse. A silence broken only by their panting breaths, by the *shush* of fine material shifting.

Pris had already dispensed with his cravat. She'd pushed his shirt up to gain access to his chest, but that wasn't enough. She wanted to see as well as to feel. Wanted to know. Everything.

From beneath her heavy lids, she captured his gaze, held it as she unbuttoned his shirt. In the shadowed dark, his eyes were impossible to read, yet his expression as he watched her still conveyed a sense of control, of knowing, of deliberation.

But there was no longer any coolness in his gaze; it was hot, nearly scorching as it lowered and swept her breasts. As he examined, then raised a hand to lazily caress.

Her nerves leapt, tightened; her senses exulted in the light, taunting touch even as her mind reeled. She closed her eyes, briefly savored. She was straddling him, naked to the waist, yet far from feeling shocked or hesitant, she wanted to be there, wanted to feel his eyes on her body, ached to feel that fleeting, teasingly promising brush of his long fingers across her sensitized skin.

Her pulse beat strongly in her fingertips, under her skin, echoing the compulsion that thrummed through her, through every vein, down every nerve. How she could be addicted to something she hadn't yet tasted was a mystery, but the effect was real. She simply wanted. And had to have.

The last button slipped free; opening her eyes, she spread the halves of his shirt wide and looked down. Visually devoured as he had, then, shaking her fingers free of the material, she reached, touched, stroked. She traced the well-defined muscles banding his chest, let her fingers tangle in the crisp black hair that lay in a mat across the width, then arrowed down to disappear beneath his waistband. She found the flat discs of his nipples beneath the dark pelt, stroked, caressed, and felt them furl. Greatly daring, she leaned down and lipped, then nipped, and felt him catch his breath, felt him stir restlessly beneath her.

Rising, she slid her hands, fingers splayed, down, over the hard ridges of his abdomen; sitting back, she followed the same path with her eyes and swallowed. He was strong, steely muscled, an altogether dangerous male in his prime.

One she had half-naked beneath her.

Her lips slowly curved. Lifting her eyes to his, she caught the dark glimmer beneath his long lashes, held it, then deliberately skated her hands slowly up his chest. Following them, she leaned in and, with reckless abandon, set her lips to his.

Covered them, kissed wantonly, with lips and tongue boldly challenged, then retreated, enticed.

His hand skated up her back to once again cup her nape; he held her immobile, and blatantly, with an irresistible power, took control of the kiss. Blatantly, arrogantly, took all she offered.

And then all he wished.

A shiver shook her, a primitive recognition that here, now, he could have whatever he wished of her, that she wouldn't resist, couldn't resist.

Didn't want to resist.

Here, now, *this* was what she wanted, what she had to have. Him.

Certain, sure, emboldened, she answered his passion with her own, brazenly incited, convinced beyond all logical question that whatever she could have of him was what she craved. What she needed.

The wild and reckless. The passionate male that lurked behind his cool façade.

That was what she wanted. That was what she was determined to have.

Regardless of the cost. Whatever price he asked, she would gladly pay. With his body hot and hard beneath her hands, with his lips hard and urgent covering hers, his tongue a heated brand tangling with hers, she wasn't in any mood to deny herself. Or him.

Wasn't in any mood to do anything other than catch her breath when his hand slid beneath her skirts. His hard palm curved about her stockinged calf, then glided slowly up, sending sensations spiraling upward. His hand continued its inexorable climb over her knee, tracing her bare thighs above her garters, pushing aside her gown and chemise to gain better access.

His questing hand found her bottom. Her heart seemed to stop as he caressed, gently fondled, then lightly shaped. His grip about her nape eased, then slid away. His fingers trailed over her bare shoulder, delicately brushed one peaked and swollen breast, sending sensations cascading through her, sending heat and molten delight flowing down her veins to gather and pool low in her body.

Those descending fingers continued on, tracing downward. He continued kissing her; she continued kissing him as he slid that hand, too, beneath her skirts. He cupped her bottom in both hands, kneaded, yet she knew he was biding his time, that his ardor was still leashed, that he was still in control and would remain so until she paid his price.

She didn't know how she knew; she simply did. The knowledge was there, inside her; she didn't question its rightness.

Hands lightly gripping, holding her, he drew back from the kiss. Caught her eyes as she raised her heavy lids, and murmured, his breath a hot promise across her lips, "I want to see all of you. Take off your gown."

She didn't hesitate. Awash on a heady tide, faintly giddy, she sat up, bunched her skirts in her hands, and drew the garment up and over her head. Extending one hand, she let it fall to the floor, then looked down at him.

But he wasn't looking at her face.

His gaze had locked on the apex of her thighs, on the dark curls her filmy chemise, in loose folds about her hips and upper thighs, veiled but didn't hide. She wondered if he wished her to remove the chemise, too.

As if he'd heard her thought, he said, "Leave the rest."

The words were little more than a low growl.

One that sent sensual anticipation streaking through her.

His hands left her bottom, slid forward around her thighs, slid down and closed around each above the knee. Slowly he eased his grip, slowly slid both hands upward, sliding beneath the insubstantial chemise, tracing the tense muscles, his thumbs cruising the quiveringly sensitive skin of her inner thighs.

Her lungs seized, clenched tight.

His hands paused in their upward sweep; he leaned back, shifted slightly beneath her as he settled back against the sofa's arm.

Distracted anew by the sight of his chest displayed before her, by tendrils of sensation as the light breeze played over her heated skin, by the strength in the hands so suggestively circling her bare thighs, it took a moment before she realized his gaze had risen to her face, that he was studying her.

She raised her eyes and met his. What he read in her eyes, her expression, she couldn't tell, but one dark brow slowly, almost insultingly arrogantly, arched.

"Shouldn't you be kissing me, Priscilla?"

She had no idea, but wasn't about to admit it. Not when he asked like that, as if she'd missed her turn in some game they were playing. She wished she could repay him with a look as contemptuous as his was arrogant; instead, she simply leaned down and did as he suggested. She kissed him—and poured every ounce of her determination to claim him, to engage with him—not the cool collected gentleman but the wild and reckless man—into the act.

And felt his control quake. Felt it shake, felt the reins he held over that other self thin and fray.

Immediately, she pressed harder, ever more blatant. She leaned closer, and her breasts brushed his chest. He shuddered, his hands instinctively flexing, fingers biting into her thighs.

She exulted, and reached for him, that elusive male she longed to meet. And he came to her, rose at last to her lure and kissed her back, ravaged her mouth even as his hands flexed again, then swept higher.

His touch was harder, more driven. More explicit as he boldly cupped the heated flesh between her thighs, then stroked, caressed. Parted the slick, swollen folds, traced her entrance.

With lips and tongue he distracted her, made her fight to match him, to appease his demands. The body beneath her seemed different, too, more steely, more powerful.

A predator unleashed.

She sensed that as he fed from her mouth; beyond thought, she returned the pleasure, equally uninhibited, equally wild.

Inciting more.

His touch between her thighs became ever more intimate, ever more explicit, until she felt she would scream. Until she was aching for something more, until she felt on fire with a greedy ravenous need.

Abruptly, one hard hand clamped over her hip, anchoring her. Between her thighs, his other hand pressed farther, then slowly, deliberately, he pushed one finger into her. Deep, then deeper still.

Her heart stopped. Her lungs weren't functioning.

She tried to gasp, to pull back from the kiss.

He released her hip, gripped her head instead, and held her lips to his. Refused to let her pull back as he withdrew that long finger, then thrust it into her again. And again, and again.

And again.

Sensations rippled through her, waves of sharp delight escalating, intensifying with every slick stroke, with every increasingly intimate penetration. Heat washed through her, rushed down to pool in a molten furnace that with every caress he stoked.

Her body wasn't her own, but his—his to command, to caress as he wished, to pleasure as he wished . . .

Desperate, she pulled back from the kiss, this time succeeded in parting their lips by an inch.

His grip on her head immediately tightened, but before he drew her back, his lashes rose, and he met her eyes. Held her gaze for an instant while their breaths mingled, hers panting and unsteady, his ragged but more even.

"Keep kissing me, all the way. I want to be in your mouth when you come apart."

She didn't understand anything more than his need. His wish, his desire. She dragged in a breath, started to close the distance, lost that breath completely as between her thighs he reached deep. Her lids fell on a moan of entreaty and surrender. His lips captured hers, his tongue invaded her mouth, and the hot tide of his kiss, of his claiming, rose and swept her away.

When you come apart.

She suddenly understood, suddenly found herself, her body, her senses, teetering on the edge of a sensual precipice, driven there by forceful, repetitive caresses, by the constant stimulation of nerves in her most intimate places, between her thighs, in her mouth, the sensitized peaks of her breasts as they rode against his chest.

Her nerves coiled tight, then tighter; every sense seemed to swoon with pleasure.

Then reality fractured, broke apart in glory, in heat and pleasure beyond imagining.

A great wave of joy and pure delight swept through her, buoyed her up and carried her on and away, then slowly, gradually receded, and left her floating. As she drifted back to earth, and her senses reengaged, she felt him drinking from her mouth as if he could taste her pleasure, as if the delight she'd experienced at his hands was a nectar he could sup from her lips.

She slumped against him; beneath her, she felt him move.

Realized that while she was close to boneless, his body was not just tense but driven, a sculpted hardness edged with passion, gripped by a need even in her innocence she instinctively recognized.

Inside, she quaked. She knew the moment of truth had arrived, but she couldn't think—and she was no longer sure.

She could no longer remember where she was, let alone where she'd been going.

Dillon lifted her fractionally, reached between them, and flicked free the buttons at his waistband. Teeth gritted, he freed his aching erection, and breathed—shallowly—again.

She was all hot, wet and welcoming, slumped in a wanton sprawl over him. The scent of her arousal rose and wreathed through him, made the animal in him flex its claws.

All he need do was lift her a fraction, and slide his throbbing staff into the scalding haven he'd so explicitly prepared. He was large, but in her present state she would take him, and take him all.

The blood pounded in his veins, an insistent tattoo driving him to action. He needed to be inside her more than he needed to breathe, but . . . there was something his more rational mind was frantically trying to tell him, battling the fogs of lust to remind him. . . .

She blew out a soft breath, a gentle exhalation against his cheek.

Her head was beside his, nestled on his shoulder. He shot her a glance, and recollection returned.

Her.

That was what he needed to remember. That he wanted *her*. Not just for a day, for a week or even a month.

For *ever.*

Once the fogs were breached, memory flooded back.

He stifled a groan, and forced his arms to, if not relax, then at least not act. Refused to let his other self rule enough to lift her . . . just that little way.

Good God! How had they come to this pass?

She'd insisted . . . but he knew damned well she hadn't meant her persuasions to go this far. Or at least, no further.

He was literally in pain, yet . . . if he took her now, like this, let his baser self loose and did as he wished—as she'd invited—and ravished her, took her aggressively in an act of primitive claiming, how would she react later?

Would she understand?

He could barely follow his own reasoning; he had no confidence he could follow hers.

But how could he let her go? How could he pretend he didn't want her? She wasn't as innocent as he'd thought; she knew what he wished of her, and would wonder . . . what she would wonder he had no clue.

She stirred in his arms; his body reacted instantly. Not just expectant, not just eager, but *clamorous.*

Gritting his teeth, he held back the driving need, could all but hear his baser self whisper that having her now would give him a hold he could use to bind her later . . .

She started to lift her head.

Jaw clenching, he reached for her hand, took it in his, then drew it down. Her eyes opened, locked on his, then widened as he closed her hand about his rigid length. His control shook; he couldn't breathe as he battled the effects of her touch.

Her eyes, wide and lustrous with reawakening desire, gave him the strength to hold his beast at bay.

Long enough to drag in a breath, and say, "Your choice."

Pris blinked. The temptation to look down, to examine what her fingers were wrapped around, was great, but she resisted, held by something in his dark eyes.

Once again she had cause to rue the dark, that she couldn't see well enough to read his emotions. They were there, roiling in the depths of his eyes, but she had to rely on senses other than sight to define them.

"Why?" That seemed the most pertinent question.

His lips quirked. He was clinging to his usual persona, but the wild and reckless man who understood her craving for excitement and thrills was very close to his surface.

"I want you—obviously. But it wouldn't be fair to take advantage of your . . ."

He broke off.

Eyes narrowing, she supplied, "Weakness? Female frailty?"

His lips thinned. "I was going to say 'inexperience.' "

She suddenly felt insulted, in a strange and peculiar way. "I started this, if you recall."

He met her gaze. "Precisely. You started it—it's up to you to decide how far you want to go, how you want to finish this."

Whether it was her temper, her normal response to a challenge, or something else that rose up and swamped her, she didn't know, couldn't tell. The end result was the same—a reckless abandon she knew quite well.

She *had* started it, and she remembered why. Recalled very clearly her wish to experience the thrills and excitement with which he was so intimately acquainted, but which she had yet to savor.

He'd taken her part of the way, whetted her appetite—did he think she'd balk?

She knew what he thought was her reason for seducing him, but she knew the truth.

And had discovered another in the last heated minutes—she truly did want him.

Wanted to know, wanted to experience, wanted to savor physical intimacy—with him.

She'd been stroking, lightly tracing the hard rod beneath her palm, very aware it had grown considerably harder in response to her touch.

Her eyes holding his, she closed her hand.

She didn't have to shift much to reclaim her position astride him; she found it easy enough operating purely by touch to guide the blunt head of his erection to her swollen and surprisingly slick entrance, ease it between her nether lips, then push back a little, then a little more, sliding him into her . . .

He was large; now that he was partway inside her he felt thicker than she'd thought, but the look on his face was worth every second of the discomfort she felt as he stretched her.

She pressed lower. His dark eyes were fixed on her as if he'd never seen a naked woman before, never had one do to him what she'd done. Was doing.

Slowly.

He'd stopped breathing; suddenly, he sucked in a huge breath, his chest swelling dramatically, then he reached for her hips.

She swore and intercepted his hands, had to sit up to do so—immediately felt the hardness of him butt against her hymen.

She closed her eyes, gripped his hands tightly, rose slightly, and swiftly bore down.

Felt a stab of pain, sharp but mercifully brief as her maidenhead ruptured. Felt an indescribable sensation as she assimilated the feel of the thick, hard reality of him buried deep inside her.

The pain started to fade.

That other sensation grew and intensified.

She cracked open her lids and looked down at him. He was still staring at her; his expression wasn't one she could interpret—he looked stunned, as if she'd clouted him over the head, and he hadn't seen the blow coming.

Of course, he now knew; that much she could read in his wide dark eyes.

She narrowed hers at him. "If you value your life, say nothing at all."

Something flared in the darkness; his jaw set. "You are the most damnable, incomprehensible female."

The words were bitten off, so low, so gravelly, she could barely distinguish them. "Rather than debating my reasoning, could we return to the matter at hand? I wanted this—so why don't you give me what I want?"

He looked at her for a moment, then his eyes blazed.

"You really want this?"

The words were low, gravelly, but now held a hint of something more. Something faintly menacing, something dangerous. A skitter of excitement slithered down her spine. She knew beyond doubt that she'd lured the wild and reckless soul, had brought him to her.

"Oh, yes." She settled more fully on him, fought to suppress a wince, boldly reached for him, grabbed his shoulders, and yanked him up to her. "This," she breathed the words over his lips, and shifted just a little upon him again, "is precisely what I want."

She leaned in to kiss him, but he kissed her.

Ravenously.

Utterly and completely without reservation.

Every inhibition she'd ever possessed went up in flames as his hard hands found her body and ruthlessly claimed. Relentlessly possessed. Every curve, every inch of skin, every sensitive, intimate place.

She tried to push her hands over and down his shoulders; his coat and shirt got in her way.

He swore, a guttural expletive, then brusquely shifted, shrugged out of coat, waistcoat, and shirt, and hauled her to him.

Crushed her body against his, her swollen and aching

breasts pressed tight against that magnificent chest, to skin that burned.

Surrounded by steely arms, by a strength that wouldn't be denied, with every nerve quivering with fevered anticipation welling from the knowledge they were intimately joined, from the overwhelming sensation of him hard and rigid thrust so deeply inside her, Pris exulted and surrendered, wrapped her arms about him, and gave herself up to the wild and reckless, to the passion and desire and the driving need that rose up and consumed them both.

Dillon couldn't believe what she'd done, could barely comprehend the power, the sheer driving need that gripped him. That she had unleashed.

Her body was hot, flushed silk, restlessly urgent, recklessly greedy as she shifted in his arms. Her sheath was a tight glove, scalding and slick, clamped hard about him. His lips on hers, his tongue dueling with hers, he fed from her, and blatantly, forcefully, gave her back the raging tide of fiery desire she and all she was sent racing through him.

Without conscious direction, he sculpted her body, settling her as he wished, then he gripped her hips, took her weight, lifted her fractionally, and thrust farther, deeper. He worked her over him, on him, quickly and efficiently forced her to take him all.

She gasped, trembled, but not once did she retreat, not once did she pull back from her greedy need.

Or his.

The instant he was fully within her, he urged her up, then brought her down.

Once was enough; she caught the rhythm and started to ride him. He kept his hands locked about her hips, not just guiding but driving, making sure she rose high enough and came down with sufficient force to rock both their senses.

Within minutes, she was reeling. Desperate, she jerked

back and broke from the kiss; eyes closed, head back, she struggled to fill her lungs.

From beneath heavy lids, he watched her, watched her face as time and again, her so-recently virginal body took him deep, as he thrust steadily, powerfully, again and again, and her sheath gave and accepted and gripped him.

For one instant, there in the darkness with the scent of lust and passion wreathing about them, with her dancing in that most primitive way upon him, with her soft gasps and fractured moans falling like a siren song from her lips, he could almost believe she was some fey creature sent to ensnare him.

Regardless, she'd succeeded.

Her desperation heightened, and infected him. Sharp spurs of need pricked him; her nails sank deeper into his shoulders as passion rose and swept them yet higher.

His gaze lowered to her breasts, undulating with her ride, heaving with the breaths she desperately drew in. Bending his head, he set his mouth to the swollen mounds, sought and found a tightly budded peak, swirled it with his tongue, then drew it deep.

He suckled powerfully.

And she screamed.

Her body started tightening, climbing the final peak. Still guiding her, driving her ever onward, he feasted on her breasts, felt the age-old power rise through them both, felt it take them, grip them, ride them, whip them.

It plunged them both into a maelstrom of passion, of molten heat and raging glory.

It raced through them, lifted them high, whirled them through the cosmos of sensation, then swept them higher, then yet higher—until she shattered about him, her cry echoing in his ears as she contracted powerfully about him. As she came apart in his arms in a glory so blinding he saw stars.

Still blind, passion-wracked, he joined her, sank deep

into her body, held her ruthlessly down, felt every last contraction of her sheath as he emptied himself into her.

And, he suspected, lost his soul in the process.

Slumped back against the padded arm of the sofa, Priscilla Dalling a warm, all-but-naked, exceedingly sated body draped in flagrant abandon over him, Dillon tried to assess just where they now stood.

She'd unquestionably started it, but just what she'd started . . . he didn't think she fully comprehended just what her reckless act had brought into being.

He was fairly sure he didn't comprehend the full ramifications himself, not yet. Regardless, he definitely wasn't up to examining, and facing and acknowledging, the depth and breadth of all she'd made him feel. It was bad enough knowing she'd breached every wall he'd ever had, that somehow, in just a week, she'd been able to gain sufficient ground with him to be able to wreak the havoc the last hour had wrought.

She stirred, and he glanced down at her, but she remained boneless, apparently senseless. Her cheek lay on his chest, her glorious hair a tumble of curls rippling across his cooling skin. Her hair was darker than his, a true black where his was sable; it felt like silk against his jaw.

He raised a hand, plucked one lock from the jumble, ran it through his fingers. Head back, he looked across the darkened summerhouse, into the immediate future.

His, and hers.

As far as he was concerned, the two were one, and nothing would ever change that. Unfortunately, he seriously doubted she saw it that way.

Yet.

So how should he proceed?

Pris felt the touch of his fingers in her hair, felt the gentle, absentminded play . . . and stayed where she was, as she was. She wasn't sure why, couldn't place the warm feeling that suffused her, of security, of peace, and something more.

Regardless, it was balm of a heady sort, a blissful taste of heaven. She was parched, and drank it in, felt it sink to her soul.

Gradually, reality intruded; her rational mind awoke and took determined stock, reminding her that she was lying naked in his arms, that he was still inside her, not as large and flagrantly impressive as he had been, but still there. Still intimately connected.

She waited for a blush to warm her cheeks, but none came.

She puzzled for a moment, then accepted; she couldn't pretend she hadn't reveled in every moment, even that instant of sharp, lancing pain, transcended as it was by the indescribable sensation of feeling him hard and solid and so very real, so deep inside her.

Of course, he'd forged even deeper yet, and she'd enjoyed and thrilled to every moment of that communion.

Every sense she possessed, every nerve, was still glowing in the aftermath.

She'd wanted, craved, excitement and thrills, and he'd given her that, and more.

He'd fulfilled her every illicit dream, did he but know it.

Her lips quirked. She was about to lift her head when his hand firmed over her hair, holding her momentarily in place.

"I'll show you the register."

It took an instant or three before she recalled what he was talking about.

A fact that spoke loudly of the rattled state of her brain and the sluggish operation of her wits. She rapidly flayed them to attention, tried to speak, and found she had to clear her throat. "I'll call at the club tomorrow morning."

"No." He sighed; his hand slid from her hair. "That won't

work. I don't show the register to anyone, and this week all the volumes are in use in the clerks' room. If I fetch one to show you, even if no one actually sees you looking at it, it's bound to cause comment."

Lifting her head, she looked into his face. "Neither of us needs that."

"No." He met her eyes. "Tomorrow night there's a party at Lady Helmsley's—we'll both be there. Helmsley Hall's not far from the club. We can slip away, you can look at the register, then we'll return to the party. There's sure to be a crowd—no one will know."

She looked into his dark eyes. "What about the guards you've set patrolling the club?"

"They won't be surprised to see me. I can walk in, then let you in via the back door. They won't see you."

She studied his face, screamingly conscious of the hard body cradling hers, of the intimacy they'd shared and that still cocooned them. She moistened her lips. "Very well. Tomorrow night, then."

Beyond her control, her gaze dropped to his lips. A moment passed, then she looked at his eyes, read in their steady gaze, in the sense of waiting that emanated from him, that his mind was following the same track as hers . . . that his inclination and hers were the same.

She'd already thrown her cap over the windmill; she no longer had anything to lose.

And having once supped from the cup of passion with him, she now knew precisely what she stood to gain.

She knew without asking, without him saying, that it was once again her choice.

Easing up, leaning on his chest, she drew his head to hers, drew his lips to hers.

And again called the wild and reckless man to share thrills and excitement with her.

Nine

Unlike the first time, he had taken charge.

The following evening, Pris stood by the side of Lady Helmsley's drawing room surrounded by a coterie of admirers, and tried to stop her mind from dwelling on the latter events of the previous night.

A vain endeavor, given the poor competition from her attentive swains. Four gentlemen, along with Miss Cartwright and Miss Siddons, stood trading quips and nonsense; their inconsequential chatter couldn't compete with her memories, with the images her mind now contained—of Dillon rising above her in the night, of him removing his remaining clothes, then hers, and showing her how much pleasure he could give her, to what degree he could make her body sing, to what rapturous heights he could take her on the way to that ultimate, soul-sating bliss.

Best of all had been those moments when she'd seen and known how much pleasure she gave him, how deeply she called to that wild and reckless man, how completely he enjoyed her, that joining with her satisfied him as thoroughly, as intensely and all-encompassingly as it did her.

The second act had been even more compelling, more fascinating, than the first.

In the end, they'd stirred, regathered their clothes, and dressed in the darkness, all shyness conspicuously lacking, then he'd driven her to the house. She'd been in her room, her candle out, when Eugenia and Adelaide had returned; she hadn't wanted to talk of anything, hadn't wanted to return to the world—all she'd wanted was to lie in her bed and dream.

"Will you be attending the race meet this week, Miss Dalling?"

She blinked, and summoned a smile for Lord Matlock, who'd been trying to impress her for the past half hour. "I suspect not, my lord. It's a minor meeting. I doubt it will prove sufficiently interesting to tempt my aunt forth."

"But what of you and the lovely Miss Blake?" Lord Matlock held her gaze appealingly. "Surely we can tempt you to join us? Cummings here will bring his sister, Lady Canterbury. We could make up a party."

Too experienced to utter a bald no, Pris played the game and let them try to persuade her. Much of that involved making plans and arguing between themselves, giving her a chance to once again scan the room.

Lady Helmsley's party was noticeably more select than Lady Kershaw's event. Lord Cromarty wasn't expected; Eugenia had inquired of Lord Helmsley when they'd arrived, citing the Irish connection to excuse her interest.

So Pris was safe for the evening, at least from that quarter.

Dillon had yet to appear; excitement thrummed through her as she surveyed the heads, impatient to see the register and learn what she could of Rus's predicament—and also to see Dillon again, to again spend time alone with him.

Their interludes to date had been largely illicit—private

meetings at night or in surroundings that freed them of social restraint. Perhaps that was why she felt such a thrill when she saw his dark head through the crowd.

Returning her gaze to Lord Matlock, she kept her attention fastened on him.

"My high-perch phaeton will do nicely as a viewing platform," Matlock appealed to her. "What say you, Miss Dalling? Are you game?"

She lightly grimaced. "I'm sorry, my lord, but I can't see my aunt permitting it." She softened the rejection with a smile. "If truth be told, Miss Blake and I are indifferent followers of the Turf."

The gentlemen politely ribbed her, pointing out that no real lady truly followed the nags. Smiling, she returned their sallies, her gaze on them while her senses twitched and tugged her attention to Dillon, drawing steadily nearer.

And then he was there, bowing over her hand, claiming the position by her side. He bowed to Miss Cartwright and Miss Siddons, and nodded to the gentlemen. "Matlock. Hastings. Markham. Cummings."

Immediately he became the focus of all attention. The young ladies, predictably, hung on his every word, but the gentlemen's reactions were more revealing; in their eyes, Dillon, a few years older, with his aura of hardness, of experience, was an enigma, but one they admired.

Given the figure he cut in the austere black-and-white of evening dress, his dramatic handsomeness only more enhanced, Pris fully comprehended the admiration of both male and female. Visually speaking, he was a pattern card depicting all an aristocratic gentleman should be.

The other men were exceedingly polite, respectful as they asked his opinion of certain runners in the upcoming races.

"I say, is there any truth in the rumor that some race here a few weeks ago was . . ." Mr. Markham had spoken impulsively; belatedly realizing to whom he spoke, he glanced at the others, color rising in his cheeks. "Well," he rather lamely concluded, "in some way suspect?"

Suspect? Pris looked at Dillon's face; his polite, faintly aloof expression told her nothing.

"I really can't comment at this point." Summoning a distant smile, Dillon reached for Pris's hand. "If you'll excuse us, I've been dispatched to fetch Miss Dalling to meet Lady Amberfield."

"Oh. Ah . . . yes, of course." Lord Matlock bowed, as did the other gentlemen.

Once Pris had taken leave of them and the young ladies, Dillon led her into the crowd.

Lady Helmsley's L-shaped drawing room was large, but the number of guests crammed into the space made it impossible to see more than a few feet in any direction. He guided Pris through the throng, grateful that the crush limited people's view of them. She was eye-catching, as always, despite the severe style of her figured silk gown. The color matched her eyes and was an excellent foil for her black hair, tonight wound high at the back of her head; the style should have looked austere, but instead evoked fantasies of the mass unraveling. The silk clung lovingly to her figure, the heart-shaped neckline displaying her breasts and the deep cleft between as well as the seductively vulnerable line of her exposed nape.

Again, she'd done her best to mute the effect with a heavily fringed, jade-and-black-patterned silk shawl; again, it hadn't worked.

His eyes feasting, he wondered at his sudden susceptibility to such heretofore undistracting feminine charms. Cynically resigned, he steered her to the end of the shorter arm of the room.

She glanced around. "Who's Lady Amberfield?"

"A local gorgon."

Pris frowned. "Why does she want to meet me?"

"She doesn't." Tacking through the last of the crowd, he halted her before a minor door in the end wall.

She considered the door. "Ah. I see."

He opened it; without a word, she slipped through, into a long, unlit corridor. Glancing briefly at the guests—all otherwise engaged—he followed, closing the door on the noise.

Through the dimness, he met her eyes. "I don't think anyone saw us leave. Are you willing to risk disappearing for an hour or so?"

She raised her brows. "To see the register? Of course."

He stared at her for a moment, then waved her on. "We can cut through the gardens. It's not far to the back of the club."

He was familiar with the house and gardens; once outside, they walked briskly through the shrubbery, through a door in the garden wall, out onto a stretch of cleared land, screened from the High Street by the backs of other properties and a line of trees; across the open stretch lay the wood at the back of the Jockey Club.

"That way?" She pointed at the wood.

He nodded. Lifting her hems free of the short grass, she stepped out.

Instinctively scanning the shadows beneath the trees, he fell in beside her. "I'll leave you at the back door, then go around and deal with the guards."

"Do you often drop by late at night?"

"Occasionally. Sometimes things occur to me, especially after I've been talking with my father."

"You said he was the Keeper of the Stud Book."

"He was." He glanced at her. "That's part of the position I now hold. You could say it's become a family interest. My grandfather was involved in developing the records of the racing industry back in his day."

The outliers of the wood rose before them. He glanced at her feet and was relieved to see she was wearing proper shoes, albeit ones with a sizable heel. Flimsy dance slippers would have already been sodden, and traipsing through the wood . . .

Reaching for her arm, he halted her at the edge of the trees. He looked into the shadows, grimaced. "Briars."

"Oh." She glanced down at her skirts and the trailing fringe of her shawl.

He stepped back, stooped, and swung her up into his arms.

She swallowed a shriek, then muttered an Irish oath—one he knew.

Hiding a grin, he hefted her, settling her weight. "Gather up the shawl."

Still muttering ungratefully, she piled the fringe in her lap.

Ducking under a branch, he carried her into the wood. There were no defined paths, but the undergrowth wasn't dense; it was easy enough to tack around the few bushes in his path.

Although she said no more, he got the impression she chafed at being so much in his control, at being so dependent on him. At having to rely on him.

The thought slid through his brain; his response was unequivocal. He might understand, but she'd have to get used to it.

Around them, the wood was alive with a muted chorus of rustlings, scratches, and snaps, but there was no hint of any person skulking in the shadows. He was aware she scanned, peering about as much as she could; clearly she didn't know if her "acquaintance" was still set on breaking into the club.

The point reminded him of how serious matters were, reminded him why he was about to break his until-now-inflexible rule and show her the register.

They reached the edge of the wood; she immediately wriggled. He set her down. She brushed her skirts down, twitched her shawl back into place, then looked across the swath of open ground at the club. "Thank you."

He grinned and looked along the side of the building toward the front. There was no one in sight. He reached for her hand. "Come on."

He led her across the drive, then over the trimmed grass to the path that led to the rear of the club. The back door was protected by a shallow porch. He whisked her into it. "Wait here," he murmured. "I'll go around and let you in."

She nodded, and he left her, walking back around the corner, then along the side of the building and around to the front door.

The two guards, chatting over a brazier, looked up. They recognized him and grinned in greeting. One tapped the bill of his cap. "Mr. Caxton."

Fishing his keys out of his waistcoat pocket, Dillon nodded back. "I'm going in for a while. I'll be in my office."

"Right you are, sir."

He started up the steps. "I'm supposedly at Lady Helmsley's—I came across through the wood. All's quiet that way."

As he'd hoped, the older of the guards grasped his meaning. "Well, then—Joe here was about to go off on another round, but seeing as it's all clear, we might as well just sit tight for a while."

"Indeed. I'll be at least an hour." Unlocking the door, he pushed it open and went in. Relocking it, he strode across the hall.

The night watchman inhabited a small booth to one side. He stuck his head out; Dillon waved. The man snapped off a salute and retreated; he was used to Dillon's nocturnal visits.

Dillon headed down the corridor, then diverted to the rear door. The instant he opened it, Pris pushed through, brushing past him.

She shivered, then drew her shawl tighter; he assumed he

was supposed to think she'd been cold. He relocked the door, then turned to discover her wandering along the corridor, peering into rooms.

Catching up with her, he took her elbow. Leaning close, he whispered, "This way."

She shivered again, not from any chill.

Aware that his libido, already aroused to a heightened state simply because she was near—let alone that they were private and alone after he'd carried her through the wood—needed no further encouragement, he steered her directly to his office.

Releasing her, he closed the door, then crossed to the large window. "Stay where you are."

He pulled the heavy curtains across, plunging the room into stygian darkness, but he knew the place like the back of his hand. Moving to the desk, he picked up the tinderbox lying beside his pen tray and struck a spark.

Lighting the large lamp on the corner of his desk, he adjusted the wick, then set the glass in place. Light spilled out across the room. He saw she'd gone to the bookcase and was scanning the volumes. "It's the missing tome."

There was a gap on the third shelf. She turned to him, brows rising.

"It's in the clerks' room. Wait here while I fetch it."

Pris frowned at the bookcase. "Is there only one book?"

Almost at the door, he paused, then turned to face her. "Do you need to see 'the register'—any volume—or one particular volume of the register?"

She stared at him; she had no idea.

He sighed, and explained, "Each volume of the Breeding Register lists the horses born in any one year that are subsequently registered for racing under Jockey Club rules. Horses aren't accepted to race until they're two years old, so this year's register lists all horses who by the first of May—the anniversary date for horses—were eligible as two-year-olds and have been formally registered. Last year's register lists all the horses who are now three-year-olds, and any new three-year-olds registered for the first time get added to that register."

She frowned. "Any register should do, but perhaps the most recent . . . ?"

Whatever Rus was involved in was happening now, so presumably the latest volume would contain whatever he was looking for.

Dillon studied her face, then nodded and left the room.

Pris wandered back to the desk. Letting her shawl slip from her shoulders, she folded and set it aside. The room wasn't cold. The prickling beneath her skin, the flickering of her nerves, owed their existence to expectation, anticipation.

Within minutes she would see what Rus was so urgently seeking. Folding her arms, she stared unseeing at the desk and prayed she'd be able to understand, to deduce from the information in the register what sort of scheme was afoot, what sort of threat Rus was facing.

Her mind rolled back over recent events, over her quest to view the register—over her clashes with Dillon, culminating in their interlude last night.

Her fall from grace, albeit in a worthy cause.

Her lips twitched; her mind blankly refused to allow her to pretend, to delude herself that she'd given herself to Dillon Caxton in order to secure a sight of the elusive register and thus to save her twin.

Her only regret was that Dillon thought she had.

Just an instant of memory and she could feel again the thrill, taste the excitement of their wild and reckless ride. Of the storm they'd created, unleashed, then gloried in. Of the sensual sharing, the pleasures and delight.

She glanced at the door, in the distance heard some other door close.

Drawing in a deep breath, she slowly let it out. Lying, deceit, even misleading by omission had never come easily to her; only the fact that Rus was involved had allowed her to so blatantly deceive their father, let alone countenance involving Eugenia and Adelaide in her scheme. She was too confident, too sure of her own self to feel the need to hide any part of her; she'd always asked the world to come to terms with her as she was and had defiantly faced whatever storms had ensued.

Footsteps, long masculine strides, drew steadily nearer.

She stared at the door. Letting Dillon—the man she knew him to be—guess the truth of her feelings, guess why she'd so wantonly given herself to him, wouldn't be wise. Instinct told her so, in terms absolute and unequivocal; rational intelligence concurred. If he knew . . . she wasn't sure what he might do. She wasn't even sure what she would want him to do.

The door knob turned. Unfolding her arms, she straightened. She would examine the register, work out what Rus was involved in, discover some way to find him and pull him free of the mess, then Eugenia, Rus, Adelaide, and she would leave Newmarket. And that would be that.

There could be no future for her and Dillon Caxton; aside from all else, he didn't know who she really was, and in the present circumstances, that was a secret she would do well to keep from him.

The door opened; he entered, carrying a large tome.

Eyes immediately drawn to it, she felt her nerves tighten, felt expectation well.

He shut the door, then came to the desk. "It's heavy—let me set it down."

She shifted to the side. He slid the register—a ledger more than six inches thick, more than a foot long, and nearly half again as wide—onto the desk; it settled with a solid *thump*.

Hand on the cover, he glanced at her as she moved closer. "Any particular entry?"

She shook her head. "I just need to see what information is listed."

He raised the cover, opening the book to a page filled with entries; with a wave, he gestured to it, then stepped back.

Pris stared at the fine writing crowded on the page. She glanced at the lamp; Dillon was already thumbing the wheel, increasing the light. Shifting to stand directly in front of the ledger, placing her hands on the desk, she leaned over it and studied the wide pages.

Columns marched across the double width, some narrow, the last on the right-hand page taking up half that page's width. Each entry was at least a few inches deep, neatly ruled to separate it from its neighbors.

The first column gave the horse's name, the second listed the date and place of foaling, the third gave the dam and her lineage, taking up many more lines. Next came the sire and his lineage, again in considerable detail.

From there, the minutiae dramatically increased. The last two columns took up nearly the entire right-hand page, one a physical description complete to the most minute color splash, the last a listing of "points." Pris knew enough about horses to understand what she was reading, but how could such details be illegally used? If Rus saw such entries, what would they tell him?

She read on, searching for some hint of the clue she was convinced must be there.

From alongside the desk, Dillon studied her face. Saw concentration claim her, watched her eyes track the small, precise lettering of his clerks.

What was she searching for? Would he know when she found it?

Would she?

That last question hung in his mind. Reaching the end of one entry, she paused, then, frown deepening, the worry clouding her lovely eyes darkening, she tracked back across the page, and started on the next.

His restlessness increased; stirring, he walked to the

bookcase and stared at that instead. And forced himself to some semblance of patience.

Last night, he'd decided there was only one way forward, one clear and obvious path. He had unequivocal plans for Pris Dalling, but before he could implement them, he needed to free her, and himself, from the tangled knot her involvement with a racing scam it was his duty to eradicate had created. While she remained caught up in whatever it was, regardless of how innocently, his loyalties were compromised, and that he couldn't afford.

That was what he told himself, how he rationalized his actions. How he tried to excuse the compulsion that gnawed at him, that had had him offering to show her the register in flagrant violation of his until-then-absolute rule.

All lies. Or if not an outright lie, than less than half the truth.

Behind him, he heard her turn a page. Glancing around, he watched her smooth the page, then lean over to read, her profile limned by the golden lamplight.

He drifted nearer, drawn to where he could see her expression. The look on her face, unguarded, spoke clearly of anxiety, of escalating concern.

Of confusion and ultimately fear.

The sight struck like a lance through his shields, impelled him to draw closer.

The truth was . . . in his heart, in his soul, in his bones, rescuing her came first. *That* was his number one priority; he had to eliminate all that threatened her.

Not for one instant had he forgotten there was danger—real danger—involved. Danger from a man who had shot at her, danger as evidenced by Collier's demise. Whatever was going on, whoever was involved, they weren't above stooping to murder, and she, with her as-yet-unexplained interest, had stepped into the arena.

He was prepared to do whatever proved necessary to remove her from the field, to sequester her safely away. Then he'd deal with whoever the villains were, and then he'd deal with her.

He'd make a deal with her, whatever it took.

Her attention remained on the ledger's page. He drew nearer, then, halting behind her, a little to the side, unable to help himself he slid one hand around her waist. Distracted, she glanced briefly back and up at him, then looked again at the page.

The feel of her, warm and supple beneath the figured silk, soothed, a reassuring sensual balm quieting the aroused and now-prowling beast. He settled his hand, fingers splayed, across her waist. When she made no demur, he edged closer, shifting so he stood directly behind her, effectively caging her between him and the desk.

Her exposed nape beckoned. He bent his head, inhaled, filled his lungs and his brain with the intoxicating scent of her. Seduced, he set his lips to the beguiling curve, traced the exquisitely fine skin.

She shuddered, caught her breath. For one instant raised her head, evocatively responsive, then he lifted his lips from her skin, and she sighed and returned to her task.

His other hand rose to join the first, bracketing her waist, holding her before him while, breath bated, he waited for the sudden pounding in his blood to subside.

Distracted, Pris gave a low chuckle, content to have him near; she found the sensation of his strength engulfing her comforting, not threatening. Focusing on the neat script, she tried to concentrate. Absentmindedly responding to his comfort, she shifted her hips against him, side to side . . .

His hands tightened, gripped.

Blinking to full awareness, she felt the hard ridge of his erection riding against her bottom. Her senses leapt; excitement sizzled down her veins. She paused, then resumed her slow swaying.

Fascinated that she could arouse him so easily.

Wondering what he would do.

He pressed closer yet; his hands rose, sculpting her body, rising to cradle her breasts. She straightened, allowing the caress, encouraging it.

Tilting her head back against his shoulder, she savored the feel of his hands on her silk-screened flesh. Marveled that she could have so acutely missed and craved something she'd known for less than a day.

His head dipped beside hers; his lips cruised the junction of throat and shoulder, warm, deliberately arousing. His hands closed, gently kneaded; his fingers stroked, caressed, found, and played.

"Did you find what you were looking for?"

The words stirred the curls by her ear; the warmth of his breath caressed like a flame.

"I don't know." Her words were as low, but more breathless. "I can't . . . interpret it."

His lips cruised her throat, found the sensitive spot at the corner of her jaw. "If you tell me why you're searching, I could probably help."

The urge to tell him was strong, but . . . "I need to know more before I'll know if I can tell you."

His hands, now restlessly, increasingly possessively, roaming her body, paused, then he asked, "What do you need to know?"

She glanced down at the ledger spread before her, at the columns marching across the page. She moistened her lips. "I need to know how the information in the register is used."

A long pause ensued, then his hands slid across her gown, one splaying over her waist, the other smoothing down her stomach to the hollow between her thighs, fingers pressing inward, through her skirts suggestively covering her mound. In a blatantly explicit manner, he tilted her hips against him.

"Are you sure?"

The words whispered past her ear, laden with heat. With

the same ruthlessly seductive power she'd encountered last night.

It was the wild and reckless man in whose arms she stood, the one man who could show her the stars and sweep her to heaven.

"Yes."

The word slipped from her lips.

She waited, nerves quivering, for him to turn her, to kiss her, to join with her as he had last night.

Instead, his lower hand left her; he reached forward and pushed the open ledger farther up the desk. "Leave your hands as they are, on the desk."

He pressed closer, nudging her hips before him, pinning her against the desk. His hand returned, palm to the silk, to cup her breast. At her waist, his other hand gripped, anchoring her before him as he closed his hand, evocatively kneaded, then settled to play.

With her senses. With her wits. With her nerves.

The first flared, then stretched, greedily drinking in the sensations he expertly orchestrated—the sharp spikes of tactile stimulation, the building, welling heat. Her wits spiraled away, unneeded, unheeded; she let them go, wholly caught in the mesmerizing play, in the promise implicit in his unhurried, almost arrogant touch, in the heavy hardness of his body pressed to hers.

As for her nerves . . . he plucked them like a maestro, tuning her body, preparing it for his use. For his pleasure, and her delight.

He bent his head, nudged hers aside, and touched his lips to her skin. Her nerves leapt, then melted. How had he in just a moment awoken her so that his lips now seared and burned? Every lingering caress, every taunting sweep of his tongue along the tendons of her throat, the evocative graze of his teeth, sent flames of need, of that heady conflagration of lust, passion, and desire of which he was a master spreading beneath her skin, rushing down her veins, pooling low, then swelling, welling, building, a volcanic furnace of fiery need driving her, compelling her.

His hand at her waist held her upright against him; his fingers at her breast artfully played, sliding over her skin, closing about her ruched nipple, and squeezing . . .

She uttered a fractured gasp. Realized he'd loosened her bodice and pressed aside the fabric to bare one breast. As if it were his to caress as he wished, to possess as he wished.

There was some element, some underlying current rippling through his touch, that spoke of that view, of how he saw her, of how he wanted her . . .

Her wits were too far distant, too veiled by the mists of passion to see more deeply, or clearly.

Her breathing was quick, shallow; its cadence escalated, breathlessness gripping her, the vise about her lungs tightening another notch as his lips returned, hot and ardent, to cruise the vulnerable line of her throat.

Giddy, her lids falling, she tilted her head and let him have his way.

Let him stoke that inner furnace and feed the flames, until they wreathed through her body, and her brain.

Behind her, she felt him shift, reach down. Grasping the back of her skirts, he drew them up, and up, until they were bunched above her waist, her chemise trapped with them, baring her, exposing the backs of her legs and her bottom to the cool night air.

To him.

His hand touched, caressed, sculpted.

Heat flared with every touch, searing her flesh, sinking into her blood to set it pounding.

To set it rushing to the swollen folds between her thighs, so she throbbed and ached. So that by the time he'd caressed and claimed every curve, by the time the dew of desire had spread across her exposed skin, by the time he consented to touch her there, to press his fingers between her thighs and stroke, then part her folds and press deep, she was urgent and ready.

Ready to moan when, his hot mouth covering the pulse at the base of her throat, he held her before him and worked his fingers deep.

Eyes closed she rode the thrusting penetration of his fingers, evocatively pressing back, rolling her hips to caress his erection in explicit invitation.

He released her breast. He shifted behind her, then leaned forward, his shoulders and chest bending her over the desk as his distracting fingers returned to her breast.

"Lean on your hands."

She did. And felt his tongue sweep over the galloping pulse at the base of her throat. Felt his fingers close once more about her tortured, excruciatingly sensitive nipple.

Her lungs tightened until they hurt, her nerves coiled, her body throbbed hotly, weeping with need as his fingers withdrew from the furnace between her thighs.

The blunt head of his erection filled the void.

He pressed in, then forged deeper, forcing her up on her toes.

The sound that fell from her, part sob, part moan, resonated with surrender. With her need, with her hunger.

He locked one hand about her bare hip; the other remained, hard and hot, about her breast. He held her anchored before him, withdrew and thrust deep, feeding and fulfilling her raging hunger with every long, heavy stroke.

She gasped, and let her head hang, let the sensations wash through her and over her. Felt the touch of his lips, the caress of his breath on her bare nape as he filled her—as pleasure bloomed, rose up, and swamped them both.

Dillon knew the instant she let go, the instant she ceded all rights to him and left him to set the pace.

It was a heady moment, one he would have liked to savor, but the heat of her slick sheath closing like a scalding glove about his rigid flesh drove him on. Gave him no surcease, no chance to use his brain.

When he had her in his arms, all he knew, all he could assimilate while sunk in her body, was feelings. They rose up, beat around him and through him; some battered him. Some pushed through the conflagration, cindering his senses and his defenses, and sank deep, took hold.

Sank talons and winding tendrils deep into his soul.

He knew, not by thought but by instinct, why they were there, how he came to be taking her so possessively, a possession veiled by his sophisticated expertise, perhaps, but he knew the truth.

Knew what drove him.

Last night . . . she might have been a virgin—initially, he'd assumed she was, but her bold and brazen temptation had made him wonder, made him doubt. But then had come that staggering moment when she'd so deliberately impaled herself upon him, and he'd known. Not simply that she'd never had a man inside her before, not just that he was by her choice the first, but that he would move heaven and earth, harness the stars, and do whatever it took to be the only.

The vow hadn't needed to be spoken, hadn't even needed to be thought. In that moment, it had simply come into being, enshrined in his soul, engraved on his heart.

And he accepted it.

The realization that he did stunned him, shook him, yet at no level was he able to shake the rigid and resolute conviction.

She. Was. His.

He'd known the moment he'd set eyes on her, and the knowledge had only grown more entrenched.

All very well. His logical mind had coped, had formulated plans to bring about what his inner self needed, and now had to have. One way or another, he would secure her; he entertained no doubts on that score.

But what ate at him wasn't rational, not within the realms

of logical thought. The need that whispered through him, that gripped and consumed him whenever she was close, whenever opportunity arose and his reckless self perceived it, was entirely conceived within the realms of passion. An unforgiving need forged in the heat of unbridled yearning, in the flames of unbounded desire.

He craved her. Craved the taste of her, the feel of her bare skin, the scent of her aroused and abandoned. Like an addict she drew him, and he simply had to have.

That was why he held her bent over the open ledger on his desk, her bare bottom and the backs of her thighs riding against him as he filled her, the fine skin covering her hip, hot silk beneath his hand, her pebbled nipple hard as stone between his fingers as he sank his rigid staff into the hot haven between her thighs, as he sank deeply into her body and claimed it anew.

He'd had to have her again, had been driven to soothe that wild and reckless self she so flagrantly provoked, with whom she so determinedly wanted to engage.

Her body tightened about him, and he felt the reins fall away. Sensed the compelling thunder rise in his blood, in his head. Felt the heat rise through her, catch her in its grip and sweep her up. High, higher.

Until she touched the stars.

Until she shattered, and with a soft cry fell from the peak.

Her sheath contracted powerfully about him, once, twice; that was all he could stand. With a guttural groan he followed her, swept away on the tide as his body joined forcefully, unrestrainedly with hers.

Consciousness returned in fits and starts, in trickles of awareness.

They were bent over the desk, breathing like horses that had just finished a race. His hand had fallen from her breast to brace beside hers, taking his weight. Her head was bowed, her nape beneath his lips.

He touched them to the delicate skin, on the whisper of a breath traced.

Wondered, in the disjointed part of his mind that had managed to realign, whether she really thought he'd claimed her in payment for information, as he'd let her believe—or whether she'd guessed. Whether in her heart, in her female mind, she knew the truth.

The truth that was written on his soul.

Ten

Pris returned to the world, warm, sated, indescribably content, and feeling strangely secure.

Dillon must have carried her to the armchair opposite the bookcase; her legs, still boneless, had certainly not supported her over the requisite yards. Slumped in the chair, he was cradling her in his lap, gently, as if she were fine porcelain.

She felt fine indeed, the glory of their joining still golden in her veins, yet despite the sensual lassitude that dragged at her body, she felt mentally energized, alert.

Expectant.

Their clothes were neat again, she presumed by his doing, for which she was grateful. Before she could gather sufficient strength to wriggle around to face him, his chest, behind her shoulders, rose and fell. His breath brushed her ear in a sigh.

"The information in the register is used in many ways." He spoke quietly, evenly. "Breeders use it—they request information on horses they're considering using as sires or dams. It's also used to track changes in ownership, as well as constituting the official race record—the wins and losses, the races run—for every registered horse."

He paused, then went on, "The information is also used to verify the identity of all placegetters in races run under Jockey Club rules."

She remembered what Rus had said in his letter—a racket run in Newmarket that somehow involved the register. Rus must have learned more, something that had made him leave Cromarty's stable and try to get a look at the register.

Dillon had told her the register's description was used to prevent "falsifying" winners. How did one "falsify" a winning horse?

She recalled the columns she'd recently perused, the countless details contained in each entry. Where in all that did the essential clue lie?

Dillon shifted; leaning on the opposite arm of the chair he studied her face. She felt his gaze but didn't meet it. Did the racket Harkness was running center on breeding, racing—or did it involve falsifying winners?

"It would be easier if you told me what, exactly, you need to know."

The quiet statement had her meeting Dillon's dark eyes. He held her gaze steadily, and simply waited. He didn't press, wasn't pressing her; to her heightened senses, he seemed resigned.

She drew a breath, then stated as evenly as he, "I need to know how the register's information can be used illegally."

He didn't move, yet she felt his reaction. Steel infused and hardened the muscles beneath her, turned the chest against which she rested to stone. The dark eyes that held her widening ones contained an implacability she hadn't seen in him before.

For a moment, Dillon struggled to find words, in the end

simply said, "I can't tell you that." His voice had flattened, grown hard. "But—"

He swallowed the unequivocal order he'd been about to utter, fought and succeeded in slamming a door on his too-violent response, succeeded in finding some degree of warrior calm. He'd known she was connected with some scam; probability had argued it was the current horse substitution one. Bad enough. That someone had shot at her had made matters worse. But to have her confirm that she was walking into the situation blind—*knowingly blind*—determined to protect her Irishman . . . !

He felt like roaring but knew better. Holding his roiling, welling emotions in check, holding her gaze, he refashioned his approach. "Whatever it is you—and that Irishman—are involved in, it's serious. *Deadly* serious."

Telling her of Collier's death, warning her that involving herself would bring her to the attention of whoever had murdered the breeder wouldn't be wise; she'd only grow more desperate to protect her friend. But just thinking of some murderer turning his attention her way sent a surge of well-nigh-ungovernable protectiveness rushing through him.

"This is *madness*." Even to his ears, his tone sounded harsh. Jettisoning wisdom, he cupped her chin in one hand; eyes narrow, he captured hers. "Some man shot at you—it was *pure luck* he failed to kill you! There's other evidence those involved in this scam have already resorted to murder." Releasing her chin, he gripped her upper arm; battling the urge to shake her, he forcefully stated, "You *have* to tell me what's going on—what you know, and who's involved."

She stared at him; in the faint light from the distant lamp, he couldn't read her eyes. But then she looked down, at his hand clamped about her arm.

Exhaling through clenched teeth, he forced his fingers to unwrap, to let her go.

Looking away, she cleared her throat, then in a sudden burst of action, she pushed up and out of his lap.

He swore, had to fight not to grab her and haul her back as she quickly put distance between them.

The action—its implications—whipped his roiling, not entirely rational emotions to new heights. He had to sit for an instant, force his body to stillness to regain some semblance of control before, jaw clenched to hold back an unprecedented urge to roar, he rose and followed her to the desk.

Stalking in her wake, he reminded himself that she didn't yet know she was his.

She stopped before the desk, in the same spot where they'd so recently come together. She ran her fingers lightly across the open register. "Thank you for showing me."

"Thank *you* for showing me—" He cut off the sarcastic, bitter words, but not before she'd caught his meaning.

The look she bent on him was reproving, and faintly, so faint he wasn't even sure of it except in his heart, hurt.

Just the suggestion slew his temper, deflated it. "I'm sorry. That was . . ."

"Uncouth."

He muttered an oath, then raked a hand through his hair—something he'd never before done in his life. He had to resist the urge to clutch the thick locks. "*How* can I convince you that this is too dangerous?" Lowering his arm, he met her gaze. "That you have to tell me what's going on before whoever's behind it finds you?"

Folding her arms, Pris frowned at him. "You can stop swearing at me for a start." Rounding the desk, she halted behind it and faced him across it. "If it's any consolation, I know what you're saying is true—that it *is* dangerous, and that I should tell you all. *But* . . ."

She watched the hardness reclaim his face; his expression grew stony and distant.

"But there's someone else involved, and you still don't trust me."

He'd spoken with his habitual cool and even delivery. She looked at him, and equally evenly stated, "There's someone else involved—and I need to think things through."

Her tone declared she was not going to be swayed by any arguments, physical, cerebral, or emotional.

For several heartbeats, they remained with gazes locked, the desk and the open register—and the memory of what had so-recently transpired—filling the space between them, then he sighed and waved her to him. "Leave the register. We'd better get back to Lady Helmsley's."

He saw her out of the back door, then went out of the front door for the benefit of the guards. Circling the building, he rejoined her, and they headed for the wood.

She refused to let him carry her; sending him before her, she hiked up her skirts and followed at his heels. She traversed the wood without sustaining any damage; dropping her skirts, she stepped out into the weak moonlight. Side by side, they crossed the open expanse, then slipped into the Helmsleys' gardens.

He touched her arm. "We should go back via the terrace."

So they'd appear to have been strolling the gardens. She nodded, and let him guide her; they followed a graveled path to the terrace.

Climbing the steps, she frowned. She couldn't see how the details in the register could have helped Rus, let alone how they might help her find him and save him.

Halting at the top of the steps, Dillon drew the delicate hand he'd held since they'd reached the gardens through his arm. He met her gaze as it rose to his face. "When are you going to tell me?"

The most urgent question he needed answered.

Her expression remained defiant. "After I've thought about it."

Holding her gaze, he forced himself to incline his head, a gesture of acceptance entirely at odds with his inclinations.

He led her to the French doors left open to the night. There were other couples taking the air; he doubted any had missed them enough to view their return as anything out of the ordinary. Together, they stepped into the ballroom, back under the chandeliers' lights.

Beside him, she cleared her throat and drew her hand from his arm. "Thank you for an enjoyable excursion, Mr. Caxton."

Instinctively, his fingers had followed her retreating ones; grasping her hand, he captured her gaze, raised her fingers to his lips, and kissed. Looking into her eyes, he let her, for one instant, see the man within. "Think quickly."

Her eyes widened, but then she arched her brows haughtily, slid her fingers from his grasp, turned, and, head high, moved away into the crowd.

He waited until Lady Fowles's party quit Helmsley House, then made his farewells to Lady Helmsley and left.

He drove home through the night, turning over all she'd said, reliving all he'd felt, all she made him feel . . . he was grateful neither Demon nor Flick had attended the party. Both knew him well enough to detect the change in him whenever Pris hove on his horizon; he was in no good mood to bear with Demon's too-knowing ribbing, let alone Flick's matchmaking instincts becoming aroused.

Just the thought made him shudder. With every year she spent at the feet of the older Cynster ladies, her innate tendencies grew worse.

On reaching Hillgate End, he saw a light glowing in his study. Driving to the stable, he learned that Barnaby had returned an hour ago, and subsequently a footman had been sent to fetch Demon, who had arrived fifteen minutes before.

Leaving his horses to the stableman's care, he walked

swiftly to the house. He made his way to the front hall; crossing the tiled expanse, his heels ringing on the flags, he glanced at the wide window at the rear of the hall, the small square panes dating from Elizabethan times, those set along the top bearing the family crest.

Caxtons had been here for centuries, had been a part of local life for all that time; uncles and cousins had moved away, but the principal branch had sent its roots deep and remained. He felt the connection as he always did when he passed the window. Looking ahead, he walked on to his study.

He opened the door on an unexpected sight. Not just Barnaby and Demon, but his father, too, was waiting.

The General was ensconced in a chair angled before the fire, a warm rug over his knees. Demon sat back from the blaze, facing the hearth in a straight-backed chair, while Barnaby had claimed the other armchair.

"Sir." With a nod to his sire, Dillon closed the door, relieved to see the color in his father's cheeks and the alert gleam in his eyes. His mind was still sharp, but his strength was waning. Tonight, however, he seemed in fine fettle.

Fetching another straight-backed chair, he set it down and sat. "I take it there's news." He looked at Barnaby. "What did you learn?"

Barnaby was unusually sober. "First, Collier was murdered, but we'll never get proof of it. He was found at the bottom of a quarry with his neck broken. He fell from the top, and as his horse came racing home in a lather with the saddle loose, it was assumed that something had spooked the horse while he'd been riding the cliff, and he'd been thrown.

"*However,* Collier was an excellent horseman. The horse was a strong, well-broken, even-tempered hack, one he habitually rode. Both the lad who saddled the horse, and the stable master who was present when Collier mounted, swear the girths were tight, that there was nothing wrong with either horse or tack. Most importantly, both thought Collier rode out to meet someone. Nothing specific said, but it wasn't the usual time he rode, the horse didn't need the exercise, and Collier seemed preoccupied."

"What time of day was this?" Demon asked.

"A little before three o'clock. I eventually found three people who'd seen another rider head up to the quarry. None saw him *with* Collier, but unless someone was in the quarry itself, or on the cliffs, if Collier met with someone there, no one could have seen them."

Dillon stirred. "So the quarry was the perfect venue for a secret meeting."

"The perfect venue," the General put in, "for murder unobserved."

"Except for those three who saw the other rider at a distance," Barnaby said, "but none could give me any description other than he wore a long coat and rode well."

"Did you search for any visitor to the area?" Dillon asked.

Barnaby's sharp grin flashed. "That's what took so long. Reasoning the man might be Collier's unknown partner"—he nodded at Demon—"whose existence you predicted, I spoke with Collier's solicitor. Collier had been on the ropes last year, but was saved by a sudden injection of cash—he said the loan was from a friend. After Collier's death, the solicitor waited for the loan to be called in, but there was no attempt to claim the money. The sum was sizable, but Collier had had an excellent run with the bookmakers over the spring, and there was plenty in his kitty when he died."

"Is that so?" Dillon exchanged a glance with Demon, then looked at Barnaby. "What did you learn about this benefactor?"

Barnaby sank back in the armchair. "Other than that he's a gentleman? Precious little. Assuming he'd ridden a hired nag, I called at all the local stables. Only one had hired a horse that day, but other than describing the man as a London 'gent,' all they could tell me was that he was about as tall as I am, dark-haired, slightly heavier build, spoke like a 'gent,' dressed like a 'gent,' but was older, although how much older they couldn't say."

Dejected, Barnaby sighed. "With only that to go on, I can't see any prospect of finding this 'London gent.' I found the inn at which he ate dinner before driving a team of post-horses south, heading down the London road."

"His carriage?" Dillon asked.

"Hired from a large posting inn," Barnaby replied. "No chance they'll remember him."

Demon was frowning. "How much was the loan?"

"The solicitor wouldn't say, but admitted it was more than ten thousand pounds."

"Great heavens!" The General's eyes widened. "Imagine . . ."

"Interesting," Demon drawled. "That might give us a trail to follow."

Barnaby frowned. "How so?"

"Because money, my fine lad, comes from somewhere. No one has ten thousand pounds sitting in his dresser. If you wanted to give someone ten thousand pounds, how would you do it?"

Still puzzled, Barnaby replied, "I'd write a bank draft . . ." His eyes widened. "Ah."

"Indeed." Demon nodded. "And we know just the person to track the transaction, if it's traceable."

"Gabriel Cynster?"

"Not just Gabriel." Dillon had worked closely with Gabriel over the past decade. "He has contacts that would make you salivate—and give your father nightmares."

Barnaby instantly revived. "How fascinating." A moment later, he said, "I rather think I'll head down to London tomorrow. Gabriel's there, isn't he?"

Demon grimaced. "At this time of year, he most definitely will be. The balls are starting up again. If you promise not to mention that horrifying fact in front of Flick, I'll write a note giving Gabriel Collier's background, and what we need to know—stop by tomorrow morning and pick it up."

"Excellent!" Barnaby looked around their small circle. "I'd thought we'd lost the scent, but it looks like the hounds are off again."

Dillon clapped him on the shoulder. They all rose. Demon took his leave of them and headed home. With renewed vigor, Barnaby headed upstairs to get some sleep; taking his father's arm, Dillon followed more slowly.

His father glanced at him as they stepped onto the landing. "And how did your evening go?"

Dillon considered as they climbed the second flight. Gaining the gallery, he answered truthfully, "I honestly don't know."

Pris woke late the next morning. Lying in her bed staring unseeing at the sun-dappled ceiling, she logically and carefully, without letting emotion cloud her judgment, considered what she knew and what she had to do.

She had to save Rus. She had to find him and help him get free of Harkness and whatever else threatened.

Regardless of all else, the impulse to find and rescue her twin was unwavering; recent events had only made the need more desperate, more urgent.

She'd fixed her hopes on the register. She'd naïvely supposed that seeing it would instantly reveal what scheme Rus had stumbled on, that she would see some connection between that and where he was hiding, or at least where to look for him, what he would be pursuing.

Instead . . .

She heaved a dispirited sigh. Beyond confirming that the register did indeed contain details pertinent to racing swindles, there'd been so *many* details, of so many different types; it hadn't occurred to her until she'd read the entries just how many ways there might be to fiddle a race.

Disappointment dragged at her, but her failure wasn't the sole source of her escalating worry. Since her arrival in Newmarket, the situation had deteriorated—or rather, she'd learned how bad it truly was. Initially, it had been possible to view Rus going into hiding as one step up from a lark. But Rus wasn't a child; years of responsibility had matured him—if he was in hiding, it was for some compelling reason, no lark.

And Harkness . . . that he'd shot at her thinking she was Rus proved Rus was still about, still unharmed, but, as Dillon had forcefully pointed out, Harkness had shot to kill. Until last night, she'd managed to push that knowledge to the back of her mind, disregard it in her push to view the register.

After her success-crowned-by-failure last night, after all Dillon had let fall, she could no longer refuse to face the grim reality.

Dillon was right—this game was dangerous.

Replaying his words, hearing his tone, she grimaced, and amended that thought. This game was dangerous on more than one front.

She'd become involved with him as a means to see the register, yet in reality, Rus's difficulties had played only a minor role in landing her in Dillon's arms. However, now that she'd landed there, more than once, her relationship with Dillon was going to make things difficult.

Last night, she'd seen something in his eyes, had heard—very clearly—a tone in his voice that had instantly made her wary. Perhaps it was being the eldest in the family, equal with Rus—a male no one imagined anyone owned—that had made her from her earliest years totally inimical to the notion of being a man's anything. Not a chattel, not a possession. Many wanted to view her that way; her beauty was something men coveted much as they might a work of art. She was a work of nature they wanted to own, to have in their homes to look at and feel smug that it was theirs. But not even her father "owned" her, nor could he control her, because she'd never ceded him the right.

But Dillon . . .

She sighed even more heavily, then stretched beneath the sheets. Sensual memory stirred; she closed her eyes, and could almost feel his hands on her body, feel him inside her.

Her mind filled in the rest, the emotional color, the niggling uncertainty over how he saw her, what he thought of her and her reasons for giving herself to him—what she'd allowed him to believe. . . .

She couldn't afford to let emotions distract her. Frowning, she moved on to the words they'd later exchanged. Did all men like him think they owned a lady once they'd slept with her, once she'd allowed them to . . . ?

Was there some unwritten rule she'd never heard of?

With a snort, she opened her eyes and tossed back the covers. Standing, she shook down her nightgown, and headed for the washstand.

If Dillon harbored any thoughts of owning her, of controlling her, he would learn his error soon enough. Meanwhile, she was going to have to tell him all and engage his help on Rus's behalf. The decision stood plainly in her mind; she hadn't had to think hard to reach it.

She'd run herself to a standstill; she had no idea which way to turn to find her twin, and that remained her principal aim. She'd put her trust in the register, and that had proved no help, but Dillon . . . he would know. He would help. He was the right person to tell.

Aside from all else, given what she'd seen in his eyes, heard in his voice last night, if she didn't tell him, and soon, he was liable to act—as men of his ilk were so fond of doing. If he thought to appeal to Eugenia . . .

She hadn't told anyone about Harkness shooting at her. If Dillon told Eugenia of the dangers Rus and she, too, now faced, Eugenia would be horrified and would certainly insist she speak to the authorities.

In this case, as far as she could tell, Dillon was "the authorities." She owed her aunt a great deal and was sincerely fond of her; it was only right she spare Eugenia the unsettling distress and speak to Dillon herself.

Her maid had already brought her washing water; Pris splashed her face, mopped it dry, then went to the armoire. Opening the double doors wide, she surveyed her wardrobe. And considered, the full circumstances being what they were, what gown she should don to most effectively deal with her lover.

"Please tell Mr. Caxton that Miss Dalling wishes to speak with him."

The clerk behind the reception desk in the foyer of the Jockey Club stared at her, then surged to his feet and bowed. "Yes, of course, miss." He bobbed again. "At once."

He started backing away, then, blushing, tore his eyes from her and hurried down the corridor leading to Dillon's office.

Pris inwardly sighed; crossing her hands over the head of her parasol, the tip resting on the tiles before her feet, head high, she pretended to be oblivious of the doorman, still staring, and the other clerks who, bustling past on various errands, stumbled in their headlong rush when they set eyes on her.

Yes, she'd dressed to kill in a gown of crisp, vertical black-and-white stripes, highlighted with thin gold stripes, with a scooped neckline and ruffled hem, and a ruffled black parasol, but her intended victim was a great deal less susceptible than the norm. Indeed, she wasn't sure he was susceptible at all.

She didn't have to wait long to find out; Dillon strode around the corner, the clerk in his wake.

"Miss Dalling." With not the slightest indication he even noticed her attire, he took the hand she offered, bowed over it, then waved to the front door. "Come—let's stroll."

Futile to gnash her teeth at his immunity to feminine wiles. She spoke quietly, aware of the clerk slipping back behind his desk. "Given the subject I wish to speak of, I would feel more comfortable discussing it in your office."

Dillon trapped her eyes, equally quietly stated, "To keep our meeting and its subject from anyone connected with racing, we should cast our interaction as purely social."

She held his gaze, swiftly debated. While she remained in town, she risked being seen by Harkness or Cromarty. She'd had Patrick drive her there in a hired closed carriage; he was waiting outside. Neither she nor he had thought it at all wise for her to appear on the High Street.

And here was Dillon proposing precisely that.

She opened her mouth to insist she could only speak in his office.

He murmured, "At this time of day, the coffee room"—with his head he indicated a corridor leading in the opposite direction to his office—"is full of owners and trainers, many not members of the club itself, but who use its amenities. Luckily, they use another entrance. However, the clerks going back and forth are often dealing with those in the coffee room. If I take you to my office, that fact will spread like wildfire via the clerks to the coffee room. Speculation will run rife as to what club business you've come to discuss."

He quietly added, "If I stroll out with you, the clerks won't gossip—they'll assume our meeting is personal, and therefore of no interest to them."

Slowly, she nodded. "There are two people—an owner

and a trainer—who mustn't see me. Can we stroll somewhere they'd be unlikely to go?"

He nodded. "Come on."

They left the building; descending the shallow steps, Pris unfurled her parasol, as she did indicating the carriage and Patrick, visible through the trees flanking the path. Dillon looked, then took her arm. "This way."

He led her away from the club, parallel to the High Street, but in the opposite direction to the Helmsleys'. The wood on that side had been thinned; it was easy to stroll beneath the trees. On some, the leaves were turning, golden and russet amid the green, summer giving way to autumn.

The wood ended at a graveled path running behind a series of properties. Dillon turned away from the High Street.

Pris relaxed. "This doesn't look like the sort of area the racing fraternity frequent."

"It isn't. This is the residential area where the townsfolk live." He indicated a space between properties farther along the path. "That's a small park—we can talk there without risk of being observed or overheard."

The park was neat and quiet, a place where well-to-do merchants' and guildmasters' nannies could take their charges. An oval pond stood at its center, while birches bordered both sides. The flagstone path wended around sections of lawn and between occasional flower beds. It was clearly a place apart from the central industry of the town, the racing folk, and all the associated visitors.

Dillon guided her to a wooden seat set beneath one of the birches. Pris sat and drew in her skirts.

As Dillon sat beside her, high-pitched voices and gurgling laughter drew her gaze to three young children tumbling on the lawn nearby, under the benevolent eye of a nanny. The children—a girl and two boys—reminded Pris of herself, Rus, and Albert when they'd been just as young and exuberant.

Just as innocent.

It seemed the right moment to say, "The Irishman who tried to break into your office was my twin brother, Rus."

Dillon's gaze touched her face; when she didn't meet it, he murmured, "Russell Dalling."

She hesitated for only a heartbeat, then nodded. She and Rus often used Dalling when they wanted to conceal their identity; if someone called him Dalling, he'd respond. There seemed little sense in unnecessarily involving the family name, the earldom, and even less their father in whatever was to come. "I came to England, to Newmarket, looking for Rus."

Opening her reticule, she drew out the letter she'd received before leaving Ireland. "I got this." Handing it to Dillon, she watched him unfold it and read. "But even before that . . ."

She recounted the entire story with few omissions, concealing only the family name. Her tale ended with her hopes for the register, for what it would reveal, now dashed. "So." She drew in a breath. "I have no alternative but to tell you all, and hope you can make better sense of the pieces of the jigsaw than I can." Her fingers clenched on her parasol's handle. "Above all, I have to find Rus."

Turning her head, she met Dillon's gaze, unsurprised to find it hard and unforgiving.

"You should have told me *all* before—from the first."

The words were condemnatory, bitten off; she raised her brows and stared him down. "I would have if it hadn't involved Rus. I would never willingly do anything that might harm him."

Slowly he raised his brows back. "So what made you change your mind?"

His voice had lowered; for an instant, the sensual undercurrents between them surged and lapped.

She ignored them and simply stated, "When I first met you, I had no idea whether you would understand that Rus was innocent of any crime, but might have become unintentionally involved. I couldn't risk simply telling you and hoping for the best. So I had to try to find him myself. I've tried everything, followed any and every clue that might tell me where he is, and what threatens him. But I haven't been able to find him, and . . ."

His eyes narrowed even more. "And Harkness shot at you."

He held her gaze for a moment, then muttered an expletive and looked away. "Harkness thought you were your brother. That's why he shot at you—and that means that as far as Harkness is concerned, Rus is still close, and needs to be eliminated."

Lips thinning, she nodded. "Yes." *And Harkness shot at me* wasn't what she'd been about to say, but if he didn't need to hear that she'd come to trust him, that would do.

Dillon leaned back against the seat. "Tell me all you know of Cromarty and Harkness."

She related their backgrounds, stressing that she had to avoid them. "If they see me, they'll know they can track Rus through me, that if they just watch me, then eventually either Rus will find me, or I'll find him."

Dillon's blood ran cold as another alternative blossomed in his brain. An alternative Harkness and Cromarty could well be, or become, sufficiently desperate to employ. If they took Pris hostage . . . she'd left Ireland, traveled to Newmarket, had even given herself to him in order to find her twin; wouldn't Russell Dalling do as much?

Dillon was aware of the special link between twins; he'd observed it often enough with Amanda and Amelia, the Cynster twins. If Cromarty and Harkness wanted Russell Dalling, all they had to do was seize Pris.

Abruptly, he sat up. "You're right. The first thing we have to do is locate your brother."

She blinked. "I'm fairly certain he's still close."

Grasping her hand, he stood and drew her to her feet,

aware his expression was tending grim. "In that case, he's still close. Come on."

Winding her arm with his, he started toward the front of the park, where it gave onto one of the main side streets. "We're going to have to risk crossing the High Street, but the chances of running into Cromarty or Harkness at this hour around here are low."

She glanced at him. "Where are we going?"

"To the lending library. Their map is the best in town."

Eleven

"Where does the Cromarty string exercise?" In the lending library, Dillon stood beside Pris, shielding her from the street while they studied the huge map.

"About here." With the tip of her parasol, she pointed to an area on the Heath, then moved the parasol tip north and west. "This farmhouse is where they're quartered."

"The old Rigby place." Eyes scanning the areas around the farm, and down in an arc to where the string exercised, Dillon mentally filled in what the map didn't show.

Pris's gaze was on his face. "You've lived here all your life, haven't you?"

"Born and raised here. Spent all my boyhood and youth here."

"You know all the abandoned buildings, the shacks—all the places Rus might hide." Excitement was creeping into her voice.

He glanced at her. "I know of a few places he might be using as a bolt-hole." Turning, he started to escort her back to the door, then stopped. "Your coachman's name is Patrick?"

"Yes, but he's rather more than a coachman."

Dillon looked around. "Wait here—I'll fetch him and your carriage. There's no sense parading you along the High Street. Go and look at some novels."

He lifted her hand from his sleeve, was about to release it when she twisted her fingers and gripped his, hard. He met her green eyes; they held an implacable expression.

"You are not—absolutely *not*—going to look for Rus without me."

She'd spoken softly, but steel rang in her tone.

He sighed. "All right." He rejigged his plans. "I'll send your coach this way, then fetch my horse. Get into the coach and wait here until I join you. I'll ride out to the Carisbrook place with you—after you change, we'll go for a nice, social ride on the Heath."

She assessed his plan, then nodded. "Tell Patrick I'll be waiting."

A nice, social ride on the Heath.

The reality was somewhat different. On horseback, Priscilla Dalling was as reckless a rider as she was in other spheres; luckily for Dillon's peace of mind, he already knew she could manage her horse.

And Solomon, his black gelding, Cynster-bred and trained, was more than a match for her flighty mare.

Thundering north and west beside her, streaking across the Heath, he scanned the open grassland for other riders while updating his mental file on Pris and Rus Dalling.

Joining her in the carriage on the drive to the Carisbrook house, he'd encouraged her to tell him more about her brother and, consequently, her family and herself.

At twenty-four years old, she and her twin were the eldest children. She'd said nothing of what had brought her brother to Newmarket, but he'd caught her hesitation in mentioning their father; he suspected some falling-out. Yet any thoughts that Rus Dalling might need to earn his keep were rendered ineligible by Pris's frequent and unconscious citings of nannies, governesses, tutors, and grooms.

An only child himself, he'd felt a pang of envy over some of the childhood exploits she'd described; she'd always shared everything with her twin—she'd had someone with her, someone who thought like she did, who reacted as she did, throughout her life.

Until now. He hadn't been surprised when she'd eventually fallen silent, then, as they'd reached the Carisbrook drive, she'd glanced at him, and asked, "You believe Rus is innocent, don't you?"

Looking into her eyes, understanding in that moment not just why she'd asked but what his answer would mean to her, he'd found himself unexpectedly grateful for his past. "I know what it's like to get caught up in such a scheme. Innocent or not-so-innocent, as was the case with me, there comes a time when such an enterprise threatens to consume you. Your brother had the sense, and the strength, to pull back of his own accord, and for that I can only admire him."

In his case, he'd needed Flick's and Demon's help to break free; it seemed entirely fitting that he should aid Russell Dalling.

Reaching the house, they'd discovered that Lady Fowles and Adelaide were attending Lady Morton's at-home. He'd kicked his heels in the parlor while Pris exchanged her mesmerizing black-and-white gown for her riding habit, that vivid confection in emerald velvet, the vibrant hue intensified by the crisp white of her blouse, with an enticing ruffle that led the eye to the deep valley between her breasts. Said valley might have been decorously concealed by thick velvet, but that hadn't stopped his imagination from eagerly following the track.

They'd left the house and headed for the fields around Swaffam Prior.

Approaching the village, he took the lead; circling the cottages, he led Pris to an outlying barn. They dismounted and went in, but there was no one there.

It was the first of many such buildings they checked, all potential bolt-holes. Every distant barn, every shack, abandoned cottage, or ruin. They swept the area around the Rigby farm; halting on a nearby rise, Pris pointed out Harkness examining a black horse. A carriage rattled up; Cromarty got out. He paused to look at the horse, then entered the house.

Tightening Solomon's reins, Dillon steadied the restive gelding. "I've been introduced to Cromarty, seen him around the coffee rooms and the club. Harkness"—his tone hardened—"I've never met."

"Your gain." Pris turned her mare away. "He's an outright bully and a brute besides."

Delivered in her soft brogue, the condemnation lacked force. Dillon studied Harkness for a moment longer, then followed Pris down the rise.

They continued their search as the day waxed, then waned. In a wide arc, they swept south across the Heath, turning aside into the bordering woodlands to check woodcutters' huts and abandoned cottages.

Pris had had the foresight to pack sandwiches, cheese, and apples; they paused within sight of the area Harkness favored for exercising Cromarty's string to consume the impromptu meal but didn't dally.

As cottage after barn after shack fell behind them, Dillon expected Pris to grow disheartened. Instead, she seemed unperturbed, still eager as they rode on. As he led her onto the northern fringes of Demon's stud, nearing the logical limit of their search, she caught his puzzled gaze, and raised a brow.

He hesitated, then said, "If our theory of your brother

hiding close enough to spy on Cromarty's horses is correct, then we're nearing the last few places he might be."

"I know." Anticipation rang in her voice. She considered him for a moment, then looked ahead. "All the places we've searched—I *know* Rus never stayed there. Don't ask me how I know—I just do. But while we haven't crossed his path, I know—*feel*—that he's . . . somewhere near."

She glanced at him, met his eyes. "I know it sounds strange . . . it's just a feeling."

He held her gaze for an instant, then faced forward, holding Solomon to a walk. "I know another set of twins—girls. They've been together all their lives until recently. Now they're married, one lives in Lincolnshire and the other in Derbyshire. I know their husbands well—neither is the fanciful sort, yet both swear that when their wife's twin gave birth, their wife knew it. Not to the hour or the day, but to the minute, the instant, despite being separated by all those miles." He glanced at Pris. "I don't understand how that can be, but I accept it happened exactly as Luc and Martin claim." He smiled. "Against that, you being certain your twin hasn't been in a room recently is easy to swallow."

Pris smiled back, then glimpsed a dilapidated cottage through the trees. "Is that where we're going?"

Dillon nodded. He set his black trotting as, excited, she urged her mare on. She felt a building expectation, a funny, deeply familiar ruffling of her senses, still distant but . . . they'd been drawing nearer to Rus, or at least to where he'd been, for the last little while.

Dillon waved to the cottage's rear. They swung that way, then dismounted. Pris studied the cottage, what was left of it. The roof had collapsed at the front and over one side. Walls were missing planks or stones; some had disintegrated entirely.

Tying their reins to a fallen tree, Dillon glanced at the cottage. "I hid here eleven years ago. Despite its appearance, the area around the hearth is dry and half a room is habitable." Raising his brows, he took Pris's hand. "Or was."

She let him go ahead, following close behind, her hand locked in his. Mice, even rats, seemed likely.

As they ducked beneath some fallen timbers, a sudden scurrying had her jumping, tightening her grip on Dillon's hand. He glanced back at her; his smile deepened as he faced forward again, but he had enough wit to keep his lips shut.

They had to clamber over debris; releasing his hand, hiking the skirts of her habit high, she stepped gingerly along a rubble-strewn corridor, then Dillon drew her into the structure proper, and she saw he'd been right. The area around the stone fireplace and hearth was clear. An old table sat before the hearth, along with a rickety stool. "The table's clean, not dusty."

Dillon turned to look, then grunted. "There's a constant stream of vagrants through Newmarket—some look for work, others look and move on." He examined the rest of the area. "Someone's been here, but whether it was your brother . . ." He glanced questioningly at her.

She scanned the room, let her senses absorb . . . when she saw the split logs stacked beside the hearth, her heart leapt. The lowest layer went one way, the next laid precisely across it, then the following layer—the three pieces remaining—sat parallel to the first. "Rus was here."

Dillon turned to her. She pointed at the pile. "He always stacks wood like that. And this place seems too neat for an abandoned ruin."

"Is Rus neat?"

"Neater than I am, and I don't like clutter and mess around me."

Dillon continued his visual search. "I see no sign of anyone staying here now."

"No." She could see no baggage. "I can't imagine Rus leaving Cromarty's without his saddlebags. He left his horse back in Ireland, so if he hasn't a horse, where are his saddlebags? If he's out spying, he wouldn't be lugging them with him—" She broke off as another thought occurred.

Dillon read her mind. "I haven't heard of any horse being stolen, and there's a very efficient grapevine about such happenings in this town."

Moving through the fallen beams, he peered into less clear areas of the cottage, but she could see the undisturbed dust from where she stood.

She was disappointed, but not disheartened. "Rus *was* here, not long ago, but he's not staying here now. I don't't"—she wrinkled her nose—"*feel* him about enough for that."

Dillon looked at her, nodded, then waved her to retreat. They made their way back out, into the afternoon sunshine.

Reaching the horses, Pris halted and faced him. "That isn't the last place he could be—it can't be."

He studied her eyes, saw hope glowing strongly, lighting the emerald green. The ruined cottage was the last likely place, but . . . "There's one other place, but it's a little way to the east, and not easy to find. Itinerants rarely stumble on it." He hesitated, then asked, "You're sure he's close, aren't you?"

She nodded, the feather in her riding cap bobbing over her ear. The sight made him smile. Standing beside her mare, with a look of impatience, she motioned commandingly for him to lift her up. Smile widening, he reached for her, closed his hands about her waist—then pulled her into him and kissed her. Thoroughly.

Eventually lifting his head, he looked down into her face; her lashes fluttered, then rose. "It's the last place—our final throw. It's an unlikely chance, but . . . let's see."

He stepped back, lifted her to her saddle, then held her stirrup for her. By the time he swung up to Solomon's back, she'd wheeled the mare and was urging her east, under the trees and into the fields beyond.

She had the direction right, so he fell in beside her. But once they reached the limit of Demon's lands, the cleared paddocks and secluded glades where his prize broodmares led a pampered life, she fell back and let him lead, tacking from one bridle path to the next, leading her steadily east into the dense, old woodland of the Caxton estate.

Some of the trees were ancient; their wide boles and thick canopies enclosed the path, screening the sun. Even now in the late afternoon of a sunny day, the air beneath the branches was cool, faintly damp. The path narrowed, then dipped through a rocky streambed; urging Solomon up the opposite bank, Dillon glanced back and saw Pris guiding her mare daintily through the rocks.

It hadn't rained recently; the leaf mold cloaking the bank wasn't slippery. The mare would manage the steep climb safely enough . . . realizing the direction of his unbidden thoughts, he faced forward before Pris could look up and read his protectiveness in his face. He wasn't even sure he approved, but the affliction seemed incurable.

A little way farther on, the path led into the clearing before their goal—an old woodcutters' cottage buried deep in the woods. Drawing rein some yards before the door, Dillon raked the cottage. Very few people knew it existed. The woodcutters came every few years to thin the woods, to gather the dead branches and reduce them to charcoal, which they sold, mostly to the Caxton household.

It was too early in the season for any woodcutters to have arrived, yet scanning the ground before the door, he saw clear evidence that horses had been standing there.

Pris had followed him into the clearing; she halted the mare alongside. "More than one horse, and recently."

Worry tinged her voice. Dillon looked up, but no smoke rose from the chimney. "We're on Caxton lands. We own this cottage, and as you've just seen, it's well hidden."

Dismounting, he led Solomon to a post with rings set into it. Securing the gelding's reins, he glanced at Pris, but she hadn't waited for him to lift her down; she led her mare to the post. While she tied off her reins, he walked to the side of the cottage and checked the small lean-to stable.

Turning back, he saw Pris watching, and shook his head. "No horse, and no sign one has been there in a good long while."

Going to the door, she waited; joining her, he lifted the latch and pushed the door wide. The hinges creaked.

He paused on the threshold, aware of Pris crowding by his shoulder. Light streamed past them, and also through the unshuttered windows, one on either side of the door. Dust motes danced in the slanting beams illuminating the rudimentary yet solid and, for its purpose, comfortable interior.

Pris sucked in a breath. Dillon glanced at her, then followed her gaze to the wood stacked beside the hearth—laid in that distinctive crosshatch. "Your brother's hallmark."

Moving into the room, he glanced around; Pris did the same. As in the ruined cottage, a certain neatness prevailed—a lack of dust, the old armchairs aligned, the two stools parallel under the table. There was no evidence of a fire in the hearth, no such obvious sign that anyone was living there, but the stones had recently been swept. Rus Dalling's mark was everywhere.

"He's been here recently." Pris glanced at him.

"More recently than at the ruined cottage?"

She nodded. "He's not near at the moment, but it's as if I've walked into his room at some house we're staying at."

He glanced around. "Let's search. If he has those saddlebags, it's unlikely he's carrying them with him."

They looked everywhere—under the narrow bed, in all the corners, on every high shelf—and found nothing. Then Dillon remembered the storeroom, built onto the cottage at the opposite end to the stable. Its door wasn't obvious, simply a section of the planks lining the wall; crooking his fingers in the gap that served as a handle, he pulled it open.

Pris pushed past him. Rough shelving ran along the outer walls. There was little light, only what seeped between the rafters and the roof, and past him as he stood in the doorway. Feeling Pris's irritated glance, he moved farther into the narrow space, reaching past her to feel along the back of the high shelves while she crouched and, despite her fear of rodents, peered and poked below the lowest shelf.

"Here!" Triumphant, she shot to her feet—courtesy of the tight space, plastering herself to him.

Something she did without the slightest hesitation, as if she barely noticed the way her breasts crushed against his chest, the way her thighs slid against his.

He sucked in a breath and flattened himself against the wall as she wrestled a pair of saddlebags up between them—only just missing doing serious damage.

Her eyes sparkled as they met his. "These are Rus's!"

"Good." His voice sounded strained; he tried to keep his expression from turning grim as he squeezed her past him and gently pushed her to the door. "Take it out in the light."

She paused in the doorway and glanced over her shoulder. "There's a traveling bag there, too."

He waved her on. "I'll get it." Once she'd gone, he took a moment to catch his breath before bending and hauling the bag from its hiding place.

Stepping into the main room, he saw Pris by the bed, busily rifling through the saddlebags. "These are definitely Rus's, but just clothes, his favorite bridle, and the quirt I gave him last birthday."

Last birthday—one she'd shared. As he put the bag on the bed, she glanced at it. "That's the bag I sent him when he wrote that he'd joined Cromarty's employ."

Swiftly rebuckling the saddlebags, she opened the traveling bag and delved within. "More clothes, a book I sent with the bag—I bet he hasn't even opened it—and . . ." Straightening, she looked at the saddlebags, then at the traveling bag. "I think this must be all his things. He has to be staying here."

She looked up at him.

He nodded. "He must be out, either in town or around the Heath. If he hasn't got a horse, then he'll be walking, so getting anywhere will take time."

"So what should we do? Wait until he comes back?"

He thought, then shook his head. "He could stay away until late." He hesitated, then met her eyes. "Those horses that were here recently . . . if someone's been looking for him, he won't risk returning until he's sure no one's likely to come calling."

Pris blew out a breath and studied his face. "All right—we'll leave a note—"

"No—no note." When she frowned and went to argue, he cut her off. "We don't know who might come searching and find your name. Even 'Pris' is too traceable—as far as I know, you're the only Priscilla in Newmarket. No—we'll put the bags back exactly as we found them, then I'll come back tonight and see if your brother's returned. Recognizing him, after all, won't be a problem."

She narrowed her eyes at him. "I don't know why you bother—you know I'm going to come here tonight, too."

He looked into her eyes, then sighed and picked up the traveling bag. "I had to try."

They returned the bag and saddlebags to the storeroom; at his suggestion, she arranged them as closely as she could to the way they'd been. "He might or might not know that someone called yesterday."

"He wouldn't have missed the hoof marks outside."

"Regardless"—he held the cottage door for her, then followed her out—"we don't want to give him cause to run. We want him at home next time we call."

He closed the door, then lifted her to the mare's saddle. On Solomon, he led the way out of the clearing along a different path—one that led to the Heath; it was the same path he'd emerged from when he'd found her fleeing Harkness three days before.

They rode through the slanting sunshine, giving the town a wide berth, circling to the east. When they clattered into the stable yard behind the Carisbrook house, they'd completed a full circuit of Newmarket.

Patrick came out of the stable. She waved gaily; kicking free of the stirrups, she slid to the ground. Handing over the mare's reins, she beamed. "We've found him! Or at least found where he's staying."

"Well, that's a relief." Patrick grinned at her, then nodded to Dillon. "Mr. Caxton."

She whirled; shading her eyes against the setting sun, she looked up at Dillon. "Where will I meet you? At the cottage?"

"No."

The word was flat, absolute. When she raised her brows at him, his lips thinned. He dismounted. "I'll meet you here." He glanced at Patrick, then at her. "I don't want you riding anywhere alone at night, much less across the Heath, no doubt dressed as a lad and astride." His eyes bored into hers. "No telling whom you might meet. Or what he might think."

She narrowed her eyes at him, opened her lips—

"Aye. Mr. Caxton's right there," Patrick cut in. "Riding alone at night's not safe, and your aunt would be the first to say so."

She glanced at Patrick, then back at Dillon—quickly enough to catch the slight, distinctly male nod he sent Patrick's way. Dillon had fetched Patrick and the carriage that morning; they'd had time to meet and get each other's measure . . .

Plastering a smile on her face, she reached out, plucked Dillon's reins from his loose grasp, and gave them to Patrick. "In that case, you'd better come in and speak with Aunt Eugenia. Riding all the way home, then all the way back here this evening will be *such* a waste of time, I'm sure she'll insist, as do I, that you join us for dinner. Especially as it's all in Rus's cause—he's far and away her favorite nephew."

She linked her arm with Dillon's, but he didn't budge.

"My household will be expecting me—"

"I'm sure Patrick can arrange for a groom to take a message." She stared at Patrick, who looked down to hide his smile.

"Aye—I can do that." He glanced at Dillon. "If you'll let me know what, where, and who to speak to, sir, I'll send a lad right away."

Dillon knew a trap when it snapped shut around him. He inwardly sighed and glanced down at Pris, hanging on his arm. "I take it your aunt will be delighted to hear we've all but located your brother?"

She smiled, and turned him toward the house. "She'll be in alt, and Adelaide will be, too." As she towed him to his fate, she blithely informed him, "They'll both want to thank you, I'm sure."

They did, several times, but to Dillon's relief, both Lady Fowles and Adelaide refrained from living up to either his or Pris's expectations. Although immensely relieved to hear that he and Pris were one step away from meeting with Rus, they were also keenly interested in the swindle he believed Rus had got wind of; they were eager to hear the details explained.

Dillon relaxed, easier in the ladies' company than he'd expected. Over the dinner table, Pris, seeing it, pulled a face at him and nearly made him choke.

He paid her back by telling Lady Fowles *precisely* what they planned that night—no carriage, but a nighttime ride—deftly swinging his legs aside so Pris couldn't kick him under the table. She tried, missed, and glared, but Lady Fowles considered, then gave her blessing. Contacting Rus took precedence over propriety.

They left the house at nine o'clock, Pris once again dressed as a lad. Their boots scrunched on the gravel as they strode into the stable yard. Patrick led their horses, refreshed and alert, out, then held the mare as Pris swung into the saddle.

"Take care," Patrick called, as they wheeled their mounts south. Dillon saluted him, then had to tap his heels to Solomon's flanks, setting the black into a powerful surge in Pris's wake.

He caught her up in short order, then rode beside her down the lane to the town. At that hour, with her dressed as she was with him beside her, there was no reason they couldn't ride straight through rather than taking the longer route around. Nevertheless, he took her down the quieter streets, rejoining the road south on the outskirts where the houses gave way again to fields and pasture. The Heath proper lay to their right as they cantered down the road to Hillgate End.

He led Pris through the main gates and up the drive, turning off the oak-lined avenue onto a bridle path that cut through the park. The house lay quiet, already slumbering in the moonlight; he glanced down at it as they let the horses stretch their legs along a cleared rise, at the long façade softened by shadow yet so solid, framed by the darkness of thick canopies to either side.

Pris, too, was looking. Over the wind of their passage, she yelled to him, "It looks so very *English*."

He grinned, nodded. It was. The quintessential English manor house in the quintessential English setting, a fitting reflection of its owners, English to the core.

Beyond the park, the woods closed in. Pris had to curb her impatience and let him lead; it took a good twenty minutes of slow and careful riding, avoiding the pitfalls with which, in the dark, the narrow paths were amply endowed, to reach the cottage.

They rode into the clearing.

No light burned behind the still-unshuttered windows.

Before he could blink, Pris was out of her saddle, dragging the mare to the post to secure her. Dismounting, he hissed at her to wait, but she didn't so much as pause. Leaving the post, she went straight to the door, lifted the latch, and pushed it open.

Dillon swore, knotted Solomon's reins, and rushed after her.

He nearly ran her down; she'd stopped just inside the door. Catching her shoulders, he steadied her; she said nothing, just continued looking around.

At the main room of the cottage, still devoid of human life, exactly as they'd left it earlier in the day . . .

He studied the stools beneath the table. "That left stool's been moved. Someone's been here."

"Rus." Pris stilled beneath his hands. "He's here . . . yet he's not."

For a long moment, she remained perfectly still, then she swung about, stepped around him, and walked out of the cottage. She stopped a few paces into the clearing. From the doorway, he scanned the dark curtain of surrounding trees for any threat.

A low, mournful birdcall sounded, reminiscent of an owl. He looked at Pris; she repeated it, haunting and long.

Then she waited. Her attention, initially swinging across the semicircle of trees facing the cottage, focused on the area to the right.

Silence fell, almost palpable. Neither of them moved.

Then an answering call came, the same mournful note repeated in a series of shorter bursts.

The effect on Pris was instantaneous. She opened her mouth; he swallowed a curse and started toward her, but before he could warn her to keep her voice down, another voice spoke, an amplified whisper reaching through the night.

"Pris?"

Dillon froze. A yard from Pris, six yards from the clearing's edge, he watched a shadow swing down from the branches, steady itself against the bole of a large oak, then slowly come forward.

Rus Dalling stepped into the moonlight, wide eyes locked on his twin sister's face. "Damn it to hell, Pris—what the *devil* are you doing here?"

With those first words, Rus Dalling assured Dillon that the two of them would get along excellently well, at least as far as Pris was concerned. She, of course, paid not the slightest heed to the implied disapproval; with a high-pitched squeal, she flung herself at her brother.

Dillon swore beneath his breath; he listened to the rustlings as night creatures reacted to the sound, while Rus Dalling sternly shushed Pris. That he'd been hiding, resigned to spending the night in a tree, told Dillon a great deal. They were assuredly not safe standing in the clearing, in plain sight.

Glancing at the cottage, Dillon saw the two horses tied to the post, realized what anyone would see if they chanced by. Turning, he joined the other two. "We can't stay out here." He caught Rus Dalling's dark gaze. "Let's get into the cottage—we can explain everything there."

"No. There are men searching—"

"I know. But if they come this way, they'll see the horses, tied like that. Mine, the black, is well-known about town—Harkness knows him by sight."

Rus Dalling had been studying him in the weak and fitful light. "You're Caxton."

Dillon nodded. "You're on my land, and that's my cottage." Grabbing Pris, he started to push her to it; Rus, still entangled, inevitably came, too. "If anyone comes by, they'll see my horse, and the mare, at this hour outside a cottage on my land—what will they think?"

Rus Dalling's face blanked. "An assignation."

"Precisely." Dillon ignored the dawning suspicion in the

other man's voice; dealing with that issue could wait. "They won't come close—aside from all else, Solomon is known to get testy. He'll raise the alarm."

He managed to guide Pris and her twin into the cottage. He paused by the door. "Wait while I close the shutters, then light the lamp."

Rus moved to do so; swiftly, Dillon crossed the front of the cottage and hauled the shutters closed. He strode back into the cottage as the tinder sparked; the instant the wick caught, he closed the door.

The lamp shed barely as much light as a candle, just enough, as they gathered around the scarred table, to illuminate their faces. Looking at Rus Dalling's, Dillon recalled Barnaby's description—a scruffy male version of Pris, a cross between Pris and Dillon. Barnaby had been very close to the mark; Rus was a few inches taller than Pris, a few inches shorter than Dillon. All three were of similar build, the only differences being the natural ones due to age and sex. The same could be said of their faces, indeed, all else about them; they were darkly, vividly handsome—at first glance, only the color of their eyes and the shade of their hair distinguished Rus and Pris from Dillon.

In those two characteristics, the twins were identical. In others . . . there were slight differences in their features, and more in the way they moved and reacted. Although highly similar in appearance and, he suspected, in character and personality, there would be, as was the case with Amanda and Amelia, significant differences, too. They were not one and the same person.

At present, Rus looked tousled and worn, a day's growth of black beard shading his jaw. He looked pale, tired, his eyes hunted; his clothes were of good quality but had taken a beating.

Pris, still beaming, was exuberantly hugging him, gaily whispering that Eugenia and Adelaide were there, too, that she'd told Dillon all, that Dillon would help him, that he'd turn green when he saw Dillon's horses, that neither Harkness nor Cromarty had realized she was in Newmarket, that they were looking for him . . . it all tumbled from her lips in a scrambled mishmash. Dillon wasn't surprised when, across the table, Rus Dalling met his eyes, sheer, stunned, incomprehension in his face.

Dragging one of the armchairs to the side of the table, Dillon seized Pris by the shoulders—by sheer surprise making her release her brother—and sat her forcefully down.

Inclined to take umbrage, she glared up at him.

He pointed a finger at her nose. "Stay there."

Drawing out one stool, he pushed it to Rus, then subsided onto the other. "First, what's been happening here?" He met Rus's eyes. "Why were you in the tree?"

Rus glanced at Pris; her gaze was trained expectantly on his face, but her lips remained shut. He looked back at Dillon. "Harkness. He's been searching for me since I left Cromarty's stable." He grimaced, glanced at Pris. "In fact, I left Cromarty's because I knew he'd be looking for me."

"You learned something you weren't supposed to—we guessed that," Pris said. "Were you in the tree because Harkness traced you here?"

Rus looked at Dillon. "I've been using whatever shelter I could find, trying to stay close enough so that I could keep an eye on the string exercising. I wanted to find proof—"

Dillon stopped him with a raised hand. "We'll get to that. Safety first." With his eyes, he indicated Pris. "Did Harkness find you here?"

"No—at least, not in person. He and his head lad have been searching as much as they can ever since I left, so I've had to keep moving. I finally found this place and thought I was safe, but then last night they rode up. Luckily, I'd gone outside to gather kindling. I saw them and hid. They watched the cottage for some time, then went in. They searched. I crept close and listened. They didn't find my things, so they weren't sure who was using the place. They went outside and hid in the trees, and waited for a few more hours." Rus shivered. "It was nearly dawn before they rode away. Even then, I didn't dare go back inside until I knew they'd be out with the string. With me gone, Harkness has to oversee all the training sessions."

Dillon looked at Pris. "It was Pris who led Harkness this way. She went spying on the string, dressed as she is now. Harkness spotted her, thought she was you, shot at her, then chased her. By chance, she fled this way."

Horrified, Rus stared at Pris, then swore—long and inventively. Dillon warmed to him even more. Pris looked bored.

"Hell and the devil!" Rus concluded. "What happened?"

"I happened," Dillon dryly replied. "I was riding by, stopped Pris, then Harkness recognized me and decided he didn't need to chase you if it meant meeting me."

Rus snorted. "Meeting you in suspicious circumstances would be his worst nightmare." His gaze returned to his sister. "But what by all that's holy did you think you were about?"

Pris elevated her nose. "Looking for you." Rus stared at her; she met his gaze levelly. "You didn't think I wouldn't, did you?"

An unanswerable question; having assessed their position, Dillon cut in, "We can't stay here—I don't even want to talk about your predicament here. The sooner we get you safely tucked away out of Harkness's reach, the better. And I know just the place." He stood.

Rising more slowly, Rus glanced from him to Pris. "Where?"

"No." Dillon caught Pris's eye as she came to her feet. "The less said here, the better. Get those bags, and let's go."

Pris turned and pushed her brother toward the storeroom. "He's right. He's pigheaded and dictatorial, but in this, he's right."

Rus cast Dillon another look, one both measuring and

suspicious, but as Dillon had hoped, Pris's acceptance of his direction if not his authority persuaded her twin to fall in without argument. Between them, they fetched the bags. Dillon took the traveling bag from Pris. "Douse the lamp."

He hauled the door open and went out, speaking to Rus over his shoulder. "You take the mare and the saddlebags. I'll take this, and take Pris up behind me."

It was the only arrangement that would work; the mare couldn't carry two people, and Dillon was too heavy for her. After one assessing glance, Rus assented with a nod. Pris came out, and dragged the door closed.

She turned to the mare and her brother. Rus caught her eye, with his head indicated Dillon. "Go with Caxton. I'll follow."

Pris hesitated, making her own assessment, then turned to Dillon.

He swung up to his saddle, then kicked one boot free to allow her to use the stirrup. He reached down; she grabbed his arm, placed her boot in the stirrup and swung up. She settled behind him, wrapping her arms about his waist. Shortening the reins, he waited while Rus adjusted the mare's stirrups and mounted, then turned Solomon's head to the west. "This way. Keep close."

Pris clung to the warmth of Dillon's back as they trotted away under the trees. Then she realized which way they were heading. She looked around, then leaned closer and whispered, "Dillon—"

"Shhh!"

She pressed her lips together and waited, but he continued along the path leading west—the same path they'd ridden in on that afternoon, the one that led to the ruined cottage. Another minute passed, and she could bear it no longer. With one finger, she poked his shoulder. "We're going the wrong way!"

She'd kept her words to a whisper; he answered on a sigh. "No, we're not." After a moment, he added, "Just wait."

Wait. It was the one thing she wasn't particularly good at. As he well knew. She wriggled.

"Sit still."

She stifled a sigh.

They reached the rock-strewn stream. Dillon eased his big black down the bank—then headed down the stream.

"Ah." Pris leaned forward so her lips brushed Dillon's ear.

He glanced briefly back at her. "Indeed."

Relieved that it was as she'd thought and Dillon was taking Rus back to his house, she twisted around to look at her twin, guiding the mare in the black's wake. She caught Rus's gaze and flashed him a reassuring grin, then turned forward, tightening her arms about Dillon as he sent the black back up the stream bank, this time heading east.

Half an hour later, they clattered into the stable yard behind the manor. The stableman and a lad appeared, and took their horses.

"We'll need them both in a few hours," Dillon said.

The stableman saluted and led the horses away.

"This way." The traveling bag in one hand, her hand in the other, Dillon turned toward the house.

Rus, his saddlebags over his arm, paced alongside her as they crossed a wide expanse of manicured lawn. She felt him glance at her hand uncompromisingly locked in Dillon's, then he glanced across her at Dillon. "You're the Keeper of the Breeding Register, aren't you?"

Dillon glanced briefly his way. "Among other things, yes."

Rus exhaled. "I've been trying to learn about that blasted register—"

"I know. Meanwhile I've been trying to learn who the hell you are, and why you wanted to know."

Pris watched as Rus, his gaze on Dillon's face, grimaced.

"That was you the other night, wasn't it? At the back of

the Jockey Club? The trap I walked into. Was the other one a friend of yours?'

Dillon's lips curved. He nodded. "You can apologize when you meet him. Actually, he was quite impressed by your pugilistic style—if you want to make amends, offer to teach him."

"I will." Rus frowned. "But what I couldn't fathom was who it was *you* went after—is there someone else trying to gain access to the register?"

"There was," Dillon said.

"Who?" Rus asked as they reached the house.

Dillon paused before a door, and met Rus's gaze. "Guess."

Then he looked at Pris.

Twelve

Rus's reaction to learning it had been *Pris* who'd lured Dillon away to allow him to escape Dillon's trap kept brother and sister engaged in a pithy, *sotto voce* exchange long enough for Dillon to herd them into his study, leave to request a plate of bread, cold meats, and ale for Rus, and tea for Pris, give orders for a room to be made up for Rus, whose existence was to be kept a complete secret from all outside the household, and return.

Shutting his study door, he cut through the still-running altercation without compunction. "Enough!" His gaze touched Pris's, then he waved them both, still standing before the hearth, to the armchairs on either side. "Sit down, and let's start at the beginning."

He waited until, still huffy, still casting irate glances at each other, they complied, then he pulled the admiral's chair from behind the desk and sank into it. He fixed his gaze on Rus's face. "What made you suspicious?"

Slumping back in the chair, Rus's gaze grew distant.

"There were two horses at Cromarty's stables that weren't his. Not part of his string. They belonged to some other owner but were with Cromarty. Apparently those were the horses that Paddy O'Loughlin, the man who held the assistant stable manager position before me, had had a disagreement over and quit."

Pris glanced at Dillon. He shook his head; he didn't want Rus distracted with the news that Paddy had subsequently disappeared.

"Thus warned," Rus continued, "I didn't say anything, but neither horse was being properly brought on. They were being run occasionally but not properly prepared." Rus looked at him. "I have no idea what that means."

"I can guess, but go on."

Rus raised his brows. "Shortly after, amid the preparations to come to Newmarket, I heard Harkness and the head lad, Crom, a mean, vicious lump who's been with Harkness forever, talking. I'd gone into the tack room to fetch a particular bridle—I knew where it was so I didn't light a lamp. Harkness and Crom came into the stable to talk privately. They didn't know I was there."

"This was the conversation you mentioned in your letter to Pris?"

"Yes. I didn't hear enough to know what was going on, but as they'd mentioned 'the register' and we were coming to Newmarket, I thought I'd be able to work it out once here."

A tap on the door heralded Jacobs with a tray. Dillon pulled a side table into the space between the chairs. Jacobs set down the tray; Pris reached for the teapot. Dillon nodded his thanks, and Jacobs retreated.

Dillon waited until Rus had fortified himself with bread and roast beef, and taken a healthy swallow of ale before prompting, "And then . . . ?

Rus dabbed at his lips with a napkin, and sat back. "The first thing that happened was that those two extra horses were brought over to England with the string, then sent off with Crom once we docked at Liverpool. I never heard where they went. As Cromarty didn't travel with the string, I wondered if he knew what was happening. He's an owner, and knows horses, but he doesn't spend much time with them, let alone do any training himself. I assumed he was unaware of whatever was going on."

Rus sipped, then went on, "The next thing . . . we had a big bay gelding, Flyin' Fury, a very good runner. Cromarty had raced him over the past two seasons, and he'd done well. We ran him in the opening meet here, and he showed the field a clean pair of heels. Naturally, he was entered for another race in the next meet, the one three weeks ago. About a week before that, I noticed Flyin' Fury . . . was odd."

Rus looked at Dillon. "Not *looked* odd—he looked exactly like . . . well, himself—but I'd take an oath the horse wasn't Flyin' Fury." He grimaced. "I know it sounds nonsense, but it just wasn't the same horse. The stable lads were uncertain—the horse didn't react to them as usual, either—but it was Crom who handled Flyin' Fury, so other than me and Harkness, none of the others spent much time with him, and, of course, Crom and Harkness weren't saying anything."

"Did you mention your suspicions?" Dillon asked.

Rus shook his head. "I said nothing, and they behaved as if Flyin' Fury was the same as ever. The real shock was that the next day, he was—meaning the real Flyin' Fury was back."

Rus took a long swallow of ale. "That was . . . hard to understand. But then two days later, the imposter was back. And then came the race, and it was the other horse that ran as Flyin' Fury, and got beaten. He came fifth."

He sighed. "I knew then, or at least guessed what had to be going on. I thought about going to the race stewards. The next morning, I went to check on the imposter, and lo and behold, it was the real Flyin' Fury again! And then Harkness decided Fury needed to be spelled, and they sent him back to Ireland.

"I was sure, then, that my suspicions were correct, *but* I didn't have an ounce of proof. Both the real Flyin' Fury and the imposter were gone, and if I said anything, it would be Harkness's and more importantly Cromarty's word against mine, and the truth is that favorites often do lose. Good runners have bad spells. There was nothing I could point to as proof of anything."

Pris frowned. "But why were they switching the horses back and forth?'

"To have the imposter in sufficiently good condition to pass the stewards' prerace check." Dillon glanced at her. "If a horse hasn't been prepared to a certain degree, the stewards can stop it from running, which is almost the same as losing the race, but won't have the same effect—the desired effect—wager-wise, and will also start an inquiry into the trainer's preparation, and that's the last thing a substitution racket needs. So they'll make sure the substitute horse is reasonably prepared, and as they can't risk both horses being seen simultaneously, they switch the substitute in and out of the string in the weeks before the race."

Pris stared at him, then looked at Rus. "So you decided to look at the Breeding Register?"

Rus shook his head. "Not then. Almost immediately, something else happened. Cromarty has a young filly, just over two years old, and she's lightning on legs. She's unbeatable in a sprint. I'd been working with her since I started with Cromarty—she's young, so needs more preparation. Blistering Belle—she went out in the first meet and left the other runners standing. In the second meet, she did even better. Then, in the week after Flyin' Fury went home, I went into the stable one morning, and it wasn't Blistering Belle."

Rus caught Dillon's eye. "I don't know how they're doing it, but I couldn't fault a single point on that horse. Physically, she was a perfect match for Belle, only I knew she wasn't Belle."

Dillon frowned. "Who rides Belle in training, at gallops?"

"Crom—Harkness's man."

"So there's no one who's in any position to corroborate your view?"

Rus shook his head. "But with Belle, I don't need anyone else's opinion. I have proof." He glanced at Pris, drawing her in. "Belle hates red apples—won't touch them—but most horses love them, of course. I tried the imposter in Belle's stall, and she lipped a ripe pippin from my palm quick smart. And that was my downfall—Harkness saw me do it. He didn't know about Belle and red apples, but he took note—nothing was more certain but that he'd mentioned it to Crom. They're thick as thieves, those two, and Crom did know—he'd see what it meant."

"And Harkness would then know that you knew," Pris said. "So what did you do?"

Rus drew a deep breath. "I made a much bigger mistake. I went to Cromarty—a gentleman and a peer. I was sure he wasn't involved, that it was Harkness and Crom behind whatever was going on. I knew I only had the time it would take Harkness to find Crom and ask about the apple. Cromarty was in his study in the manor—I went in and told him all I'd learned, all I suspected.

"He was shocked. Appalled and shaken." Rus's lips twisted. "I realize now that it was because I'd found out, but at the time his reaction fitted. He told me to leave it all to him, that he would deal with the problem immediately. I agreed, and left. I heard him give orders to have Harkness summoned."

Rus paused, then went on, "By the time I reached the stable yard, my thumbs were pricking. Things didn't feel right—shouldn't Cromarty have tried to dismiss what I'd said? He'd just sat there and goggled at every assertion I'd made. He *never* protested. And he hadn't questioned me on any of the details." His lips thinned. "I didn't go back to my room. I hid in the yard until I saw Harkness go in, then scooted around the house, and listened under Cromarty's study window."

Rus blew out a breath. "I heard Cromarty tell Harkness that I knew of their scheme, and then they discussed how to get rid of me—to silence me. I didn't wait to hear their decision. I raced back, packed my things, and hied out into the night."

"Where did you go?" Pris asked.

Rus grinned. "I spent the first night in the church at Swaffam Prior. I reasoned it was the last place Harkness and Crom would look. After that I moved either at night or during training times. But I knew I had to get proof, unequivocal proof of whatever's going on." His gaze switched to Dillon's face. "Until I have that—enough so the authorities can arrest Cromarty, Harkness, and Crom—it's too dangerous to come out of hiding."

Dillon held Rus's gaze and gave thanks that he, unlike his sister, had a healthy respect for the situation they were facing. A good grasp of it, too, if the fear shadowing his green eyes was any guide. Rus had cheated death by minutes, and he knew it. Thoroughbred racing was known as the sport of kings, and just like the kings who'd established it, the sport had a darker side.

Easing his shoulders against the chair's back, Dillon nodded. "So what do we have? You've witnessed one successful substitution, that of Flyin' Fury, but we have no evidence to prove it."

Rus nodded.

"You know of another substitution, one that's in the process of being set up. Blistering Belle, and I know just which race they'll change her in—the October Handicap."

"Precisely. By then, she'll have run three races and won

by miles in each. She'll start favorite, without a doubt."

"But this time, we have proof—a way you can tell the real Belle apart from her double."

"But," Rus cut in, "we need both horses to demonstrate the substitution. Just pointing to one horse, whether it be Belle or the other, proves nothing. And we haven't got both horses. I've been trying to find where Harkness and Crom are hiding the substitutes and the real champions when they're away from the stable. I know which direction they head off in, but without a horse, I haven't been able to follow."

Dillon nodded. "That's something we can investigate."

After a moment, he glanced up and saw Rus frowning at him; he raised his brows.

"You seem predisposed to believing me. To taking this seriously." Rus glanced at Pris, then back at Dillon. "Why? It's an amazing tale, and could be just that for all you know."

Dillon smiled. "Quite aside from your sister dragooning me into rescuing you, what you've discovered is the other half of what we—myself and others—have already been investigating." Briefly, he described the rumors about the races in the spring season, how he'd been asked to investigate, how the initial inquiries Barnaby made had turned up little, then how, ironically, Rus's efforts to gain access to the register had spurred them to push harder.

What they'd subsequently uncovered—the likelihood of substitutions, Collier's involvement and his suspicious death, his elusive partner, and the rumors of a suspect race run at Newmarket a few weeks ago—made Rus sit up. "That had to be Flyin' Fury."

"We should have confirmation from London soon." Dillon eyed Rus. "Did you ever hear mention of Cromarty having a partner?"

Rus shook his head. "He's been in the game for decades.

I've not heard any whisper that he's hard-pressed." Then he grimaced. "Of course, a man like Cromarty wouldn't trumpet such a thing. Who knows?"

"My thinking entirely. So it's possible."

After a moment, Rus looked at Dillon. "This register—is there any information in it we could use as proof? To help with proof?"

Pris snorted. "It's *full* of information, but proof?" She met Dillon's eyes, and prayed she wouldn't blush.

His lips curved, but then he looked at Rus. "If there was any point on which the substitutes and the real champions differed, yes, the register would help—it lists the points used to verify horses' identities, and if I so decree the stewards could do a full check on any horse before any race. However, if the horses are as alike as you say, that won't help."

Rus nodded. "Can we look through the register to identify the substitutes? They're Thoroughbreds, and by no means poor specimens. Chances are they'll be in the same age groups as Flyin' Fury and Blistering Belle. I'm thinking that whoever owns them could be asked to explain."

"Assuming that's not Cromarty himself." Dillon considered. "It's not illegal to own two very similar horses. However, if he does own both those champions *and* their look-alikes, it would certainly give us reason to focus a great deal more attention on him and his runners."

Reaching across his desk, he pulled a sheet of paper to him. Selecting a pen, he dipped it in the inkpot; resting the paper on the flat of his chair's arm, he scrawled.

Craning her neck, Pris read *Flyin' Fury* and *Blistering Belle.*

"Tell me all you can about these horses." Dillon glanced at Rus. "I'll set my clerks scanning the register tomorrow morning—let's see what we turn up."

Rus gave a general description, then a more technical listing of the horses' points. Pris sat back, thinking rather than listening. When Dillon and Rus finished, she asked, "How are we going to find where they're hiding Blistering Belle and her imposter?"

Both Dillon and Rus looked at her, then exchanged a glance.

Dillon sat back, met her eyes. "*We* aren't. None of us can. We're all too recognizable."

She frowned. He went on, "The last thing we need is for Cromarty and Harkness to know we're watching them. They know Rus has guessed enough to raise questions, but having seen me with *you*"—Dillon angled his head at her—"they'll assume Rus has already spoken with me, but I've taken no action and it's been three days, so presumably he failed to convince me of anything. With luck they'll feel safe again, enough to go ahead with the Blistering Belle substitution. If they run scared and don't, then we—myself and the authorities—won't have any chance to catch them and shut the racket down."

Dillon paused, considering, then looked again at her. "Exactly how best to handle this situation . . . I admit I don't know, especially when you add in the possibility of a 'silent partner' lurking in the background. I want to expose him, too, not just bring Cromarty down. If his actions with Collier are any guide, at the first hint of trouble, this man will eradicate any link to himself and simply switch the substitutions to some other stable next season."

He looked at Rus. "I don't want to act precipitously and show the villain our hand before we're ready to act, before we've identified him. And we're not in any position to do anything yet—we need more information, then we'll plan."

Rus was nodding. Dillon switched his gaze to Pris. "So we'll find out who owns the imposters, and we'll have someone track Crom to learn where they're hiding the switched horses. One of my grooms—"

"Patrick." She sat forward. "He's at the Carisbrook house,

much closer to the Rigby farm, and he'll understand and be careful."

Dillon nodded. "Good idea."

Rus was frowning. "Patrick's here?" Then he grimaced. "I suppose he would be, if Eugenia is." He shook his head. "I still can't take it in that you all upped stakes and came after me."

Pris regarded him with affectionate scorn. "I can't believe you ever imagined we wouldn't."

"Yes, well." Dillon glanced at the clock over the mantelpiece. "It's late—we need to get you back to Lady Fowles." He glanced at Rus as he stood. "I'll introduce you to Jacobs—he'll show you your room. Other than our staff, all of whom have been with us forever, the only one here is my father, and he already knows the official side of this."

"He was the Keeper of the Stud Book before Dillon." Pris rose as Rus got to his feet.

Dillon led the way to the door, then paused and turned around. He studied her for a moment, then looked at Rus. "Lady Fowles, Miss Blake, and *Miss* Dalling will no doubt be keen to visit you. Luckily, our recent social appearances will serve as an excuse—no one will be surprised to see your aunt's carriage turn into the Hillgate End drive, or to find Lady Fowles taking tea with my father." He glanced at her, and smiled. "The perfect camouflage."

She saw the fleeting gleam in his eyes, part amusement, part . . . was it male satisfaction? She wished she could read what was going on in his brain. "We'll call tomorrow morning." Stretching up, she kissed Rus's rough cheek, then hugged him hard. "Patrick will come, too, and you can tell him about Crom, and in which direction he takes the horses to be hidden."

Rus kissed her back, patted her shoulder. Then he looked at Dillon and held out his hand. "Thank you. It might be your duty to investigate this matter, yet I'm still in your debt."

Dillon caught the flick of Rus's eyes Pris's way; lips curving, he grasped Rus's hand. "Don't worry—when we get to the end of this, the shoe might well be on the other foot."

A nicely ambiguous statement; from the look in Rus's eyes, he caught both meanings. With Rus handed into Jacobs's care, Dillon ushered Pris away; he felt Rus's gaze on his back as he steered Pris down the corridor, heading for the stables and the long ride across the moonlit fields to the Carisbrook house.

Even before they left the stable yard, Pris's relief, until then deflected by their talk, was welling, threatening to spill over. Dillon saw her mounted, then turned away. Swinging up to Solomon's back, he looked across—and saw her cavorting giddily, letting the mare prance and dance as her emotion communicated itself to her flighty mount. "Pris!"

She flashed him a glorious smile—a wild, reckless and dangerous smile. "Come on—let's ride!"

A light tap to the mare's flanks was all it took to send her racing; jaw setting, Dillon sent Solomon surging after her. He caught up before she'd left the manor drive; she laughed and matched him, stride for stride. The pounding of flying hooves on the packed gravel, an insistent tattoo, was a drumbeat they both responded to.

They shot out of the drive and the fields lay before them. Dark, deserted, all theirs. With a whoop, Pris whirled her quirt and raced on.

Dangerous, reckless, and wild.

Mentally gritting his teeth, Dillon herded her. He was too wise—understood too well the reckless passion that had her in its grip—to try to head her, to hold her back. To restrain her. Instead, using Solomon's bulk and strength, and his own knowledge of every foot, every yard of the surrounding land, he guided the mare in her headlong dash, through the physical outpouring of Pris's joy.

Finding her brother, knowing he was safe—touching him, seeing him—had released a dam of pent-up emotions, of stresses and strains, worries and cares. Pris wasn't just free, she was soaring—carefree, lighthearted.

Light-headed; he was certain of that. She seemed breathless, her laughter spilling out, the silvery notes falling like fairy dust all around them. They thundered through the night; every faculty stretched, he picked their route, keeping to well-beaten tracks that in the darkness only showed in his mind.

Over fields, through paddocks, flying over low fences, they streaked through the night. Anyone seeing them would have sworn they were mad; he knew they were both sane, just out of control.

Or at least, she was; he was doing his best to remain levelheaded, not to let her infect him with her wild and reckless passion. Having to concentrate helped; knowing that any error of judgment on his part could see her thrown and injured helped more.

Then the Carisbrook house loomed ahead, a dark monolith rising up out of the shadowy landscape. The mare was tiring, but far from blown; she was as game as her rider. He was about to correct course for the yard behind the house when Pris called a challenge; dropping her reins, she caught the mare's flying mane, crouched low, and put on a turn of speed that in less than a minute left Solomon two lengths behind.

And on a wrong heading. Dillon cursed, checked, and went after her. Pushing Solomon on, he closed the gap, but then they burst through the bushes lining the drive, crossed it in a lunge, and swept into the scattered trees beyond.

They had to tack this way and that around the trees, slowing them both, for which he was grateful. But then the mare reached a path and leapt forward again. And he knew where she was going—where she was leading him.

His sane self cursed; this was not a good idea.

Most of him, that side of him she never failed to speak to, was already with her.

With her, close on her heels as she pulled the mare to a halt beside the summerhouse, tumbled out of her saddle, looping the reins about the stair rail before, laughing giddily, she raced up the steps.

With her, mere steps behind her as she flew across the summerhouse straight for the central pole. With her as she reached it, wrapped both hands around it and, leaping high, exuberantly swung herself around. Dropping back to the floor, she faced him, her smile brighter, more glorious, than the sun.

"We found him!"

She flung herself at him.

Caught his face between her hands and fused her lips to his.

He caught her, staggered back, steadied, then pressed her back until her spine hit the pole.

And devoured.

Took all she not just offered but pressed on him, that she lavished and tempted and defied him to take.

He didn't take control of the kiss—it took control of him. And her. They fed from each other, hungered and burned until all either knew was a desperate want. An urgent need to conquer and surrender, to seize, to possess, to simply have.

Her mouth was his, his tongue was hers, their breaths beyond ragged and urgent. Fire flashed and raced through them; desire swelled and crashed through them. Passion rose in a tidal wave and swept them both away.

Madness. It gripped them. Wild, reckless, dangerous.

It whipped them, consumed them, drove them. Harried every breath, every gasp, every too-desperate touch.

He wrenched open the shirt she'd worn under her jacket, found the ties of her chemise and yanked it down, wrapped his palm about her breast and nearly groaned. He flexed his fingers and she did; he kneaded possessively and she gave voice to their hunger, even as her hands worked desperately at his waist, hauling up his shirt, then sliding beneath to spread hungrily over his chest.

Clothes flew. Her boots skidded across the floor, dispensed with so he could tug her breeches down and off her legs. His jacket and shirt disappeared, eaten, for all he knew, by her greedy hands.

Hot, grasping, urgent.

Needy, greedy, and wanting.

Heat throbbed beneath every inch of his skin. When she pushed aside the flap of his breeches and, reaching within, wrapped her hand around him, for one instant he thought he might die.

The desperation was that great.

His need was even greater.

As was hers.

Her tongue was in his mouth, taunting and pleading even while her fingers played.

His hand was on her naked bottom, gripping, possessing. His other hand toyed with one swollen breast, almost idly stroking the tightly furled nipple.

She tightened her grip, then with her nails lightly scored.

He couldn't breathe. Releasing her breast, he slid both hands down, gripped her thighs, and hoisted her.

With a surprised gasp, she released her hold, but even before he pinned her to the pole, she was winding her long bare legs about his hips. Before he pressed closer, she pulled him to her.

He thrust deep inside her.

Drew back and thrust again, harder, farther.

She broke from the kiss gasping; head back, she wriggled, adjusted about him, then she tightened her legs, holding him close, urging him into a deep, steady, forceful rhythm. One that rocked them both. One designed to fuse them beyond recall.

He caught the pole above her head and pushed her higher, pushed deeper and still deeper into her.

She caught her breath on a sob, found his head with her hands, tipped his face to hers, bent her head, and kissed him.

And they were lost.

Lost to the tempest, to the roiling turbulent need that rose up and swamped them. To the fire and hunger that roared through their veins, igniting flames beneath every inch of skin, spreading and searing, consuming the last shreds of sanity, the last vestiges of reservation, the last shadows of inhibition.

Until they knew only this.

This need, this want, this desperation.

The wild, the reckless, the dangerous—the all-consuming. The elemental power that poured through them both.

That gripped them, ripped them apart, and offered their souls to some higher power as ecstasy swept through them.

As it shattered them, battered them, then flung them, boneless, into some limitless sea.

Into the balm of aftermath that sealed them, healed them.

That finally, uncounted minutes later, receded, and left them clinging to each other in the dark of the night, in the cool shadows of the summerhouse by the lake.

Thirteen

"Hel-lo! What have we here?"

Comfortably seated in his study opposite Rus Dalling, Dillon looked up to see Barnaby framed in the doorway. Barnaby's gaze had locked on Rus—whom he'd last seen in the moonlight behind the Jockey Club.

Rus had recognized Barnaby; cocking a brow at Dillon, he slowly rose to his feet.

Dillon did the same, waving Barnaby in. "The Honorable Barnaby Adair, allow me to present Russell Dalling. And yes," he added, seeing the speculation in Barnaby's eyes, "Rus is Miss Dalling's twin."

Rus offered his hand. "My apologies for the nature of our previous encounter. I had no idea who you were, and I had good reason not to dally to find out."

Strolling forward, Barnaby glanced at Dillon, then gripped Rus's hand. "I take it you've thrown in your lot with us—on the side of the angels, as it were."

Rus's brilliant smile flashed. "I was always on that side. I just didn't know who else was, who I could trust."

Barnaby rubbed his jaw; the bruise there had almost faded from sight. "Speaking of trust, you could earn mine by showing me some of those maneuvers you used. I've been in brawls aplenty, but that was something new. And effective."

Rus exchanged a smile with Dillon, then glanced back at Barnaby. "He said you'd say that."

"Yes, well, predictable, that's me." Barnaby looked at Dillon. "So you succeeded in persuading Miss Dalling to tell you all?"

"Not without considerable effort. Eventually she ran out of options and elected, at last, to tell me about Rus, and what she knew of his problems. Once you hear, you'll understand, but it was immediately apparent Rus was seeking to expose the same swindle we're pursuing."

"From the other end, as it were," Rus said.

"Excellent . . ." Barnaby's voice died away. Consternation dawning, he glanced from Rus to Dillon.

"What?" Dillon asked.

Barnaby nodded at Rus. "You've scrubbed up well—I do hope you're in hiding?"

Dillon frowned. "He is, but you haven't yet heard the reason why."

"I can *see* a damned good reason why," Barnaby returned. "Just look at us. One sighting by the local mamas of the three of us together and the news will be out in a flash. Well—you saw how it was when it was just you and me. Add Rus here, and I guarantee the news will reach London within hours."

Looking at Rus, Dillon saw Barnaby's point. Barnaby was a golden Adonis, he himself was dark and dramatic, while Rus, a touch younger, was the epitome of devilish. He grimaced. "We'll need to remember that."

Rus grinned. "It can't be that bad."

"Oh, can't it?" Barnaby said. "How much time have you spent socializing in the ton, here or in London?"

Rus raised his brows. "None, really. Not socializing."

"Well, you just wait. Take it from us—we're old hands. It's not safe for men like us in the ton." Barnaby looked around for a chair. "You're young—you'll learn."

"Learn what?"

They all looked around. The door was open; Pris stood on the threshold. Her gaze was on Barnaby; she inclined her head in greeting. Then her gaze traveled, slowly, from Barnaby to her brother, then finally to Dillon.

Her gaze lingered, then she blinked, and stepped into the room.

"There—see!" Barnaby turned to Rus. "Even she paused, and she's your sister and arguably the least susceptible female in the ton. I rest my case."

Pris frowned. "What are you talking about?"

"I'm just trying to warn your brother of a danger he doesn't yet appreciate he'll face."

Before Barnaby could say more, Dillon waved Pris to the armchair he'd vacated and drew his admiral's chair from the desk. Rus sat again; Barnaby pulled up a straight-backed chair and elegantly subsided.

"Right then." Barnaby looked at them eagerly. "Enlighten me. Start at the beginning."

Exchanging a glance with Pris, Dillon started at the point where she'd finally told him of Rus, described how they'd found him, then let Rus explain all he'd discovered before they'd joined forces.

While Rus talked, Dillon studied Pris. He hadn't been surprised by her arrival; today was the second day Rus had been hiding at the manor.

Yesterday, she, Eugenia, Adelaide, and Patrick had arrived midmorning. Having made Rus's acquaintance and heard his tale over breakfast, the General had been in excellent form, delighted to welcome the visitors to Hillgate

End, to play host and sit chatting with Eugenia and Adelaide when, with Rus and Patrick, Dillon had withdrawn to discuss searching for where Harkness was concealing the substitute horses.

If the three of them had had their way, Pris would have been excluded from that discussion; they were as one in wanting to keep her apart from what they knew to be dangerous. Regardless, their wishes had been overridden by a display of feminine will they hadn't been able to counter. Rus had tried to argue; with her, he had the freest hand. Having listened to the needle-witted exchange, Dillon felt certain that Rus was the elder twin; he was more responsible and openly concerned for Pris's safety. The fact he understood, indeed shared, her wild and reckless streak only sharpened his concern.

But he hadn't succeeded, so Pris now knew that, always late at night, Crom took the horses north and east, away from the Rigby place, farther from Newmarket and the Heath. Patrick would watch the Rigby farm until they learned what they needed to know; he hadn't seen any activity last night.

Pris was watching Rus and Barnaby talk, impatient to get on, accepting that Barnaby needed to know all they'd learned, yet chafing at the time necessary to inform him. While Barnaby questioned and Rus answered, Dillon let his gaze slide from Pris's vibrant face to her figure, today elegantly gowned in forest green twill.

He wasn't sure which of her incarnations—the unconventional female dressed in breeches or the exquisite, faintly haughty lady—distracted him more. The former reminded him of that heated interlude in the summerhouse two evenings before, while the latter evoked potent memories of the night just passed—and the provocative promise arising from that.

Last night . . . he'd been restless beyond bearing. Driven by he knew not what—by some impossible-to-deny impulse he hadn't want to examine closely—he'd surrendered and, close to midnight, had saddled Solomon and ridden to the Carisbrook house.

To the summerhouse. He hadn't expected her to be there, had had no thought in his head other than simply to be near her. He'd imagined sitting on the sofa and looking over the lake, until his restlessness had faded.

He'd been doing just that, sitting staring over the still water, when he'd seen a wraith moving through the trees. Her, in a pale gown with a shawl about her shoulders.

They hadn't made any arrangement; it hadn't been an assignation. Yet she'd entered the summerhouse without hesitation. Showing no real surprise at finding him there, she'd walked directly to him, halted before him, and let her shawl slide from her shoulders.

She'd spent the next hours in his arms, in an interlude unlike any other he'd ever known. She'd taken his restlessness, and shaped it, transmuted it into something else, something she'd wanted, and had taken into herself.

Much later, at peace in a way he'd never before been, he'd walked her back to the house, seen her slip inside, then had returned to Solomon and ridden home.

That sense of peace still lingered, even now.

Just gazing at her somehow soothed some part of him he hadn't before realized needed anyone's touch.

"So!" Barnaby turned to him. "Did your clerks find anything?"

He shifted, refocused. "They've found something, but we don't yet know what it means. The two horses Rus identified as look-alikes for Flyin' Fury and Blistering Belle are owned by a Mr. Aberdeen. He's a gentleman, owns a reasonable stable of runners, and employs his own trainer, yet it appears he's sent—or is it lent?—those horses to Cromarty."

Barnaby frowned. "He's not a local owner?"

Dillon shook his head. "Based near Sheffield. He usually runs his horses at Doncaster or Cheltenham. My clerks are trying to identify the two horses Cromarty had in Ireland, that Crom took somewhere after the string landed in Liverpool. If those horses are Aberdeen's, or are Cromarty's but are look-alikes for two of Aberdeen's runners, then it's possible the groundwork for substitutions at Doncaster and Cheltenham is also in hand."

Barnaby looked at him. "This is not a small enterprise."

"No," Dillon agreed. "And that brings us to today's news. Yours."

"Indeed!" Barnaby glanced at Rus, then Pris, then looked at Dillon. "Perhaps we ought to adjourn to Demon's house? His opinion would be useful, and it would be better if we were all there to hear it."

Dillon nodded. "Good idea. He was away all yesterday looking at horses. I've yet to introduce him to Rus or Pris, and fill him in on all we've learned. Flick and he were expected back this morning."

"Demon," Rus said as they all rose. "Demon Cynster?"

Recognizing the awestruck look in Rus's eyes, Dillon grinned. "There's only one Demon, believe me. He's my cousin-in-law, but you can interpret that as brother-in-law. I grew up with Flick, now his wife. Demon's stud is the neighboring estate."

"Oh, I know." Rus fell in beside him as he followed Pris and Barnaby to the door. "While I was hiding in the woods, I used to fill in time by sneaking close to his paddocks and watching the horses. He's got more prime 'uns in one place than I've ever set eyes on before."

"For Demon, horse breeding is more than a hobby—it's his passion." Dillon caught Pris's eye as she glanced his way, and smiled. "After Flick, that is."

He didn't hear her sniff, but was quite sure she did.

They walked the short distance to the Cynster house, discussing various points, filling in details Rus and Dillon had skimmed over earlier. No matter how they probed, Barnaby refused to divulge anything of what he'd learned, not until they had Demon there, too.

Both Demon and Flick were at home; both were eager to hear their news, even more so when they learned who Rus was.

Pris hung on to her patience and waited with what decorum she could muster; what she really wanted was to pace, plan, and act. She'd assumed finding Rus would be the same as finding peace, yet although she'd been immensely relieved to have her twin back hale and whole, the existence of a continuing threat to his life wasn't something she could bear with any degree of equanimity.

She wanted that threat ended, eradicated, and she wanted that now. But she needed Dillon's, Barnaby's, Demon's, and Flick's help, so she bit her tongue and forbore to hurry them.

At last, once Dillon had noted the as-yet-unclear involvement of Mr. Aberdeen, all eyes swung to Barnaby. She'd expected him to relish the moment; instead, he looked grave.

"What I have to report"—he glanced around at their faces—"when added to all you've learned, suggests the whole is more serious, indeed blacker, than we'd thought. Gabriel and his contacts tried to trace the ten thousand pounds Collier received. Montague, who I gather you both know"—Barnaby nodded to Dillon and Demon, who nodded back—"assured me that had the transfer been made in the normal way of business, they would have found some trail, but they didn't. Wherever that money came from, it didn't move through any bank. Collier must have received it as cash—literally a bundle of notes. Both Gabriel and Montague suggested the most likely source was a wealthy gamester, someone who regularly handles such sums."

Barnaby paused; his expression grew harder. "Then Vane appeared with the latest he'd gleaned, not from the clubs but from various rather seedier locations. The latest gossip concerning the suspect race run here a few weeks ago"—Barnaby looked at Rus—"and yes, the horse involved was Flyin' Fury, is that positively *huge* sums were laid *against* Flyin' Fury winning.

"Certain bookmakers are wailing and gnashing their teeth, but, of course, few have any sympathy. However, Vane learned enough to estimate the winnings solely from those bets as more than one hundred thousand pounds. The point that most interested everyone was that the individual bets weren't large—nothing out of the ordinary, all to different people or betting agents. So while the bookmakers are certain they were stung, they have no way of knowing who to blame."

Demon looked grim. "If they did know who, that person would no longer be a concern."

"No, indeed." Barnaby nodded. "Gabriel sent a message. He, Montague, and Vane believe that whoever's behind this will prove deadly. This is not the usual sort of scam, but one operating on a massive scale. The monetary risks being taken are enormous, the potential gain gargantuan. Consequently, if threatened, whoever's behind this won't hesitate to deal death into the game.

"I told them we believed that particular card had already been played with Collier." Barnaby looked at Demon and Dillon. "Vane sent a message, too. *Beware.*"

Demon exchanged a glance with Dillon. "Sound advice."

Pris got the distinct impression that to them that *Beware* meant something different, certainly carried more weight than the usual interpretation. She noticed Flick watching Demon, faintly narrow-eyed, but couldn't guess the direction of her thoughts.

Everyone paused, piecing together all they knew. Demon summarized, "So we've yet to find where the switched horses are hidden. Once we know that"—he met Dillon's gaze—"we'll have to give serious thought as to how best to proceed."

Dillon nodded and rose. "We'll let you know what we discover."

Demon and Flick saw them to the front door. The conversation along the way revolved about the runners they were preparing for the upcoming race meet—the first October meeting, a major event in the Newmarket calendar.

"Dillon and I feel sure that's the meet at which they'll switch Blistering Belle," Rus said.

Demon concurred. "If we can't thrust a spoke through their wheel, they'll make a killing." He looked at Dillon. "In the circumstances, I don't know what help we'll be. We'll both be up to our ears in preparation."

"Actually . . ." Flick eyed Rus appraisingly. "I could use an extra pair of well-trained hands, and as there's nothing you can do at present since you must remain in hiding, and as our training track is well screened, out of bounds and out of sight to any but our most trusted lads, why don't you slip over and lend a hand? I'll put you to work, and you can show me what you Irish can do."

There was enough challenge in the words to allow Rus to grin and accept with alacrity rather than fall to his knees and kiss Flick's feet. Pris smiled, relieved that Rus would be kept occupied, delighted that the occupation was his passion. Catching Flick's eye, she inclined her head in thanks. Flick grinned and patted her arm.

A moment later, they set off, walking across the fields and through the belt of woodland separating the stud from Hillgate End. Rus was in alt, his head already in the clouds.

Dillon laughed. "Tell me—how do you see Flick? Sweet, delicate, a Botticelli angel, gentle temper, all smiles?"

Rus looked at Dillon, shrugged. "Something like that."

His grin wide, Dillon clapped Rus on the shoulder. "Just wait, boyo—she's a sergeant major around horses. I guarantee she'll run you ragged."

The next morning, Pris came down to breakfast to find Patrick hovering in the dining room. She stared at him. "Did you find them?"

He grinned. "I did."

She sank into her chair; ignoring Adelaide's and Eugenia's exclamations, she demanded, "Where?"

Patrick told her.

Ten minutes after she'd consumed a hasty breakfast, she was in the gig, the reins in her hands, Adelaide beside her, as she tooled them down the lanes to call on the household at Hillgate End.

"They switched the black fillies late last night." Pris unfolded a map she'd drawn. "It's a tiny cottage, more a hovel Patrick said, but there's a lean-to stable alongside big enough to hold two horses."

She laid her sketch on Dillon's desk; he, Rus, and Barnaby crowded around. The General had been present when she and Adelaide had been shown in. Dillon and Rus had frowned, signaling with their eyes; they hadn't wanted Adelaide involved.

She'd felt like she would burst, holding in the news while Adelaide shyly greeted them, then started chatting with Rus; he'd just returned from his first session working with Flick and seemed both exhilarated and stunned. But then the General had risen to the occasion and claimed Adelaide's attention and her arm for a stroll about the garden. Mentally blessing him, Pris had lost no time imparting her news.

"There." She pointed to a cross some miles northeast of the Rigby farm. "It's little more than four walls and a chimney on the other side of this stream." She traced a squiggly line. "There are trees along the rise behind it."

"Which horse will it be?" Barnaby looked at Rus.

He shook his head. "Sometimes it was a day between switches, at other times three." He glanced at Dillon. "I'll go there and check which horse it is."

"Not in daylight," Pris said. "Harkness might see you out riding. Who knows what he'll be up to?"

Rus grinned. "Actually I do know, at least for a few

hours every day. This afternoon he and Crom will be overseeing the string exercising on the Heath."

"Can you be sure?' Dillon asked.

"Without me, unless Harkness has managed to hire another assistant trainer—and how likely is that in Newmarket just before a major meet?—then he and Crom both have to attend the training sessions. Cromarty has a good few horses entered, and aside from the substitution, he doesn't like to lose any more than any other owner."

"Right, then." Dillon straightened. "This afternoon it is."

Pris bit her tongue; they did have to know which horse was where, and only Rus could be certain which was which—and she couldn't think of any way to argue him out of what she, nevertheless, viewed as a dangerous journey.

She met his eyes—amused yet understanding—and pulled a face at him. He laughed, hugged her, and wisely made no comment.

She and Adelaide stayed for luncheon. The General seemed delighted by their presence; he confessed he missed having young ladies around. "Flick was here for years, and even though she's just across the fields, it's not the same."

He glanced down the table at Dillon, old eyes twinkling. "I sometimes think I should invite Prudence, Flick and Demon's daughter, to stay for a few weeks."

Dillon groaned. "Heaven preserve me!" To Pris and Adelaide, he explained, "Imagine a cross between Flick and Demon—a hedonistic female, convinced she's right, and who will stop at nothing—absolutely nothing—to ensure matters fall out as she decrees they ought." He shuddered. "She's a terror now, and will be utterly unstoppable in a few years."

Barnaby nodded. "I'm just grateful that by then we'll be ancient, and probably far distant, so she won't turn her beady eyes on us."

"They aren't beady." Pris felt forced to defend the young girl she'd once glimpsed. "They're quite lovely."

Barnaby nodded even more. "Precisely. Weapons of the highest caliber. Just wait until she uses them on Rus, then ask him whether we're not right."

The conversation continued in a lighthearted vein. At the end of the meal, they made plans to meet at the Carisbrook house later that afternoon—to go for a ride. Adelaide reluctantly ruled herself out without them having to say anything; she wasn't a sufficiently confident rider to keep up with them.

Pris went out of her way to be extra pleasant as she drove them back, detouring to the lending library so Adelaide could find a new novel—and to check the large map on the wall. Assured she had the position of the cottage properly fixed in her mind, she drove on to the house, where Eugenia and Patrick waited.

She and Eugenia, with Patrick trailing behind, went for a walk around the lake while she explained all they knew and their present direction.

Eugenia nodded. "Mr. Caxton—Dillon—seems an estimable gentleman, and Mr. Adair, too—his connection with the new police force does give one confidence. While I'm hardly happy that Rus must stay in hiding, I'm glad he"—Eugenia glanced at Pris—"and you, my dear, have found yourselves in such excellent company. I'll admit that in coming here, I feared matters might turn out far worse."

Pris nodded. They continued to amble around the lake's shore.

"I do hope," Eugenia continued, "that your brother curbs his enthusiasm and doesn't do anything reckless and dangerous."

"Actually, I don't think there's much likelihood of that." Pris described Flick's invitation, and what Rus had recounted of his first session beside her on the training track. "He hadn't realized that she, herself, rides the horses she trains. Once he found out, he thought he'd have to hold his horse back. Instead, she left him floundering."

Smiling, Pris wondered if Flick had deliberately let the situation play out as it had, guessing how it would spur Rus on and put him on his mettle.

"Hmm," Eugenia said. "I did think Mrs. Cynster was an exceptionally intelligent lady."

Smile deepening, Pris strolled on.

As the afternoon ticked by, she forced herself to patience, to not look at the clock every ten minutes. Regardless, when her three coconspirators clattered into the stable yard, she was mounted and waiting.

Eugenia, Adelaide, and Patrick came out to wave them off. Minutes later, they were galloping across the fields—north, to the tiny cottage.

Pris held her mare alongside the three larger horses—Dillon's black, a raking bay carrying Barnaby, and the strong gray that Rus was riding. Before they'd appeared, she'd been just a little worried that, despite the arrangements, they would give the Carisbrook house a wide berth and leave her waiting "in safety." She was pleased they hadn't, pleased with them, her mood buoyant as they raced toward the cottage.

They had to reach it, Rus had to examine the horse stabled there, then he had to get back to Hillgate End before dusk heralded an end to the day's training. So they wasted no time; letting the horses stretch out, they flew.

A rocky streambed appeared ahead, cutting through the relatively flat fields. Dillon drew rein, then swung Solomon to follow the bank. The others followed. From the opposite bank, the land rose gently to where, tucked into the side of a rise, the tiny cottage nestled against a protective band of trees.

Finding a crossing place, Dillon sent Solomon down the bank. The big black took the opposite bank in one leap. Pris came next, waved on by Barnaby and Rus; her mare stepped daintily, picking its way, then climbed the rising bank at an angle. Barnaby and Rus quickly followed; Dillon turned and set Solomon for the cottage, surging up beside Pris's mare, already striking out for their goal.

Eyes on the cottage's door, he called, "You and I—let's head straight for the cottage. We can knock on the door—if there's anyone there, you can beg a drink of water." He glanced at her.

She nodded to show she'd heard. Her lips curved, her eyes alight, she raced up the slope beside him.

He signaled to the other two to hold back. Facing forward again, he kept pace with Pris, tamping down the urge to recklessly race.

She was reckless enough, racing enough for them both.

She pulled up before the cottage, laughing, letting the mare circle. She waited until he halted and dismounted, then trotted the mare up and let him lift her down.

Setting her on her feet, he took her hand. "Come on."

He led her to the cottage door, and pounded on it. They waited, both breathing quickly, sharing a long glance as a minute ticked by.

"I can't hear anything," she mouthed.

He knocked again, louder, longer. "I say! Is anyone there? Could a lady beg a drink of water?"

Silence. Then from around the corner came a muffled whicker.

Stepping back, he studied the cottage. It had only a single story, no attic, its one small window so grimy it was impossible to see inside. "I think we're safe." He beckoned to the other two, who'd hung back as if merely pausing on their way somewhere else.

Pris tried to slip her fingers free of his hold; he tightened his grip, scanning the surroundings as the other two rode up. Satisfied there was no one to see them, he met Pris's narrowing eyes. "All right—let's see."

They strode around the corner. The entrance to the stable faced the rear, well screened and protected by the trees. It was in better condition than the cottage, better even than its outward appearance suggested.

Ducking beneath the heavy beam over the doorway, Dillon glanced around, taking in the bridles and reins neatly hung on one wall, the two stalls, both strong and of surprisingly good size, with half doors across their mouths. The floor was stone, clean and swept; the sweet smell of straw hung in the warm, still air.

The second stall was occupied. Pris headed for it. His fingers still locked about hers, he followed. A black filly with four even white socks and a white blaze on her chest watched them from within the stall, curious but wary, making no move to come to the half door and get acquainted.

Brisk footsteps heralded Rus, with Barnaby close behind. Rus slowed to take in the surroundings, then he met Dillon's eyes. "At least they take proper care of them."

Dillon waved to the occupied stall, drawing Pris back. "Which is she?"

Rus stepped to the half door; the instant the filly set eyes on him, she gave a delighted whinny and came eagerly forward. She butted Rus in the chest. Laughing, he scratched between her ears, then stroked her long black nose. "This is Belle."

The horse snuffled and butted again.

Rus reached into his pocket and drew out a ripe red pippin. He offered it; Belle literally curled her lip, snorted in disgust, and knocked his hand aside. Rus chuckled, repocketed the pippin, and drew out a lump of sugar. Appeased, Belle lipped it from his palm, blowing softly.

Then she butted him again, pressing against the front of the stall.

"No, girl," Rus crooned, Irish accent soft and lilting. "You have to stay here, at least for a while."

"We'd better go." After witnessing the evidence of the

apple, Barnaby had retreated beyond the stable door, keeping watch down the valley. "The sun's going down." He glanced at Dillon. "How much longer will the training sessions last?"

Reluctantly, Rus drew away from Belle; Dillon and Pris followed him from the stable. Behind them, Belle whickered forlornly.

Dillon looked west, then out across the slope to where the shadows were lengthening. "We've just time enough for Rus to reach Hillgate End before Harkness and Crom start scouting."

"Even if they send the string back to the Rigby place and head straight to your woods?" Pris glanced worriedly at Rus as they walked quickly back to their horses.

"Even so." Rus grinned at her. "With the meet so close, Harkness won't be cutting corners and rushing through training."

Pris stopped arguing, but from the way she glanced at Rus, she wasn't convinced. In the circumstances, Dillon left Rus to lift her to her saddle.

Within minutes they were across the stream and flying over the fields to the Carisbrook house.

When they clattered into the stable yard, Patrick was waiting. He caught Pris's mare. "Did you find her—the black filly?"

Rus nodded. "Blistering Belle." He glanced at Dillon. "What now?"

"Now we think." Dillon settled Solomon, prancing as Patrick lifted Pris down. "We can't afford a misstep." He caught Pris's eye, then glanced at Patrick. "It's short notice, but do you think Lady Fowles will agree to an impromptu dinner at Hillgate End this evening? I know my father would be delighted, and it'll give us a chance to review what we know, consider the possibilities, and decide on our goal. Then we can make plans."

Pris nodded. "I'm sure Aunt Eugenia will be delighted to join your father for dinner."

Dillon raised his hand in a salute. "We'll see you then."

The other two called farewells, then the three wheeled. Pris watched them spring their mounts and charge away, racing. With a sniff, she turned to the house. "I'd better go and tell Eugenia that we've arranged her evening for her."

Fourteen

Pris hadn't expected Eugenia to object to their commandeering of her evening, yet she was puzzled by how pleased her aunt was at the "invitation."

Descending the stairs at six o'clock, ready to set out, she discovered Eugenia preening—definitely preening—before the mirror in the hall.

"Oh—there you are, dear. Tell me"—Eugenia tweaked the delicate lace collar she'd fastened about her discreet neckline—"do you think this makes me look too old?"

Pris blinked, but when Eugenia glanced her way inquiringly, she went to view her aunt in the mirror—actually looked at the soft-featured face, at the gently waving blond hair only lightly streaked with gray. At the nicely rounded figure, matronly but Rubenesquely so, at the intelligence that shone in the clear blue eyes. She shook her head. "I don't think you look old at all."

Purely feminine pleasure lit Eugenia's smile. "Thank you, dear." Turning, she surveyed Pris, then raised her brows. "That shade of lilac becomes you. I take it you're abandoning the severe bluestocking look?"

Straightening her amethyst skirts, Pris shrugged. "It's only Rus, Dillon, and Barnaby—it's not as if there'll be anyone there I need to fool."

Eugenia looked much struck. "Very true."

The twinkle in her eyes stated that she wasn't fooled, either—that she understood perfectly that there would be one male present Pris was quite happy to expose to the full force of her charms.

Adelaide came clattering down the stairs, content now she knew where Rus was, that he was safe, and thrilled to be seeing him that evening. "I'm ready." Halting at the foot of the stairs, she looked at Pris and Eugenia, eagerness lighting her face. "Can we go?"

Pris glanced at Eugenia; Eugenia glanced at Pris. Then they both laughed.

"Come along." Eugenia waved them to the door. "Patrick is waiting."

The drive to Hillgate End was accomplished in an atmosphere of pleasant anticipation. The General met them at the manor door and bowed them in. Dillon, Rus, and Barnaby were waiting in the drawing room.

Walking in behind Eugenia, Pris was glad she'd seen Dillon in evening dress before; she managed not to stare, but it was only after she'd greeted him, then turned, and Rus grinned at her, that she even remembered her twin was there. She blinked, dragooned her wits into order, and moved to greet Barnaby.

What followed was the epitome of a warm, relaxed, very comfortable evening spent among good friends. The dinner was excellent, the wines light; the talk was effervescent, engaging, a simple delight. By mutual accord no one spoke of the matter that had brought them together, of the decisions that hung suspended, waiting to be made. Instead, they spoke of London, and Ireland, of scandal and news, of horses, too, but of breeding them, not racing them.

The laughter was genuine, the appreciation sincere. Rus spent time chatting quietly to Adelaide; while Barnaby entertained the General and Eugenia, Dillon and Pris exchanged opinions on card games, curricle racing, and dogs.

But when the last course was cleared and the covers drawn, the General looked around and smiled. "Perhaps, in the circumstances, Lady Fowles, Miss Blake, and I will retire to the drawing room and leave you four to your deliberations."

"Indeed." Eugenia pushed back her chair. "But don't take too long. We'll expect you to join us for tea."

The men stood as she did. The General offered Eugenia his arm; with Adelaide on his other side, the three left the room, already chatting.

Dillon sank back into his chair next to Pris. Barnaby remained opposite; Rus switched chairs to sit beside him. Before they could say a word, the door swung open and Jacobs entered carrying the port decanter on a tray.

He halted, blinked.

Dillon glanced at Pris, but she was frowning at the tabletop. He jogged her elbow; when she looked up, with his head he indicated Jacobs, waiting, uncertain what to do. Pris stared, then looked back at Dillon. He opened his eyes wide at her.

She realized. "Oh! Yes—do go ahead." She waved distractedly. "Whatever it is you do."

"Pour three glasses," Dillon instructed Jacobs, "then take the decanter to the General in the drawing room. I'm sure Lady Fowles won't mind."

"Very good, sir."

Jacobs set the three glasses at Dillon's elbow. He passed two to Rus and Barnaby, then lifted his and sipped.

"To success," Barnaby said, and drank.

Rus and Dillon murmured agreement, then Dillon set

down his glass. "The first thing we need to decide is: do we have the full picture? Or at least enough of the picture to act?"

Folding his arms, Barnaby leaned on the table. "Let me paint what we have so far. There's someone, possibly a single man—let's call him Mr. X—a gentleman and a hardened gamester who wagers and wins massive sums. For men like that, it's not just the money but the thrill of winning that matters, and to play at the level that gives them thrills, they have to have money. Buckets of it.

"Let's start from last autumn. Collier wagered heavily and lost. Mr. X heard of it. Over winter, he approached Collier, who was facing ruin, became his silent partner, and set up the conditions for running horse substitutions. Over the spring season, at least two substitutions were successfully run, proving for Mr. X that he had all the necessary pieces—the owners, trainers, horses, betting agents, sharp bookmakers—everything needed to generate very large sums of cash."

"But after the season ended, he fell out with Collier." Dillon met Barnaby's eyes. "Mr. X acted decisively to remove a threat to his scheme—he killed Collier."

Barnaby nodded. "Mr. X might already have had Cromarty and Aberdeen lined up, but regardless, his racket rolled on without a hitch."

"It's possible," Dillon put in, "that changing stables every season was always a part of his plan. That makes it almost impossible for the authorities to stop his scheme—we're only alerted after the race is run, usually not until weeks later, and then it's the end of the season. Even if after this season we started monitoring Cromarty, if next season's substitutions are run by Aberdeen . . . the authorities will always be one very big step behind Mr. X."

Barnaby frowned at the tabletop. "One thought occurs—given his gambling connections, did Mr. X organize for Collier, and Cromarty and Aberdeen, to be *induced* into debt so he could then recruit them?" Barnaby looked at Dillon. "I'm not saying Collier, Cromarty, and Aberdeen are angels acting wholly under duress, but their roles in Mr. X's scheme might not have been by choice."

Dillon stared at Barnaby. "That's . . . a distinctly black twist. But yes, given the way owners sometimes bet on their runners, it's possible Mr. X is preying on the industry in that sense, too."

Pris shivered. "This Mr. X seems not only black-hearted, but conscienceless, too."

Dillon, Rus, and Barnaby shared a glance, then Barnaby went on, "So to this season. Mr. X ran a highly successful substitution early through Cromarty, here, with Flyin' Fury, netting very large sums."

"However," Dillon said, "running substitutions at Newmarket has side effects Mr. X might not appreciate. Because Newmarket is the home of the Jockey Club, running substitutions here strikes at the core of the industry itself. If this keeps on, there'll be anarchy. Literally. The Flyin' Fury substitution was bad enough, but substituting Blistering Belle will be immeasurably worse—a premier race in one of the premier meets at the premier racetrack. The wagering will be intense, the furor afterward commensurately enormous. The punters won't stand for it, and nor will the ton."

"But," Barnaby said, "regardless of the outcry, and it'll be you and the Committee who'll have to weather the worst, there will still be no way to stop Mr. X, especially not if he keeps switching stables and tracks."

Grimly, Dillon nodded. "Knowing a substitution scam is active doesn't make it any easier to stop."

"Unless," Rus put in, "you know about a substitution before it occurs. Which brings us to Blistering Belle."

Barnaby considered, then shook his head and sat back. "Even so . . ."

Dillon grimaced. "Halting the substitution of Blistering Belle by stopping the substitute from running will switch some wagers to the next favorite in the race and void others entirely. Money will still be lost and won through the bookmakers, it just won't be as much. And while Mr. X won't get his accustomed and undoubtedly expected reward, he won't lose much either—certainly nothing he can't afford. Most worryingly, however, it won't shut down his scheme. He'll just shift to using Aberdeen, and even if we manage to expose Aberdeen's runners before any substitutions are affected, Mr. X will just lie low for the season."

"Or use some other owner we've yet to link to him." Pris frowned. After a moment, she continued, frustration clear in her tone, "There's no simple, obvious way forward, is there? No obvious 'this is what we should do'?"

Rus and Barnaby shook their heads.

"It's the trickiest, messiest crime I've ever heard of," Barnaby said. "Quite aside from Mr. X, there's an enormous cast of wrongdoers here, all of whom deserve some measure of retribution, yet even though we know of the impending crime and how to stop it, if we do, we won't touch the majority of those involved, and Mr. X and his scheme not at all."

"He's a spider in the center of his web," Dillon said, his gaze on his fingers slowly tapping the table. "We can break a few connections, even destroy part of the web, but that won't harm the spider. Once we retreat, he'll just crawl back out of hiding, re-spin his web, making new connections, and then continue to lure, catch, and devour his prey."

They could all see the analogy; all were silent, thinking, then Barnaby stirred. He looked at Dillon. "What's our minimum here—what damage can we do if we expose Cromarty with Blistering Belle?"

When Dillon glanced at him, Barnaby fleetingly grinned. "You've looked into it, haven't you?"

Dillon returned the grin, but then sobered. "I have, and the answer's not heartening. The only way we can prove anything illegal is to expose the substitute for Blistering Belle immediately before the race is run. Cromarty,

Harkness, and Crom will be charged with attempting to perpetrate a substitution. But if Harkness was persuaded to protect Cromarty by swearing Cromarty knew nothing about it, Harkness and Crom would face jail—Newgate most likely—but Cromarty would get off with a fine and a reprimand for not paying sufficient attention to what was going on in his stable."

"That's all?" Pris looked shocked. "Everyone else gets away?"

Meeting her eyes, Dillon nodded. "A few fingers singed over wagers, but that's all the effect exposing the Blistering Belle substitution will have." He glanced at Barnaby and Rus. "There'll be no evidence to implicate anyone else."

"And little to no likelihood of Cromarty telling us the names of all others involved." Disillusioned, Rus polished off his port.

"Doubly so if he knows what happened to Collier." Leaning back in his chair, Dillon looked at the others. "I can't see any chance of us learning anything new about Mr. X through halting the Blistering Belle substitution."

Barnaby drained his glass, then set it down. "There has to be a better way."

Dillon met his gaze. "We need to think of some way to reach the spider."

The October Meeting and the two-year-old stakes in which Blistering Belle was due to be switched were still four days away. With no obvious solution to their dilemma, they agreed to take one day—twenty-four hours more—to rack their brains before deciding on their course.

They adjourned, joining the others in the drawing room in time to pass the teacups. Later, Dillon stood with Barnaby and Rus on the front steps and waved the carriage with Eugenia, Pris, and Adelaide away.

Later still, with the moon riding the sky and the fields silent about him, he rode north and east to the summerhouse by the lake.

Once again, they'd made no arrangement, had not even exchanged a meaningful look, but Pris was there, sitting on the sofa waiting for him.

Waiting to smile, mysterious and feminine, take his hand, and draw him down. To her. To the wonder, the magic, he found in her arms, to the wildness and thrills of a reckless ride, to the golden glory that claimed them in aftermath, to the completion that reached to his soul.

That healed him, that in some way he didn't understand welded the two halves of him and made him whole.

Lying sprawled on his back on the sofa, more or less naked, with Pris slumped, very definitely naked, over him, he was staring into the shadows, thinking of that curious melding, mulling over it, how it felt, when she shifted, settling in his arms, turned her head to look over the lake, and murmured, "There has to be a way."

While crossing the dark miles to the summerhouse, a flicker of an idea had flared; unexpected, radical, he wasn't sure how it might pan out.

Eyes on the shadowed ceiling, he lifted one hand, caught a lock of her hair, twirled the silky curl between his fingers. "I've always considered that my disgrace years ago ultimately resulting in me becoming one of the elected few charged with defending the sport of kings was a monumentally ironic twist of fate." He paused, then went on, "Now I wonder if fate had some longer-term goal in view."

She was silent for a moment, then, "Because the racing industry is now facing a serious threat, and due to your past you have a better understanding of that threat?"

"In part. But I was thinking more of the nature, mine, that long ago led me into trouble. I'm not my father. He hasn't a wild and reckless bone in his body. If my past trouble hadn't happened, if I hadn't been disgraced, hadn't wanted to make restitution, would I have followed in his steps and later assumed his position?"

"You mean would *you* have been the Keeper of the Breeding Register now—the one facing the problem now?"

He glanced down at her. "Would a man like *me* be facing this problem."

She lifted her head, met his eyes. Folding her hands on his chest, she rested her chin on them, and narrowed her eyes on his. "You've thought of something."

Amused by her comprehension, he wished the light was strong enough to see the color of her eyes, to better appreciate the rest of her. "A possibility, a glimmer of a chance. I'm not sure."

If, on reflection, on further development, the idea proved to be more, then his wild and reckless side would be fundamental to carrying it through, to bringing it to fruition. The same wild and reckless side she not just evoked, not just wantonly engaged with, but had somehow found a way to weld, to integrate seamlessly with his more responsible, sane, and sensible self.

When he was with her, he no longer felt torn, as if he were shifting from one persona to the other, as if he were two people within the one skin. That long-ago disgrace had caused a schism, a distrust of sorts, a wariness he'd been aware of for years—a concern that his wild and reckless side was a liability, a danger. A side he should never give free rein. Yet now . . .

What was fate telling him?

"Regardless of whatever we do, we need to stop Cromarty, Harkness, and Crom, and slap them behind bars." From where they would no longer be a threat to Pris, Rus, or any of their family. He knew, none better, how unprincipled those inhabiting the underside of racing could be, how they would retaliate against their chosen scapegoats. "That's the absolute minimum we have to accomplish."

He and Demon had both understood Vane's injunction, to beware—to watch and shield their families, to ensure that whatever action occurred did not and could not rebound on those they cared about, those under their protection.

A justified and timely warning.

Pris continued to study his face. "Just removing Cromarty, Harkness, and Crom . . . all very well, but none of us are going to accept that as success."

He refocused on her eyes, noting the determination conveyed by the set of her jaw, her lips. Wondered what gave rise to it. "As long as we remove those three, Rus will be safe."

She snorted. "While I would be the first to rejoice in Rus's safety, that's hardly the end of it." She frowned into his eyes, as if sensing the other side of his comment—the question buried in it. "Knowing this sort of *evil* is going on, that we know about it but haven't done anything to end it would never sit well with either Rus or me. I can't imagine Barnaby shrugging and letting it go either—he's already gnashing his teeth." Her expression turned skeptical. "And as for *you*—you will simply never rest. Well, how could you? It's your calling, isn't it?"

It was.

Within him, something quivered, resonating with her words, at the clear-sighted recognition not only implied but visible in her face. He'd never heard it—his life's work—stated so simply, summarized so succinctly, as if it really were that obvious . . .

Perhaps it needed someone as uninhibited as she to simply say it. To render his purpose, his motives in facing the current threat, in such clear-cut fashion. To condense it to two words: *his calling.*

His because the responsibility was primarily his, not only by virtue of the position he held, but because the Committee had requested his help, handed the problem to him to solve, and were counting on him to deal with it.

Calling because that's what it was. His wasn't a paid position, but one conferred in recognition of what had come to be his vocation. Quite aside from the familial connection, he'd grown into the position, and it, in turn, had truly become a part of him.

And that, all of that, was why he had to do more than just remove Cromarty, Harkness, and Crom, why he had to free the industry he'd served for well-nigh half his life—the industry around which his life revolved—from an evil that threatened to poison it to the core.

Her eyes, fixed on his, narrowed to gleaming slits. "What have you thought of?"

He met her gaze, then let his lips curve. "Patience—it was only a first inkling. I'll tell you once I've thought it through, once I've worked out how it might help us."

He'd kept his tone low, soothing. The fingers of one hand still toying with her hair, he ran his other hand up from her thigh, palm to satin skin, up over her naked bottom to her hip, skimming the side of her waist to the swell of her breast—deliberately distracting her.

Only to be distracted himself by the way her lashes fluttered, then sank, the way she all but purred with pleasure.

"Hmm . . ." She leaned into the caress, offering her breast more fully to his hand, then lasciviously, sinuously shifted up his body, found his lips with hers, and kissed him.

Deciding that in light of Vane's injunction, distracting her was clearly his bounden duty, he released her hair, framed her face, and kissed her back.

"Much to my disgust, despite racking my brains, I've singularly failed to discover any way to bring down our spider. We can shake his web, but . . ." Barnaby grimaced, and looked around the circle of faces gathered in Dillon's study.

It was the following afternoon; since parting from Dillon

in the small hours of the morning, Pris had spent all her waking hours trying to think of something that would connect Cromarty to his secretive partner, something they'd overlooked.

Like Barnaby, her travail had been in vain. Despite her cajoling, Dillon had refused to enlighten her as to even the direction of his "possibility." Hoping against hope that his subsequent cogitations had revealed it to be real, she'd driven Adelaide and herself to Hillgate End; Adelaide was presently chatting with the General.

When Barnaby held up his hands in defeat, Pris looked at Rus in the armchair opposite hers.

Her twin caught her glance; as Dillon and Barnaby looked to him, he shook his head. "The scope of this . . . I'm out of my depth. Cromarty, Harkness, and Crom—catching them is straightforward. But the only way we might reach further is if Cromarty not only identifies Mr. X but has evidence to prove his involvement. But if he was so careful with Collier, he'll have been the same with Cromarty."

His chin sunk on his chest, Barnaby nodded glumly. Lifting his head, he looked at Pris. "Any advance?"

Lips compressed, she shook her head. She looked at Dillon.

He caught her gaze, then looked at the other two as they turned to him. "I agree—exposing Cromarty, Harkness, and Crom is well within our grasp, but that won't get us any further. It won't attack the wider scheme, it won't even significantly damage it. Chances are, once we remove Cromarty and company, the scheme will sprout at Doncaster and Cheltenham, and even if we manage to expose Aberdeen, the scheme will simply go to ground and reemerge next season, somewhere else."

Barnaby heaved a dejected sigh. "So our only option is a far-from-satisfactory one. One that won't actually address the crime." Looking down, he studied his boots.

Pris watched Dillon, saw him hesitate. He glanced at her, then drew a breath and evenly stated, "That isn't our only option."

Barnaby lifted his head; he studied Dillon's face. "You've thought of something. *Hallelujah!* What?"

They all looked inquiringly at Dillon. His expression—serious, obdurate, committed, and determined—was echoed by his tone. "I've thought about this from every angle. My overriding concern has to be for the industry—we should do whatever holds the best promise for the widest gain. As far as I can see, there's only one alternative to exposing Cromarty and company before the race is run." He held up a hand. "Don't say anything, just hear me out to the end." He glanced around the circle, his gaze coming to rest on Pris. "I'm going to suggest we perform a double switch, put the real Belle back in the race and let her run."

Pris blinked; Rus and Barnaby did, too. Like her, they frowned, thinking, trying to see . . .

Dillon gave them a moment, then explained, "If the real Belle runs, and wins, the repercussions will be enormous. No one who's innocent will be harmed in any way—all those who wager on her in good faith will reap their just reward. However, on the other side of the ledger, those who wager against her, or offer long odds knowing the race is supposed to be fixed, will also reap their just rewards. They'll lose, and lose heavily."

He paused, then went on, "It's the only way I can think of that attacks the whole web, rather than just Cromarty. If Belle runs and wins, every strand of Mr. X's enterprise will be burnt—almost certainly every strand will collapse. We know how vicious the underside of racing can be—it's even more cutthroat, literally, when the betrayers are themselves betrayed. Mr. X couldn't have grown his enterprise to the size Gabriel and Vane suspect without involving some powerful, very shadowy figures. Belle winning would obviously not be a deliberate ploy on Mr. X's part, but to those shadowy, powerful figures that will count for nought. It's his scheme—he'll be blamed for its failure, for their losses. It won't, unfortunately, put those gentlemen out of business, but it will, most assuredly, put Mr. X out of business."

"And," Barnaby said, his eyes lighting with dawning zeal, "what happens to Mr. X will serve as an exemplary warning to anyone thinking of trying a similar scheme." He met Dillon's dark gaze. "This is an absolutely *brilliant* idea."

Dillon grimaced. "As with all such ideas, there's one aspect that's not quite so brilliant."

Like Barnaby, Rus had been transformed, reinvigorated, but now he hesitated. "What?"

"Cromarty, Harkness, and Crom." Dillon held Rus's gaze, then looked at Pris. "If we switch Belle back, they won't have committed any crime. We'll have eradicated all evidence that they were even contemplating it."

"They'll get away with not even a reprimand?" Pris asked.

Dillon's lips twisted. "Not an official one. However, they won't escape unscathed. Cromarty will doubtless wager against Belle winning—how much losing those wagers will hurt him depends on how much he puts at risk. But the repercussions won't stop there—he and Harkness, especially, will be in very hot water with all the other players in the game—the sharp bookmakers who quoted long odds for Belle, Mr. X himself, and even those shadowy figures. No one will understand how they could have let it happen."

Rus was smiling widely. "Including Cromarty, Harkness, and Crom. Oh, to be near when Belle whistles past the winning post!" Green eyes afire, he met Dillon's gaze. "Barnaby's right—this is a brilliant idea. Even with the caveat that we'll be erasing all evidence of the immediate crime, it's still a brilliant idea. It achieves so much more—much, *much* more!"

"Indeed." Barnaby nodded decisively. "And we won't be doing anything illegal along the way. We'll just be being helpful and giving Cromarty his real champion back—how can he complain?"

Rus chuckled. "Precisely."

Dillon looked at Pris, waited. She studied his eyes, wondering why he was being, if not diffident in putting forward what they all saw as a fabulous idea, a near-perfect answer to their dilemma, then strangely careful. She could neither see nor feel any hint of his being swept along by enthusiasm, of being charged with eagerness as both Rus and Barnaby were.

Nevertheless . . . she smiled and nodded. "I agree—it's a wonderful idea. It may be unconventional, but it'll achieve what needs to be achieved."

His dark eyes remained on her face for an instant longer, then he stirred, and glanced at Rus and Barnaby. "One thing we must ensure—Harkness, Cromarty, and Crom must have absolutely no inkling that any of us"—his gaze swept their circle—"are involved. To them, how the real Belle comes to be the horse that runs the race must remain a perfect mystery."

Barnaby blinked, then nodded. "Yes, absolutely. No recriminations invited. Switching Belle back has to be achieved by the most complete sleight of hand." He looked from Dillon to Rus. "So—how do we do it?"

The ensuing discussion was fast and furious, possibilities and suggestions canvassed rapidly and decisively. They all contributed. Despite Dillon's wish to keep Rus's involvement to a minimum—a stance Pris appreciated—there was one essential aspect in which her twin necessarily featured.

"Belle will need to be put through her paces—prepared as she normally would be before a race. Chances are, since we found her out at the cottage, she'll have been left there without any regular runs. If they follow the same pattern they did when substituting Flyin' Fury, they won't bring Belle back to the string until after the race. They'll need that time—at least four days—to bring the substitute along well enough to make a decent showing, to pass her off as the real Belle."

Dillon held Rus's gaze for a long moment, then grimaced. "What are you suggesting?"

"Other than Cromarty, only Harkness and Crom know of the scheme, so only they can check on Belle. I'm sure they would at least once a day, but with the meet only days away, during training times, both Harkness and Crom will be out on the Heath." Rus glanced at Pris. "Well away from the cottage."

He looked at Dillon. "What I'm suggesting is that during the training times, I go to the cottage and work with Belle. We've three days left, and she's been stabled for nearly two. If I start working her later this afternoon, I'm sure I'll have her raring to go come Tuesday."

Dillon didn't like it, but reluctantly agreed. Belle had to be prepared. It was the one true risk in their scheme—if she ran but still didn't win.

Pris understood that; what she still didn't understand was his underlying gravity.

"It'll be best if I move to the Carisbrook house," Rus said. "It's much closer to the cottage—I won't lose as much time going back and forth, and there'll be less chance of anyone sighting me and reporting it to Harkness."

Dillon grimaced, but nodded. "With one proviso—you take Patrick whenever you set foot outside the house."

"You needn't worry." Pris caught Dillon's eye, then met her brother's. "He won't be leaving the house alone."

Rus grinned.

They organized for Pris to take Rus's bags in the gig when she drove back with Adelaide. The three men would ride straight to the cottage to give Belle her first training session in days.

Satisfied Rus would be well protected, Pris accepted the arrangements with good grace. "Now, how do we go about reswitching Belle?"

That necessitated much discussion, but Dillon and Rus had more than enough knowledge of the movement and housing of horses before a race, and the scramble of activities that filled the morning of a race day, to formulate a plan.

"Cromarty's using Figgs's stable, just off the track." Pulling a low table between their chairs, Dillon sketched a rough map of Newmarket and surrounds, marking in the relevant spots; they all pored over the map as he indicated Figgs's stable with a box.

"We'll need to bring Belle down to Hillgate End during the training session the afternoon before." Dillon glanced at Rus, who nodded. "The best time to make the switch is just before dawn, as the day starts for the stables and all in them. I assume Crom at least will be sleeping in the stable?"

Rus nodded. "It's usually only him from Cromarty's, but there's Figgs's night watchman as well."

"He'll be easily distracted, at least long enough for our purposes, but Crom we don't want to do anything with at all—nothing to trigger the slightest suspicion that anything might be going on. With the two fillies being all but identical, as long as we switch them *without* jolting Crom's suspicions, it's unlikely he'll notice the reswitch, especially not with the usual hullabaloo of a race morning distracting him. Cromarty has three runners as well as Belle in the morning's races. Crom will be too busy to dwell on little things like a horse's personality. As long as he continues to believe that the horse in Belle's stall is the substitute, that's what he'll see."

Rus nodded. "I agree."

Dillon again looked around the circle. "So here's what we're going to do—how we're going to put Belle back in the race."

"Good evening, General." Demon nodded to Dillon's father as he walked through the doorway of Dillon's study. It was later that evening; after dinner, Dillon and his father, alone again, had retired to the room in which they both felt most comfortable.

Noting the hardness in Demon's blue eyes as they fixed on him, the crispness of the movement as he shut the study door, Dillon wasn't surprised when he growled, "As for you, you infuriating whelp, what the devil do you think you're up to?"

Having long ago learned that Demon's bark was worse than his bite, and that that was almost always driven by concern, Dillon raised his brows mildly, and replied, "Doing what's best for the racing fraternity."

The words, along with his even tone, gave Demon pause. He blinked, then, frowning, grabbed the chair from behind Dillon's desk and hauled it around to face Dillon and his father in the armchairs before the hearth. Dropping into the chair, crossing his long legs, Demon fixed Dillon with a steady, very direct gaze. "Explain."

Then Demon's eyes flicked to the General, briefly scanned the older man's face. "He hasn't told you either, has he?"

With unruffleable calm, the General smiled. "Dillon was about to explain all to me." His gaze switched to Dillon's face. "Do go on, m'boy."

Dillon hadn't been about to do any such thing—if he'd had his way, he would have shielded his father from any possible anxiety—but he appreciated his father's tacit support and the unshakeable faith that lay beneath it.

"So what have you heard?" Setting aside his glass of port, he rose to pour one for Demon.

Demon watched him, still frowning. "Rus Dalling dropped by midafternoon to beg off assisting Flick for the next few days. Incidentally, she's of a mind to kiss your feet for bringing him to her attention—he's a natural, and she's in alt. But this afternoon she was out—Rus found me." Demon took the glass Dillon offered him. "He told me he had to work on the real Belle, because you had some plan afoot to pull what amounts to a double substitution."

Pausing to take a sip of port, Demon eyed Dillon as he resumed his seat. "I didn't interrogate Dalling—in the circumstances, I thought it wiser to come and interrogate you."

Dillon smiled, outwardly relaxed, inwardly unsure how the next few minutes would go. "This is the situation—what we now know." Succinctly, he described the racket run by Mr. X, then outlined the options they faced.

"So I could deal with the scenario entirely as prescribed by the rule book, and achieve nothing more than removing Cromarty and Harkness from the industry. Or we can grasp the chance and shatter the entire scheme, and its perpetrator, too."

Dillon paused, his gaze on Demon's now seriously troubled face. He hadn't been surprised that Rus and Pris had so readily embraced his plan; it was tailor-made to appeal to their wild and reckless natures. Barnaby, too, possessed a certain devil-take-the-hindmost streak. And Barnaby didn't know enough of Dillon's past to comprehend that in proposing, let alone undertaking, such a plan Dillon was taking a personal risk. That was something Demon and the General understood. There were, however, other issues here.

He chose his words with care, let his passion color them. "You understand what's at stake. If we can strike at the heart of such a scheme, turn it back on itself so that the perpetrator and all his minions get badly stung rather than the gullible public they think to prey upon, that will be a more effective deterrent, one of infinitely greater magnitude, than the slight risk of a corrupt owner being exposed and tossed in jail."

He caught Demon's eye, faintly raised a brow. "Which of the two alternatives would you expect me to choose?"

Demon swore; he looked down at his hands, clasped about his glass. He'd listened with barely an interruption. Looking up, he scowled at Dillon. "It galls me to admit you're right—that your tack *is* the right decision. However"—he grimaced—"you can't expect me to like it."

He tossed off his port, then looked at the General. "If anything goes wrong . . ."

The General smiled benignly; despite his occasional vagueness, both Dillon and Demon knew the mind behind his worn façade still functioned with considerable incisiveness. But the General possessed something neither of them yet had, a deep well of experience and understanding of the human condition, and all that encompassed.

Calmly, he nodded at Demon, acknowledging his concern. "If anything about the reswitch becomes known, it will impinge very badly on Dillon. Once the reswitch is in hand, if any learn of it, then because the reswitch will destroy all evidence of the initial substitution, it will appear that whoever is involved in the reswitch is actually carrying out a substitution."

Turning his head, the General met Dillon's gaze. "You're risking your reputation—something you've worked for the last ten and more years to rebuild. Are you sure you want to do that?"

There was neither condemnation nor encouragement in the General's tone—no hint of how he thought Dillon should answer.

Dillon held his father's gaze steadily, and evenly asked, "What would my reputation be founded on if I didn't? If I weren't willing to do what now needs to be done for the good of the industry that's been placed in my care?"

A warm, openly approving smile spread across the General's face; he inclined his head, then looked at Demon, and mildly raised his brows.

Demon exhaled through his teeth. "Yes, all right. He's right." He frowned at Dillon. "But I want a hand in this, too."

"I don't think that's wise." Even Demon's reputation could be besmirched.

"Well, I do—think of it as a little extra protection." Demon smiled, all teeth. "To appease me."

Dillon read Demon's eyes and inwardly sighed. No point arguing.

Demon didn't wait for him to agree. "Getting Belle from here to the track on the morning of the race—walking her in as a lone horse is bound to attract attention, no matter the hour. The night watchmen at least will see and take note." He caught Dillon's eye. "I assume you're planning to leave here an hour before dawn?" Dillon nodded. Demon went on, "We'd normally leave about an hour later, walking our runners to the holding stalls by the track—on that day, we'll leave earlier. As we pass here, Belle can join our group. No one will notice an extra horse, and no one will think it odd that we might arrive a little earlier than usual to avoid the inevitable scramble."

Dillon blinked, seeing the scenario Demon was painting. The Cynster string didn't exercise on the Heath, but on a private track buried within Demon's now considerable estate and thus out of bounds to the racing public. Consequently, when the day's Cynster runners appeared at the holding stalls, touts, bookmakers, jockeys, owners, and trainers flocked to the stalls to assess what these days represented a significant portion of the competition.

Even extra early—indeed, especially if the Cynster horses made an unexpectedly early appearance—crowds would gather. Word would fly, people would come running. The ensuing melee would fix all attention on the holding stalls—away from the stables that stood just back from the track. What better cover in which to perform their reswitch?

Refocusing, Dillon found Demon watching him.

"A worthwhile addition to your plan?"

Dillon met his eyes, inclined his head. "Yes, thank you. That'll make things much easier."

* * *

Half an hour later, Dillon walked Demon to the front door.

"Where's Adair?" Demon asked, as they entered the front hall.

"He had the idea of alerting our London friends to keep their ears open in the hope that in the aftermath of the race they might learn something of those involved." Dillon halted by the door. "He was going to speak with his father and an Inspector Stokes he thinks highly of, as well as Gabriel and Vane, who will no doubt pass the word to the others in town."

Demon nodded. "Good idea. No telling what the ripples might reveal when you drop that filly back into her race."

Smiling, Dillon hauled open the door.

Demon stepped out, then turned back. "I will, of course, have to tell Flick all—you'll have to take your chances on a lecture." He paused, then added, "And you may as well warn Dalling that he's liable to sustain a visit from her during one of the training sessions." Turning to head down the steps, he continued, "And of course, that means I'll have to come, too."

Dillon grinned. He stood watching as Demon strode away across the lawn, then swung the door closed and headed for his bed.

Fifteen

Over the next days, their plan evolved, was refined and polished. With Rus staying at the Carisbrook house, Dillon curtailed his nocturnal visits to the summerhouse by the lake. He had too much respect for the connectedness between twins to risk it.

What Rus would make of his liaison with Pris he didn't know, but now—while all three of them were immersed in a highly secret and dangerous endeavor—wasn't the time to find out. However, he made a vow to, at the earliest opportunity, make his intentions, the honorable nature of them, clear to Pris's twin. No sense courting any unnecessary misunderstandings.

Their social connection had excused Pris and Adelaide calling at Hillgate End; now it excused him frequently visiting the Carisbrook house and spending hours there. Barnaby returned from London fired with zeal, carrying good wishes from all involved, including Inspector Stokes;

everyone had agreed that the opportunity to shatter the entire scheme was too valuable a chance to pass up.

Pris and Patrick remained adamant that Rus shouldn't visit the isolated cottage alone; all three rode forth every morning and afternoon, as soon as they judged Harkness and Crom would have left for the Heath. As Demon had prophesied, Flick rode up one morning in breeches and coat, Demon beside her. She'd taken charge of the training session, put Belle through her paces, then glowingly commended Rus, giving him encouragement and various tips.

When he saw Dillon later, Demon had growled that Rus had all but groveled at his wife's dainty feet—a position, Dillon knew, Demon reserved for himself.

They were all committed, heart and soul and in some cases reputation, and increasingly confident their plan would work. Flick's frank assessment that she'd never seen any two-year-old faster than Blistering Belle went a long way to easing the unvoiced fear that despite their best efforts, Belle might, in the end, lose her race.

Rus had remained unswervingly certain Belle would lead the field; Flick's endorsement brought relief to all other minds.

After finalizing the details of how they would effect the switch, Dillon spent hours drilling the Hillgate End stable lads and grooms. It had been agreed they were the best small army to use; all were familiar faces around the racetrack, the associated holding stalls, and nearby stables. No one would even register their presence on a race day morning, yet unlike Demon's lads, none had any actual job to perform.

In addition, all were, to a man, unswervingly loyal to the Caxtons.

That last was vital. It was impossible to conceal from such necessary minor players that the intent proposed would normally be viewed as illegal, yet when Dillon outlined what he needed them to do, their reactions made it clear they took it for granted that his reasons were sound, that despite appearances, he hadn't stirred one inch from the path of the angels.

He was grateful for their unquestioning support, but also humbled. Their blind faith left him only more determined to ensure that, by noon on the second day of the October meeting, the substitution scam would be in ruins.

He and his father had discussed at length whether or not to tell the three stewards of the Jockey Club—the Committee who oversaw the running of the club and its regulations. Despite the risk, they decided against it; neither felt sure the three stewards could be counted on to keep their lips shut.

Not even for a few hours on the morning of the race.

The first day of the October meeting dawned fine and clear. The races on that day were showcase events for five-, six-, and seven-year-olds, followed by a series of privately sponsored challenges. With the weather cooperating, a carnival-like atmosphere prevailed. Dillon, the General, Flick, and Demon spent most of the day at the track. They were local identities, making their absence too notable to risk.

For that first day, Pris, Rus, and Patrick were strictly forbidden even the environs of Newmarket, the former two because, with the influx of visitors, many from London and also Ireland, the chance that someone might recognize them had escalated. Patrick was delegated to ensure that the wild and reckless duo didn't conspire to egg each other on in some foolhardy scheme to join the crowds.

As the hours of Monday ticked by, there wasn't one of their band who didn't feel the spur of impatience, who wasn't eager to see the next day dawn.

A slew of trophy races, including the two-year-old stakes in which Blistering Belle was scheduled to feature, were slated for the second day. The morning session would comprise five races, all with outstanding fields—all certain to generate considerable excitement among the hordes of gentlemen and the select group of ladies who had descended on Newmarket, home to the sport of kings.

At last, the sun went down, and the end of Monday was nigh. Night fell over Newmarket, leaving the town a bright sea of lamps as parties and dinners and all manner of entertainments kept the crowds amused. But beyond the town, beyond the houses, out around the track and all over the Heath, quiet darkness descended, and enveloped all.

The hour before dawn was the chilliest, and the darkest. On that Tuesday morning, the Cynster runners left their warm stable at the ungodly hour of four o'clock; watched over by Demon, with Flick mounted beside him, they started their slow, ambling walk to the holding stalls beside the track. Accustomed to early-morning track work, the horses were unperturbed, content enough to walk slowly along between the mounts of their stable lads, riding beside them, leading reins in hand.

As the cavalcade of six runners, their accompanying crew, and sundry other accompanying horses drew level with the Hillgate End gates, another pair of horses emerged from the shadows and became one with the larger group.

Lips tightening, Demon nodded to the slight figure atop one of Flick's older hacks; disheveled, a cloth cap pulled low over her eyes, a woollen muffler wound about her throat and chin, Pris held Blistering Belle's reins loosely in one hand. Slightly slouched, at first glance indistinguishable from the stable lads leading Demon's and Flick's runners, she led the horse all their hopes rode upon toward the track.

Her position in their plan had very nearly brought the whole undone. Dillon, Rus, Patrick, Barnaby, and Demon himself had all argued hotly against her taking the role of

Blistering Belle's "lad," leading the horse to the track, then into the stable and performing the actual switch before leading the other black filly away. It was the most dangerous as well as the most vital role of all.

They'd ranted and raved, only to have the wind taken from their sails by Flick's acerbic comment that Pris was the only one who could do what needed to be done. Acceptance of that truth had been painful, for Rus and Dillon most of all, but there'd been no other choice.

Blistering Belle had formed a close bond with Rus; she trusted him implicitly and would follow him anywhere. Unfortunately, she didn't like Rus leaving her; every time he did, she whinnied, kicked her stall, did everything in her female equine repertoire to bring him back.

Rus couldn't lead her into Figgs's stable and switch her for the other filly. Belle wouldn't stand for it—she'd create such a ruckus that everyone, led by Crom, would come running. However, as Rus couldn't risk being seen by Harkness or Crom anyway, especially not with Belle or her look-alike, he hadn't been a contender for the role.

Initially, no one had seen the problem looming, but when they'd tried to get Belle to allow one of Dillon's grooms to lead her, they'd discovered she'd grown wary of being led by anyone she didn't trust. She hadn't liked being stuck in the isolated stable and was now not prepared to let just anyone lead her away.

They'd tried everyone, even Barnaby. The only one Belle would accept was Pris, almost certainly because she could lower her voice to an approximation of her twin's, and the cadences of their speech as well as their accents were strikingly similar—even, it seemed, to equine ears.

Belle recognized Pris as a friend. She would happily walk with Pris leading her; most importantly, she would with perfect equanimity allow Pris to put her in a stall and leave her, even when Pris took out another horse instead.

Pris leaving her was acceptable; Rus leaving her was not.

The male mutterings such feminine perversity provoked had lasted for hours, but nothing could change the hard fact that Pris it had to be.

Last night, she'd remained at the stud, being coached by Demon, Flick, Rus, and Dillon as to what she might expect, how to behave in various situations. Eyeing her as they ambled along, Demon uttered a silent prayer that they'd covered all possible eventualities. He glanced at Flick riding beside him. Although it went against the grain, he would have preferred her in Pris's position; Flick had grown up about Newmarket racetrack, knew everything there was to know about the stables and race mornings—she knew everything Pris didn't.

The road reached the edge of the Heath; instead of continuing along the beaten surface, the cavalcade took to the turf, taking the most direct line to the track, the shortest distance for their runners to walk. The steady *clop* of iron-shod hooves changed to a muted *thud*.

Away from the trees, the air seemed colder, the wreathing mists damper, chillier. Demon lifted his head, scented the faint breeze, studied the clouds overhead. The day would be fine; once the sun rose, the mists would burn off. It would be another perfect day for racing.

He glanced again at Pris and saw her shiver. He was wearing a thick greatcoat; Flick was well wrapped in a warm pelisse. Pris wore a threadbare ancient jacket, not thick enough to keep the morning chill at bay, but she had to appear to be the stable lad she was emulating. Jaw setting, Demon forced himself to look away.

Pris wasn't sure that the shivers that rippled through her had anything to do with the misty chill. She was so tense, it was a wonder her horse wasn't jibbing and shifting and dancing with impatience. And nerves; hers were stretched tighter than they'd ever been.

Beside her, Belle plodded along, content to be among her kind again. Her head lifted now and again as she looked ahead, almost as if she could sense the track. While watching Rus train her over the last days, Pris had learned that some horses simply loved to run, and Belle was one; she seemed eager to race, to run, to win.

Everything hung on her doing so, but after the last days, that was the least of Pris's worries. Getting Belle into the stable and the other horse out without Crom knowing, and without Rus doing anything to call attention to himself along the way, loomed as the biggest hurdle.

Other than the odd comment between the lads, the occasional breathy snort of a horse and the muted jangle of a harness, the cavalcade advanced in silence across the wide green sward.

Eventually, the first of the stables dotted around the track materialized through the thinning mist. Searching the area behind it, Pris saw mounted figures waiting—a gentleman in a greatcoat, and three lads with three racing Thoroughbreds on leading reins.

She glanced at Demon, riding on the other side of Belle.

He caught her gaze. "Wait until we're closer."

She nodded. The cavalcade advanced on a line that would take them along the front of the stable and on toward the track.

"Now."

At Demon's quiet command, she turned her mount and Belle; the lads alongside slowed their charges to let her draw away from the group. Keeping to the same steady pace, she headed for the riders behind the stable; Demon's timing had ensured that she and Belle were visible as separate from the cavalcade for only the minute it took them to walk down the screening side of the stable and around the corner to join the other group.

Dillon was waiting, as was Rus. Her twin briefly smiled, the gesture one more of relief than excitement. She smiled back, rather tightly. Rus set his mount walking, leading one of the three retired racehorses Demon and Flick had provided. Their still-elegant lines made them perfect camouflage for Belle; they closed around her. Falling in behind Rus, the group made their way along the rear of a succession of blocklike stables that stood in a wide arc a little back from the track, an outer ring behind the inner ring of holding stalls. To any who sighted them, they would appear to be a small group of runners walking in from an outlying stable for the day.

A few lads and touts slinking around the stables saw them, but all attention quickly diverted to the holding stalls as the news that the Cynster runners had arrived early spread. Everyone rushed to take a look.

No one gave the small band trudging along a second glance.

Dillon, as ever on his black, rode beside her. Other than meeting her eyes, exchanging one powerful, very direct glance, he'd merely turned to ride beside her, on the outside of the group. No smile; his face could have been granite, his expression carved from stone. He was dressed for a day at the track. His role was, as himself, to watch over every stage in the execution of their plan, and if something went awry, to step in and wield his authority to deflect attention as required.

At their final meeting last night, he'd briefly outlined what they—meaning he—would do once Belle was safely exchanged and in place. While for the rest of them, their active roles ended at that point, his continued, at least until Belle's race was run.

They clopped slowly along; Pris struggled to drag air into her lungs—it felt like a lead weight was pressing on her chest. She felt compelled to try to look every way at once, watching for Harkness or Cromarty even though she knew both had retreated to the Rigby farm last night and were unlikely to appear for at least another hour.

Dillon had had stable lads and grooms out and about all day yesterday, keeping watch on those whose movements they'd needed to know. It had been a piece of luck that Harkness had gone out to check on Blistering Belle yesterday at noon, before returning to the track; that had left them free to bring Belle down to the Cynster stud by a circuitous route during the afternoon, train her on the private track under Flick's expert eye, then walk her across to the Hillgate End stables, where she'd spent the night.

The sky started to lighten, shifting from black to indigo, to gray. They passed another stable, slowly working their way around to Figgs's stable, where Cromarty's runners for today's races had been stabled for the night.

That had been another fortunate factor. Having rented cheaper premises farther from the Heath, Cromarty couldn't walk his runners in on race day. He had to bring them in the afternoon before and quarter them overnight at one of the stables that specialized in such housing. If that hadn't been so, their window of time in which to switch Belle for her look-alike would have narrowed to the almost impossible.

As it was . . . drawing in a tight breath as Figgs's stable loomed just beyond the one they were nearing, Pris prayed she would have enough time—that all that everyone did left her enough time—to get Belle into the stable, and the other filly out, without any of Cromarty's crew noticing.

Dillon eased Solomon forward; Rus glanced his way, met his gaze, and slowed. They halted behind the stable next to Figgs's. Everyone dismounted, handing their reins to Dillon's grooms, the other two "lads" with them; the pair remained with the horses, keeping the larger older horses screening Belle, while Rus, Pris, and Dillon went to the corner of the building.

A quick glance and they shifted around the corner, but stopped just beyond it. Pris and Rus lounged back against the stable's side, giving every appearance of lads wasting time until they were summoned to work. Dillon stood before them, apparently chatting; hanging open from his shoulders, his greatcoat, long enough to brush his calves, gave both Pris and Rus some cover. From where they'd stopped, they could see along the front of Figgs's stable, angled slightly to the one they stood against. Unfortunately, they couldn't see the main stable doors, only the forecourt immediately before, but couldn't risk getting a better angle by moving farther down the sidewall; that would make them more visible—too visible.

Aside from the main double doors facing the track, located along the stable's front at the end farthest from them, Figgs's stable, like most, had another door in the sidewall at this end, fifteen yards from where they stood. No more than the main doors would that door be locked—fire was too real a threat and racehorses too valuable—which was why the stables employed night watchmen, and owners renting stalls had employees sleep with their charges, as Crom had done last night and the night before.

Glancing over his shoulder, Dillon scanned the area before the stable, noting two of his grooms ambling about, idling—ready to intervene if needed. Barnaby would be watching from the shadows of the next stable along; disguised as a tout, his role was to coordinate any intervention or distraction necessary to keep Crom and the night watchman away from Figgs's stable long enough for Pris to switch Belle and get away.

They were all in position, all ready to act—all they needed was for Crom and the night watchman to wake and leave the stable.

Dillon could feel impatience riding him, lashing with invisible whips. He could sense the same rising tension in the other two, yet this was the point where caution had to rule, where one moment of inattention or one impulsive act could wreck their plans.

About them, the environs of the track stirred and came to life. The sky lightened, the dark gray of predawn giving way to streaks of pink and silver, the rising sun tinting the clouds. The light strengthened, not yet direct sunlight but sufficient to cast the scene in crisp clarity.

The shadows were gone. And still they waited.

"At last," Pris breathed, peeking around his shoulder. "There goes the night watchman."

Dillon glanced around; sure enough, the night watchman, a grizzled veteran jockey too old to ride, came shuffling from the stable, scratching and yawning and stretching. He paused in the forecourt, blinking, looking around, then stumbled off in the direction of the nearby latrines.

Glancing at one of the idlers—the majority of those loitering near Figgs's stable were members of their "army"—Dillon saw the groom look in Barnaby's direction, then push away from the stall against which he'd been leaning and head after the night watchman.

If the old boy headed back to his post before they'd passed the "all clear," the groom would delay him, and if that didn't last long enough, there was another pair stationed closer to the latrines with orders to intervene.

The night watchman was taken care of.

Dillon turned back to Pris and Rus. "Now for Crom."

It was still early, even in race day terms; except for those keen to get a glimpse of the runners as they arrived at the holding stalls—and they were fully occupied studying the Cynster horses—all others were bleary-eyed, just starting their day. Not at their best, not sharply observant.

"Damn!" Rus stiffened, then swore. "*Harkness!* What the devil's he doing here this early?"

Dillon swung to look in the direction Rus was staring—past the back of Figgs's stable to the open area beyond—simultaneously shifting closer to Pris so she remained concealed.

Harkness—big, burly, and black-haired—was striding up from one of the roped lines where racegoers could leave their nags. His attention was fixed on Figgs's stable, clearly his goal.

Dillon grabbed Pris's arm, half dragged, half shoved her, gathering Rus on the way, back around the corner to the safety of the milling horses. "Wait here." His tone brooked no argument. "I'll take care of him. You two stick to the plan!"

Without waiting for any acknowledgment, he swung on his heel, quickly strode back around the corner and across onto the forecourt of Figgs's stable, then slowed to a walk. He passed the main doors, now propped wide; he glimpsed activity within—it looked like Crom was stirring. Reaching the gap between Figgs's stable and the next—glimpsing Barnaby lounging against a holding stall farther on, staring, frowning, at him—Dillon paused; lifting his head, he looked past the holding stalls to the track beyond, as if surveying his domain and finding all well.

Harkness was coming up from behind, approaching through the gap between Figgs's stable and the next. Dillon had stopped at a point where Harkness would pass him. As the man's heavy footsteps neared, Dillon turned. Expression easy, he glanced at Harkness, mildly inclined his head in a polite but vague gesture—an action Harkness warily mirrored—then walked on.

Dillon took two paces, halted, and glanced back. "Harkness, isn't it?"

Harkness stopped, and looked around.

Dillon smiled easily. "You train for Cromarty, don't you?"

Slowly, Harkness faced him. "Aye."

Dillon retraced his steps, a slight frown in his eyes. "I've been meaning to ask—how have his lordship and you found the going this season?"

Harkness's face was closed, his expression rigid, his beady black eyes watchful. Dillon kept his questioning gaze steady on his face; after a moment, Harkness shrugged. "Much as last season, more or less."

"Hmm." Dillon glanced down, as if considering his words. "No problems with staff, then?"

Looking up, he caught a flash of fear in Harkness's eyes; he'd definitely recognized Dillon with Pris—who he'd thought was Rus—on the Heath days ago.

Dillon waited, gaze still inquiring. Harkness shifted his heavy frame, then said, "Not really—nothing major."

"Ah." Dillon nodded, as if accepting completely what Harkness was saying. "I did wonder—I had a young Irishman come to me with some convoluted tale. Used to be your assistant, I believe. I gather he left under a cloud—naturally, I listened to his story with that in mind. We all know what it's like to have troublesome staff. Indeed, the man's tale was so nonsensical it was clear he was simply intending to cause trouble."

Meeting Harkness's eyes, Dillon smiled genially. "I just thought I'd let Lord Cromarty know that I wasn't taken in by the man's tale."

Despite the harshness of his face, the hardness of his expression, Harkness's relief was obvious. His lips eased; he bobbed his head. "Thank you, sir. One never knows with people like that. I'll be sure to tell his lordship."

Behind Harkness, Dillon saw a wizened gnome come out of Figgs's stable. Crom. He glanced about; noticing Harkness talking to Dillon, he hesitated, then hitched up his belt and lumbered off to the latrines. There was no reason Crom or Harkness would think their runners were under any threat. All activity around the stable was following the usual pattern of a racing morning, with the usual lads, jockeys, and hangers-on drifting past.

Crom lumbered across the gap between Figgs's stable and the one behind which Pris and Rus were waiting. They would see him; within seconds, Pris would be in Figgs's stable with Belle. Two Belles.

His genial smile in place, Dillon swung toward the increasingly noisy gathering farther along the arc of holding stalls. As if just realizing what it meant, he murmured, "I heard the Cynster runners had come in early."

He glanced at Harkness. "I haven't seen them yet—but you must be keen to cast your eye over the competition." Looking back at the milling crowd, he grinned. "It looks like half the trainers with runners in the morning's races are already there."

They were; Dillon gave thanks for Demon's foresight in creating such a useful diversion. Meeting Harkness's black gaze, he inclined his head toward the crowd. "I must take a look—coming?"

Harkness might have been a villain, but he was a trainer first and last; he didn't need to be persuaded to legitimately spy on the competition.

With absolutely no suspicion that anything was going on, Harkness accompanied Dillon to the Cynster stalls.

From the corner of the stable where he'd been keeping watch, Rus turned back and met Pris's eyes. He hesitated, clearly torn, then nodded. "Go!"

She immediately stepped out, head down, Belle's reins in her hand. Beside her, Stan, Dillon's groom, kept pace. As they approached the side of Figgs's stable, Stan loped ahead. He opened the single door, took a quick look in, then stood back and held the door wide for her to lead Belle through.

Without hesitation, Pris did—as if Belle and she belonged in that stable.

Stan closed the door, leaving it open a sliver, keeping watch, ready to let her and the other filly, Black Rose, out again.

Abruptly enveloped in the warm gloom of the stable, Pris waited a moment for her eyes to adjust, and said a quick prayer. Blinking, she stepped out, scanning each stall, each horse, looking for Black Rose—praying she'd be closer to this end than the other, that, nightmare of nightmares, she wouldn't be in one of the stalls facing the open main doors.

Fate smiled; she found the black filly looking inquisitively out of a stall midway down the line. Giving thanks, she quickly led Belle nearer, then looped her reins about a convenient post. She'd brought another leading bridle for Black Rose; taking a precious moment to croon to the filly and stroke her nose, she slipped into the stall and quickly fitted the bridle.

Black Rose was a much more even-tempered horse than Belle; Pris sensed it immediately—wondered if that edge of temper was a necessary element in the makeup of a champion.

She scoffed at herself, amazed she could even think. She was so keyed up, her brain felt like it was literally racing, along with her heart. Her senses were fractured, scattered, trying to keep track of so many things—alert to any hint of danger—while she quickly led Black Rose out of the stall, tethered her farther down the aisle, then turned to Belle, and the most fraught moment in their entire plan.

Belle looked down her long black nose at her while she tugged the reins loose. Pris looked back, into the large, intelligent eyes. "Good girl. Now let's get you into the stall, and then later you'll get to race."

Belle lifted her head, then lowered it—twice. Pris's heart leapt into her mouth—was Belle going to be difficult? Was she going to rear?

Instead, Belle nudged forward; Pris snapped her mouth shut and quickly led the champion filly into the stall. She turned her, then slipped the bridle and reins off the sleek black head.

Belle snorted, and nodded twice.

Pris wished she could sigh in relief, but she was too tense—her stomach felt cinched into hard, tight knots. She patted Belle one last time, then slipped out of the stall and latched the door.

Stuffing Belle's reins and bridle into her pocket, she returned to Black Rose and tugged the filly's reins free. Her heart thudding in her chest, she set out for the door at the end of the aisle.

"Here—you! Yes, *you*."

Barnaby's voice brought her up short. His voice, but not his usual drawling accent; he sounded like a London tough. She froze, then glanced back at the main doors—but there was no one there.

From over her stall door, Belle looked inquiringly at her.

"I was wondering . . ." Barnaby's voice lowered, became indistinct.

He was talking to someone just outside the main doors. Crom, or the night watchman.

Pris looked down. The aisle was beaten earth and straw. They had no option anyway; hauling in a tortured breath, she held it and quickly led Black Rose on. The aisle seemed much longer than before; they went faster and faster as they neared the end, then the door swung open and daylight lay ahead. She led Black Rose straight through. Stan swung the door shut behind them, silently latched it, then scrambled to catch up as she trotted Black Rose on—not to the back of the stable where they'd waited but straight into the group of horses Rus and the other groom were leading along.

In seconds, Black Rose was concealed within the group. Rus, who'd been leading his and Pris's horses, boosted her into her saddle, then swung up to his. Slouching, they took the reins the grooms handed them, then settled to lead their plodding charges on.

"Where's Harkness?" Pris asked, when she'd caught enough breath to speak, when her thundering heart had subsided out of her throat so she could form the words.

"I don't know." From beneath the brim of his cap, Rus was searching in all directions. After a moment, he said, "We trust Dillon and follow the plan, at least until we know otherwise."

She nodded. Ten paces farther on, they crossed into the open as they ambled past the gap between Figgs's stable and the next. They all looked toward the track—to the open area before Figgs's stable—but the only people about were strangers.

It took discipline to keep to their slow walk; even a trot would have attracted attention. They reached the next stable and were about to pass out of the most risky area; Pris glanced back at the last moment, just before the stable would block her view—and saw Barnaby taking a few steps backward, apparently parting from someone standing before Figgs's main doors.

Looking ahead, she drew in a breath.

And told herself not to jinx anything, to stay alert until they reached the Heath proper and the wood in which they were to take cover after that.

Thirty nerve-racking minutes later, she, Rus, Stan, and Mike, the other groom, entered the small wood to the east of Newmarket, beyond the town's fringes and the outlying fields. Pris drew rein—then took what felt like her first real breath of the morning.

She glanced at Rus and met his eyes. Felt a smile spread across her face. "We did it!"

With a whoop, she sent her cap soaring. Rus, grinning fit to burst, did the same, as did Stan and Mike.

Once they'd quieted, however, they were eager to get on. Stan and Mike would return the Cynster horses to the stud, then would rejoin the crowd at the track. Pris and Rus would ride north, taking Black Rose with them; they'd stow the look-alike in the isolated stable for Harkness or Crom to find.

"Then," Rus said, as he wheeled his horse, "we'll head back to the Carisbrook house, get changed, and get ourselves back to the track in time to watch Belle win."

Pris had no argument with that plan; with a giddy laugh, she urged her mount on.

"As I'm sure you've heard, there have been rumors concerning suspect race results over the spring, and again a few weeks ago, here at Newmarket." Dillon looked around the sea of faces watching him with varying degrees of suspicion, caution, and trepidation. He'd had all the jockeys scheduled to ride that day herded into the weighing room for a special address.

"In response to this threat to the good name of the sport, the Committee has decreed that on at least one day of every meet more stringent checks than usual will be carried out by the race stewards." His suggestion, but the Committee had been very ready to agree. Anything to dampen the rumors and the consequent speculation.

Dillon waited until the inevitable groans died away. "Nothing too onerous, but there will be more stewards watching each race. Their particular aim today will be to verify that you all ride your horses to their best."

Scanning the room, he saw resigned shrugs, no hint of a grimace or any other indication the extra watch would discompose someone's plans. He'd expected as much, but had wanted to ensure the jockey riding Blistering Belle—an experienced jockey named Fanning—would have every incentive to urge Belle to give her best.

With a nod, he concluded, "I wish you all good riding, and every success."

The morning crawled. Barnaby had joined Dillon after he'd trailed Harkness back to Figgs's stable and watched the man enter. Barnaby reported that despite a close call with Crom, he assumed the switch had been successfully accomplished; he'd glimpsed the group of horses clustered around a set of black legs disappearing around the next stable. The lack of any subsequent drama seemed a clear enough indication that Belle was back in her appointed stall.

Later, he'd walked the holding stalls with the race stewards conducting the first prerace check; each horse's points were matched to those listed in the register. A black filly was in Blistering Belle's stall; Dillon studied her while the stewards checked her over. He thought she was the champion Rus had been training, but he couldn't be sure.

After addressing the jockeys in the weighing room, he retreated to his customary position before the stand, talking with the various owners and members who sought him out while waiting for the first race to get under way.

Eventually, a horn sounded; excusing himself, he returned to the track, joining the race stewards by the starting post.

As each horse was led up, a more stringent survey of points was done. At last, all the runners were cleared, ready, and in line—then with a deafening roar, the race was on.

The next hour went in confirming the winner and placegetters by applying the most stringent of checks, including having a veterinarian check each horse's teeth to confirm age. When all the assessments were completed and weight confirmed, the winner and placegetters were declared, and paraded before the stand to the applause of the assembled members.

Trophy presented, gratified owner duly congratulated, and then it was time to repeat the process with the horses for the second race.

One of Demon's runners took that prize—the Anniversary Plate. While the horse was being paraded, Dillon scanned the top row of the stand and saw Pris. She was wearing a veil, but he knew it was her. Rus sat alongside, a hat shading his features, with Patrick next to him and Barnaby beside Pris.

The twins had been banished to the heights, forbidden to descend until the third race had not just been run, but the winner declared, paraded, and the trophy awarded. Barnaby and Patrick had strict instructions to ensure that edict was followed. The chances of Cromarty or Harkness catching sight of the pair were slight, but all had agreed that there was no reason for either villain to know the part Rus and Pris—or indeed anyone else—had played in the unraveling of their grand scheme.

Mr. X's grand scheme.

None of them had forgotten Mr. X; letting his gaze slide over the wealthy, aristocratic crowd filling the stand, Dillon wondered if Mr. X was there, watching. He truly hoped he was.

"Time to head back, sir."

Dillon glanced around to find his head race steward waiting to walk back to the starting line. He smiled in almost feral anticipation. "Indeed, Smythe—let's go."

The starting post for the two-year-olds was closer; once there, they waited while the first of the runners was brought up. Dillon could barely harness his impatience. He'd never felt so . . . focused, intent—so *stretched* in his life. He had more riding on Blistering Belle than in any wager he'd ever made.

When she came clopping up, alert and clearly keen, her attention already on the winning post, he had to fight to remain outwardly impassive; fists clenched in his greatcoat pockets, he stood back and observed while Smythe and another steward checked her over, then waved her on.

He barely registered the seven horses that followed her into line.

As the lads stepped back and the jockeys took control, he glanced up at the distant stand, to the top row.

He focused on Pris, wondered what she was feeling, whether her lungs were tight, her heart thumping, whether her palms were as clammy as his were.

The white cloth was waved. He looked down as it was released; he watched as it fluttered to the ground.

Then it touched—and they were off.

Sixteen

The thunder of heavy hooves, the roar of the crowd—noise filled Dillon's ears, swamped his mind as he strained to see down the track. Along with the race officials, he moved out to stand on the starting line itself. This race was run on the straight, a long sprint to the finishing post in front of the stand; from the starting line he shouldn't have been able to be sure of the winner—except that a black horse was showing the rest of the field a clean pair of heels!

He couldn't breathe; he stared down the track at the dwindling black streak, so far in front and forging farther ahead that she seemed to be shrinking against the rest of the horses.

His heart raced along with her; for one giddy instant, he felt as if he were teetering on some edge. Not even in the days he'd bet heavily on the nags had he been this involved. This time his emotions were engaged; never had he had so much riding on a race.

The stand erupted; yells, whoops, and whistles reached them—they could see people cheering and waving wildly as the crowd favorite came romping home. And then she was there, flashing past the winning post; the ecstatic punters roared, then turned, laughing, to hug their friends, to thump each other on the shoulder, grinning widely.

Eyes fixed on the row at the top of the stand, Dillon could just make out Pris and Rus, dancing about, hugging each other and Patrick and Barnaby.

"Well, then."

Dillon glanced around to find Smythe by his elbow.

Smiling widely, the head steward surveyed the outpourings of joy all along the track. "It's good to see a favorite win. Gives the punters heart."

"Indeed." Dillon was finding it near impossible to keep his own smile within bounds. "We'd better get down there. I want the checks to be beyond question on this one."

"That they'll be," Smythe assured him. "There'll be no questions to dim the mood."

"For everyone except the bookmakers." Dillon paced beside Smythe as they strode down the track, the other race stewards following.

"Aye." Smythe shook his head. "There were some offering ridiculously long odds on that filly. Why was beyond me—her form's been excellent, and whoever Cromarty's had training her has brought her along well. Perhaps they thought that like that other runner of his, this one would take a breather—more fool them. They'll have had their fingers burnt, no mistake."

Dillon certainly hoped so.

The crowd about the dismounting yard was twenty deep as gleeful racegoers pressed close to call congratulations to Fanning and get a better look at the latest racing legend in the making. Flick, with Demon protectively hovering, was in the front row; beaming, she caught Dillon's hand, and tugged him down to whisper, "I'd congratulate you, but she's not your horse. But she was *magnificent*!"

"Which means"—Demon leaned near as Dillon straightened—"that we have to buy her." He glanced at his wife; she was staring at Belle with the rapt attention of a lover.

Dillon's lips twitched. "Of course."

He turned as a cheer heralded the appearance of the winner's owner and trainer—Cromarty, with Harkness behind him, both looking stunned, both struggling not to look like their world had ended while people called congratulations, grabbed their hands to pump them, and thumped them on the back. Cromarty looked green; Harkness's expression was utterly blank.

Making no effort to hide his smile, Dillon crossed to speak with them. "Congratulations, my lord." He held out his hand.

After blinking at him, Cromarty clasped it, gripped. "Ah—yes. An . . ." He tugged at his neckcloth as if it were too tight. "An amazing win."

"I don't know about amazing." Dillon nodded to Harkness. "Good training will show."

Already pale, Harkness blanched.

A flicker of an idea teased; his pleasant façade in place, Dillon watched Cromarty and Harkness closely—noted the surreptitious, disbelievingly horrified glances they exchanged while the three jockeys, Belle, and both placegetters were put through the various postrace assessments.

Then Smythe returned. Offering Dillon the race sheet, with the details duly noted, Smythe nodded at Cromarty. "Excellent win, my lord. And all's right here, so you'd best be on your way to the winner's circle."

Cromarty managed a weak smile. "Thank you."

Dillon initialed the race sheet, then handed it back to Smythe. "I'll catch up with you at the starting post for the next."

Smythe went on his way. Dillon turned to Cromarty. "Well, my lord—shall we? The Committee will be waiting to make the presentation."

Cromarty looked as if he were reeling. "Ah . . . yes. Of course."

Draped with a blanket and led by Crom, also stunned and subdued, with Fanning walking beside her, Belle stepped daintily along a narrow corridor that opened up through the adoring crowd. The filly accepted the accolades as her due, content now she'd had her run and left every other contender in the dust.

Dillon glanced at Cromarty as, side by side, they followed in her wake. His complexion was ashen; he was starting to sweat.

That tantalizing flicker of a possibility strengthened.

The winner's circle, an arena before the stand that the crowd obligingly drew back from, opened ahead of them. Delivering the hapless Cromarty to Lord Crichton, the Committee member officiating that day, waiting with a beaming Lady Helmsley to present the trophy, a silver cup, Dillon walked to the edge of the circle, then turned.

Cromarty was barely coherent. He stumbled through the presentation, the strained smile he'd plastered across his face frequently slipping. Those unfamiliar with such moments might imagine his odd behavior to be due to befuddled yet still-gratified astonishment. Those with more insight would start wondering why the owner of a filly already known to be an up-and-coming champion should be so staggered, even given the nature of the win.

Dillon looked at Harkness and saw the same turmoil, not just in the trainer's black-featured face, but in his stance, in his stilted, forced responses to well-wishers in the crowd. That Cromarty might have had so much riding on Blistering Belle losing that he was now facing ruin wasn't hard to believe. Why Harkness would feel the same . . . that suggested he knew that Blistering Belle winning posed a danger much more potent than mere financial ruin.

Unobtrusively, Dillon left the winner's circle, found two of his senior race stewards, and drew them aside.

"Lord Cromarty and his trainer, Harkness." He didn't need to say more; suspicion hardened in both stewards' eyes. They knew the industry they worked for, knew the games played. Dillon kept his expression impassive. "Give them time to enjoy the adulation, then approach them, but separately. John, you speak to Harkness first. Tell him, politely, that the Committee and I would like to ask him a few questions." Such a request wasn't one any trainer could refuse. Nevertheless . . . "Make sure you have two others with you. Ask him to go with you to the club. Keep him there in one of the smaller rooms until I return. Don't let him speak with anyone in between."

Turning to the other steward, Dillon continued, "Mike—wait until Harkness is on his way to the club, then tell Cromarty the same thing. I don't mind if they see each other in the distance, but I don't want them to have a chance to talk privately, not until after I've finished with them."

"Indeed, sir." Mike Connor exchanged a meaningful glance with John Oak. "We'll keep them at the club—how long will you be?"

Dillon smiled. "I doubt I'll be there before midafternoon." His smile took on an edge. "Let them wait. Alone."

"Yes, sir." Both stewards saluted and turned back to the crowd.

Glancing up at the stand, Dillon found himself smiling widely; he raised a hand, resisting the urge to wave as wildly as Pris was waving at him. He hesitated, but it was nearly time for the next race. He didn't always officiate at the starting post, but given his declaration to the jockeys that morning, many would expect to see him there.

Besides, he needed to think, to further develop that

tantalizing possibility that what Cromarty's and Harkness's reactions suggested might be there for the grasping. If he joined the others now, joined their celebrations, the one thing he was sure of was that he wouldn't be able to think; drawing in a breath, he saluted the group at the top of the stand, then swung around and headed for the starting post.

After the last race of the morning, something of an anticlimax after the excitement of the third, after the winner had been declared, the trophy presented, and the crowd started to disperse, Dillon made his way to the back of the stand, to the private room tucked beneath the large structure, and the party to which one of Demon's lads had summoned him.

Demon and Flick had hired the room, and gathered everyone involved to toast their collective success. Pausing outside the door, Dillon heard the hum of voices, the gay sound of laughter and good cheer. For most of those within, today had been their moment, and all had gone supremely well.

For himself, however, Belle streaking past the winning post was only the first battle—one they'd won through sheer impudence and the unexpectedness of their attack. If all went as they hoped, and the web collapsed and took Mr. X with it, then all would indeed be well. Until he was sure of that . . .

Regardless, it wasn't hard to feel buoyed by the victories of the day.

Opening the door, he stepped inside; shutting it behind him, he looked around. The room wasn't large, so it was crowded; scanning the faces, he noted his grooms and Demon's lads, Eugenia, Patrick, Adelaide, his father, as well as the members of their wild and reckless band.

And the three stewards of the Jockey Club, two gathered

around his father, the other, Lord Sheldrake, chatting animatedly to Barnaby. The sight brought him up short. Under his breath, he swore.

Flick and Pris were standing a little way into the room; they both turned and spotted him.

"Here he is!" Her face wreathed in the most glorious smile—one Dillon drank in, and felt sink to his soul—Pris swept forward to take his arm.

"At last!" Flick swooped, took his other arm and dragged him forward. "Where's a glass?"

Stan rushed to offer Dillon a glass of champagne; Demon strolled up with another for Flick—Pris already had a glass in her hand.

"To Dillon and the success of his plan!" Flick raised her glass.

"To a more honest future for racing!" Demon added, hoisting his glass.

"To the death of a spider!" Pris raised her glass high.

"To Blistering Belle and all who rode with her!" Rus yelled.

His easy smile in place, Dillon raised his glass. "To all our efforts, and our success today!"

Everyone cheered, then drank.

Lowering his glass, across the room Dillon met Barnaby's eyes; one person, at least, shared his reservations.

As people returned to their conversations, he looked down at Pris, hanging on his arm, looked into her eyes, bright emerald and enchanting. Different from before; he only needed that one look to know she was—for the first time since he'd met her—carefree. As she should be.

His own smile deepening, feeling his heart lift in response to her clear happiness, he took her hand, moving her back a pace, out of the pressing crowd. "Barnaby mentioned you were nearly caught by Crom."

Luckily, Barnaby had prefaced the news with the information that all had gone well, so he hadn't reacted as he might have, for which small mercy he was grateful.

Pris's smile didn't dim, but her eyes widened. "Thank God he was there—Barnaby, I mean. He stopped Crom just before he walked in. I was halfway down the aisle with Black Rose—I would never have got out if Barnaby hadn't intervened."

"He's useful in such situations. So how did it go?"

She was very happy to tell him; he listened, not just to her words but to the music in her voice, to the lighter notes in the soft brogue that never failed to mesmerize him, to the burbling lilt of happiness that made music of her joy.

It was a lighter, brighter melody he hadn't heard from her before; the sound wrapped about his heart and warmed him in some mysterious way he couldn't begin to describe.

"But what of you?" She opened her eyes at him. "How did you fare with Harkness?"

He told her, then, straightening, looked over the heads. "Speaking of Harkness, let's go and talk to Barnaby—there's more that happened later."

Taking her hand, he led her through the crowd, stopping when she insisted he partake of the sandwiches and delicacies laid out on a table. With a plate in one hand and her by his side, they tacked through the company, pausing to acknowledge and thank those of his household and Demon's lads they encountered along the way.

The three stewards each made a point of coming up to him, congratulating him, shaking his hand, thumping his shoulder. All three were not just pleased but deeply delighted at the outcome of his actions, his response to their request he investigate the rumors.

"To have struck such a blow against the felons plaguing our industry—well, m'boy, what more could we ask?" Lord Canterbury clapped him on the shoulder again. "Not even your father could have done better."

It was clear someone had explained all to them; Dillon was left to wonder who.

The General was sitting beside Eugenia; after she added her warm congratulations, he met Dillon's gaze and simply smiled. "Well done, m'boy. It was the right risk to take."

Looking into his father's old eyes, Dillon clasped his hand, held it for a moment, then with a smile, released it. If his father had told the stewards, it was because he'd felt the need to protect him—to ensure that having taken the risk, he wouldn't face any unnecessary repercussions. An understandable action, yet . . .

Putting his misgivings aside, he allowed Pris to steer him to Barnaby, who was chatting with Rus, Adelaide, and Patrick.

Pris stood beside Dillon while he and the others exclaimed and exchanged comments, recounting and reliving their glorious plan. She couldn't stop smiling; she couldn't recall the last time her heart had felt so light—she literally felt like dancing with happiness. It took discipline not to jig.

"I can't believe it's all over." Adelaide beamed at Dillon, then looked up at Rus beside her. "It's such a relief."

Smiling every bit as much as Pris, Rus glanced down, then tapped Adelaide's nose. "All's well that ends well."

Pris laughed, and agreed. Given the light shining in Adelaide's eyes, given that Pris knew her twin was far from blind, she was starting to suspect that Rus wasn't as unaware of Adelaide's plans as he pretended to be. Indeed, she was starting to wonder if he was considering falling in with them, in his own, eccentrically wild way.

She hoped he did; she'd known for the past year that Adelaide was the right lady for him. She was quieter, steadier—an anchor for his mercurial temperament—but she didn't shock easily, nor was she weak. Her strength wasn't the obvious, outgoing sort, but the type that endured. She would be the steadfast rock around which Rus's life could revolve.

Glancing up, Pris met Patrick's eyes and saw a similar

speculation there. She let her own smile widen; grinning, Patrick nodded.

He turned to Rus. "You were going to introduce us to the Cynsters' head lad."

Distracted from his contemplation of Adelaide's face, Rus blinked, then nodded. "Yes, indeed! Come on—he's over there."

Flashing a grin at Pris, Dillon, and Barnaby, Rus led the other two off.

To Pris's surprise, Barnaby instantly sobered; the change was dramatic, as if he'd dropped a genial mask to reveal the sharp mind and hard intelligence behind it.

"What's up?" Hard blue eyes fixed on Dillon's face, Barnaby raised his brows.

She glanced at Dillon in time to see his lips twist, wry but deadly serious.

"I would have greatly preferred the news of our accomplishment to have remained among friends, so that any potential recriminations concentrated on Cromarty and Harkness, and reached no further. However . . ." Looking across the room at the three stewards, Dillon grimaced.

"But it was clearly not to be," Barnaby returned, "and with any luck we'll have driven Mr. X from the field sufficiently forcefully that he'll be too busy licking his wounds to worry about lashing out at anyone."

Barnaby's voice faded toward the end of that sentence; Pris inwardly frowned when he glanced—ruefully?—at Dillon.

Dillon caught the glance, fleetingly raised his brows. "Precisely." He spoke quietly. "Badly injured curs are at their most dangerous—they feel they have nothing left to lose."

Barnaby grimaced. "Too true."

"However"—Dillon's voice strengthened—"that's apropos of what I have to report." He met Barnaby's instantly alert gaze. "We assumed Cromarty and Harkness, not wanting to incriminate themselves, would resist any inducements to tell us more—for instance who Mr. X is. After witnessing their reactions after Belle won, I believe we should revisit that assumption."

Barnaby's eyes lit. "You think they'll talk?"

"I think that, with a little judicious persuasion, they might come to view self-incrimination as the lesser of two evils."

"Oh-ho! Right, then." Barnaby rubbed his hands together. "When are you thinking of paying them a visit?"

"I've had my race stewards invite them, separately, for an interview—they're at the Jockey Club awaiting my return."

"Ah." Barnaby nodded in understanding. "In that case, let's give them another hour or two to dwell on the future."

"My thinking exactly."

Pris had listened without comment, her joyful smile still in place, her tongue firmly fixed between her teeth. She longed to demand a place—at least a listening brief—at the interviews with Cromarty and Harkness, but . . . that wasn't possible. Such a request would be unreasonable, too difficult to arrange . . . and while before, she'd felt a part of their team, now . . . now she'd found Rus, and he was free and no longer under any threat, her part in the adventure had ended.

And Dillon was moving on without her, as he should. He and Barnaby would pursue Mr. X as far as they could. Everyone would expect it, and of course, they would forge on . . .

She no longer had any part in their game. The knowledge caused a definite pang, but she quelled it. She kept her expression bright, and smiled encouragingly when Dillon glanced her way.

Demon appeared, collected as always, as if viewing the

assembled celebrating multitude from a lofty but benign height. Pausing beside Dillon, he sipped, then said, "It was I who told the club stewards."

Dillon's gaze swung to him; he raised his brows.

Demon faintly smiled. "You were watching Cromarty and Harkness—you didn't see how many others were watching them, too, how many others were visited by sudden suspicions. *Not* telling the stewards what had gone on became untenable at that point. Ye gads!—Cromarty looked beyond bilious, and Harkness couldn't crack a smile. Everyone with any nous knew *something* had gone on. When I reached the stewards, all three pounced on me—they were gratified to be given the true story. Of course, as Sheldrake was honest enough to say, they wouldn't have wanted to know if your plan hadn't worked, but as it had . . . at least, this way, the story that does the rounds will present the tale in the most favorable light." Demon shrugged. "Admittedly, it would have been preferable if they said nothing at all, but we can't hope for miracles."

Barnaby snorted. "If there's one thing I've learned during my short sojourn in Newmarket, it's that this industry thrives on talk. Gossip, information, speculation. Without it, nothing would work."

Demon and Dillon exchanged a glance, then smiled.

Pris had followed the exchange . . . more or less. She understood Dillon's stance that the fewer who knew of his plan, successful or not, the better; what she couldn't fathom was why Demon had felt it necessary to include the club stewards, who were plainly not expected to be discreet. Demon had clearly weighed up *something* against the stewards' continued ignorance, but what? What had Demon decided was more important than the secrecy Dillon had tried to maintain?

Everyone was happy, indeed thrilled that his plan had succeeded so well; there was clearly no problem . . . yet the question, the unknown, niggled. Still smiling as Flick came bustling up to join them, Pris made a mental note to ask Dillon later . . .

She lifted her gaze to his face. Later when? Tonight?

He hadn't come to the summerhouse for the past three nights. He'd been caught up with their plans, but now it was all over and triumph was theirs, would he come tonight to celebrate privately with her?

Her heart leapt, her nerves tightened, her breath slowed. Realizing Flick was speaking, she hauled her wits back to the present and forced herself to pay attention.

"I'm absolutely set on it." Flick leaned on her husband's arm, and flashed her blue eyes and a teasing smile up at him. "And you know you agree, no matter your grumbles."

They all glanced up as others neared—Rus with Adelaide on his arm.

"And here he is now." Flick beamed at Rus and gave Demon a nudge.

Demon sighed, but he was smiling. He met Rus's eyes. "What my wife wants me to say is that we've been thinking for some time that we need an assistant trainer, and we'd like to offer you the position."

Rus's face had blanked at the words "assistant trainer"; when Demon's voice faded, Rus didn't smile—he glowed. "*Yes!* I mean, I'd be honored—of course, I would!" Enthusiasm blazing in his green eyes, Rus grasped the hand Demon held out.

Watching, delight in her twin's just reward spreading through her, Pris felt another pang—an unexpected one. A *mortifying* one—how could she feel jealous that Rus was finally getting everything—every chance—he'd ever dreamed of? Mentally horrified, she buried the unnatural emotion deep. Her smile had never faltered; she made it brighten. "How *wonderful*!"

Rus released Adelaide, who he'd embraced and who'd

squeaked, and turned to her. Pris hugged him tightly, and grabbed the moment to whisper, "Even Papa will understand the honor in that."

Rus met her eyes; his lips tightened. He hugged her back, then released her.

He swung to Flick. "You won't regret it." He swept her hands together between his. "You can work me as hard as you like." His glowing gaze included Demon. "It'll be a joy to work alongside you both."

Pris listened to her twin babbling, and felt his happiness.

Adelaide shifted to her side. She, too, was watching Rus. "I'm so glad—this is *just* what he needs, isn't it?" She glanced at Pris, who nodded. Gaze returning to Rus, Adelaide asked, "Do you think your father . . . ?"

The thought echoed Pris's own. "I'll certainly do my best to make sure he understands, not just the position, but the honor, the status. He's never seen it that way, you know."

"I know." Grim determination threaded through Adelaide's gentle tones. "But he'll have to open his eyes."

"Eugenia will help." Pris glanced across at her aunt, still sitting beside the General . . . Pris blinked, and looked closer, took in the warmth in Eugenia's smile, and the gentle, yet appreciative light in the General's eyes. . . .

She glanced at Dillon. Was she the only one who'd been blind?

"Actually, I've been thinking." Adelaide's gaze was also fixed on Eugenia and the General. "Aunt Eugenia's truly enjoyed her time here." Adelaide's gaze swung to Rus. "I thought I might suggest that after we go to London so we can say we swanned around there, and then go back to the Hall with you, she might want to visit here again. We all know Rus is her favorite—she'll want to check up on him, don't you think?"

Pris couldn't stop her smile; Adelaide, for one, hadn't missed a trick. She squeezed her arm. "I think that's very likely. Indeed—"

She broke off. After a moment, Adelaide looked inquiringly her way. "Indeed what?"

Holding on to her smile, Pris shook her head. "Never mind."

She'd been about to suggest that she, too, would be happy to return to Newmarket, then reality had struck. She and Dillon weren't like Adelaide and Rus; even less were they similar to Eugenia and the General, whose relationship Pris judged to be one of fond companionship rather than passion. She and Dillon . . .

Their coming together had been a moment out of time, an engagement driven by the reckless, irresponsible, all-but-unthinking desire that sparked and arced between them. An irresistible force, it had swept them both away. Their relationship had not simply been born of passion—it *was* passion. Of passion.

Ephemeral. Insubstantial. Something that with time would surely fade.

She glanced again at Dillon. Rus, Flick, and Demon were engrossed in a discussion of horses, with Adelaide quietly listening in. Dillon and Barnaby had their heads together, no doubt plotting how best to extract all they could from Cromarty and Harkness.

Pris looked around, saw the still-smiling faces, sensed the glow of achievement, of triumph, still lingering in the air.

Everything had worked out; all their prayers had been answered, and on far more than one count. From the stewards of the Jockey Club, to the General, to Demon and Flick, Rus, Adelaide, Eugenia—even Barnaby—all had reaped the rewards of the angels.

In their different ways, all had taken a chance, and gained more than they'd asked for. Indeed, Dillon and Barnaby had yet to plumb the depths of their potential gain; they might yet unmask the villainous Mr. X.

As for her . . . head tilting, gaze growing distant as she looked at Dillon, she recalled her purpose in coming to

Newmarket. She'd found Rus, had helped drag him free of the coil into which he'd tumbled, and now had the pleasure of seeing him succeeding in the arena that meant so much to him. That would help immeasurably in reconciling him with her father, and then her family would once again be whole. All was well in her life, except . . .

For the one extra thing, the unexpected gift fate had handed her.

She refocused on Dillon, let her eyes drink in his dark beauty, the starkly handsome lines that would have been too perfect if it hadn't been for the powerful virility and sensuality that rippled like a warning beneath his smooth façade.

She looked, and felt the response within her, felt the tug that reached to her heart, and further, to her soul. Felt the connection that had grown ever stronger, that with each day, each night, each moment together had deepened and burgeoned and bloomed.

A treasure, or a curse? Which was it fate had handed her?

When this was over and they were apart, which would she name it?

Had fate blessed her or damned her? Only time would tell.

And time for her, for them, had run out.

Amid the pervasive happiness, the festive cheer, her heart suddenly felt like lead.

As if he sensed it, Dillon looked up—looked at her, met her gaze, his own suddenly intent.

She summoned a light smile, forced her lungs to work and drag in a breath, then moved past Adelaide to join him and Barnaby. "Have you decided how to approach them?"

She tried to sound eager; Barnaby grinned, and answered.

Dillon continued to study her; she didn't dare try to read his dark eyes in case he read hers. She didn't know what he was thinking, why he'd suddenly looked at her like that, why he was now so quiet, leaving Barnaby to outline their plan. "Do you really think they'll give you Mr. X's name?"

"Not readily," Barnaby quipped. "But persuasion is my middle name."

She managed a laugh, then turned as Rus came up, Adelaide on his arm. He was still bubbling with delight, still barely able to believe his good fortune.

Dillon watched Pris twit Rus on his unbounded enthusiasm, laughing when he jokingly attempted to disclaim, saying he was only behaving so in order not to hurt Flick's feelings. He listened as she, Rus, and Adelaide turned their attention once more to Barnaby and the upcoming interrogations . . . he'd almost convinced himself nothing was wrong—that the disturbance he'd sensed, some nebulous elemental ruffling of his instincts, had had no foundation—when he caught Rus glancing at Pris, and saw the same uncertain anxiety he himself felt mirrored in her twin's green eyes.

He focused more intently on Pris, but no more than Rus could he see past the shield she'd erected, one of easy good cheer, of transparent happiness that was simply too bright, too polished, to be true.

Something was troubling her, and she was hiding it from him. From Rus, too, but he didn't care about that. What he did care about was that she was doing it deliberately, that she was shutting him out of her life—he didn't care how small the matter bothering her was.

Barnaby turned to him. "We should go. If we manage to get a name, I'll head straight to London—we'd better get to it so I can be away before dark."

Dillon blinked, looked at Barnaby, then nodded. "Right."

Stepping back as Barnaby turned to the door, he glanced once more at Pris, but she was looking beyond Barnaby, toward the door . . .

He waited. She looked his way, and her smile was back—but that wasn't what he wanted to see.

A chill touched his soul. He didn't know what she was thinking, feeling—how she thought and felt about him, about them. He'd assumed . . . but he knew better than to assume he understood how women thought.

Summoning a smile, he inclined his head to her. He was about to turn and leave, then suddenly knew he couldn't. Not without . . .

Rus and Adelaide had turned away; stepping closer to Pris, he caught her green gaze. "Tonight?"

Her eyes, fixed on his, widened. For an instant, she ceased to breathe. Then she did, and whispered, "Yes. Tonight."

Her gaze dropped to his lips for a fleeting instant, then she turned away.

He forced himself to do the same, and follow Barnaby to the door.

"I don't know what you're talking about. What man?"

Belligerent and bellicose, Harkness glared at them.

They'd spoken to him first; he was the greater villain, therefore more likely to grab what he could from the situation. However, he'd got his second wind and had reverted to denying any part in any wrongdoing whatever.

Dillon ambled to the wooden table behind which Barnaby sat studying Harkness, seated in a hard chair on the other side; he touched Barnaby's shoulder. "Leave him. Let's go and chat with Cromarty and see what he has to say."

Harkness's beady eyes blinked. Until then, he hadn't known they'd brought Cromarty in for questioning, too.

Glancing back as he followed Barnaby from the room, Dillon saw Harkness, staring straight ahead, start to gnaw a fingernail.

Leaving his stewards watching over Harkness, he and

Barnaby walked to another of the small rooms reserved for interviews with jockeys, trainers, owners, and occasionally the constabulary.

He followed Barnaby in. As with Harkness, he introduced Barnaby as a gentleman with connections to the metropolitan police. All perfectly true, although from the way Cromarty, seated on a similar chair to Harkness, before a similar table, blanched, he'd leapt to the conclusion that Barnaby wielded all sorts of unspecified powers. Precisely what they wanted him to think.

"Good afternoon, Lord Cromarty." Sitting behind the desk, Barnaby placed an open notebook upon it. Withdrawing a pencil from his coat pocket, he tapped the point on the page, then looked at his lordship. "Now then, my lord. This gentleman who went into partnership with you—your silent partner. What's his name?"

Cromarty looked acutely uncomfortable. "Ah . . . what did Harkness say? You've asked him, haven't you?"

Barnaby didn't blink. He let two seconds tick by, then said, "This gentleman's name, my lord?"

Cromarty shifted; he darted a glance at Dillon. "I . . . um." He swallowed. "I'm . . . er, bound by privilege." He blinked, then nodded. "Yes, that's it—bound by commercial privilege not to divulge the gentleman's name."

Barnaby's brows rose. "Indeed?" He looked down at his notebook, tapped the pencil twice, then looked at Dillon. "What do you think?"

Dillon met his gaze for an instant, then looked at Lord Cromarty. "Perhaps, my lord, I should tell you a story."

Cromarty blinked. "A story?"

Pacing slowly behind Barnaby's chair, Dillon nodded. "Indeed. The story of another owner who had dealings with this same fine gentleman."

He had Cromarty's full attention; he continued to pace. "This owner's name was Collier—you might have met him. He was registered and raced for more than twenty years."

Cromarty frowned. "Midlands? Races out of Doncaster mostly?"

"That's him. Or was him, I should say."

Cromarty swallowed. "Was?"

His fear was almost palpable. Dillon inclined his head. "Collier . . ."

He told Collier's tale, using his voice, his tone, to deepen Cromarty's unease. Cromarty stared, pale as a sheet, the whites of his eyes increasingly prominent. Concluding with a description of Collier's body being found in the quarry, Dillon met Cromarty's starting eyes. "Dead. Quite dead."

The only sound in the room for the next several seconds was Dillon's footsteps as he continued to pace.

Once the full implications had sunk into Cromarty's panicking brain, Barnaby said in his most reasonable tone, "That's why, my lord, given the outcome of today's race, we would most strongly advise you to tell us all you know about this gentleman, most especially his name."

Cromarty had dragged his gaze from Dillon to Barnaby; he swallowed, then, in the tones of a man facing the hangman, simply said, "Gilbert Martin." Cromarty looked at Dillon. "He's Mr. Gilbert Martin of Connaught Place."

Fifteen minutes later, they had what amounted to a full confession from Cromarty, extracted by Dillon, assisted by Barnaby's musings on the likely reaction of the less-reputable bookmakers once they fully absorbed the dimension of the calamity that had befallen them; Cromarty had told them everything they'd wanted to know.

Thus armed, they returned to Harkness. His resistance lasted only as long as it took Dillon to inform him that Cromarty had told them all. Harkness confirmed Gilbert's name and direction, and also the man's description—tonnish, well turned out, tall, dark-haired, of heavier build than Barnaby.

Harkness confirmed their reading of him as the more experienced villain; unlike Cromarty, he didn't beg for leniency but dourly stated that if there was a choice between Newgate and transportation to the colonies, he'd rather transportation.

About to leave, Barnaby cocked a brow his way. Harkness simply said, "More chance of surviving on the other side of the world."

In the corridor, Dillon motioned to the constables sent by the magistrate, who he'd notified earlier. Leaving them to deal with Cromarty and Harkness, he led Barnaby to his office.

Sprawling in the chair behind his desk, he watched as Barnaby subsided into the armchair, a silly, beatific smile on his face. Dillon grinned. "What?"

Barnaby flashed that smile his way. "I didn't believe we'd get a name—I hadn't let myself believe it. Mr. Gilbert Martin of Connaught Place."

"Do you know him?"

"No." Barnaby shrugged. "But he shouldn't be hard to locate. Tonnish gentlemen have a tendency to overestimate their cleverness."

"Speaking as a tonnish gentleman?"

Barnaby grinned.

Dillon glanced out of the window. It was nearly four o'clock; soon the sun would sink and the light would dim. "Are you still set on starting for London immediately?"

"Absolutely." Barnaby sprang to his feet. "It just seemed right to spend a few minutes here, where this more or less started."

Dillon rose, too, and came out from behind his desk. "What are your plans once you reach town?"

"Home." Barnaby flung the word over his shoulder as he made for the door. "The pater's there—he'll be the first I tell. Tomorrow, I'll call on Stokes. He's already very interested in the whole business—I'm sure he'll be keen to be in on the kill."

Flashing Dillon another smile—this one of predatory intent—Barnaby led the way out of the door. "Who knows? Once we catch our spider, we might discover there's even more to his web than we already know."

"I sincerely hope not." Dillon followed Barnaby into the corridor. "I've had a surfeit of our spider's coils. I'm just glad to be free of them."

At last. As he strode from the Jockey Club by Barnaby's side, Dillon let that fact sink in, let himself embrace the notion of devoting his mind, and all his considerable energies, to dealing with coils of an entirely different sort.

Those he could use to bind one wild and recklessly passionate female irreversibly to him.

Seventeen

It was a strange night, mild, but the wind had turned waspish, unpredictable and unsettled, whipping past in gusts one minute, dying away to nothing the next. Clouds had rolled in, heavy enough to trap the day's warmth beneath them; slipping away from the house, Pris didn't need more than a light shawl.

With the moon well screened, the night closed darkly about her. She found it comforting. The route to the summer-house was engraved in her mind; she walked quickly along, keen—incipiently desperate—to reach her destination.

"Damn Rus." She muttered the words without heat; she didn't truly begrudge her twin his jubilation, but he'd chatted and laughed over the tea tray until she'd thought she'd scream—or even more revealingly plead a headache. She never suffered from headaches; such a claim would instantly have focused all attention on her. So she'd been forced to wait patiently until Rus had run out of words on which Adelaide and Eugenia could hang and everyone had at long last retired before she could attend to her own urgent need.

The need to see Dillon again.

The need to be with him again, alone in the night. To be in his arms, to feel them close around her, to *feel* again—*live* again—for what might very well be the last time.

She hurried on, her feet silent on the grass as she ducked into the shrubbery. It wasn't as well tended as a shrubbery ought to be, yet wasn't impossibly neglected, not overgrown so much as escaping from the confines gardeners had sought to impose—she'd always felt at home in its less than stringently correct surrounds.

Thanks to Rus, she was late, later than she'd ever been. She could only hope Dillon had waited, only pray that he hadn't thought she'd forgotten, or simply decided not to come to him . . .

Why wasn't she running?

Grabbing up her skirts, she did just that. Weaving past branches, leaping over steps, surefooted she raced down the narrow paths lined by thick bushes, screened by high hedges. Her heart raced, too, not in panic but in desperation—yes, definitely desperation. An emotion she didn't appreciate feeling, yet accepted she did. Accepted that she had this one night, this one time, and that would likely be all.

Ever.

Quite when that truth had slid into her mind and taken up residence she didn't know, but it was there now. After Dillon, instead of Dillon—she couldn't imagine any man taking his place. She ran on, faster, more frantically, needing to grasp this last night, this last moment—to have it shine, and then enshrine it in her heart.

She pelted into the central grassed court—and ran straight into a wall. A warm wall of muscle and bone.

Dillon caught her, steadied her. Instantly alert, he looked over her head, scanning the path along which she'd come. "What is it?"

Finding nothing, he looked down at her. His hands remained locked about her upper arms, holding her upright, protectively close. "Why are you running? What from?"

She couldn't tell him why, but . . . she moistened her dry lips. "Not from. To." She stared into his face, drinking in the dramatic beauty, visible even in the poor light. "You."

Reaching up, she cradled his face; stretching up on her toes, she pressed her lips to his.

Told him why with her lips, with her tongue, with her mouth. Told him why with her body as he gathered her in, as his arms slid around her and locked her to him.

Above them, the wind gusted, then abruptly rose to a wail, a wild, elemental power unleashed. It raced through the branches and rattled them, whipped up to the sky and set the clouds roiling.

In the grassed court, her hands framing Dillon's face, Pris heard it, sensed it, felt it. She drew the power in, let it fill her, flow through her. Let it take her own wildness and fashion it anew, into something finer. Something shining and glorious. Something infinitely precious.

It was she who drew away to sink to the ground, to the lush grass, a sweet-scented bed as it crushed beneath her.

His hand locked about hers, Dillon looked down at her, through the darkness trying to read her eyes. "The summerhouse . . ." When she shook her head, he drew in a ragged breath, his chest rising and falling. "Your room, then."

"No." Reaching up, she caught his other hand; exerting a steady pull, she drew him down. "Here. Now."

Under heaven.

He came down on his knees, let her draw him into a kiss, another heated exchange that set their pulses racing. The next time he drew back it wasn't to argue; his face etched with passion, his expression one of stark desire, he shrugged out of his coat, spread it behind her, then followed her down as she lay back upon it.

Dillon sank into her arms, let her welcome him, let her

hold him and trap him—let her dictate. Her, only her. Only with her—for her—would he do this, cede control and let her lead. Only she made him feel like this—that nothing was more important in his life than having her, appeasing her, worshipping and possessing her, doing everything in his power to keep her forever his.

So he gave her what she wanted, let his wildness free, let it mate with hers and drive them. Let the sparks flare, let the flames ignite, then roar—let the conflagration take them and consume them.

She wanted to rush, to race, to greedily grasp and devour; he held her back, forced her to slow—forced her to know, to feel, to appreciate every iota of worshipful strength he had it in him to lavish on her, every last scintilla of passion he tithed to her, every last gasp of surrender he laid at her dainty feet.

How would she know if he didn't tell her?—and for this, he had no words. So he showed her instead.

Showed her, as the wind raged overhead but left them untouched, cocooned in the long grass, protected by the shrubbery, to what depths passion could descend, to what heights it could reach—to what bliss it could lead.

Clothes . . . he shed them, his, and hers, until she lay naked beneath him, until their bodies met, brushed, touched, and caressed without restriction. His hands, his mouth, his lips and tongue played upon her beauty, possessed her, claimed her anew. She was his, became his in even more wondrous ways as about them the night deepened and cooled, while in the drifting, shifting shadows of the grassed court they burned with incandescent fire.

With heat, with longing, with a bone-deep raging need.

She cried out as with lips and tongue he sent her reeling over the edge, over the precipice of sensual abandon into the abyss of exploded sensation. Cried again as he drove her further, sobbed as he spread her thighs and settled between, gasped when he lifted her long legs, wound them about his hips, then drove into her.

Again, and again.

Pris writhed beneath him, clutched tight and sobbed, let her body beg and caress and drive him on. Drive him to take more, to seize and possess to the limit of his nature, to the depths of his passionate soul, to give all she wanted, to surrender and be hers—to be all she needed in this, their last moment out of time.

Reaching beneath her, he tipped her hips to his, and thrust deeper, harder, more brutally explicit as he claimed her, exactly as she wanted, exactly as she wished.

She arched, desperate to match the undulations of her body to the plundering rhythm of his, to appease and be fulfilled, to gather all that was her due, and reach her sensual limit, too.

To find where that was, and go beyond, with him.

He bent his head and his lips found the furled peak of her breast. The wind caught her scream and whipped it away, greedily gathered every sob and moan, every sound of her surrender, and hoarded them. Gloated over them as beneath him, breathless with ecstasy, she shattered again, but he still wasn't content, wasn't finished with her.

Wasn't yet ready to cede and be vanquished.

But it was his turn now.

His turn as he rose above her in the dark night, a primal figure, some primitive god, arms braced, holding himself above her, looking down on her, passion deeply etched in the hard lines of his face as he watched her body rise to each powerful thrust, as with total abandon she took him deep within her, as he lost himself in her.

She couldn't see his eyes, but could feel their fire, knew when he closed them, knew when the power caught him, when it whirled through her, through him, and without mercy fused them.

Under that sensual, physical assault she shattered anew; this time, with a guttural groan, he went with her. Joined with her as their bodies danced, as their senses spun and coalesced, as their hearts thundered, attuned, their souls aware, in concert.

They simply let go, both of them. Even though they were blind, as one, they simply knew—simply reveled in the wild winds that buffeted them, in the unremittingly untamed release that swept through them, that caught them, buoyed them, lifted them free of passion's fire, propelled them high.

Then let them fall.

Let them feel.

Every heartbeat as they fell back to earth.

Back to the sharp scent of crushed grass, to the mingled musky scents of their sated bodies, to the softness, the hardness, the warmth, and the wetness. The heat that still held them, cradled them, soothed them. The night that enveloped them in comforting dark as their lips met, and held.

And the moment lingered.

Caught at the cusp between reality and the ephemeral.

Filled with the indescribable joy of being one.

As one.

Him and her. Wild, reckless, and true.

Dillon's head was still spinning when, hours later, he swung up onto Solomon's back and turned the black gelding for Hillgate End.

She'd blindsided him. Again.

She'd wanted and needed with a passion as dark and as turbulent as his own; he hadn't been able to deny her—hadn't even been able to slow her down enough to learn what he'd gone there to discover—what she was thinking.

God knew, when she was like that, thinking was the last thing on either of their minds. He wasn't even sure his brain was functioning properly now.

Him, them, their future—her thoughts on those points were what he'd intended to probe. Preferably subtly, but if that hadn't worked, he'd been prepared to simply ask—to say the words, no matter how vulnerable that left him. He had to know.

Then again . . . eyes narrowing he stared sightlessly into the night, and wondered if, perhaps, she'd already told him. Perhaps, like him, she found words inadequate. They were, after all, very alike.

Whether it was that similarity that made him so sure she was the one, or what followed from that, he wasn't sure. All he knew was that she understood him, the real him, better than anyone else ever had. Anyone. Not his mother, not his father, not even Flick understood him as she did. Because she was largely the same.

Because the demons she possessed—the wild and reckless passions inside her—were of the same type, the same caliber.

Her comprehension not just allowed but encouraged him to be . . . all that he could be. To not hold back, not suppress his passions and keep them in check, their exercise a danger to be guarded against, but to allow them free rein, to let them flow and give him strength and insight, trusting that he, the rest of him, was strong enough, sane enough to guide and harness them.

With her, he was one. One being, one whole person. When she was with him, he was so completely himself, such an integrated whole—no reservations, no part of him guarded and held back—it sometimes came as a shock. She gave him a strength that without her he couldn't wield—his own nature.

And while he needed and wanted her, if tonight was any

guide, she needed and wanted him, too. Perhaps all they had to do was to take the next step? To trust enough in what was already between them and go forward?

The clop of Solomon's hooves as they reached the road brought him back to his surroundings. The gelding headed down the last stretch to the manor, to the warmth of his stall. Dillon thought of his bed, cold and empty, and grimaced. The conclusion was clear enough.

What he should do was, therefore, clear enough. As for the when . . .

Flick always threw a major ball for all the luminaries of the sport of kings who were in Newmarket for the week. As usual, her ball would be held tomorrow night, after the last day of the meeting, and, of course, Lady Fowles and her household would be present.

With Rus rescued and restored, with the substitution scam unraveled and no more, tomorrow night seemed tailor-made for his purpose.

Turning Solomon in at the gates of Hillgate End, Dillon made a firm vow. Tomorrow night, he'd ask Pris to marry him.

Everybody at Flick's ball seemed intent on pleasure, on enjoying the moment knowing all was right in their world. Pris couldn't share their enthusiasm. To her, the end seemed nigh, looming nearer with every passing minute.

But she hadn't forgotten her manners. Smiling delightedly, she followed Eugenia into the ballroom built out from one side of the Cynsters' house, and gaily greeted Demon and Flick.

Flick pressed her hand, then surveyed her guests—a glittering crowd that would have done credit to any tonnish London ballroom. "I know Dillon's here somewhere, but I'd advise you to avoid as many of the racing fraternity as you can. They become a trifle tedious when discussing their obsession."

Pris laughed. "I'll bear that in mind." She moved on in Eugenia's wake, with Rus and Adelaide behind her.

They'd spent the afternoon making plans. They'd told her father they would spend time in London; now Rus was free and his immediate future settled, Eugenia had declared that to London they should go, even if for only a few weeks. The autumn session of Parliament was under way, and the so-called Little Season, the social round occasioned by the return to London of many of the ton, likewise in full swing. A few weeks in London would give them plenty to report, and many would see them.

Rus had surprised them by insisting he would accompany them. He'd been adamant, certain Demon and Flick would agree that his place was with them during their stay in the capital; his new job could wait. As Demon had dropped by to have a word with Rus and had unequivocally agreed, Rus was now a part of their London jaunt.

Pris didn't know whether to be relieved or perturbed. Having Rus about would keep Eugenia's and Adelaide's attention from her, but there was little she could do to hide her less-than-joyous state from her twin.

And as she most definitely could not explain why she felt as she did—as if an enthralling challenge that had fulfilled her in ways she'd never imagined could be was over—then having Rus watching her, concerned, was yet another cross to bear. Especially when he was so happy himself.

She hated putting a damper on his spirits, yet come tomorrow, she had a strong suspicion she was going to feel as if she were in mourning.

For tonight, however, she was determined to keep her smile bright, to seize as much of Dillon's company as she might, although doubtless he'd be a focus of interest for the many notables from the racing world attending. Whatever time he could give her, she'd take, and be glad. It would be the last time she would see him; they'd decided to leave for London in the morning, and his duties at the ball would surely claim him until the small hours.

Somewhere, sometime tonight, she would have to find a moment in which to say good-bye.

The crowds parted before them, revealing a chaise on which the General sat, chatting to two gentlemen standing before him. Behind the chaise, his hand resting on the carved back, Dillon stood talking with Lord Sheldrake.

Smiling brightly became easier the instant Dillon's eyes met hers, the instant his spontaneous expression of unbounded pleasure registered. The warmth in his eyes, the curve of his lips—the way his focus had shifted so definitely that Lord Sheldrake broke off and turned to see who approached—all buoyed her.

Everyone exchanged greetings. Eugenia sat beside the General, who welcomed her warmly. He drew her into the conversation with the other two gentlemen, aldermen of the town. Rus and Adelaide stood at the end of the chaise, Rus pointing out other guests, Adelaide engrossed.

Dillon excused himself to Sheldrake, who, smiling, bowed to Pris, then wandered into the crowd. Rounding the chaise to join her, Dillon reached for her hand. His gaze lowered as he took in her emerald-and-ivory-striped silk gown with its revealing heart-shaped neckline, then he raised his eyes to hers, and arched a brow. "No shawl tonight?"

She smiled. "I didn't deem it necessary."

Dillon wasn't sure he agreed. Setting her hand on his arm, he could only hope the crowd prevented too many men from ogling the charms eloquently displayed by the snugly fitting bodice and the filmy, clinging skirts. The intense emerald hue echoed the color of her glorious eyes while the ivory highlighted the creamy richness of her skin.

Her black hair, as usual fashioned in a teasing, flirting

confection of curls, capped the whole in dramatic fashion, drawing his eyes at least, again and again, to the vulnerable, intensely feminine curve of her nape.

Just glancing at that evocative line, letting his eyes linger for an instant, was enough to have him evaluating the logistics of getting her alone, of indulging their shared passion again . . .

As if sensing his thoughts, she glanced up and met his gaze, her eyes slightly wide, widening even farther as she briefly searched his.

Recalling his intent—having it return to him in full force—he didn't hide his desire, the fact she evoked it simply by being beside him, but let her see, let her feel, let her understand.

She blinked, and glanced away. "Ah . . ."

Smoothly, he said, "Flick only allows waltzes at these affairs—or rather, Demon refuses to countenance anything else. Lady Helmsley's beckoning. Let's chat with her while the musicians get ready."

Lady Helmsley was delighted to have the chance to congratulate him and to talk with Pris again. Then the musicians started up and they left her ladyship for the dance floor. Drawing Pris into his arms, Dillon put his mind to capturing and holding her attention, and succeeded well enough to have her blinking dazedly at the end of the measure.

Then she focused on his face, read his commitment—to her, to her pleasure. A puzzled frown formed in the depths of her emerald eyes; smile deepening, he led her to speak with Lady Fortescue, a friend of his mother's who'd come up for the racing. From her, they progressed to Mrs. Pemberton, and Lady Carmichael.

Sweeping a lady off her feet—never before had he devoted himself to the task with such unwavering zeal. He was determined that when he asked her to marry him, Pris wouldn't even pause to think. If he had his choice, she wouldn't be capable of thinking, but sadly he couldn't—didn't dare—risk kissing her first. If he did, he might well not be thinking either, and that wouldn't do. After the last days, especially after last night, he wanted their strange courtship ended, brought to its inevitable conclusion, tonight.

So he kept her by his side, boldly laid claim to her evening, and brazenly displayed her as his for all to see.

They waltzed twice. He permitted Rus, Demon, and Lord Canterbury to waltz with her, too, but no one else. There was a limit to his forbearance—a limit to what his nature would allow, at least with respect to her.

It felt strange yet right to be in thrall in such a way, that with her, he was the victim of his own possessive passion, that it dictated and drove him, and no amount of debonair sophistication was enough to blunt its bite.

For years he'd witnessed the effects of that affliction on Demon; although he might have wished otherwise, he could hardly claim surprise that now it had infected him, too. He knew whence it sprang.

And with *that,* he had no argument. Indeed, with that, he was fully in accord.

He waited until after supper; the interlude when guests were wandering back to the ballroom was the perfect moment to slip away. Guiding Pris to the side of the ballroom, he glanced around at the reassembling throng, then turned to her.

Pris met his eyes; she assumed his attentiveness was because he, too, acknowledged tonight as their last contact. She'd enjoyed spending the evening beside him, a last taste of some of the pleasures to which he'd introduced her, but her nerves had progressively stretched and grown taut, knowing this moment must come. Facing the prospect resolutely, summoning a smile and firmly fixing it on her lips, she instructed herself to bid him farewell, and wish him a happy future.

She lifted her chin, and he murmured, his dark eyes

steady on hers, "I want to talk to you alone. The family parlor will be empty."

He'd said "talk"; searching his eyes, she sensed he meant that. And what she wanted to say would assuredly be easier said in private. "Yes. All right."

Glancing at the crowd, she gave him her hand.

Behind him, a distinguished gentleman stepped free of the throng; peering around Dillon, he saw her, and beamed.

Her jaw dropped. She froze.

Dillon saw, turned.

She gripped his fingers tighter, stopping him as he instinctively moved to shield her. "Ah . . ." Her eyes couldn't get any wider. She gulped. Forced what must have been a travesty of a smile to her face. "Papa! How . . . ?"

She didn't know what to say. A fact her father, thankfully, comprehended. With a wry, somewhat rueful smile, he stepped forward and drew her into a huge hug, the sort of hug she hadn't had from him in years.

Blinking rapidly, she hurriedly returned the embrace—and suddenly felt like she was fifteen years old again. "Er . . . Rus. Have you seen him?"

"Yes." Releasing her, her father drew back. His smile was warm; it filled his eyes—something else she hadn't seen in years. "And yes, I've heard all about your adventures here. I've met the Cynsters and General Caxton and Lord Sheldrake, too, and spoken with your brother, and Eugenia."

He paused, studying her, as if searching for evidence that she was well. "I've been looking for you, and . . ." Turning, he looked at Dillon—looked properly, shrewd eyes striking straight through the handsome mask. Used to her and Rus, her father wasn't distracted by a classically perfect face.

"You must be Dillon Caxton." Her father held out his hand. "I'm Kentland."

Dillon inclined his head, clasped and shook the proffered hand.

Her father glanced at her, his smile—a proud one—still curving his lips. "For my sins, the father of Lady Priscilla and her brother."

Dillon didn't blink. Releasing her father's hand, he slowly turned his head and looked at her.

She couldn't read his eyes, much less his expression, now perfectly, politely impassive. To his credit, he didn't parrot "*Lady* Priscilla?" although she was certain the words echoed in his brain.

Oblivious of any undercurrents, her father went on, "I understand I have you to thank for Russell breaking free of his recent predicament."

Dillon blinked, and turned back to her father. After an infinitesimal pause, he said, "He did well to learn what he did, and to escape in time. After that, it was more a case of our best interests following a parallel course. Our success has benefited us all, including the racing industry as a whole, as I'm sure Lord Sheldrake will have told you. Believe me, I'm very grateful your son acted on what he'd learned, rather than just lying low. And, of course"—eyes emotionless, he glanced at her—"it was thanks to your daughter, through her agency, that we met."

"Indeed." Her father beamed. He met her eyes again, held her gaze for a moment, then more quietly said, "It took you leaving to bring me to my senses. I had a long talk with Albert. Rus and I . . . well, we'll work out some arrangement." He glanced at the company, many of them of the haut ton. "I now see I was overly hasty in forming my opinion of Rus's chosen path."

Turning back to her, he smiled, then glanced at Dillon. "I didn't mean to interrupt. My daughter and I will have plenty of time to catch up later. I daresay you wish to dance . . . ?"

The musicians had just started up again. Dillon smiled—

a smile she read as a warning—inclined his head to her sire, and reached for her hand. "Thank you, sir." He looked at her, and arched a brow. Opening his mouth, he caught himself, then evenly enunciated, "Lady Priscilla?"

She smiled a touch weakly, bobbed a curtsy in acceptance, fleetingly touched her father's arm, then allowed Dillon to draw her away. Her father and his amazing appearance weren't the reasons her heart was thumping. When, reaching the floor, Dillon swept her into the dance, straight into a powerfully controlled turn, she sensed just how high his temper had flown, how hard he was riding it, reining it in.

Before she could say anything—even think what to say or do, where to start—he asked, his voice hard, his consonants sharply clipped, "I'm not currently *au fait* with the Irish peerage." His gaze remained fixed on the dancers he was steering them through. "Assist me, if you would. Kentland. Would that be the Earl of Kentland?"

"Yes." Pris struggled to draw breath into suddenly tight lungs. "Of Dalloway Hall, County Kilkenny."

"Dalloway?" His jaw clenched; a muscle jumped along the stony line. Dark eyes filled with roiling anger swung down and locked on hers. "Is that your surname—your *real* surname, then?"

A huge weight pressed down on her chest. She couldn't speak, simply nodded.

A second passed, then his chest swelled as he drew in a breath that seemed every bit as tight as hers.

"Always nice to know the name of the lady I've been—"

Pris shut her eyes, wished she could shut her ears, but she still heard the word he used. She knew what it meant, knew what men meant when they used it.

He swung her into a viciously tight turn, one that brought her body up hard against his. She fought to stifle a gasp. A second later, he softly swore.

She opened her eyes, but she couldn't meet his. Yet if he

continued to waltz with her so *intensely,* people would notice.

He must have realized; he swore softly again. Then without a hitch, he whirled her to the edge of the floor, released her, seized her hand, and dragged her out of the room.

Before she could ask where he was taking her, he snapped, "The parlor, remember?"

She swallowed, trying to ease her heart down into its proper place. Desperately she tried to marshal her wits, but . . . she'd never expected this. She'd all but forgotten he knew her as Miss Priscilla Dalling—that although he knew her in every sense that counted, she hadn't corrected that long-ago lie.

Hauling her down a distant corridor, taking her far from the ballroom, he threw open a door, stormed in, whisked her through, then, releasing her, slammed the door shut.

Pris swung to face him. This was definitely not how she'd intended to say good-bye.

But what she saw in his eyes, intent and fixed on her, erased every thought from her head.

"*Lady Priscilla Dalloway*—have I finally got that right?"

He took a step—a distinctly menacing step—toward her; she promptly took a step back. She nodded.

"An *earl's* daughter."

"Yes." It hadn't been a question, but, lifting her chin, she answered anyway; hearing her own voice rather than just his roaring, growling one helped.

He continued to advance as she retreated. The word that leapt to her mind was panther—or was it a jaguar she meant? Whichever was more lethal, that's the one she meant.

That was what he reminded her of as he stalked her across the room, his dark eyes burning with an unholy fury—a temper she fully understood, but had absolutely no clue how to assuage.

"I . . ." She bit her lip; the words that came to her tongue were so pitiful.

"Forgot who you were?"

His tone pricked her on the raw. She halted, tipped her chin higher as he drew nearer, and narrowed her eyes at him. "Yes, as it happens. In a manner of speaking, I did."

Her temper swelled; she welcomed it, let it fill her. Let it give her the strength to meet him eye to eye. "When we first met, there was no reason you needed to know my real name, and Dalling—it's a name Rus and I use when there's reason to keep the family name apart from whatever's going on. Naturally, I used it when we first met. Afterward . . ."

His smile held no humor. "Do let's get to afterward."

Leaning forward, she returned that smile with interest. "Afterward, it didn't *matter. Yes*, I forgot about it—because my name is not who I *am*. It's just a *name,* and me by any name is the same person! So yes, I forgot—and so forgot to correct what you knew. *So* I apologize for the shock you just had to endure, but as for anything else . . ."

Her voice had risen, gaining in strength. Flinging out her arms, she held his gaze, her own now scorching. "This is me. *Pris*. Whether it's Dalling or Dalloway, whether there's a lady in front of it, what the devil difference does it make?

"Why on earth should my being an earl's daughter make any difference to us? To what happened, or where we are now? It certainly doesn't change what's to come."

Dillon looked into her face, all blazing eyes and unwavering certainty—and realized she'd just told him all he wanted to know. Her name, her title, didn't matter; she would marry him anyway. Good. Because he was definitely marrying her, and the sooner the better.

There was no reason he couldn't offer for an earl's daughter. His family was one of the oldest in the haut ton, connected to several of the principal families. His estate might be described as tidy, but his private fortune was immense, and his status as one of the select few elected to govern the sport of kings, a status their recent triumph had only elevated, ensured that Lord Kentland would have no reason to refuse his suit.

"Marry me."

She blinked. Then, lips parting, she stared at him, her emerald eyes growing wide, then even wider. "Wh-what? What did you say?"

His jaw clenched; he spoke through gritted teeth. "I said: *marry me.* You heard me perfectly well."

She drew back. Looked at him as if he were the strangest specimen of manhood she'd yet encountered, but then, as he watched, suspicion, then wariness, flooded her eyes. She drew a breath; her voice wobbled as she asked, "Why?"

"Why?" A host of answers flooded his incredulous brain. Because if she didn't, soon, he'd go insane? Because he needed her in his life and she needed him? Because it was obvious? Because they'd been intimate and she might be carrying his child . . . the thought made him weak-kneed.

Very definitely weak-brained. "Because I want you to."

Before she could demand "why?" to that, too, he leaned closer, bringing his face level with hers. "And you want to, too."

He was one hundred percent sure of that.

To his astonishment, she paled. Her lips set, as did her expression. "No, I don't." She bit the words off.

It was his turn to stare. Equally disbelieving. Equally astounded.

Before he could say anything—before he could argue and press—Pris held up a restraining hand. Temper and sorrow, hurt and anger were a powerful mix, roiling and boiling and rising inside her. "Let's see if I have this right."

From the sudden hardening of his expression, she knew her eyes had flashed, that soaring emotion had again set them alight. She pointed toward the ballroom. "Ten minutes ago, a pleasant evening—our last evening together—was drawing to a civilized close. We were about to part amicably and, with fond farewells and Godspeeds, go our separate ways." She folded her arms; chin high, she kept her eyes on his. "But then you learned I'm an earl's daughter—that the young lady you've been dallying intimately with is a nobleman's daughter—and you suddenly perceive that we need to marry."

She gave him only an instant to absorb that summation before stating unequivocally, "*No.* I *don't* agree! I will never agree to marry because society deems it necessary."

There was so much anger surging beneath her words they wavered, but it was the sorrow swirling through her that shook her to her core. She dragged in a breath and went on, clinging to her temper, drawing on its strength. "I knew what I was doing from the first—I never imagined marriage was any part of our arrangement, because it *wasn't,* as you and I both know. What we had was an affair, a succession of mutually agreed interludes. There was a reason for the first. And the second, if you recall. The rest came about because we both wished them to."

His face had turned stony, a set of hard angles and unforgiving planes in which his eyes burned. "Do you seriously imagine—"

"What I *know* is that you didn't seduce me—*I* seduced *you.*" She gave him back glare for glare. "Do *you* seriously imagine I did that so that now you would feel obliged to marry me? That I did what I did—dallied intimately with you—in order to trap you into offering for my hand?"

Hurt fury laced her voice as she gave her temper free rein. Better that than any of the other emotions coursing through her.

Confused exasperation disrupted the intensity of his dark gaze. "I never said . . ." He frowned, scowled. "That *wasn't* how it was."

"*Yes, it was!*" Her voice had grown shrill; she was close

to crying with the frustration and futility of it all—the sad irony of fate. Until he'd said the words, raised the specter, she'd been able to ignore it, pretend it didn't exist—convince herself that she didn't want to marry him, that dalliance and experience were all she'd ever wanted. That they were enough.

But now he'd said the fateful words—for all the wrong reasons. For the *worst* of wrong reasons. And in doing so he'd raised the prospect and she could no longer hide from the truth. Marrying him, being his wife, was the dream she hadn't allowed herself to acknowledge, the one she'd pretended she hadn't had.

There was no way to turn back the clock, to start again as if they were simply gentleman and lady, to ignore the reality of what had passed between them over recent weeks.

No way for them to marry without knowing that it was not love but social dictates that had brought them to it.

And that was something she would never accept.

Especially not with him. Better than anyone, she knew it was impossible to trap a wild soul without harming it.

She held his gaze, clung to her composure, tilted her chin. "Regardless, I have absolutely no interest in forcing you to marry me. Indeed, I'm no longer sure I have any interest in marrying at all."

He stared at her, still scowling, then exhaled through his teeth. Lifting one hand, he raked it through his hair.

She seized the moment; she couldn't bear to stand there and argue, not when it felt like every word, every phrase, was another stone hitting her heart. "I wish you every success in your future endeavors." Ducking around him, she rushed to the door. "And I hope—" Pausing with her hand on the knob, she looked back.

He'd spun around and now stared at her, an absolutely stunned, totally incredulous look on his face.

She stared back for an instant, drinking in her last sight

of his dramatic male beauty, then hauled in a quick breath. "I hope you have a fulfilling life."

Without me.

His expression changed; she didn't wait to see to what. Opening the door, she rushed out; shutting it behind her, she picked up her skirts and ran toward the ballroom.

Behind her, she heard a bellow, then he opened the door—called "*Pris!* Damn it—come back!"—but then she turned a corner, and heard no more.

In the doorway to the parlor, Dillon stared down the corridor, but she didn't reappear. For a long moment, he just stood there. It was the—what? third time?—she'd left him feeling like she'd taken a plank to his head.

Turning back into the room, he shut the door. Frowning, he crossed to the well-padded sofa and slumped down on it. And tried to sort out his feelings.

That she didn't want him feeling forced to marry her was all well and good, but that *she'd never at any time thought of marrying him . . .*

He wasn't sure what to do with that—couldn't see how it fitted with what he'd thought was going on, with what he'd thought had grown between them. Until she'd said that, he would have sworn that she was . . . as emotionally enmeshed with him as he was with her.

Yet when he'd tried to correct her view that marriage hadn't been any part of their arrangement, she'd been adamant. Clearly, it hadn't been in her mind, even if it had, from the first, been in his. And she'd just as clearly been planning to bid him a fond farewell—affectionate, perhaps, but she'd made it clear her heart wasn't involved. Hadn't been touched.

Unlike his.

He was suddenly very aware of that organ constricting. Leaning his head against the sofa back, he looked up at the ceiling, and swore.

And heard a rustle behind him, and a familiar little "Humph!"

Swinging around, up on one knee, he peered over the back of the sofa. And goggled. "Prue!"

She looked up at him; not one whit discomposed, she wrinkled her nose, and got to her feet.

"What the devil are you doing there?"

Calmly smoothing down her robe, she cinched it tight. "My bedchamber is above the ballroom. Mama and Papa said if it got too loud, I could come down here and read or sleep."

Sinking back onto the sofa, Dillon realized all the lamps had been lit.

"I was reading." A book in her hand, Prue climbed into one of the armchairs by the fire. "Then I heard someone coming, so I hid."

Rapidly reviewing all she must have heard, Dillon narrowed his eyes at her. "You hid so you could eavesdrop."

She looked superior. "I thought it might be instructive." Her blue eyes—bluer than her father's, sharper than her mother's—fixed on his face. "It was. That will probably be the poorest attempt at a proposal I'll ever hear." She frowned. "At least, I hope it will be."

He spoke through his teeth in his most menacing voice, "You will forget everything you heard."

She sniffed. "All that gammon about you offering for her hand because you'd found out she was an earl's daughter. I can't see what else you expected. She was quite restrained, I thought, at least for her. She has a fabulous temper, hasn't she?"

Dillon ground his teeth. He remembered the emotions lighting Pris's eyes—temper, yes, but also something else, something that had bothered him, distracted him, and slowed him down. "That wasn't why I proposed."

The words had slipped out, a statement of fact, more to himself than anyone else. Realizing he'd spoken aloud, he glanced up and found Prue watching him, a pitying light in her eyes.

"It's what she thinks that matters, and she thinks you offered because you feel obliged to. She asked why, and you let her think that, more fool you."

"It wasn't only that."

"No, indeed. One minute you're roaring at her—you did realize you were roaring, didn't you? Then you don't ask, but tell her—order her—to marry you. *Huh!* In her shoes, I would have sent you to the right about, too."

Dillon stared at Prue, at her direct, scathingly unimpressed expression, for a full minute, then, jaw setting, he hauled himself to his feet and headed for the door.

"Where are you going?"

Hand on the door knob, he looked back to see Prue opening her book. She looked at him inquiringly. He met her gaze, and smiled dangerously. "I'm going to find her, drag her off somewhere where there will be no one listening, and explain the truth to her in simple language impossible to misconstrue."

Hauling open the door, he went out and shut it with a definite click.

Eighteen

The following afternoon, a mix of frustration, exasperation, and uncertainty riding him, Dillon turned his blacks into the Carisbrook house drive, not at all sure what he would face when he finally ran Pris to earth, or what he would do when he did.

Last night he'd returned to the ballroom only to discover her nowhere in sight. He'd eventually found Humphries, Demon's butler, and learned that Lord Kentland's party had left some ten minutes before, Lady Priscilla having taken unwell.

In his mind he'd heard one of Prue's unimpressed snorts, but Pris running away had left him uneasy. If she'd been defiantly angry, she would have stayed and flirted with every gentleman willing to fall victim to her charms; there'd been enough of those present to have made her point.

Instead . . . if she'd pleaded illness and run, she must have been upset.

That was what had distracted him in the parlor—the hurt

he'd glimpsed in her eyes. She distracted him in any case, but her being hurt in any way whatever was the ultimate in distraction. His mind seemed instantly to realign, to focus on finding what had upset her and eradicating it. Even if it was him.

According to Prue, Pris believed he'd offered for her only from a sense of moral obligation. Tooling his curricle on, he frowned. Regardless of her view of things, moral obligation did play a part—or would have if he hadn't already intended to marry her.

He was what he was; honor was a part of his character, not something he could deny, could pretend didn't matter. He might also be reckless and wild, but that didn't preclude him behaving honorably. Nevertheless, in this instance, honor and moral obligation were entirely by the by; they weren't why he wanted to marry her.

A long night of thinking—easy enough when tossing and turning alone in his bed—had forced him to concede that he'd made a mistake, a major one, in even for an instant allowing Pris to think that moral obligation had played any role whatever in prompting his proposal. In even for a heartbeat contemplating using that to hide his real reason.

He'd been a fool for all of ten seconds—far less than a minute—and look where it had landed him.

Prue, he was certain, would, with withering scorn, point out the implication.

Which was why he was looking for Pris, prepared and determined to make a clean breast of it regardless of his sensibilities. He'd tried to think of words, to rehearse useful phrases; horrified by what his mind had suggested, he'd stopped, and given up.

Sufficient unto the moment the evil thereof, the words he might be forced to utter. Dwelling on them ahead of time wasn't helpful.

Especially as, lurking around his heart, was a cold and

murky cloud of uncertainty. What if he'd been wrong? What if, regardless of all he'd thought they'd shared, she truly viewed him as nothing more than her first fling? As her first lover only, not her last?

The cold cloud intensified; he pushed the thought away. The house neared; he checked his team, then guided them into the stable yard.

Patrick came out of the stable. He nodded and walked to where Dillon halted the curricle. "Morning, sir. If you're looking for Lady Pris, I'm afraid you're too late. They left after an early lunch."

He managed to keep his expression impassive, to not let any of the shock he felt show. "I see." After a blank moment, he had no choice but to ask, "Left for where?" Ireland?

"Why, up to London." Moving to the restive horses' heads, Patrick glanced at him. "I thought Mrs. Cynster would have told you."

Dillon blinked. What did Flick have to do with this? "I . . . haven't caught up with my cousin after the ball."

But he would. She'd kissed his cheek and sent him off last night—and had said not a word about Pris and her family fleeing to the capital.

"Aye, well, they were going to stay at Grillons, but Mrs. Cynster said she was just itching for an excuse to go up to town." Patrick was admiring the horses, stroking their long noses. "She invited the whole party—Lord Kentland, Lady Fowles, Miss Adelaide, Lady Priscilla, and Lord Russell—to stay at her house in town. In Half Moon Street, it is."

Dillon nodded. He usually stayed there when he went to London.

Patrick nodded at the house. "I'm just seeing things packed up here, then I'll be following. Lady Pris was keen to get off as soon as they could."

Dillon met Patrick's eyes, wondered how much he'd guessed. "I see."

"Seemed a trifle under the weather, she did, but hell-bent on getting on the road and away."

Dillon inwardly frowned. She was running, still. A question he hadn't asked himself before swam into his mind. If she was running, she was upset. But why was she upset?

He could comprehend anger; she'd thought he'd thought she'd schemed to force him to offer for her, and was understandably incensed. She'd seen the notion as a slur on her integrity; although he hadn't thought any such thing, he could appreciate her point. But what was behind her . . . he didn't have the words to describe her emotions; he could sense them, but the turmoil inside her—pain, hurt, regret—what else?—it all came under the heading of "upset."

What was going on inside her head?

What, when it came down to it, did she truly want? Him? Or not?

Not in the way she'd believed he'd meant, that much he knew, but did she truly not want him whatever his motives?

His frown materialized. His head had started to ache. Jaw clenching, he met Patrick's eyes and caught a hint of grim sympathy.

"It is so damn complicated," he ground out, gathering the blacks' reins, "trying to think like a woman!"

"Amen!" Patrick's grin flashed as he stepped back and saluted. "I've never yet managed it myself."

With a curt nod, Dillon whipped up the blacks and headed back to Hillgate End.

One sleepless night, one brooding, restless god-awful day when he could think of nothing, concentrate on nothing, convinced him he couldn't simply sit and wait—and even less could he let Pris go. Let her slip out of his life without trying his damnedest to get her back in it.

He wasn't even sure he could live without her—whether his life, whether he, had any meaningful future without her; his mind seemed already to have arranged his entire future life around her, with her at its center—if she wasn't there, where she belonged, everything would fall apart.

How that had happened, why he was convinced it was so, he didn't know—he only knew that was how he felt.

In his heart. In his soul. Where she and only she had ever touched.

He had to get her back; he had to get her married to him. What he needed to work out was how to achieve that.

It was the middle of the autumn racing season, but the major Newmarket meeting was behind them, and the substitution scam was no more. For the rest of the season, matters ought to run smoothly, enough for him to leave the reins in someone else's hands, at least for a week or so.

He waited until that evening, when he and his father were sitting quietly in the study. Eyes on the port in the glass he was twirling, he said, "Despite it being the middle of the season, I'm thinking of spending a few weeks in London."

He looked up to see his father's eyes twinkling.

"That's hardly a surprise, m'boy. Of course you must go up to town. We'd all be disappointed if you didn't."

He blinked. His father went on as if everything had already been arranged. "I'll take over for you here. Indeed, I'm looking forward to getting back to things for a while, knowing it won't be for long. Demon will lend a hand if necessary. I know all the clerks—we'll hold the fort while you go after Pris."

Dillon frowned. "How did you know?"

The General's smile turned wry. "Flick dropped a word in my ear at the ball, then looked in yesterday on her way to town. She said when you finally bestirred yourself and followed, to tell you Horatia would have a room ready and be expecting you."

Everything *had* already been arranged . . . he stared at his father. "Did Flick say anything else?"

The General consulted his memory, then shook his head. "Nothing material."

"How about *im*material?"

At that, his father chuckled. "The truth is, everyone who knows you both thinks you deserve each other. More, that you're right for each other, and that no one better is likely to exist for either of you. Consequently, the collective view is that you should hie yourself to London and convince Pris to marry you as soon as may be. Quite aside from there being no sense in wasting time, there's the other side of the coin to consider."

He was lost. "What other side, and of which coin?"

His father met his gaze, his eyes shrewd and wise. "The side that will make Pris a target for every rake and fortune hunter in town. It won't be just her appearance, nor just her temperament, but also the simple fact of you not being there."

An iron-cold chill touched Dillon's heart; he could see all too well the tableau his father was painting. "Right." He drained his glass and set it aside. "I'll leave in the morning."

"Excellent." The General smiled approvingly. "I was told to inform you that should you require any assistance whatever, you only need ask. The ladies will be most happy to assist you."

By "the ladies," he meant the Cynster ladies and their cohorts—a body of the most powerful females in the ton. Although warily grateful, Dillon was bemused. "Why?"

The twinkle returned to the General's eyes. "As it's been put to me, by marrying Pris you'll earn the undying gratitude of all the ton's hostesses as well as all the mamas—not just those with marriageable daughters, but also those with marriageable sons. Dashed inconvenient, the pair of you, it seems—you distract the young ladies, and Pris distracts the gentlemen, and everyone forgets who they're supposed to be focusing on. The consensus is that the sooner you and she marry, and take yourselves off the marriage mart, the better it will be for the entire ton."

Dillon stared. "Flick actually said that?"

The General smiled. "Actually, she said a great deal more, but that was the gist of it."

Dillon was thankful to have been spared. One thing, however, was now clear. "I'd better drive up to London first thing."

"Oh—thank you, Lord Halliwell." Pris accepted the glass of champagne she'd forgotten she'd sent Viscount Halliwell to fetch, and bestowed a grateful smile.

Patently basking in such mild approval, the viscount rejoined Lord Camberleigh and Mr. Barton, all vying for her interest, all doing their damnedest to engage it.

A futile endeavor, but it was impossible to explain that to them, or indeed, anyone; Pris had to smile and let them drone on.

About them, Lady Trenton's ballroom was filled with the gay, the witty, the wealthy, and the influential, along with a large contingent of hopeful young ladies and gentlemen. The next few weeks were the last in the year in which society congregated in London; once Parliament rose in November, the ton would retire to their estates, and all matchmaking activity would become confined to the smaller, more select house parties that would fill in the months until March, when everyone would return to town again.

For those interested in making a match, these next weeks would be crucial in determining whether they would further their aims through the winter months or have to bide their time until spring.

In originally suggesting they visit London, Pris hadn't realized how frenetic the search for suitable mates would be, much less how high on the list of eligibles she would feature. Now she knew, and was quietly aghast, but there was nothing she could do but smile. And pretend the gentlemen who flocked around had some chance of winning her hand.

Of course, they had even less chance of accomplishing that than they had of fixing her wandering attention. The man who succeeded in winning her hand would first have to win her heart—that was a vow she'd sworn years ago, when following her come-out she'd realized the reality of many matches in her circle. A temperate union, based on affection and trust at best, would never do for her; worse, such a marriage would potentially be dangerous, inviting trouble. Her emotions, her temperament, were too strong, too intense; she would never find peace in a passionless existence.

Such had been her thoughts before she'd met Dillon Caxton.

And lost her heart to him.

The gentlemen who pursued her could not win from her something she no longer possessed. Forcing a smile in response to Lord Camberleigh's tale, she tried not to think of the yawning emptiness inside her.

It was her third night in the capital. Flick had prevailed on Pris's father to accept her hospitality at her house in fashionable Half Moon Street. As soon as they'd assembled there, Flick had taken them under her wing and introduced them to her wider family, the other Cynster ladies, both of Flick's generation and the one before. A more formidable collection of ladies Pris had never encountered; somewhat to her surprise, they'd welcomed her, Eugenia, and Adelaide warmly, and set about assisting them into the ton.

She'd allowed herself to be swept along, to be presented to this lady, that *grande dame,* with Eugenia to accept invitation after invitation and appear at three balls every night. She'd hoped the activity would ease the cold, dull ache where her heart used to be; she'd prayed the London gentlemen would distract her thoughts—in vain.

They were all so . . . weak. Pale. Insignificant. Lacking sufficient strength to impact on senses grown accustomed to the darkly dramatic, to the decisive, the dangerous, and the wild.

Yet she didn't regret refusing Dillon's suit—*couldn't* regret rejecting an offer that hadn't come from his heart. Her heart might have—all but unknown to her at the time—been ready and willing to accept his, but it hadn't been his heart he'd offered her, only his hand, his name.

During all her time in Newmarket, through all they'd done, all they'd shared, her only regret, an abiding regret, was that she'd allowed the fiction that she'd given herself to him as an inducement to view the register to stand.

Aside from her name, that was the one other lie she hadn't corrected for him. It was a big lie, a serious lie, but the situation between them meant she'd never be able to address it.

If she confessed she'd seduced him, had first taken him into her body purely because she'd wanted him, and had repeated the exercise because she'd craved the closeness, the connection, he'd see the truth, that she'd been in love with him from the first, and feel even more compelled to marry her.

So she wouldn't tell him, and the lie would stand.

She told herself it didn't matter, that in the wider scheme of things she'd accomplished all she'd set out from Ireland to do. Rus was safe and free, and the racing world was now his oyster, her father and he had reconciled, and her family was once again whole.

She should be grateful; her heart should be light.

The yawning emptiness within her grew colder and ached.

A squeak from a distant violin broke through her thoughts, made her blink and refocus on Mr. Barton, who'd been laboring through a description of the latest play at the Theatre Royal. The three gentlemen shot glances at one another. She dragged in a breath, dragooned her wits into action—anything to avoid an invitation to waltz. "What was your sister's opinion of the play, sir?"

Mr. Barton put great store in his sister's opinions; chest inflating, he was about to launch forth when something behind her caught his eye.

He blinked. Mouth open, his words dying on his tongue, he stared.

Pris glanced at the other two; they'd followed the direction of Barton's fixed gaze and were now staring, apparently dumbstruck, too.

It would be rude, and too obvious, to swing around and look, yet it appeared that whatever—whoever—was occasioning the gentlemen's consternation was approaching, drawing nearer.

Then she felt it—a ruffling of her senses, like a hand stroking the air a mere breath from her skin.

Felt the touch, the burning caress of his gaze on her nape, fully exposed by her gown and upswept hair.

She hauled in a breath, and swung around.

Her heart leapt. Her traitorous senses teetered, ready to swoon.

He was there. Right behind her, large as life. Darker and more sinfully handsome than she recalled.

One step, and she would be in his arms.

The battle not to take that step nearly slew her; she literally swayed.

He took her hand—she wasn't aware she'd offered it—and bowed, an abbreviated gesture that shrieked of closeness, of something a great deal more than mere acquaintance.

His eyes had searched her face; now they fixed on hers. She couldn't read his, dark and impenetrable, could read nothing in his rigidly impassive expression.

The feel of his fingers closing warm and strong about hers effortlessly locked every iota of her consciousness on him.

"What are you doing here?" The only question that mattered; the only question to which she needed an answer.

One dark brow arched. He held her gaze. "Can't you guess?"

She frowned. "No."

The violins interrupted with the prelude to a waltz. He looked up—over her head at the three gentlemen she'd completely forgotten. Recalling her manners, she shifted so her back was no longer to them, just in time to hear Dillon say, "If you'll excuse us, gentlemen?"

No real question. Camberleigh, Barton, and Halliwell all blinked.

Pris blinked, too—at the wealth of confident, arrogant assumption carried in his tone. Temper sparking, she swung to face him—only to find him, now at her side, winding her arm in his, settling her hand on his sleeve.

And leading her to the dance floor.

She tried to catch his eye, but he was looking ahead, steering her through the guests. She tried to halt. Smoothly, he changed his hold on her arm and stepped back—so he was half behind her, herding her with his body through the crowd.

The thought of stopping and letting him run into her sent shivers down her spine; she bundled it out of her mind. Physical resistance was clearly not an option.

"I haven't agreed to waltz with you." She hissed the words over her shoulder as they approached the dance floor.

For an instant, he didn't reply, then his breath caressed her ear. "You haven't refused . . . and you won't."

Her breath hitched; she fought to quell a reactive shiver—one of pure, anticipatory pleasure. Arguing was clearly not an option either. Not if she wished to hold on to her wits, and she had the distinct impression she was going to need them.

That was confirmed the instant he swept her into his arms and into the sea of swirling couples thronging the floor. It was the middle of the evening, the crowd at its height; they should have been anonymous amid the revolving horde.

Of course, they were anything but. Alone, each of them drew eyes; together, they could, and were, transfixing the entire crowd, even some of their fellow dancers.

Not that she had eyes, or ears, or wits for anyone else.

He looked down at her, his expression unreadable, his eyes the same. He was waltzing very correctly, not taking advantage of the dance as he might have to tantalize her senses and addle her brain.

Her senses were tantalized anyway, but at least her wits remained hers.

Keeping her expression outwardly serene, she let a frown infuse her eyes. "You haven't answered my question."

"Which question is that?"

His tone—one of drawling male arrogance—seemed designed to prick her temper. Suspecting that might indeed be the case, she met his gaze steadily. "Why are you here?"

The answer came back, not in that irritating tone but in his usual deep voice, as if it were the most obvious thing in the world. "I came for you."

She stared into his eyes, fell into the beckoning darkness; the world was spinning—she wasn't at all sure it was due only to the dance. "Why?"

"Because I haven't finished with you—I want more from you."

She felt the blood drain from her face, but forced herself to continue to meet his dark eyes. "No. What we had in Newmarket—it ended there. A clean break, a finite end. You shouldn't have come, shouldn't have followed me."

"But I did. I have."

There was something—some edging of tone, some elusive light in his dark eyes—that set her senses on full alert.

He seemed to see it; smoothly, he gathered her in for a tight turn, bent his head, and whispered in her ear, "And I would suggest this is not a wise time or place to pretend you don't want me."

She turned her head. Their faces were close, their lips mere inches apart. She looked into his eyes, at this range nearly black, still unfathomable. "What are you doing?"

His lips curved lightly. Unbidden, her gaze dropped to them; she realized and hauled it back to his eyes.

"As you've been so assiduous in reminding me, it was you who first seduced me." He held her gaze. "Now it's my turn."

Her lungs had stopped functioning; it was an effort to find breath enough to whisper back, "I don't want to be seduced."

One dark brow arched. Straightening as their revolutions took them down the room, he calmly stated, "I don't believe you have a choice."

Temper was such a useful emotion; she let it fill her, let it infuse her eyes, her glare, while keeping the rest of her expression serene. "I suspect you'll discover you're mistaken."

His other brow rose to join the first; his disgustingly confident male arrogance was back. "Are you willing to put that to the test?"

No! Innate caution leapt to catch her tongue, to grab back the gauntlet her temper—and he—had very nearly goaded her into flinging at his feet.

"I believe," she returned, in her haughtiest, iciest tone, "that I can live without that particular amusement."

The final chords of the waltz sounded. He whirled her to a halt, smiled as he raised her hand to his lips. "We'll see."

Battling to ignore the warmth that spread from the contact, the lingering touch of his lips on her fingers, a subtle seduction in itself, she turned away, glanced around. "I should return to Eugenia."

He looked over the heads. "She's over there."

Somewhat to her surprise, he led her straight to her aunt, seated on a chaise to one side of the room with Lady Horatia Cynster and the beautiful and intriguing Dowager Duchess of St. Ives. Pris set eyes on the three ladies with relief; in their company, she was sure to be safe.

Her first intimation that that might not be the case came when all three ladies saw Dillon by her side. Eugenia positively beamed; Lady Horatia and the Dowager welcomed him effusively. Standing beside him, Pris heard their teasing, lightly arch comments—and had to fight not to stare.

They were *encouraging* him!

She managed to keep her mouth from falling open. She caught enough of the assessing glances all three ladies sent her way, understood enough of the subtle prods couched in their repartee to realize that safety did not lie with them.

Glancing around, she saw Rus standing a little to one side, Adelaide, as ever, beside him. She'd saved her twin; now he could save her.

Sliding her hand from Dillon's arm—registering that his attention immediately swung her way—she kept her sweet, innocuous smile in place and bobbed a curtsy to the three ladies. "I must speak with my brother."

Two steps—and Dillon had excused himself and was on her heels. She'd expected nothing else, but his speed confirmed that the older ladies were on his side.

How had he managed to outflank her with them, gain their support, and all before she'd even known he was in town? What had he told them?

Her mind seized, but then her wits reengaged. He wouldn't have told them all—all was too shocking; they wouldn't have been so openly approving of him and his suit. He might have allowed them to guess how close he and she had grown without being specific . . . she inwardly grimaced. She knew enough of tonnish life to know that he might not even have had to do that.

On all counts, he and she would make an excellent

match. And promoting excellent matches was the principal activity of the senior ladies of the ton.

Reaching her brother, she smiled, with a gesture indicated the prowling figure beside her. "Dillon's arrived."

Rus grinned at the devil and offered his hand. "Excellent."

There was something, some element in the glance Dillon and her brother exchanged as they shook hands that jarred her nerves, that had her looking sharply from one to the other.

But no, she reassured herself. He couldn't have corrupted her twin.

Two minutes was enough to assure her he had.

Adelaide, of course, beamed at Dillon, entirely content given she had Rus beside her. For his part, Rus had quickly realized that in this arena, he didn't need to shield Adelaide, but she could, and would, shield him; he'd been quick to avail himself of her services.

If Pris hadn't had good reason to believe Rus's interest, until now predictably fickle, was well on the way to becoming permanently engaged, she might have entertained some concern for Adelaide. As matters stood, the only one she was left feeling concerned about was herself. Astonishing though it was, even Rus and Adelaide seemed to believe that Dillon and she . . .

She would have to talk to Rus and explain the whole.

But before she could drag her brother aside, the damned musicians struck up. Rus turned to Adelaide, and with a certain glint in his eye, invited her to share a country dance with him.

Adelaide accepted, and with smiles they whisked off. Pris watched them go, a frown in her eyes. Her brother was . . . engrossed. Enthralled. Busy. Engaged in an enterprise she didn't wish to interrupt, or disrupt.

She could, she was sure, regardless of how Dillon appeared to him, convince Rus that her best interests lay in avoiding him, but . . . did she really want to, just at this moment, focus her not-always-predictable twin on her less-than-happy state?

Dillon had remained beside her; she could feel his gaze on her face. He hadn't asked her to dance, for which she was grateful. It was a Sir Roger de Coverly, involving lots of whirling in each other's arms, and she knew beyond doubt that she'd be giddy—seriously giddy with her defenses in tatters—by the end of it. He would know that, too . . . she glanced suspiciously up at him.

He met her look blankly, and inclined his head down the room. "Your father's over there."

Her *father*? She couldn't believe it, but had to find out. Regally accepting Dillon's arm, she allowed him to steer her through the unrelenting crowd.

Lord Kentland turned from the gentlemen he'd been conversing with just as they came up. Seeing them, he beamed.

"Caxton!" He clasped Dillon's hand, smiling delightedly as he shook it, then looked at Pris, his pleasure and pride in her—her appearance, her presence, everything about her—transparent.

Dillon hadn't been sure how the earl would choose to play this scene. After a moment, Kentland glanced at him, a direct and challenging gleam in his eye. "Glad you're here, my boy. Now you can watch over her." He glanced around at the crowd, at the rakes, roués, and assorted wolves of the ton dotted among the ranks, all of whom had noticed Pris, then looked back at Dillon. "I've gray hairs enough."

Dillon let his lips curve, but it wasn't in a smile. "I'll do my best, sir."

Kentland clapped him on the shoulder. "I'm sure you will."

He looked at his daughter; Dillon didn't need to glance her way to know she was staring, all but openmouthed, incredulous and disbelieving, at her father. Stunned by his defection, or so she would view it.

Kentland, however, was made of stern stuff. Ignoring the incipient ire, and the *Et tu, Brute?* accusation flaring in her eyes, he smiled and nodded at her. "I'll see you later. Enjoy your evening, my dear." He looked up, and signaled to an acquaintance. "Yes, Horace, I'm coming."

With a nod and a bow, the earl headed for the card room.

Dillon watched him go. From beside him came silence. Complete and utter silence.

As Pris no doubt now suspected, he'd had a busy day. After driving down from Newmarket, he'd left his bags and his horses in Berkeley Square, in Highthorpe's, Horatia's butler's, care, and had gone posthaste to Half Moon Street. As he'd devoutly hoped, the ladies had been out at some luncheon, but Lord Kentland and his heir had been in. It was the earl with whom Dillon had requested an interview.

Adhering to the principle that the truth would serve him best, he'd given his lordship as much of it as was wise. While he hadn't stated in so many words how close he and Pris had grown, the earl was man of the world enough to fill in the gaps—and as had quickly become clear, his lordship was well acquainted with his daughter's character, with her wild, willful, and passionate ways.

That to the earl it was a relief to be able to hand his daughter into the care of someone who actually understood her had slowly dawned; by the time he'd left the study in which their discussion had taken place, Dillon had understood that the earl was counting on him to succeed in overcoming any and all resistance, to one way or another sweep his twenty-four-year-old headstrong daughter off her feet. The earl fully comprehended that his path to success might involve meetings of a nature of which society would not normally approve; assured of Dillon's commitment and intent, his lordship had dismissed such risks as necessary to the cause.

Paternal approval and more, outright encouragement, were his.

He'd had his card taken up to Rus, who'd come quickly down to join him. The earl had passed them in the front hall. While his lordship headed to White's, Rus had been eager to visit Boodle's, of which Dillon was a member. Along the way, Dillon had explained the situation between himself and Pris, much as he had with their father. Even more forthrightly than his sire, Rus had accepted Dillon's proposed suit for his sister's hand and pledged his aid.

It was only later, when he'd been dressing for the evening, that Dillon had realized that Rus's encouragement meant rather more than the norm. Rus and Pris shared that special link twins possessed, and Rus had been convinced, even before Dillon had spoken, that Pris belonged with him.

He'd set out to find her more confident of success than when he'd driven into town. The first necessary elements of his strategy were in place.

When laying siege, the first requirement was to cut off all escape.

Glancing down at Pris, he wasn't surprised to discover a seriously black frown on her face; she slowly turned and aimed it at him, emerald gaze sharpening to twin arrow points as she narrowed her eyes.

A fraught moment passed, then with awful calm, she stated, "If you'll excuse me?"

Glacial ice encased the words; with a distant nod, she turned away.

He reached out and shackled her wrist. Met the green fire of her furious glance as she swung back to face him, ready to annihilate him. "Where to?"

Lips thin, she drew in a breath, breasts rising ominously beneath the abbreviated bodice of her aqua silk gown. "To the withdrawing room." She breathed the words on a rising current of seething anger.

It was the one place he couldn't follow her.

Pointedly, she glanced down at his fingers, locked about her wrist. He uncurled them, released her.

Without another glance at him, she swished her skirts around and glided, with quite lethal grace, to the nearest door.

Dillon stood and watched her. As she passed out of the ballroom, his lips slowly curved—this time, in a smile.

Pris had no need to use the withdrawing room's amenities, nor had she any torn flounce or trailing lace to pin up. There were a number of mirrors propped about the room; she stood before one, pretending to readjust the curls tumbling in artful disarray from the knot on the top of her head.

Pausing, she looked at her reflection—looked dispassionately, and considered what others saw. A lady of medium height, her features dramatic and arresting, her black hair gleaming, her full lips rosy red, her slender but distinctly curvaceous figure encased in aqua silk, the coruscating hues created with every movement reminiscent of the shifting sea.

Pulling a face at the sight, at her bosom mounding above the low-cut, tightly fitting bodice, she wished that, on coming to London, she'd thought to resurrect her bluestocking look. That might at least have spared her the most deadening aspect of her emergence into the ton's ballrooms—the relegation to superficial young miss, to being nothing more than a face and a body in gentlemen's eyes.

They certainly looked, but they didn't see.

They looked at her face and saw only her perfect features.

They looked at her figure and saw only her sumptuous breasts, the evocative and graceful lines of her hips and thighs, her long legs.

They didn't see her. Not as Dillon saw her . . .

For a long moment she stared at the mirror, then, lips tightening, she turned away. She was not going to weaken in this; she wouldn't alter her stance, not even for him. If she couldn't find it in her to harden her heart against him, then she'd simply have to harden her head—and think faster and more quickly than he.

She caught a few glances from the other ladies, many of whom had entered after she had. She couldn't hide here, and she was simply too noticeable to fade into the background, for instance in the card room.

An instant's consideration warned that if she waited too long, Dillon would ask Adelaide to come and check on her. That would be embarrassing.

Resolutely she headed for the door. There had to be some other way.

The door closed behind her; pausing in the poorly lit corridor, she looked along it to where, twenty yards away, light and gaiety spilled through the ballroom doors giving onto the foyer at the head of the main stairs.

There was no one in sight. A situation that wouldn't last long. She could hear ladies' voices in the withdrawing room; soon, they'd step out and return to the ball.

She swung around. Beyond the withdrawing room the corridor was unlit. A little way along, it reached a corner, then turned down a wing.

Glancing back, she confirmed that she was still alone in the corridor. The sound of ladies approaching the door at her back decided her; lifting her skirts, she hurried away from the ballroom. The withdrawing room door opened, and a wash of chatter rolled out just as she slipped around the corner.

Into darkness, and peace.

She started down what she guessed would be a wing of bedchambers. Behind her, the ladies' voices faded and died. She glanced back—and halted.

And smiled; she could barely believe her luck. The other side of the wing, beyond the main corridor from where she stood, ended in a room, recessed so its door wasn't visible from the main corridor. The door to that room stood open; faint light glowed from within.

Such rooms were often left prepared in case a lady needed to retire in privacy and peace.

A lady such as herself; in the circumstances, she felt she qualified.

Retracing her steps, she peeked around the corner. She waited until two giggling young ladies disappeared through the withdrawing room door, then scurried across the corridor to the recessed door, and her haven.

Quietly, in case some other lady was already there, she walked in. It was a small parlor with two large armchairs angled before the hearth. A fire burned in the grate, more for show than for warmth. On a side table against the wall, a lamp was turned low; it shed enough light to see that neither chair was occupied.

She heaved a sigh of relief and quietly closed the door. She looked at the key sitting in its lock, then turned it. The loud click faded, taking with it some of the rather odd panic that had been brewing inside her.

Feeling strangely alone, she walked to the hearth, then, more out of habit than any real need, bent to warm her hands before the blaze.

She sensed him draw near the instant before his palm cupped her bottom and too knowingly caressed.

With a smothered oath, she shot upright—straight into his arms.

He smiled down at her as if she were his next meal. "I wondered how long you'd be."

He turned her more fully into his arms. Stunned, she braced her hands against his chest, drew in a huge breath.

Before she could release it in the tirade he so richly deserved, he bent his head, sealed her lips. And kissed every thought from her head.

Nineteen

He kissed her until she was gasping, until the scent of him, the taste of him, had overwhelmed and seduced her, until she had to cling to him to stay on her feet. The melding of their mouths, the twining of their tongues, was hungry, ravenous—ravishing. Every particle of her parched being seized, clung, and yearned, drinking him in as voraciously as he did her.

Regardless . . . she retained enough sanity to grasp the moment when his lips slid from hers to feather along her jaw. Sinking her fingers into the hard muscles of his arms, denying the compulsion to slide her arms up and twine her fingers in his hair—and hold him to her—she closed her eyes and whispered, "Let me go."

"No." He gathered her more securely, more fully against him.

Every nerve leapt at the contact. Her head spun as her body reacted to the hard promise of his. But . . . "Why?"

Her most urgent question. She opened her eyes, caught

his, only inches away as he lifted his head. She watched as he studied her, both saw and sensed his search for words, for how to answer with the truth.

Then his lips firmed. "Because you're mine."

The words should have sounded merely dramatic, but his tone made them much more. Even more than a statement of fact—his flat implacability made them a statement of certainty, of life as he saw it.

She caught her breath, searched his eyes, struggled to put a name to what she saw in the dark depths. "This is madness."

He paused, then closed those last few inches. As his lips brushed hers, he murmured, "And more."

Dillon took her mouth again, laid claim to all she couldn't deny him. She was right; having her was a madness, a humor of the blood, an addictive ache that only she could assuage. Having her was a madness he now needed and craved, knowing he could, knowing she would. That no matter her denials, her disbelief, when it came to him and her, together, alone like this, their needs and wants converged and became one.

One compulsion, one hunger, one overwhelming craving to taste the wild and reckless, the soaring, greedy, fiery, all-consuming passion that only with each other could they reach.

Her father had remarked to him that when it came to her, he possessed an advantage no other had ever had—he understood her. Not completely, but in many ways he thought as she did, felt as she did.

Wanted with the same fire and passion that coursed through her wild and reckless soul. And felt the consequent lash of desire every bit as keenly.

In this, always, they were as one. Well matched. The ladies had it right.

Yet even while she met him, matched him, even while he sensed the passion rising and welling and building inside her, he also sensed her confusion, her lack of understanding—her need to understand. Her struggle to hold against the inexorable tide, her innate caution holding her back until she'd learned where he was headed, until she knew what giving herself to him again would mean, until she understood where the road down which he was determined to lead her led.

He could sweep her resistance away; if he wished, he could simply overpower her senses and drive her into intimacy. She might be able to stand against his passion, but not his and hers combined. He knew well enough that telling her simply what his ultimate goal was would only lead to more arguments, to more resistance, not less. If he wanted to win her quickly and surely, before he revealed his goal, he had to establish the truth, as he'd set out from Flick's parlor to do nights before, to state his reality in a way she couldn't misconstrue.

But this was Pris—she, like he, mistrusted words. Deeds spoke louder, and more truly. And that was why he was there, with her alone, so he could show her the truth. So he could start revealing to her what she was to him.

They were both heated, the engagement of lips and tongues no longer sufficient to meet the rapacious hunger spiraling up within them. He spread his hands, let them rove, over her back, over the aqua silk screening her skin.

He felt her responsive shudder to his bones, ached when, against her better judgment, she sank against him, fingers tightening on his lapel as she fought the compulsion to urge him on. Fought to hold on to her wits even while she shifted closer, hips and thighs moving into him, making his control quake.

His fingers found what they were searching for. Her gown laced up the back.

Lifting his head, dragging in a breath, he turned her and drew her back—trapped her against him, her back to his chest.

Her luscious bottom to his groin. He bit back a groan, and concentrated—on her. Raising his hands to her breasts, he closed them, locked her against him as the contact made her gasp, made her momentarily more malleable.

Pris kept her eyes closed and battled to quell the shivers coursing down her spine. She wasn't cold, wasn't in need of more clothes, but less.

He kneaded her breasts, but there was no desperation in his touch, only a knowing confidence, one that screamed of how well he knew that each evocative caress sank into her mind, captured her senses, weakened her will.

Before she could gather her wits and respond—resist, break away—one hard hand left her already aching breast. His chest shifted back. A second later, she felt the quick, deft tugs as he unpicked her laces.

Why was he here? Why was he doing this—what did he hope to achieve?

Her mind wasn't sure; her heated body didn't care.

But she knew she should say something, do something, before—

Her bodice gaped; the tiny off-the-shoulder sleeves weren't designed to hold it up. Drawing her fully back against him again, he slid one hand beneath the loose silk, tugged down the gathered top of her chemise, and lifted first one breast, then the other, free.

She sucked in a tight breath, had to lean back against him, had to grip the long muscles of his thighs as the remembered pleasure of his hands and fingers on her naked skin swept through her again. His hands sculpted and shaped. He pandered to her senses, openly, flagrantly, until her breasts were heavy, aching and swollen, firm and sensitive to every seductive touch.

His fingers circled her ruched nipples, then closed, squeezed.

She gasped, and he bent his head, with his lips traced the curve of her ear.

"Open your eyes. The mirror—look."

It took effort, but she raised her lids, looked across the room, and saw what he saw. He was a dark male presence, clothed in black, holding trapped before him a slender siren in aqua silk, her bodice loose and lowered, revealing two creamy flushed mounds that his tanned hands possessed and caressed, as if he had the right, yes, but that wasn't all she felt in his touch.

Wasn't all she saw when she raised her gaze and in the mirror searched his face.

Soft light spilled over them, golden and flickering from the fire, muted and white from the lamp. In that gentle illumination, she both felt and saw something that made her breath catch.

She—the siren—might be trapped and helpless, but . . .

Her breath suspended, her body all his, she watched as he watched her watch him. As he caressed with a reined need that was powerfully reverent, as he worshipped her openly, without disguise.

Every touch, every brush of his fingertips across her taut skin was a testament, a prayer. It wasn't simply the physical but something more ephemeral, as if he valued the needs raging inside her, without question appreciated the wild passion she longed to let free . . .

Her gaze had dropped to his hands; now she looked back at his face, confirmed that he did indeed worship that. The wild compulsive beat in her blood.

No other had ever heard it, let alone responded. No other had ever appreciated it, shared it, as he did.

That was what she read in his face.

That was when she felt the reins of her will start to slide from her grasp.

She dragged in a breath, tried to wrench her senses from the gentle but overpowering seduction. She licked her dry lips. "I don't . . ."

He looked down at his hands. "Want this?" His fingers

found her nipples and squeezed; she closed her eyes on a hiss of pleasure, and he murmured, "Don't lie—you do."

His voice was a dark rumble in her ear. His touch changed, became more flagrantly possessive. "What of this?"

Sudden pressure—burgeoning pleasure—made her gasp.

"Do you know . . . one thing I love about you is how you respond. To every touch, every brush, every caress." He demonstrated, and her shameless body, her witless senses swooned, and proved him right.

"Yes, that." His breath was another caress. "But not only that. With you, with me, it's not just your body that rises and meets mine, that aches and hungers, but your senses, your soul. You come to me, join with me, fly with me." He shifted slightly, his strength surrounding her as one hand left her breast and reached down. "And that's something infinitely more precious."

She heard her skirt rustle, felt it rise, felt the cooler touch of air as he drew the front up. Not in any rush, not bunching and crushing, but carefully sweeping it up and to the side; opening her eyes, she stared, mesmerized, as he released her other breast, draped her raised skirt in the crook of that arm, then his fingers returned to her heated skin, firming around one breast again while his other hand slid beneath the angled hem, and skimmed up one leg.

To the curls at the apex of her thighs. He stroked them once, then reached past, sliding his fingers along the swollen folds, then caressing.

In the mirror, he watched her face. "And this?" His fingers were slick with her arousal; he slid one into her sheath, lightly probed.

She shuddered and closed her eyes.

Felt his lips at her temple, felt his breath against her cheek.

"I didn't tell you before, but I should have . . . this, having you in my arms, feeling you respond to me, is one of the things I most love about you." Between her thighs, his fingers probed; at her breast, his fingers squeezed. At her ear, his voice deepened and roughened, and drew her deeper into his thrall.

"This." And her body answered.

"And this." Her senses quaked.

The deep rumble of his words, explicit and evocative, kept her with him, held her to him—in those heated moments, through the rising flames, showed her herself through his eyes.

A revelation that made her ache. That made her want with a need she'd felt before but only now understood, only now saw for what it was.

And in that, he was right. She did want him—would always want him. Would always want to give herself to him in just this way—not just to please him, but to take for herself the joy of knowing she could, that she did.

His hands caressed, his voice ensnared, but it was her own needs that flamed within her. That drove her passion to ever wilder heights.

And she knew. She might have the strength to deny him, but once he'd stirred her senses and given them passionate life, she didn't possess the will to deny them.

She couldn't, now he'd revealed something of his fascination with her, quench the drive to know more—to take him into her body once more and experience again the connection . . . knowing what she now knew.

If she could understand what that connection was, what gave it its power, she would know what to do, how to deal with it. How to conquer it.

That, unquestionably, was what she most urgently needed to know.

Her body started to coil, to tighten—but she needed him inside her, needed the physical joining to reveal the ephemeral.

As if he heard her thoughts, his stroking eased, slowed.

Eyes still closed, she sensed his hesitation before he asked, his voice gravelly with desire, "Do you want me inside you?"

She opened her eyes, across the room met his in the mirror. "Yes." She held his gaze for a second, then boldly asked, "How?"

The abruptness of his response spoke volumes. His hands left her; he urged her to an armchair—a high-seated wing chair. "Kneel on that—be careful not to crush your skirt."

She could only just make out his words; she wasn't the only one at the mercy of their shared passion. Lifting her skirt, she clambered up onto the seat, dropping the aqua silk over her knees.

"Lean forward and hold on to the top."

His hands at her waist steadied her; when her fingers curved about the carved wooden edge, he released her and lifted the back of her skirt.

They were at an angle to the mirror; turning her head, she watched as he flipped her skirt over her waist, saw his face as his hands made contact with her bare bottom, as thumbs and palms caressed, then, still engrossed, he reached blindly for the buttons at his waist.

Two flicks, and his erection sprang free.

She caught her breath, held it, eyes wide as he guided the thick rod between her thighs . . . as she felt the broad head part her slick, throbbing flesh, as she watched his face as his lids fell, as he slowly, with blatantly reined strength, eased his way inside her. Then he thrust home.

She lost her breath on a gasp. The passion she'd held back rose and roared within her, howled and kicked as she clamped around him, embraced him, welcomed him.

For one instant, he held still, his thighs to her bare bottom, his face etched with passion, with ravening desire—and something more. Something starker, more powerful, more elemental.

More important.

For that one instant, she stared, drinking in the sight, trying to fathom just what it was that held him so effortlessly.

Then he dragged in a huge breath, withdrew, and returned. Her breath shuddered; her lids fell.

And she gave herself over to him, to pleasing him, and pleasing herself.

To being pleasured to oblivion.

Thoroughly.

Twice.

Pris woke the next morning, and stretched languidly beneath the covers. Relaxing, she lay there, wallowing in the lingering aftermath of the glory that had, last night, coursed her veins.

She'd missed it, missed this feeling of wonderful wholeness, of completion. Of feeling female in the most all-encompassing sense.

Last night . . . he'd held her, and loved her, gently cradled her until she'd recovered enough to stand, then he'd set her bodice to rights, smoothed her skirts down, and escorted her back to the ballroom.

No one, it seemed, had missed them. She'd had no idea how much time had elapsed, but not one *grande dame* directed so much as a cocked eyebrow their way. She wasn't entirely sure what that meant, but she was twenty-four, an age by which society expected ladies of her station to wed.

And within the ton, dalliance was an accepted part of the rituals leading to the altar.

Frowning, she drummed her fingers on the comforter. She would need to bear that in mind—that help in avoiding Dillon would likely not be all that forthcoming. She couldn't—patently could not—rely on society to erect hurdles in his path.

Of course, now her biggest problem was that she was no longer sure of his path. After last night . . .

They'd parted in Lady Trenton's front hall; she'd uttered not one word of warning or reproach—either would have been hypocritical, and given his temper where she was concerned, so much wasted breath.

She hadn't missed the honesty—the raw reality—of his desire for her. Or hers for him. However, he'd said not one word about marriage.

So what was his direction now?

All he'd said was that he would see her today.

With a humph, she threw back the covers and rose. Briskly washing, then dressing, she glanced at the clock. Eleven o'clock. She stopped. Stared. *Eleven?*

She glanced at the window, paused to listen to the noises about the house. "Damn!" She'd slept in.

Grumbling, she rushed through her toilette.

Her immediate goal where Dillon was concerned seemed obvious enough. Until she knew what he was about, she would do well to avoid him, or at least avoid situations in which they would be alone.

Despite the forces arrayed against her, she was her own woman; she remained determined to dictate her own life. She was not going to marry any man who didn't love her. Regardless of their beliefs, the ton would simply have to swallow that fact.

Primed for battle, she went downstairs, wondering a little at the silence. She turned into the dining parlor—and saw Dillon seated at the table.

Halting, she stared. She hadn't expected any action before breakfast!

His chair was pushed back from the table, a coffee cup by his elbow. Lowering the news sheet he'd been perusing, he smiled. "Good morning." His gaze swept over her mint green gown. His smile deepened. "I trust you slept well."

She waited until his gaze returned to her face to blandly state, "I did, thank you. What are you doing here?"

"Waiting for you." He waved her to the sideboard.

Reluctant though she was to take her eyes from him, she went. "Where are the others?"

"They left fifteen minutes ago in Flick's barouche. I have my curricle—we're to meet them in the park."

She glanced at him; his attention had returned to the news sheet. The ham smelled wonderful; she helped herself to two slices, then returned to the table and sat opposite him. The butler appeared with a fresh pot of tea and a rack of warm toast; she thanked him, and settled to eat.

Adult males, she knew, rarely chatted over the breakfast cups; content enough with Dillon's silence, she applied herself to assuaging an appetite in large part due to him.

The instant she lifted her napkin to her lips, he folded the news sheet and set it aside. "I'll check on my horses. Come out when you're ready."

She inclined her head and rose as he did. It felt strange, walking out to the hall side by side, without ceremony parting at the foot of the stairs . . . as she reached her bedchamber, she realized what she meant by "strange." Domesticated. As if he and she . . .

Frowning, she opened the door and went in to don her bonnet and pelisse.

She was still frowning inwardly when she went down the front steps, ready to pounce on any uncalled-for, too-possessive action he might think to make. Instead, while their private interactions—his comments, her replies as he tooled them through the streets of Mayfair—remained at a level that attested to their intimacy, his outward actions were impossible to fault. He behaved with unwavering propriety, as a gentleman should to an unmarried lady of his class.

She was still wondering what he was up to—not just what his direction was but what fiendishly arrogant steps he might take to steer her down it—when he guided his pair through the gates of the park. They bowled along under the trees, but then the Avenue, lined with the carriages of the fashionable, hove into sight, and he had to check his team.

They were the same beautiful blacks she'd admired in Newmarket; Dillon held them to a slow trot as they tacked between the stationary carriages and the smaller curricles and phaetons that passed up and down the crowded stretch.

"Flick's carriage is royal blue. See if you can spot it."

She looked around. When other ladies saw her, and smiled and nodded, she responded in kind. They seemed to be attracting a significant amount of attention, but then it was her, him, and his horses all together. She glanced at him, took in his many-caped greatcoat hanging open over a coat of black superfine, a gold-and-black-striped waistcoat and tight buckskin breeches that disappeared into glossy Hessians, and had to admit, all together, they must present quite a sight. Something akin to an illustration in the *Ladies Journal*—"*fashionable lady and gentleman driving in the park.*"

"What's so amusing?"

His words brought her back to the moment, to the realization she'd been smiling to herself. "Just . . ." He glanced at her; she met his eyes, mentally shrugged. "Just the picture we must make." Looking ahead, she nodded at the ladies in the carriages before them. "We're creating quite a stir."

Dillon merely inclined his head; inwardly, he grinned. They were creating a stir for a more potent reason than their glamorous appearance. He didn't, however, feel any great need to explain that, not yet.

Indeed, if ever. From the point of attaining his goal, there were some things it might be better she never learned.

He saw a flash of blue ahead. "There they are—to the left."

The space beside Flick's carriage was just wide enough for him to ease his curricle into. He'd borrowed one of Demon's London grooms as a tiger; consigning the blacks to his care, he rounded the curricle and handed Pris down.

Eugenia and Flick were settled in the carriage. As he and Pris drew near, Rus assisted Adelaide to the lawn.

As soon as Pris had greeted Eugenia and Flick, Adelaide, all but bubbling with exuberance, said, "We've been waiting to stroll the lawns."

Pris had to smile at her eagerness. "Yes, of course. Shall we?"

She looked at the carriage, received Eugenia's approving nod, then turned—and found Dillon waiting to offer his arm. She hesitated for only an instant before laying her hand on his sleeve. It was only a walk in the park, after all.

A walk she frankly enjoyed. Strolling with just Dillon, Rus, and Adelaide was relaxing; she didn't have to be on guard socially. Although other couples and groups crossed their path, all merely exchanged greetings, swapped comments on the weather or the entertainments they expected to attend that evening, then moved on.

Following Rus and Adelaide down the gravel path that led to the banks of the Serpentine, it was on the tip of her tongue to mention that yesterday, she'd had to fight off the gentlemen, both the eligible and the not-so-eligible, when caution, and suspicion, caught her tongue.

She glanced at Dillon; while she might know what lurked beneath his urbanity, there was nothing in his appearance as he gazed about to declare his possessiveness. Nothing she could see that could possibly be warning other gentlemen away—off, as if he owned her.

He sensed her gaze, turned his head, and caught her eyes. Arched a dark brow.

She looked ahead to where the slate waters of the lake rippled beneath the breeze. "I was just thinking how pleasant it was to walk in the fresh air." She glanced at him. "I haven't walked this way, or so far, before. Indeed, yesterday there were so many around, I got barely ten yards from the carriage."

Dillon kept his smile easy and assured. "One day, a few appearances at balls, can make a big difference in the ton. Once people know who you are . . ."

She tilted her head, and seemed to accept the suggestion.

He studied her face, then looked ahead, and reiterated his earlier wisdom. There was absolutely no sense in explaining just how the good ladies and the interested gentlemen were interpreting his driving her in the park, and strolling with her over the lawns, at least not yet, not given the suspicion he'd glimpsed in her eyes.

After the standard half hour, he gathered Rus and Adelaide and steered the three back to the waiting carriages.

Flick beamed at him; she was thrilled to her teeth that he was behaving as he was. He could only pray she didn't do anything to give Pris's nascent suspicions some direction.

"Celia's?" He did his best to distract Flick as Rus handed Adelaide into the carriage. He kept his hand over Pris's on his sleeve.

"Yes." Flick glanced at Eugenia, who smiled at him.

"Lady Celia insisted that we impose on you—her very words were: be *sure* to bring him, too."

Dillon had no difficulty believing that. "In that case, Pris and I will follow in my curricle."

Flick waved. "Go ahead. Your horses will hate to be held back behind us."

He looked down at Pris. "Would you rather travel in the carriage?"

The look she bent on him was measuring. Turning, she surveyed his blacks. "Flick's horses are well enough, but given the choice, I prefer yours."

They parted from the others. He led her to the curricle

and helped her up to the seat. He was climbing up to sit beside her when she asked, "Can I handle the ribbons?"

He grasped the reins and sat beside her. "Only after I die."

She narrowed her eyes at him. "I'm perfectly proficient."

"Really?"

While they rattled over the London streets, she tried to persuade him to entrust his prize cattle with their velvet mouths to her. In vain.

She was distinctly huffy when he drew up outside Lady Celia Cynster's house, but the gathering inside distracted her.

He found it distracting, too; he was constantly on pins that one of the assembled ladies—those of the wider Cynster clan as well as many of their connections and a significant collection of their bosom-bows—would make some comment that would alert Pris to his strategy. While the ladies certainly saw and understood it, and were quick to twit him over it, while those like Horatia, Helena, and Honoria came tantalizingly close to saying one word too many in Pris's hearing, all deigned to let him escape. For the moment.

The implication was obvious. They expected action. They expected success.

"The truth," he growled, in response to Flick's query regarding progress, specifically his, "is that I'd rather be reporting to the Jockey Club Committee on yet another substitution scam—one I had no notion existed—than face this inquisition if I fail."

Flick arched her brows at him. "But you aren't going to fail, are you?"

"No. But a trifle less pressure would be appreciated."

She grinned and patted his arm. "Gentlemen like you respond best to artfully applied pressure."

She swanned off before, astonished, he could reply.

"Artful?" he grumbled to Vane, Flick's brother-in-law,

when he unexpectedly appeared. "They're as artful as Edward I—the Hammer of the Scots."

Vane grinned. "We've all had to live through it. We survived. No doubt you will, too."

"One can but hope," Dillon muttered, as Pris came up to join them.

He introduced her to Vane. Straightening from his bow, Vane shot him an intrigued glance—as if he now understood Dillon's uncertainty. None of those who'd run the Cynster ladies' gauntlet before had had to deal with a lady quite like Pris.

One in whom the wild and reckless held quite so much sway.

"I wanted to congratulate you"—Vane included them both, and Rus nearby, in his glance—"on your success in bringing the substitution racket to such a resounding end. It was a significant risk, so Demon tells me, but from all I'm hearing, the results have been extraordinary."

"What have you heard?" Pris asked.

Vane smiled at her. Watching, Dillon noted that the legendary Cynster charm had no discernible effect on Pris; she waited, patently undeflected. Vane glanced briefly at Dillon, so fleetingly Dillon was sure Pris didn't catch his infinitesimal nod.

Looking back at her, choosing his words with a care Dillon appreciated, Vane replied, "The atmosphere in the gentlemen's clubs is one of open glee. Further down the social scale, there's much nodding and wise comments, and a gratifying spreading of the word to beware of being drawn into such schemes."

Glancing at Dillon, he continued, "Lower still, and comments are rather hotter and a great deal sharper. It's like a seething cauldron, with everyone looking for who to blame."

Dillon raised his brows. "No word on who that is?"

"None that I've heard, although there's quite an army searching." Vane looked across the room. "But here's one who might have some light to shed on that."

Turning, Pris beheld yet another tall, elegant, patently dangerous gentleman. All the Cynster males seemed to be cast from the same mold; glancing back at Dillon while they waited for the other to finish greeting Lady Celia—from her comments he was one of her sons, by name Rupert—Pris found no difficulty seeing Dillon as part of the crew.

The same elegance—languid in repose, like a sated cat, but that could change in a flash to a hard-edged ruthlessness that the outer cloak of civilized behavior did little to mute or disguise. The same strength, not just of muscle and bone, although that was plainly there, but a strength of purpose, of decision and execution.

She narrowed her eyes at the pair of them—Dillon and Vane—trying to put her finger on the other similarity that hovered at the edge of her perception. The same . . . was it protectiveness?

Glancing across at the newcomer, she saw that same element in him; as he detached from his mother and made his way toward them the description came to her as an image without words—a knight fully armored, sword drawn. Not in aggression, but in defense.

Knights sworn to defend. That's how they appeared to her.

All three, including Dillon.

"Lady Priscilla?" The newcomer reached for her hand, and she surrendered it. He bowed. "Gabriel Cynster." He nodded to Dillon and Vane. "I have news—not as much as I'd hoped, but something."

"I was just telling Lady Priscilla and Dillon that the underworld is seething."

Gabriel's gaze remained on Vane's face for an instant, then switched to Dillon's. After a fractional hesitation, he said, "I see. Well." He smiled at Pris. "What I have to report tallies with that."

Pris listened as Gabriel—whose mother called him Rupert, just as Vane's mother called him Spencer and Demon was Harry; there was doubtless some story there, but she'd yet to hear it—described how his contacts in the world of finance had confirmed that numerous criminal figures had been badly singed if not terminally burned by the collapse of the substitution scam.

"Boswell is under the hatches and unlikely to resurface, and at least three others are close to plunging underwater permanently, too. While no one is openly cheering, many, including the new police force, are exceedingly pleased."

Neither Gabriel, Vane, nor Dillon appeared quite as thrilled as she'd expected. Indeed, they all looked a trifle grim.

"Whoever was behind the scam, they've taken a good portion of London's criminals down with them. Some will survive; others won't. All, however, will want revenge." Gabriel cocked a brow at Dillon. "Any word from Adair?"

"Not yet. He's out of town, hot on the trail of Mr. Gilbert Martin, supposedly of Connaught Place."

Vane humphed. "For Martin's sake, let's hope Adair and the police catch up with him first."

Pris had remained silent throughout, judging it wise to leave those protective instincts she'd sensed unstirred. She'd been expecting them to try to exclude her; instead, she'd caught Dillon's surreptitious signal to Vane that he could speak freely in front of her.

She appreciated that. Appreciated the fact he hadn't sought to treat her like a child, to be protected and cosseted and patted on the head and told to go and play with her dolls. She knew there were dangerous people involved in the substitution scam; she hadn't, however, until Gabriel had spoken so soberly, understood just how dangerous they were.

Instincts of her own were stirring, even before Vane glanced at Dillon, and said, voice low so the ladies around them wouldn't hear, "One thing. While I was trawling for news, I heard your name often. If not general knowledge yet, it's at least widely known that you were the crucial player in bringing the scam crashing down. Everyone, grudgingly or otherwise, regardless of which side of the street they inhabit, is acknowledging your strategy as brilliant—as just the sort of response the villainous least want to see from the authorities."

Dillon grimaced. "Once the club stewards were told the truth—by Demon, I might add—it was impossible to put the lid back on the pot."

Gabriel shifted. "As matters now stand, you'll need to stay alert."

Dillon met his gaze, then nodded. "I know."

Pris wasn't sure she caught the full implications of that exchange, but Vane nodded, too, then, with his charming smile, gracefully took his leave.

"You might have a word with young Dalloway," Gabriel murmured, "although as far as I know, his involvement has remained unremarked."

"I will," Dillon said. "Come—I'll introduce you."

With her by his side, he led Gabriel to Rus. A few minutes later, they left her brother chatting to Gabriel about horses and his future assisting at Demon's stud.

A number of ladies waylaid them; when they finally won free, she suggested they stroll by the long windows giving onto the gardens.

Few ladies present were interested in horticulture.

She paused to gaze out at a manicured lawn. "Mr. Cynster intimated there was some threat . . . ?"

Halting beside her, Dillon replied, "Not a specific threat—a potential one." He caught her questioning gaze, lightly grimaced. "Now it's become known that I engineered the collapse of Martin's scheme, it's possible those who've suffered major losses might feel moved to revenge, and in the absence of Martin, or even after they've dealt with him, there's a chance they'll lash out."

"At you?" She searched his dark eyes, calm as night-shrouded pools; she didn't like the cold, deadening sensation that had locked about her heart. "That's . . . *monstrous*! They took a risk—if they lost, they should . . ."

Dillon smiled ruefully. "Be gentlemen enough to accept their losses?" Once, he'd been naïve enough to think the same.

But her outrage on his behalf warmed his heart, and his smile, as he lifted her fingers to his lips, and kissed. "Unfortunately not, but don't worry about them." He brushed her fingertips again and saw her mind shift focus, watched her eyes fix on his lips. He let his smile deepen. "You've enough on your plate."

She blinked, lifted her gaze, narrowed her eyes at him, but he merely smiled imperturbably and turned her back into the room. And set himself to distract her until she forgot Gabriel's warning.

He hadn't needed to hear it; he'd already seen the threat. But as he intended to spend every waking hour—and as many of his sleeping hours as possible, too—by Pris's side in the immediate and subsequent future, he would be there to deflect any action against her, which was what Gabriel had meant.

A threat against him he would have viewed with dismissive nonchalance; a threat to him that might evolve into a threat against her was another matter entirely.

Twenty

Pris couldn't believe it. When Dillon at last returned her to Half Moon Street, a hackney carrying Rus and Adelaide following his curricle, it was nearly time to dress for dinner; somehow she'd spent the entire day with him!

At the conclusion of Lady Celia's luncheon, he'd suggested that a visit to the capital, however short, should take in at least some of the more notable sights. As the day had turned cloudy, the wind rising, he'd suggested she, Rus, and Adelaide allow him to show them the museum.

Rus and Adelaide had been keen; she'd seen no reason not to indulge them all, but as she'd allowed Dillon to squire her out of Lady Celia's house, she'd glimpsed a certain satisfaction in the older ladies' faces.

But Dillon's behavior had been faultless, even though he'd remained assiduously by her side; although there'd been moments when her senses had leapt, when his fingers had brushed her silk-twill-covered back, or when he'd lifted her down from his curricle, she could hardly blame him for that. That was her witless senses' fault, not his. And while at times she'd been uncomfortably aware of a flickering of her nerves, of heat beneath her skin, she'd also found it easy to relax in his company—in which Rus and Adelaide had largely left her.

She'd attempted to remonstrate with her brother, in a whispered aside pointedly suggesting that it was unwise for him to slip away with Adelaide out of her chaperoning sight. He'd looked at her as if she were mad, and uttered one word. "Poppycock!" He'd promptly taken Adelaide's arm and headed off to view the Elgin Marbles.

Resigned, she'd remained with Dillon, strolling about a series of exhibits of Egyptian treasures. Somewhat to her surprise, there'd been numerous others strolling about the hall. When she'd commented on the crowd, he'd explained that the recent artifacts from Egypt had caused quite a stir.

She mentally shook herself as he drew his blacks to a halt before the steps to Flick's door. Tossing the reins to the tiger, he climbed down and came around to lift her to the pavement. As usual, when his hands closed about her waist, her breathing suspended, but she was growing used to the effect, enough to disguise it. She smiled up at him. For an instant, as his eyes met hers, held hers, he seemed to sober, to look deeper . . . her heart gave an unexpected flutter, but then he returned her light smile. Releasing her, he escorted her to the door.

Reaching the porch, he rang the bell, then turned to her. Raising her hand, he caught her eyes, brushed her fingertips with his lips, then, smile deepening, he turned her hand and, her gaze still trapped in his, pressed a hotter, distinctly more intimate kiss on the inside of her wrist. *"Au revoir."*

His deep, rumbling tone reverberated through her, an evocative wave that left a sense of empty yearning in its wake.

Releasing her hand, with an elegant nod, he turned as the

hackney carrying Rus and Adelaide drew up behind his curricle. Descending the steps, he made his farewells to them, then leapt to the curricle's box seat, took the reins, glanced her way, smiled and saluted her, then gave his horses the office.

The door at her back had opened. Pris dragged in a breath, turned, and walked into the hall, lecturing her unruly senses to behave and subside.

She listened with half an ear to Adelaide's bright chatter as together they climbed the stairs. As they gained the gallery, she murmured, "It's Lady Hemmings's musicale tonight, isn't it?"

"Yes! I've never been to such an event—Aunt Eugenia said there's to be an Italian soprano, and a tenor, too. Apparently they're all the rage."

Pris smiled noncommittally; she parted from Adelaide at Adelaide's door, then walked on to her own, at the end of the hallway.

An Italian soprano and a tenor; that didn't sound like the sort of entertainment at which gentlemen of Dillon's ilk would be found. Given the state of her treacherous heart, that was undoubtedly just as well.

"Are you truly enjoying this caterwauling?"

Pris started, then turned; she only just managed to keep her jaw from dropping as Dillon sank into the chair beside hers, then struggled to arrange his long legs beneath the chair in the row in front. Flicking open her fan, she raised it, and hissed from behind it, "What are you doing here?"

His dark eyes slid sidelong to meet hers. "I would have thought that was obvious."

When she raised her brows even higher, he nodded to the front of the room where the Italian soprano had launched into her next piece. "I couldn't miss the chance to hear the latest sensation."

"Shhhh!" The lady in front turned and scowled at them.

Pris shut her lips, held back her disbelieving snort. There were a total of five males present, aside from the tenor and the harried accompanist. Of those five, four were clearly fops. And then there was the gentleman beside her.

Not even Adelaide had been able to convince Rus that he should attend.

She glanced at Dillon, mouthed, "Where's Rus?" She'd thought her brother was with him.

He pointed to the lady in front, and mouthed, "Later."

She possessed her soul with very little patience until the soprano had ended her piece.

"He's with Vane at the club," Dillon answered without waiting for her to ask again. "He's safe."

He turned his head and smiled at her, and she wondered if she was.

She summoned a frown. "I thought gentlemen like you never attended"—she glanced at the buxom singer at the front of the room, shuffling sheets of music with the pianist—" 'caterwauling' sessions such as this."

"You're right. We don't. Except on certain defined occasions."

She fixed her eyes on his face. "*What* occasions?"

"When we're endeavoring to impress a lady with the depth of our devotion."

She stared at him. After a moment, she somewhat faintly asked, "You choose the middle of a recital to say something like that?" She had to fight to keep her tone from rising.

He smiled—that untrustworthy smile she was coming to recognize; catching her hand, he fleetingly raised it to his lips. "Of course." He lowered his voice as the pianist rattled the keys. "Here, you can't argue, nor can you run."

The soprano gave voice again. Pris faced forward. He was right. Here, he could say what he wished, and she . . . in the face of his presence, found it very hard to argue.

Assuming she wished to argue. Or run.

Her head was suddenly whirling, and it had nothing to do with the musical contortions the soprano unerringly performed. She'd refused his offer, dictated by honor as it had been. He'd followed her to London, refusing to let her go. Now . . .

Her entire day snapped into sharper focus. The entire day in which he'd remained by her side, demonstrating to everyone who'd seen them—the better part of the ton's ladies—just how intent, how committed he was to having her . . . *as his bride*!

Temper surged. Leopards didn't change their spots; apparently jaguars didn't either. He hadn't changed his mind about marrying her; he'd simply changed his line of attack.

And he'd gained her father's and her twin's approval—and Eugenia's, and everyone else's who mattered. The scales fell from her eyes with a resounding crash, and she suddenly saw it all.

Before her, the soprano shrieked. Pris's eyes narrowed, unseeing; she set her lips. She wasn't going to be bullied into marrying him because he thought she should—because he thought it right and proper—even if the ton, her family, and everyone else thought so, too.

That wasn't enough, not nearly enough. Not enough to hold her, or him.

The singing finally ended; the ladies rose—all noting Dillon's presence, all alert and intrigued. And approving; she saw that in one glance. There was not one person in the entire room who would support her in avoiding him.

No point taking him to task—not there—and she couldn't dismiss him, either, not unless he chose to be dismissed.

She treated him with unreserved iciness; he saw, smiled, and refused to react. Appropriating her hand, then gathering Adelaide, he led them to Eugenia, remained chatting politely, then escorted them downstairs, joined them in the carriage—where he and Eugenia discussed the Egyptian treasures—and ultimately saw the three of them into Flick's house.

Eugenia and Adelaide thanked him for his escort, bade him good night, and started up the stairs.

Pris watched them go, waited until they were out of sight before turning, grimly determined, to face him.

"I'm off to the club to roust your brother." He smiled at her. "I'll make sure he gets safely home."

That smile was the one she didn't trust—the one that reminded her of a hunting cat. And his gaze was serious, direct, and far too intent for her peace of mind. She drew herself up, clasped her hands before her, drew in a breath—

His lashes lowered; he tweaked his cuffs. "What room has Flick given you—the one at the end of the wing?"

She blinked, effectively distracted. "Yes . . . how did you know?"

Dillon raised his brows. "A lucky guess."

A predictable guess. When he'd reached Horatia's house, there'd been a packet waiting, addressed to him in Flick's neat hand. It had contained a key—one he'd looked at, puzzled; he'd had a key to Flick's front door for years. Seeing his confusion, Horatia had informed him that Flick had left the key to make amends for whisking the Dalloways to London; she'd believed it would prove useful.

The truth had dawned. The key was to Flick's side door—the one beside the stairs at the end of the wing.

He'd been shocked, especially when Horatia had seen his comprehension and smiled. They were shameless, the lot of them, but . . .

It was his turn to smile shamelessly—at Pris. "I'll see you later."

With a nod, he turned to the front door.

"What . . . ? Wait!"

Glancing around, confirming they were alone, Pris

started after him, reaching to catch his sleeve. "What do you mean—later?"

He halted, and looked at her. "Later tonight."

She frowned at him. "Later tonight *where*?"

His brows rose; his eyes smiled—laughed—down at her, but there was an intentness behind the expression that had been growing sharper with each hour that passed. "In your room. In your bed."

Shocked speechless, she simply stared at him. She finally managed to get her tongue to work. "No."

Lifting her hand from his sleeve, he kissed her fingertips and released them. "Yes." Turning, he walked to the door; hand on the latch, he looked back. "And don't bother to lock your door."

With a nod, he let himself out, leaving her staring at the closing door. When it snapped shut, she shook her head—shook her wits into place, shook her resistance back to life.

"No." She narrowed her eyes at the door. "No, no, no."

Swinging on her heel, she marched up the stairs and headed off to barricade her door.

She was not going to allow him to "persuade" her into marriage.

Standing to one side of the closed and definitely locked window in her bedchamber, Pris looked out at the dark night and wished he wasn't so determinedly honorable, that he'd accepted her refusal, heaved a sigh of relief, and let her go. That would have been so much easier.

Regardless, his determination was only making her even more adamant, even more sure of her mind, heart, and soul. It was love—wild, reckless, passionate, and unbounded—or nothing. Love was the only bond she would accept.

It was the only one he should accept, too.

They were who they were. One way or another, he was going to have to face that fact.

She glanced at her door. It was closed; she'd tried to lock it only to discover that while it had a lock, the lock sported no key. She could hardly go and ask Flick for it, especially not at that hour, and even then, what excuse could she give?

Looking out once again at the garden below, poorly lit by the waning moon, she drew the shawl she'd thrown over her nightgown tighter and wondered how long she might have to wait . . . wondered where he was. She'd heard Rus come in a little while ago. Had Dillon brought him home? Was he down there, cloaked in the shadows, shifting as the bushes threshed in the stiffening wind?

A storm was rolling in, heavy clouds swelling, darkening the sky. The wind shrieked and rushed around the eaves. She smiled. She liked storms. She glanced down again. Did he?

Pressing closer to the glass, she peered out and down.

The footfall behind her was so soft, she almost missed hearing it.

Whirling, disbelief swamped her when she saw Dillon prowling halfway across the room.

He halted at the foot of the bed, shrugged out of his coat, tossed it onto a nearby chair, then calmly sat on the end of the bed, and glanced at her. "What are you doing over there? Did you imagine some Romeo and Juliet encounter?"

Eyes narrowing, she folded her arms, and walked closer. "Far from it. I wasn't going to open the window."

Dillon's fleeting smile as he shrugged out of his waistcoat was quite genuine. Looking down, he reached for his boots. "How farsighted of Flick," he murmured.

"What?"

Glancing up, he saw confusion and rapid calculation in Pris's eyes. "Nothing." Setting aside one boot, he reached for the other, but kept his gaze on her. He was closer to the door than she. Even though she didn't glance that way, he sensed her tensing. "Trust me—you won't make it."

She looked at him and glared. Then she threw her hands in the air and turned away. "This is *ridiculous*! I am not going to change my mind and marry you simply because you and society deem I should. This"—pacing before him, she gestured, including the bed behind him—"*won't work*."

He lowered his second boot to the floor.

She dragged in a breath. Folding her arms, eyes spitting green fire, she halted before him, her fine nightgown whispering about her legs. "Why don't you just ask me again, and then I can refuse you, and then you can leave—"

Pris swallowed a shriek as he grabbed her, as his hands clamped about her waist and he lifted her, tossed her—suddenly she was lying on her back in the middle of her bed, and he was leaning over her.

"No."

She stared up into his shadowed face. She'd left a single candle burning on the nightstand, but it was screened by his shoulders, leaving his face unlit—mysteriously male, impossible to read. She frowned direfully up at him, valiantly ignoring her thudding heart, her already racing pulse. "No what?"

His concentration shifted to the tiny buttons closing the front of her nightgown. "No, I won't ask you to marry me again—not yet. Not until you won't refuse me."

The words were even, his tone matter-of-fact, as if he were discussing some business strategy as he steadily slipped buttons free. "And as for leaving you . . ." He'd unbuttoned the gown to her navel; raising a hand to her shoulder, he pushed the material aside, baring one breast. He studied it; his features set. "That's not going to happen."

Bending his head, he took the furled nipple between his lips—and she forgot how to breathe. His tongue knowingly swirled, and she gasped and arched beneath him.

Beneath his hard frame, her body came alive, responding

to his nearness, to the wicked temptation he was, to the illicit desires he so consummately stirred.

Her own wild desires; she knew that any second they would rise to his call—to his touch, his nearness—and sweep her senses away, leaving her wits struggling to cope, to control . . . something uncontrollable. She couldn't—shouldn't—let that happen.

Lids at half-mast, she focused on him, and was caught. By the expression on his face as he drew her nightgown down to her waist, baring her other breast, then reverently caressed both ivory mounds with fingertips that burned. His gaze was pure flame; his intent concentration had only one name. Devotion. Selfless worship beyond question.

Her voice shook, weak and breathless as she forced herself to plead, "Just ask me again."

His dark gaze flicked up to her eyes, then returned to his obsession. Sexually pleasing her, pleasuring her. "No." After a moment, he added, as she gasped and closed her eyes, as she felt him draw her nightgown farther down until it pulled taut across her hips. "That wouldn't be fair."

Fair? His hand splayed across her naked stomach, then pressed, and slid lower . . .

"Fair to whom?" She forced open her lids, forced herself to look at him, but he wasn't looking at her face. He was watching his hand as he slid it beneath the band her nightgown had formed, as his fingers reached for and found her curls, stroked, gently played, then pressed on.

And found her, already swollen and wet for him, heated and welcoming as he stroked, lightly caressed, then he shifted his hand, boldly pressing her thighs wide, and slid one finger into her.

Then and only then did he look at her face.

He stroked, watching her, and evenly replied, "Fair to us. Me and you." He reached farther; she shuddered and closed her eyes.

Felt him lean nearer, felt his breath washing over one aching nipple. Then his lips touched, closed; he suckled, and she fought to swallow a scream.

She gripped his upper arms tight, hung on as he feasted and fed her rioting senses. As he swept her and them away as she'd known he would. She longed to rail at him, to tell him he was wrong—that there was no *"us,"* no him and her—but he was right.

There was.

No matter how hard she fought to deny it, he knew, and so did she. Knew that in passion they were not just alike, but somehow linked. Bound.

He drew her gown away, replaced it with his hands, his mouth, his passion. Stroked her with flame until she burned. Until desire and need ignited, then he pushed her on until she shattered beneath his hands, until the sun and stars claimed her.

She lay on the rucked coverlet, panting; through half-closed eyes, she watched him as he traced sensual patterns on her flushed skin.

"This . . ." He spread his hand and traced a wide swath over one breast, through the curve of her waist to the swell of her hip—and watched her body's helpless response. "Is what fascinates me—what holds me, binds me. Bids me." His lips quirked, wryly self-deprecating. "Even commands me."

She blinked.

"Beauty"—turning his hand, he brushed the backs of his fingers across her stomach, and made her breath catch, made her nerves shiver—"is transient, and as we both know, it's no guarantee of anything, now or tomorrow. But this—" Raising his hand, he brushed the underside of her breast, and her shiver became a reality. "Is a promise of incalculable worth."

His dark gaze rose to meet hers, and there was no veil to screen his meaning, no guile to blur it. This was how he felt—about her, about them. "It's the woman in you I love—the goddess in you I worship. Not the outward trappings, but the female within. That's who I join with, that's who I want to link my life to, who I want to live it with."

He paused, then, still holding her gaze, he lowered his head and placed a burning kiss just below her navel. "That's who I covet. Who I serve." His breath washed heat over her skin, sent warmth sinking through her belly. "Who I need. That's the woman who makes me complete."

His lips touched again, and she closed her eyes against the words that had struck to her heart, to her core; she closed her eyes tighter still against the swirling sensations as he traced a path lower, his mouth branding her sensitive skin. Then his lips whispered over her curls as he spread her thighs, and . . .

"Oh, God—*Dillon*!" She had to swallow her shriek, had to remember not to scream. Helpless, she moaned instead as he covered her with his mouth, then with his tongue claimed.

One fist to her lips, smothering her moans, she tangled her other hand in his hair, gripped tight, shamelessly clung as he drove her mindless. Beneath the heat and passion, beneath the lash of his intimate ministrations, she writhed and panted.

Heat filled every pore, then overflowed. Passion took its place, burning and consuming every shred of resistance until she surrendered, until she became the goddess he knew her to be, and welcomed him into her temple, until she embraced all he gave, all the passion and desire he brought to her—and gave him hers.

Far beyond sanity, her world shook; reality tilted and quaked. Then existence itself fragmented, and glory poured through, filling her, buoying her—and yet she was waiting, hovering, yearning.

He left her; she felt empty and lost. She wanted to protest, but couldn't form the words. She cracked open her lids instead, and was reassured.

He was dispensing with his remaining clothes. A naked god, he rejoined her on the rumpled coverlet. Settling between her thighs, he lifted and wound her legs about his hips, caught her heavy-lidded gaze, then thrust smoothly, forcefully into her, and joined them.

Filled her, and linked them.

He lowered his head and found her lips with his. Within seconds, they were rocking deeply, journeying again, rapidly pacing through that achingly familiar landscape, clinging, then desperately striving as the storms of their merged passions raged, raked, and swept them both away.

And the wildness was back, infusing, feeding and driving them, compelling them, whipping them on to ever greater heights, ever higher peaks, until passion itself ruptured, and there was nothing but blinding light, and a heat and fire that sank to the soul.

To their souls, both, welding, fusing, binding them ever more tightly.

In some higher plane of her mind, she saw it, wished she could deny it but knew she could not.

Knew, as she drifted slowly back to earth, her hands gently stroking the long planes of his back, that this was the real truth.

Him and her together. *Us.*

She didn't know what to do with that revelation. Didn't know how, couldn't immediately see how *us,* even now, could come to be. Not with any certainty. Not in the real world—the world beyond her bed, beyond the circle of his arms.

How could she ever be sure? How could she know all that he'd shown her—even that—wasn't simply his too-knowing persuasions?

She'd woken some time ago, her mind sliding back to reality with a disconcerting thud. The room was dark, the candle long since guttered; the house remained shrouded in its nighttime silence, but the pall of darkness beyond her window had started to lighten.

Dillon lay behind her, spooned around her, warm and strong and strangely reassuring.

Also distracting. His arm lay over her waist; one leg was tangled with hers. The unaccustomed rasp of hair-dusted limbs against her soft skin constantly tweaked her senses.

She needed to think—to assess and reassess—to remember all he'd said, all he'd revealed. All she'd come to see and understand.

She needed to know where she stood, whether anything had changed. Whether, as he believed, there was some way forward for *us,* or whether, as she feared, it was all a sham.

Carefully, she edged toward the side of the bed, easing out from under his arm. She was about to slip free when his hand and arm flexed, and he yanked her unceremoniously back against him.

"Where are you going?"

She managed to draw a breath. "I need to think."

He sighed, his breath stirring the curls over her nape. "You don't. That's our problem—you think too much."

He shifted, sliding his other arm under and around her, then one big warm palm slid from her shoulder along her side, and down to fondle her bottom. She sucked in a breath and tried to wriggle away, but he splayed his other hand over her stomach and held her in place.

"If you really must think . . ." He shifted closer; she felt his erection against her bottom. His lips traced the curve of her ear, while his fingers caressed the soft flesh between her thighs. "Then think of this. Who are you running from? Me, or you?"

She bit her lip against a moan, and closed her eyes. She knew exactly who she was running from—who her logical mind was trying to pretend didn't exist. The woman within, the *her* she became in his arms. The *her* she became with him and him alone. The woman inside her he made her see, the wild, reckless, freely passionate female that was all and everything she could be.

The *her* he connected with, and who loved him, so deeply now she knew her heart would shatter if he didn't love her back. Didn't love her with the same mindless passion, the selfsame commitment and devotion.

He lured *her* forth, with shockingly explicit caresses made her flower for him, then he filled her, joined with her, and that wild hoyden gloried.

Eyes closed, she wished she could close her mind, but she couldn't. Couldn't not see the truth, acknowledge it as it blazed within her.

Her body moved rhythmically with his; it felt as if he were surrounding her, possessing her, but it wasn't that she feared. She feared she couldn't possess him in the same way.

His lips grazed her temple. She caught her breath on a gasp. "I don't . . ." She paused, then whispered, "I don't understand."

Truth, at least; she was too deeply caught to be helped by lies.

His possession didn't falter; his lips returned to trace her ear. "Understand this." His words were gravelly, rough with desire, edged with the growl of unleashed passion. But she heard them, felt them as he thrust repeatedly into her body, as he held her trapped and made her his.

"I didn't offer for your hand because of any moral obligation."

He shifted fractionally, and thrust deeper into her.

"And regardless of what you thought, you didn't seduce me. I *let* you seduce me—*not* the same thing. Not at all."

The last words were barely audible, a whisper of sound across her shoulder, followed by a searing kiss.

And the conflagration flared, and took them again, consumed them again, and she went with him gladly, eagerly, the wild goddess within her free.

And his. As he was hers.

At least in that arena. In *that,* she believed.

One thing was clear. As he'd warned her, she could forget about running.

In the following days, everywhere she turned, he was there. He was constantly in her thoughts, all but constantly by her side.

Constantly stealing her away to indulge in the wild and wicked, the reckless and illicit; even while surrounded by the very haut of the haut ton he fed her a diet of the thrills and excitement he more than anyone knew she—the wild and reckless hoyden—gloried in.

And with every interlude, every hour that passed, it became harder to deny him—and harder to rebury the hoydenish goddess and revert to the, if not prim and proper, then at least logical and sensible lady she needed to be.

When, driven to distraction, astride him in Lady Carnegie's gazebo, she pointed out he was corrupting her, he calmly replied that as it was only with him, and he was going to be her husband, it didn't count as corruption. Even through the shadows, she'd seen the expression that had flashed across his face, temporarily hardening his features. Only with him—who was going to be her husband.

Her expression must have changed; before she could say anything, he drew her head to his and kissed her—kept kissing her until desire ignited and cindered her wits.

Enough was enough. It couldn't go on.

She had to do something—make some decision and act.

Her first decision, her first action, was to beard the one person who knew him best. She ran Flick to earth in the back parlor, thankfully alone, idly studying the *Ladies Journal.*

Walking to the window, restless and bold, she opened without preamble. "You know Dillon well, don't you?"

Flick looked up, mildly smiled. "From the age of seven. He's older by a year, but we were both only children, with few other children about, and with my interest in horses and riding, as you might imagine we spent a lot of time together, far more than would be the norm."

Sinking onto the window seat, Pris met Flick's blue eyes. "Can you . . . explain him to me? I can't quite . . . that is, I don't know . . ."

"Whether to trust him?" Flick grinned. "A wise question for any lady to ask. Especially of a man like him."

Pris blinked. "A man like him?"

"A heartbreaker. Oh, not intentionally, never that. But there are hearts aplenty among the ton that carry a crack because of him. Some of them remarkably hard hearts, I might add. But of that, he—like most males in similar circumstances—remains oblivious."

Flick paused. "But you were asking about trust." Frowning, she closed the magazine. "Hmm . . . I'll do you the courtesy of not simply saying you should. So let's see if I can help."

She stared across the room. "Let's stick to recent events, ones we both know of. For instance, dealing with the substitution racket." Shifting on the chaise to face Pris, Flick went on, "He's told you about his past, hasn't he? How he once became involved in fixing races?"

Pris nodded. "You and Demon helped disentangle him."

"Yes, but in the process Dillon blocked a pistol shot aimed at me. Perhaps he saw it as redeeming himself, but regardless, when the instant came, he acted without hesitation. And after all the brouhaha, it was he himself who rebuilt his reputation. Steadily, doggedly. More than any other gentleman, he knows how much his reputation is worth."

"Because he once lost it." Pris nodded.

"However!" Flick held up a finger. "When it came to dealing with this latest scam, Dillon chose the best way for the industry, the sport whose ideals he champions, even though that meant putting his hard-won reputation at risk. And it was a real risk, one he saw and understood. If anything had gone wrong, if Belle had lost, any hint of his involvement would have made his position as Keeper of the Register untenable, and you'll have seen how much that means to both him and the General, yet he didn't hesitate in what was, once again, a selfless act in defense of something he considers his to protect."

Flick paused, then continued, "I've met a great number of powerful men." Her lips quirked; she met Pris's eyes. "I married a Cynster, after all. But not one of them has the same reckless abandon when it comes to risks that Dillon has. If there's something he's committed to protecting, something he cares about, then he never weighs the risk to himself." Flick grinned. "Luckily, fate tends to smile on such passionately reckless souls."

Pris tilted her head, her gaze far away. "So you're saying he's unwaveringly loyal, courageous, and . . ."

"True. There's not an ounce of deceit in him, not in terms of intending to harm. He can prevaricate and manipulate with the best of them, but the instant things turn serious, and action becomes imperative, everything else falls away, and he's unfailingly direct."

Pris thought of what he'd said, revealed, over the past days and nights. She refocused on Flick, to find her regarding her pointedly.

"And then there's you." Flick nodded. "A very revealing enterprise, how he's dealing with you."

"Revealing?"

"Consider the evidence. First, despite his unwavering loyalty to the racing game, he's put you ahead of it—he followed you here rather than watch over the rest of the season in Newmarket. Then he capped that by doing everything—making absolutely every possible gesture—to make it *publicly* clear that he wants you as his wife, despite the lack of any encouragement on your part. He's taken the risk of laying his heart not just on his sleeve, but at your feet, and in the most public way imaginable. This from a man who passionately abhors being in the public eye.

"In matters concerning ladies, he's normally discretion incarnate. All his previous affairs—I know they existed, but even *I* don't know which ladies were involved." Flick paused, then shook herself. "But I digress. What I was attempting to point out was that in typical fashion, Dillon has knowingly and intentionally taken a massive social and emotional risk, all in pursuit of you."

Pris frowned. "What risk?"

Flick opened her eyes wide. "Why, that you might refuse him. You can still refuse him, you see—and you're strong enough to do it, regardless of what he does or causes to happen, and he knows that, too."

Pris sat frowning, fitting together the insights Flick had offered.

Flick watched her for a minute, then leaned across and briskly patted her knee. "When you're deciding whether to trust him, don't forget this—he's trusted you. Because of his actions, because of what he is, he's put his life and his heart into your hands. There's not much more a man like him can yield." Flick paused, then reiterated, "When making your decision, remember that."

Pris held Flick's blue gaze for a long moment, then drew a deep breath and inclined her head. "Thank you."

Flick grinned and sat back. "For the advice? Or for pointing out the responsibility?"

Pris studied her, then smiled back. "Both."

Twenty-one

Absorbed with her side of the equation, she hadn't considered his. Now that Flick had pointed it out, along with the implications, Pris had a great deal more to think about—a much wider view of Dillon Caxton and his pursuit of her.

She still couldn't be certain of his reason for wanting to marry her, but, with Flick's revelations, the scales had tipped.

If belief had yet to surface, hope at least had bloomed.

Later that evening, whirling down Lady Kendrick's dance floor, she listened to Rus enthusiastically describe his plans—not just for the next months, but for the rest of his life.

"We'll go back to the Hall eventually, of course, but first . . ."

He hadn't specified, but it seemed clear that "we" meant he and Adelaide. He'd slipped into the habit of referring to them in the plural—just as Dillon insisted on doing with her and him. It was always them. *Us.*

Suddenly aware that Rus had stopped speaking, she looked, and found him regarding her with unusual seriousness.

What are you going to do? was on the tip of his tongue; instead, he looked over her head. "If you're still at the Hall, you might well be an aunt by then." His lips curved lightly. "You could help take care of our children."

Pris narrowed her eyes to slits, but he refused to meet her gaze. "It's no use, you know. I won't be prodded."

He glanced at her. "Adelaide suggested a little nudge might help."

She widened her eyes in an affronted glare. "You know better."

He sighed. "Well, anyway." Blithely, he returned to his life, his future, and left her to plan her own.

Which still wasn't any easy matter. Adelaide had known where to prod.

Returned to Dillon's side at the end of the measure, she grasped the excuse of a trailing flounce to escape to the withdrawing room. While repairing the damage, she tried to bring some order to her thoughts, to approach the vexed question of her future—as Dillon's wife or not?—from a different angle.

If she didn't marry Dillon, what would she do?

The answer wasn't heartening. What, outside marriage, remained for her to achieve?

Rus was safe, welcomed into his chosen field, and he and her father were reconciled. Indeed, they were all three in greater harmony than she could ever recall. Her younger siblings were happy and well cared for, largely as a result of her planning; they didn't need her to be there, on hand. While she would instantly return should any trouble threaten, with her father, Eugenia, Rus, Adelaide, and

Albert all present and in league, it was difficult to imagine what such trouble might be.

As for the Hall, her home, she'd grown up knowing it would never be hers to run; the reins would pass to Adelaide, Rus's wife. Leaving, establishing her own home . . . she'd always assumed she would one day.

She'd traveled with Eugenia to Dublin, to Edinburgh, to London. She enjoyed cities well enough, enjoyed their distractions, but she enjoyed the country more.

She'd felt at home in Newmarket.

The thought slid through her mind. Wrinkling her nose, she sat before a mirror to tidy her curls.

A movement to her left drew her attention. A lady, elegantly gowned and coiffed, sank onto a chair alongside and simply stared.

Slowly, Pris turned and looked—directly—at the lady.

She blinked. "Oh." Her eyes remained round as she studied Pris's face. She seemed disposed to simply stare.

"Is there something I can help you with?" Pris asked.

The lady's eyes lifted to hers, then her shoulders slumped. "No. That is . . ." She frowned. "You're very beautiful. My sisters warned me, but I didn't really believe . . ." Her frown deepened. "You've made things very difficult."

Pris blinked. "In what way?"

"Why, over Dillon Caxton, of course." The lady, blond and brown-eyed, regarded Pris with increasing disfavor. "It was supposed to be my turn—mine, or Helen Purfett's, but if I say so myself, my claim is the stronger."

"Your claim?" Pris frowned back. "To what?"

Glancing about, the lady leaned closer and hissed, "To *him*, of course!"

Pris looked at her; she didn't appear demented. "I don't understand."

"Every time he visits London, there's a . . . a competition of sorts. To see who can catch his eye and lure him to her bed. We all know the rules—only matrons of the ton, only those he hasn't indulged before. My sisters—all three of them—have had their turns. We're all acknowledged beauties, you see. So I was quite determined that next time he came to the capital, he would be mine. But instead"—the lady glared at Pris—"he's spent all his time chasing you. He hasn't spared so much as a glance—not for me, or Helen, or anyone else!" The lady leaned back; surveying Pris, she spread her hands. "And just look at you!" Her lower lip quivered. "It's not *fair*!"

Pris understood the plight of the bored matrons; they'd married for the socially accepted reasons and consequently were reduced to searching for excitement outside their marriage vows. They epitomized the reason she refused to marry other than for love; she felt a certain compassion for their straits. However . . . "I'm sorry. I can't see how I can help you. I can hardly change my face."

The lady's frown grew more pointed. "No, and I daresay it's senseless asking you to refuse him. Besides, he seems totally committed. But you could at least marry him quickly, then, once you're settled, he'll be free again for us."

Pris blinked. It took effort, but she managed not to react, not to, succinctly and with great clarity, disabuse the lady of that notion. *If* she married Dillon, he'd look at another lady at his peril. However, as she read it, this was a matter of the ladies looking at *him*—almost as . . . as if he were she. This was a mirror image of the way men too often viewed her.

Her wild and reckless self stirred.

She summoned a smile—a sweet, Adelaide-like expression of willing but uncertain helpfulness. Deception might be beyond Dillon; it was definitely not beyond her, not in a good cause, specifically theirs.

Theirs. The word rang in her mind, made her hesitate for one instant, then she accepted it. "I'd be happy to marry him with all speed, but . . ." She shrugged lightly. "To do that, I need to bring him to the point sooner rather than later." She looked innocently at the lady. "You—or at least your three sisters—must know him well. Perhaps you could give me some hints of how to . . . *encourage* him?"

For a moment, she feared the lady wouldn't be gullible enough to share her sisters' knowledge. Her eyes narrowed, her lips pursed, but then she grimaced. "It will probably shock you, and goodness knows, it'll certainly shock him coming from a naïve young lady like you, but . . ."

The lady tapped a finger to her lips, glanced around, then leaned closer. "First, you must arrange a private interlude. *Then*—"

Pris listened, and learned. The lady was most helpful.

Later that night, Pris waited in her bedchamber for Dillon to appear. They'd attended the usual three balls, then he'd seen them home and gone off, she presumed to his club. Soon he would return, to her room, to her. A robe belted over her nightgown, she paced before the hearth, and waited.

She'd made up her mind. It hadn't been Flick's insight that had tipped the scales irrevocably, but rather what the lady—Lady Caverstone—had revealed. It had suddenly dawned that if she didn't accept Dillon—didn't take the risk, grasp the chance, and make of *them* what might be—she would condemn him to precisely the sort of life she would never accept for herself.

They were very alike. Outward beauty set them apart, yet few understood the dramatic passions that lay beneath. Regardless, until now, she hadn't perceived just how closely their mirror-destinies matched.

If, as Flick had suggested, she was special to him, the only one he'd ever pursued with a view to matrimony, if, as he'd told her, she was the one woman with whom he felt complete, then . . . if she didn't embrace all she was, and allow herself to be who he needed her to be—his wife, and more, that wild, tempestuous, passionate goddess who could hold his heart and soul—if she instead refused his suit and went back to Ireland to live a quiet, unchallenged life, where would that leave him?

At the mercy of ladies such as Lady Caverstone and her sisters.

A deadening existence, one with no fire and passion, no wild and reckless thrills, no real comfort.

No. Not that road.

The idea of him dwelling in such soul-eating aloneness, the emotion that notion had evoked, had not just answered her questions but dismissed them. They didn't matter; this—he—did.

It was time to make an end, to declare her decision, to make her direction known.

After listening to Lady Caverstone, she knew precisely how.

When the door to her bedroom opened, she was ready.

Ready to smile, to herself more than him, ready to offer him her hands, and lead him to her bed. To the side of it, where she halted, braced her hands against his chest and stopped him from drawing her into his arms and kissing her. "No. Not yet."

He blinked, studied her; suspicion and wariness slid through his eyes.

She met them, arched a brow in challenge. "My turn to lead."

Suspicion fled. His lips quirked. "This being the sort of dance where you can?"

"Exactly." She breathed the word as she pushed his coat off his shoulders and down his arms. She left him to free his hands from the sleeves, and gave her attention to his cravat.

Unraveling the knot, she drew the ends free, then pulled on them to bring his head down to hers, to kiss him—

openmouthed and eager, hungry and wanton. The instant she felt his arms slide around her, the instant he moved to take control, she drew back.

"Uh-uh." Stepping back, out of his arms, she wagged a finger. "No touching. Not until I give you leave."

He cocked a brow at her, but obediently lowered his arms. He stood passive as she set her fingers to the silver buttons of his waistcoat. She slid the garment off, flung it aside, then set to work on his shirt. The buttons dealt with, she wrestled the tails from his waistband, spread the halves wide—then paused. To admire. To gloat.

All this could—and would—be hers. Lady Caverstone and her sisters could go begging.

Dillon sucked in a long, slow breath, felt desire slide and coil through him as he watched her, saw in her face a possessiveness he hadn't thought to see there. Why not, he couldn't have said, but the sight . . . surely it could mean only one thing?

Carefully, he reached for her, intending to draw her to him and learn what that expression truly meant.

"No." She batted his hands away. Frowned at him as she wrenched his shirt over his shoulders, trapping his arms. "Stay still."

They were speaking in whispers even though the room next door was unoccupied. Swallowing his impatience—she'd taken the role he usually played; he wasn't accustomed to submission—he waited for her to free his hands. Instead, she spread hers on his chest, blatantly possessively caressed, then set her lips to his already heated skin.

Her teeth came into play, distracting nips, a subtle grazing over one tight nipple. Then her tongue swept across it and he sucked in a breath; shifting his weight, he leaned down and tried to nudge her head up—for a kiss, not a touch.

She avoided him, commanded, "Don't move."

Impossible. There was one part of him not even she could command; it was already straining against the flap of his trousers, and she knew it. He gritted his teeth. "Pris . . ."

She laughed, low, sensuous, the waft of her breath against his skin a subtle torture. "Wait." She drew back.

Jaw clenched, he sighed, and stared—martyred—at the ceiling, then he heard a muted thump—her robe hitting the floor—a second later glimpsed a flash of white nightgown. His eyes locked on her in time to see her wriggle the long gown off over her head.

He stared; his chest ached. Grudgingly, he freed enough of his mind to breathe. He'd seen her naked only in bed, or shrouded in darkness. Now . . .

Clothed in a seductive mix of moonlight and candlelight, she was the goddess he dreamed of. Pagan, wild, untamed. Her black curls cascaded over her shoulders, silken locks framing the furled peaks of her breasts. Her long limbs, graceful, skin pearlescent, were a deity's bounty.

She came to him, softly smiling, emerald eyes smoldering, and something within him shook. Broke. Then she was there, and her hands spread, her breasts touched, and he was lost.

Lost in wonder as she pandered to a dream he hadn't known he'd had. She moved against him, sinuously supple, her promise implicit, yet for the moment withheld.

Behind his back, he freed first one hand, then the other from the tangle of his shirt, barely daring to breathe as she dealt with the buttons at his waist, then, crouching, drew his trousers down.

At her direction, he helped her dispense with his shoes and stockings, at her prodding stepped clear of his trousers and allowed her to sweep them away.

He sucked in a too-tight breath. He couldn't think clearly, not enough to take control, not when she was in this mood. He had to see what more she'd planned; that she *had* planned had finally sunk into his distracted brain. Instead of the usual single candlestick on her nightstand, a four-armed candelabra stood there, shedding ample light over the bed.

And her as, still crouched at his feet, she swiveled to him, and looked up—let her gaze travel slowly up his body, from his knees up his thighs, past his jutting erection, past his taut abdomen, past his locked chest to reach his eyes.

For a heartbeat, she held his gaze, her own a blaze of emerald intent, then she smiled and slid to her knees; spreading her hands on his thighs, she sent them cruising. Upward.

He nearly swallowed his tongue when she clasped both hands around his rigid length. Nearly lost his mind when she calmly leaned close, and licked. He literally shuddered when she followed one bulging vein with the tip of her tongue, then lightly traced the rim of his shaft.

Then she smoothly took him into her mouth, and his brain died.

He couldn't breathe. Every muscle he possessed had locked tight. As she suckled gently, then drew him deeper, he closed his eyes, and felt his world rock.

Her injunctions held no power against his reaction; as she freely and wantonly pleasured him, no power on earth could have stopped him from tangling his fingers in her silky mane. She suckled more powerfully, and his fingers spasmed, clutched as he fought not to thrust into her hot, wet, welcoming mouth.

Her hands drifted, circled his thighs, rose, caressed his buttocks, then tensed, flexed, as her lips and tongue played . . .

She might be a goddess; he was only human.

Smothering a groan, he dragged in a labored breath. "*Pris!* Enough."

He didn't know whether he felt relief or disappointment when she obeyed and released him.

Breasts rising and falling, she looked up at him, the expression in her eyes frankly calculating.

Before she could return to her recent obsession, he reached for her. To his relief, she let him draw her to her feet, but planted her hands on his chest, held herself from him. She met his eyes, met his experience with determination. "No—*not* enough."

He frowned, arched a brow.

She arched one back, more pointedly, very much a goddess in control. "How much are you willing to give? To surrender?"

For me. For my love.

Pris let her eyes say the words, with them told him unequivocally what the prize she was offering was.

His palms curved around her shoulders, gripped. He was breathing as rapidly, as shallowly as she; heat poured from him and lured her, drew her, but not until he paid, and admitted he did, would she appease them both.

He'd been studying her eyes; he hauled in a tortured breath. "How much do you want?"

The right answer. She smiled. Intently. And prodded his bare chest with her fingertips. "Lie on your back in the middle of the bed."

He hesitated, but, his hands falling from her, did as she asked.

She watched while he arranged himself, head on the pillows, hands by his sides, legs slightly spread. Smile deepening, she clambered up on the bed, then around to kneel between his feet.

She paused to admire the view, then set her hands to his calves, sent them sliding slowly upward—and followed, lowering her body to his, feeling muscles harden, contract, and shift as she slid skin to skin over him, up to where she could angle her knees to either side of his waist and rise up, straddling his abdomen as she caught one of his hands, lifted his arm and pushed it back—over his head and out to where the silk scarf she'd left tied to the headboard lay waiting.

He turned his head, stared incredulously as she swiftly secured his wrist. Mouth open, jaw slack, he turned his head, watching as she did the same with his other hand, leaving him, theoretically at least, helpless. At her mercy.

He narrowed his eyes at her as, delighted, she settled back across his lower chest. "What are you about?"

The tone of his voice assured her he wasn't intending to argue.

She smiled; placing her hands on either side of his chest, she leaned low, and licked. "Possessing you." She breathed the words across the spot she'd moistened, and felt the hard body beneath her react. Without taking her eyes from his, she added, "As I will. As I wish."

She let her eyes add the *As you deserve.*

He looked deep, read her message, then groaned and closed his eyes.

She smiled even more, and set her lips to his skin. And set about fulfilling her sentence. Set about taking all she wished of him, all that he willingly surrendered. All that he usually demanded of his lovers, she demanded of him; all he usually gave them, she gave him. With lips, tongue, and teeth, with her hands, with her body, with the tips of her breasts, she caressed him, and drove him wild.

Drove him mindless. As mindless as he usually made her, as wild and reckless, as urgently, openly needy. Greedy.

What she hadn't counted on was his rising hunger feeding her own.

Heat raged as she moved over him, as she twisted and twined, explored and caressed. As he answered every demand, gave her his mouth when she wished it, then when she moved lower, closing his eyes, setting his jaw, and letting her have her way.

Without restriction letting her take every shred of his self into her, then letting her give it back. Over and over, a worship unending, until neither could wait any longer, and she rose over him and sheathed him and took him in. And rode him.

Wild, uninhibited, paganly wanton in the moonlight, abandoned and erotic as the candlelight flickered and gilded her skin.

Dillon watched her, barely able to believe what he saw, what he sensed, what he felt reaching through the thundering in his veins, an emotion deep and true. Reaching for his heart, closing about his soul.

Holding him, embracing him as she shattered above him. Teeth gritted, jaw clenched, he held to sanity and watched as passion took her, as for that timeless moment glory filled the void and rushed through her, and him.

She slumped over him, then eased down to collapse on his chest.

Shutting his eyes, he breathed deeply, prayed for control, then lifting his lids, he looked down, and nudged her head with his jaw. "My hands." His voice was barely working. "Untie them. Pris—*please*?"

For a moment, she lay dead, then he felt her breasts swell as she drew in a huge breath. Then she shifted, reached for one wrist, stretched, and tugged.

The instant he felt the silken shackle give, he wrenched his hand free, reached across, tipping her on his chest, and with one yank had his other hand untied.

Then he caught her, kissed her, claimed her mouth, and let all he felt for her free. He rolled, and she was beneath him; deep in the kiss, he reached for her thighs, spread them, lifted them, and sank home.

Deep. Where he belonged.

She thought so, too. On a gasp and a sob, she wound her legs over his, tilted her hips, and pulled him even deeper.

He filled her, savoring every inch of her tight clasp, of her complete and willful surrender. Then he took, filled his soul, his heart, his senses with her. Let the thunder in his veins drive them both. Felt her join him, felt her clutch, heard her moan.

Then they were flying far beyond the edge of the world, well beyond perception's reach, one heart, one soul, two merged minds, two bodies in thrall to that elemental hunger. Driving, reaching, striving, wanting.

She fragmented, came apart, and took him with her; hand in hand, fingers tightly laced, they gained their private heaven. And felt the glory close around them, welcoming them in, assuring them beyond words, beyond thought, that this truly was their home.

That this was where *Us* belonged.

"Ask me again." Pris lay slumped, exhausted, beside him, the glory of aftermath a golden warmth in her veins.

He lay spooned around her, cradling her against him, her back to his chest. "No." A mumbled rumble.

She tried to frown, failed, then remembered he couldn't see. "Why not?"

"Because neither of us is thinking straight—capable of thinking straight. I'm not going to risk you giving me the wrong answer, or, heaven forbid, later forgetting what answer you gave."

Flick's words whirled in her mind; Pris managed an inelegant snort. "You thrive on taking risks, especially with what matters."

"Not when I might lose more than I'm willing to lose."

She thought that over and realized it was a statement with which she couldn't possibly argue.

She also realized she couldn't recall ever winning an argument with him. She grumbled on principle, but he held firm, finally silencing her with, "Besides, you're not the only one who can plan."

Before she could decide if that was a threat or a promise, she fell asleep.

The next morning, Dillon was seated at Horatia's dining table, happily alone, even more happily putting the final touches to his plans for the day, when the knocker was plied with considerable force.

Highthorpe strode past the dining room door; Dillon heard voices, then Barnaby walked in.

A disheveled, bedraggled, exhausted Barnaby.

"Good God!" Dillon sat up; setting down his coffee cup, he waved to a chair. "Sit down before you fall down. What the devil happened?"

Through two days' growth of beard, Barnaby grimaced wearily. "Nothing a cup of strong coffee, breakfast, a bath, a razor, and a day of sleep won't cure."

"We can start with the first two." Dillon nodded as Highthorpe placed a cup before Barnaby and filled it.

He waited until Barnaby had taken a long sip, eyes closed, clearly savoring the relief. When he opened his eyes and looked over the breakfast dishes spread on the table, Dillon said, "Help yourself—just talk while you do. You're hardly a sight to calm nerves."

Barnaby fleetingly grinned and pulled a platter of ham his way. "I drove all night. And most of the day and night before that."

"Martin?"

Barnaby nodded grimly.

Dillon frowned. "You found him?"

"Yes, and no." Barnaby stabbed a piece of ham. "Stokes and I visited the house in Connaught Place." He put the ham into his mouth, waved the empty fork as he chewed, then swallowed. "It wasn't Martin in the house, but a family renting from Mr. Gilbert Martin. We found the agent, and Stokes persuaded him to give us Martin's address."

Barnaby looked at his plate. "Northampton. Stokes went with me. When we got there, it was the same story. Someone else in the house, renting via an agent from Mr. Gilbert Martin. And so we found that agent, and went on to Liverpool."

Dillon held his tongue while Barnaby ate.

"After that, it was Edinburgh, York, Carlisle, Bath, then Glasgow." Barnaby frowned. "I might have missed one or two towns, but the last was Bristol. That's where we ran Mr. Gilbert Martin to earth, entirely by accident, through an acquaintance in the town."

Barnaby met Dillon's eyes. "Mr. Gilbert Martin is seventy-three years old, has no son, knows of no other Gilbert Martin, and although he does indeed own the house in Connaught Place and rents it via that first agent, Mr. Martin hasn't the faintest idea about his supposed new address in Northampton or any of the other houses."

Barnaby paused, then added, "The rental monies from the London house are paid into an account in the city, and Mr. Martin draws on that. There's been no change there, so he had no idea anything was going on."

Dillon's frown deepened. "So *we* have no idea who that other Mr. Gilbert Martin is?"

"Other than a devilishly clever cove? No, none."

After a moment, Barnaby went on, "During our travels, Stokes and I had plenty of time to dwell on various scenarios. Once we learned what a goose chase Mr. X had sent us on, and how neatly it had been arranged, more or less guaranteeing that even the head denizens of the underworld would never be able to trace him, it became clear just what danger you, especially, now face."

He looked at Dillon. "If Mr. X decides on revenge, we'll have absolutely no idea from which direction the blow might come."

Impassive, Dillon nodded. "Yet there might be no blow, no revenge. I can hardly go through life constantly expecting it. Mr. X has to have been savaged financially. He might already have fled the country."

"There's that, but . . ." Barnaby met Dillon's eyes. "It doesn't feel right. He went to all that trouble to hide his identity—what are the chances he's one of us, a member of the ton?"

"Gabriel's continued searching, but as of yesterday, he'd found no trace, no trail, not an inkling."

"Just so. Mr. X is a past master at hiding his tracks. He could be the gentleman at your shoulder next time you stop by your club, or at the next ball you attend. I don't suppose you'd consider repairing to Newmarket?"

"No."

Barnaby sighed. "I told Stokes so, but, like me, he's sure Mr. X will have a try at you, even if he then scurries off overseas. He's probably planning to, so killing you just before will fit nicely into his plans."

Dillon couldn't help his smile. "Are you trying to frighten me?"

"Yes. Is it working?"

"Not quite as you imagined, but . . . I have an idea. As you're both so convinced Mr. X will come after me, doesn't that suggest we have an opportunity—possibly our last opportunity—to lay our hands on him?"

Barnaby blinked. "You mean use you as bait?"

Dillon raised his brows. "If I'm the one lure we're all agreed he'll come after . . . why not?"

He called for Pris at eleven, bullied her into her pelisse, then drove her to his chosen place.

As he led her through the doors and down the nave, she looked around, then leaned close to whisper, "Why are we here?"

About them, the sacred peace of St. Paul's Cathedral held sway. "Because," he whispered back, winding her arm with his, "I wanted a place where despite being alone, we wouldn't run the risk of distracting ourselves. We need to talk, and for that we need to think."

She considered protesting, then thought better of it; she looked around with greater interest. "Where?"

He'd planned that, too. "This way."

The day was cool, clouds scudding overhead, a brisk wind debating whether to unleash some rain or not. An assortment of sightseers wandered both nave and transept, studying the plaques and monuments, but when he escorted Pris through the door at the rear of the side chapel, as he'd hoped there were no others enjoying the peace of the ancient courtyard beyond.

A narrow, walled rectangle, in days gone by the courtyard had provided herbs for the infirmary attached to the cathedral. Now it was simply a quiet place for contemplation.

The perfect place to consider and decide the rest of their lives.

He led her to a gray stone bench thickly cushioned with thyme. Gathering her skirts, she sat and looked up at him. After an instant's hesitation, of gathering his thoughts, he sat beside her.

"Never having done this before, I'm not sure of the best approach, but I can't see that going down on one knee is going to help."

"It won't." Her voice was noticeably tight, a touch breathless.

"In that case . . ." He took her hand in his, gently tugged off her glove, tossed it in her lap, then clasped her hand palm to palm in his. He looked across the courtyard at the ancient walls—as old as time, a fitting setting for them. In some ways they were "old souls," too, more pagan than most.

"We're not like other people, other couples, you and I." He glanced at her; he had her full attention. "I knew that the instant I set eyes on you, on the steps of the club. You were . . . so unlike any other woman I'd ever met, ever seen. You saw me, the real me. Not through a veil but directly. And I saw you in exactly the same way. I knew then, and I think you did, too. But for both of us, the concept didn't fit what we'd thought would be, so . . . we prevaricated."

His lips curved; he looked down at her hand, tightened his about it. "You more than me, I think, but then came the confusion of why I'd offered for you, and that was my error. I knew why all along, but fate's intervention and a moment's hesitation meant you weren't sure. I've since told you something of my reasons, *but* I haven't told you all. I've told you what I feel for you—that you're the woman who makes me feel whole and complete, the natural other half of me—but I haven't told you why you . . . are so precious to me."

Her eyes on his profile, Pris gripped his fingers, from her heart softly said, "Isn't that implicit?"

She saw his lips curve, then he shook his head.

"No more prevarications. The truth is, if I hadn't met you that day on the steps of the Jockey Club—if you hadn't been there, searching for Rus—then I seriously doubt I would ever have come to this point. I don't think I could ever have married, not because I don't wish to, but because marriage to a woman who couldn't see me, who could never truly know me, would be . . ."

"Something very like prison."

He nodded. "Yes—you see that. But few others ever would." He glanced at her, lips still curved, yet with seriousness and honesty in his dark eyes. "The truth is, you're my savior. If you'll accept me as your husband, if you'll take my hand and be my wife, you'll be freeing me, replacing the specter of that prison with a chance to live the life I would, if I could, choose."

His eyes locked with hers, he shifted to face her. "And my chosen life would be to live with you, to renew Hillgate

End as a home with you, to have children with you, and grow old with you."

He paused, then, his eyes still on hers, he raised her hand to his lips, and kissed. "Will you marry me, Pris? Will you be my savior and take my hand, and be my goddess forever?"

It took effort not to let her tears well to the point where they would fall. She had to take a moment to find her voice, conscious, even through that fleeting instant, that he was watching her, that the tension in him rose a notch even though he had to know how she would reply.

He embodied everything she wanted, all she needed. Drowning in his dark eyes, in the steady light that shone there, she had no doubt of her answer, yet he deserved more than a bare acceptance. She drew in a not quite steady breath, held it for an instant, then said, "Yes, but—" She held up her other hand, staying him as he drew her nearer. "If we're to speak truth here, then my truth is that you're my savior, too. Perhaps I would have married, but what are the chances I would have found another gentleman who not only recognizes but appreciates my 'wild and reckless ways'?"

She looked into his eyes. "The truth is, if I hadn't found you, I would have suppressed that side of myself, and it would have been like a slow death. But if I marry you—if you marry me—I won't have to. I can simply be *me,* become the best me I can be, for the rest of my life."

Her heart leapt, then soared at the prospect. Her lips curved irrepressibly as joy filled her, steady and sure.

He studied her eyes, her dawning smile; to her surprise, he remained sober. Then he drew in a breath, tightened his hand about hers. "I have a caveat to make."

It was her turn to study his face. "A caveat?"

"Your 'wild and reckless ways' . . . do you think you could promise to indulge in them only when I'm with you?"

He was serious and uncomfortable, uneasy in making the request.

She blinked. "Why?"

Jaw setting, he looked down at her hand, trapped in his, then looked up and met her eyes. "Because"—his expression had changed to one she knew well, all arrogant, domineering male—"losing you is the one risk I will *never* take."

You are my life. You mean too much to me.

That message was blazoned in his eyes, etched in the hard planes of his face, carried in the defined lines of muscles that had tensed. She felt that reality, unequivocal and unyielding, reach out to her; she hesitated, breath caught, but then she closed her eyes and let it wrap about her.

Accepted it. Accepted him.

As he was. As she needed him to be.

Wild and reckless, passionate—and possessive.

That was the real truth of him. Of them. Of *us*.

She opened her eyes, looked into his, still burning with possessive heat. "Yes. All right."

He wasn't sure whether to believe her, to put his trust in the bright joy in her eyes. He hesitated, then asked, "All right? Just like that—all right?"

She considered, then nodded. Decisively. "Yes. Yes to everything." Rescuing her glove from her lap, she stood. Happiness was welling, flooding through her, threatening to spill over; better they left before it did.

Dillon rose with her, retaining his hold on her hand. "So you agree not to take any risks—any risks at all—unless I'm with you?" Feeling a trifle off-balance, he tried to see her face as they walked back to the chapel door.

"Yes! Well, as far as I can." Reaching the door, she halted and faced him, met his eyes directly. "And no, I am not *pleased* to have to make such a promise, but . . ." Tilting her head, she searched his eyes. "You won't rest unless I do, will you?"

He'd forgotten she saw straight into his soul. He looked into her eyes, saw all the joy he could wish for, along with too much understanding to deny, and surrendered. "No."

She nodded. "Precisely." She turned to the door. "So I'll try my best—"

"Please tell me you'll do more than *try*."

"—to accommodate you." She glanced sideways at him, caught his eye. "Isn't that what wives are supposed to do?"

There was a subtle smile on her lips, a light in her emerald eyes—more than teasing, an outright challenge—another element of her understanding.

His gaze fastened on those distracting lips.

She stiffened. "No. Not in a cathedral. This was your plan. You have to live with it."

He closed his eyes, groaned, and opened the door for her. He followed her into the church, now as eager as she to leave, and mildly amazed that the deed was done, that despite all, their path was set and agreed.

She glanced at the altar as they went past, then looked at him as he took her arm. "Have you given any thought as to when we should wed?"

The point didn't require thought. "How about as soon as humanly possible? Most of your family's here—we could send for your younger brothers and sisters." He hesitated. "Unless you want to marry in Ireland?"

"No," Pris shook her head. That would make it too hard for many of her new friends to attend, and besides, there was nothing for her there; her future lay . . . she glanced at Dillon. "Let's marry in Newmarket."

He met her gaze as they emerged through the main doors, into brilliant sunshine lancing through the broken clouds. "If you're happy with that?"

"Yes." Smiling delightedly, she felt her heart soar; all their decisions felt unequivocally right.

They stopped on the porch. Dillon signaled to the tiger to bring the curricle and pair to them, then swept her into his arms and kissed her—thoroughly. When he released her, the smile on his lips set the seal on her joy. She looked about; the sun warmed her; everything seemed sharper, cleaner, more crystal clear. More finite and settled, outside and within, as if from that first meeting in Newmarket she'd been living in a kaleidoscope of ever-shifting possibilities, but now the kaleidoscope had stopped, revealing the fabulous, exciting pattern that her future—their future—would be.

Eagerness gripped her. Impatience welled. The instant they were in the curricle and Dillon had set his horses pacing, she asked, "Where should we go first?"

"First?"

"Where should we go to start the arrangements? Our wedding isn't simply going to happen, not without a great deal of discussion and organizing."

Dillon grimaced, but didn't take his eyes from his blacks. "I'll make a deal with you—you make the arrangements, tell me where to be when, and I'll be there. Just don't ask me for an opinion on anything."

She laughed; the sound curled around his heart and warmed it.

"Done." She leaned lightly against his shoulder, then straightened. "So where should we call first, to tell them our news?"

"Flick's, or she'll never forgive me, and Eugenia and Adelaide will be there, too. I suspect they won't have gone out yet." They'd be waiting to see what had transpired, he had not a doubt. "And no doubt Flick will then rush us around to Horatia's."

Pris happily agreed.

Dillon tooled the curricle through the city streets, reassured that he could safely leave her in the Cynster ladies' company, especially in the throes of planning a wedding. All attention would be focused on her; she would be the center of the gathering.

With her safety assured, he could turn his mind to his latest risk—one last throw of the dice to flush out Mr. X, and ensure that Pris and he did not remain at the mercy of a vengeful villain, possibly for the rest of their lives.

That shared life had now taken shape in his mind; with Pris, he would make it a reality. And there was very little he wouldn't risk to make it safe, to protect it, and her.

Twenty-two

Rus was the first person Pris set eyes on as they entered Flick's front hall. Her smile exuberant, she flung herself into his arms. "You're going to have a brother-in-law. I'm going to marry Dillon."

Rus's face creased in a smile to match her own. "Excellent!" He swung her around and around; Pris laughed, eyes alight.

Adelaide and Eugenia appeared in the drawing room doorway, followed by Flick, all eager to learn what was going on.

With his habitual charm, his eyes on Pris, Dillon told them.

Adelaide shrieked and hugged him wildly. Eugenia beamed, patted his arm, then kissed his cheek. Flick's smile held a touch of gloating as she lined up to do the same. His smile easy yet arrogantly proud, Dillon received and responded to their congratulations and eager questions.

Pris turned to Rus, eyed him accusingly. "You knew."

He grinned. "Of course. You were both so obviously in love, you can't expect us not to have noticed. Even Papa noticed after just one ball."

She frowned. "How? What did we do that was so revealing?"

He studied her, confirmed her question was serious. "It's the way you look at each other, react to each other. I've seen you with any number of gentlemen, some nearly as striking as Dillon, and you behave as if they're mere ciphers. You see, smile, talk, even dance with them, yet it's as if you're not truly aware of them, as if they're too weak to impinge on your consciousness. With Dillon . . . if he's in the same room"—Rus grinned as her gaze drifted Dillon's way—"you're aware of him. Your attention instantly focuses on him. He doesn't have to do anything to claim your regard—he simply has it."

Rus squeezed her hand. "And he's the same, if not more so, with you. For instance, if you tried to slip away, he'd know and look up before you managed to leave his sight."

Still puzzled, she asked, "And that's enough for you—and Papa—to be sure he loves me?"

Rus laughed. "Trust us—for a man like him, it's an infallible sign."

Pris wondered what he meant by "like him."

"I'm more than delighted you've found him," Rus went on. "You've done so much to make my life right—to give me what I need to be happy—it's only right that along the way, you found your happiness, too."

She snorted. "You make Dillon sound like my reward."

Rus's eyes twinkled. "If the shoe fits . . ."

Before she could think of some pithy retort, Flick came rustling up to embrace her, then Eugenia and Adelaide were there, and before she and Dillon could do more than exchange a glance, they were swept up in a giddy whirl of arrangements, questions, decisions, and yet more congratulations. As Dillon had predicted, Flick herded them straight to Horatia's to spread the news.

Within half an hour, the Cynster ladies were gathering, all eager to assist in organizing the engagement ball Horatia had immediately claimed the right to host.

Dizzying mayhem ensued, principally feminine, although some of the men, like George, Horatia's husband, looked in to congratulate them and shake Dillon's hand—then glance around at the company, and quietly escape. Dillon, Rus, and Pris's father all remained for some time, but once their agreement to the principal event had been elicited, they became largely redundant.

Pris wasn't surprised when Dillon touched her shoulder, then murmured, "Your father, Rus, and I are going to my club. I have a business meeting this afternoon—I'll join you for dinner."

She smiled. "Yes, of course." She squeezed his hand, let him kiss her fingers and go.

Squelching the errant thought that she would much rather be escaping with him, she turned back to the ladies and surrendered to the inevitable with good grace.

Their engagement ball was held four evenings later at Horatia's house in Berkeley Square. A formal dinner preceded it, during which the announcement of their engagement and impending wedding was made to a glittering gathering of over fifty guests.

Pris gave thanks for the hours of training she'd endured at the hands of various governesses. "Just as well I *am* an earl's daughter," she whispered *sotto voce* to Dillon as they stood in the receiving line just inside the ballroom. "How else I would have coped with this I shudder to think."

Beside her, Dillon snorted. "You'd have coped." She felt his gaze briefly caress her bare shoulders. "That damn gown alone tips the scales your way—the ladies are almost as distracted as the gentlemen."

As the extremely haughty Countess Lieven had just bestowed her exceedingly haughty approval, her gaze lingering on Pris's stunningly designed gown, Pris hid a smile at his growl, and murmured back, "One has to make the most of the weapons one is born with."

Lord Carnegie reached them at that moment, forcing Dillon to let that comment lie.

His lordship's dazzled reaction only buoyed Pris's confidence more. Her gown was one of the few details that the ladies had left entirely to her, judging, correctly, that they could safely leave sartorial matters in her already experienced hands. The creation that graced her person, in figured silk of her favorite shade of emerald green, was an exercise in simplicity and illusion. It didn't just flatter her figure; while entirely decorous, the tightly fitted, low-cut bodice overlaid with gossamer silk of the same shade and print teased the imagination. The skirts were cut in the latest fashion, slender and sheathlike in front, gathered and spreading at the back.

With Dillon in black and crisp white beside her, they appeared the very epitome of a tonnish couple at their engagement ball.

She could barely wait for their first waltz, for the ball to get under way, to move on and ahead with their lives, but the receiving line stretched as far as she could see. Keeping her delighted smile in place, she shook hands, curtsied, and received the guests' congratulations.

Somewhat to her surprise, many ladies with daughters in tow seemed quite sincere in their avowals.

"I'm so *very* glad you've both made your choice." Lady Hendricks, her niece behind her, smiled graciously, shook their hands, then swept into the ballroom, intent on assessing likely victims.

Grasping a momentary hiatus as an old friend paused to

chat with Horatia and George, Pris leaned closer to Dillon, and murmured, "Your father told me we'd pleased all the matchmakers by becoming engaged to each other." She tipped her head at Lady Hendricks. "It seems he was right."

"Apparently," Dillon murmured back, "we'd attained the status of 'too dangerous'—the ladies are delighted we've removed ourselves from the lists. With us gone, they hope to get their charges refocused on the main chance."

Pris laughed and turned back to dazzle the Montagues.

The General had arrived the day before; she'd been touched when he'd spent most of the afternoon with her, both calming and distracting her with talk of Hillgate End, of Dillon's mother, of his happiness that she would soon be there with Dillon. The simple family life he'd painted had not just appealed to her, but ensnared her; his gentle words had filled her with both expectation and longing, stirring her usual impetuous wildness to seize the moment and act.

She wanted to be there, at Hillgate End, its mistress, wanted, with Dillon, to grasp the life there and live it.

Impatience was building; she'd harnessed it, lecturing herself that this ball, and all the rest leading up to their wedding in a few weeks' time, was the necessary prelude to that—to gaining all her heart desired.

As they chatted and welcomed and responded to congratulations, she reviewed her mental lists, her preparations for that life ahead, scanning for anything she'd missed or left undone. Any potential cloud that might dim their path, any potential hurdle that might get in their way.

One small item nagged. Barnaby had returned to London, apparently with no news of Mr. X. Amid all the distractions, she'd had no time to hear the whole story, only the conclusion; they'd reached a dead end in trying to identify their villain.

All the men seemed to have shrugged and accepted that whatever financial damage Mr. X had sustained would have to stand as sufficient retribution. She wasn't so easily appeased, but from what little she'd heard, there was nothing more they could do. That seemed an unsatisfying end to their adventure; she made a mental note to dance with Barnaby and make him tell her the details of his search.

"Lady Cadogan." Pris curtsied. "How delightful to see you."

Dillon smiled and bowed over her ladyship's hand. A twinkle in her eye, Lady Cadogan rapped his knuckles with her fan and advised him to keep his eye on his bride-to-be. He assured her he had every intention of doing so, then watched as her ladyship gathered her husband from the web of Pris's loveliness and bore him away.

To Dillon's relief, the stream of incoming guests eased, then the musicians struck up a brief prelude.

As he turned to Pris, took her hand, bowed, and led her to the steps leading down to the ballroom floor, he felt not the slightest tremor of nervousness or hesitation; what he felt was possessiveness and a driving need to have done with all the outward trappings, to have her wed, and his, at home in Newmarket.

It was she who hesitated at the top of the steps, he who, her hand in his, caught her eyes, her entire attention, and, holding it, led her down, out onto the floor as the guests fell back, led her into their engagement waltz.

She came into his arms light as air, a magical Irish maiden. As he drew her close, and the rest of the room dissolved in a whirl around them, he murmured, "You've captured me—you know that, don't you? My heart, my soul, they're yours forever."

Emerald eyes, jewel-bright, smiled into his. "You're the only man I see—that I've ever seen. I don't know why that is, but it's so."

They said nothing more; anything else would have been redundant. They revolved around the ballroom, alone as far as they and their senses knew. Other couples joined them;

others laughed and smiled. They remained oblivious, unaware.

Nothing beyond their cocoon could break the spell.

When the music ended, it took effort to wrench their minds from their private world and return to the mundane, to the hundreds waiting to chat and claim their company. They both did it because they had to, but just a glance, a touch of gazes, was enough to emphasize just how alike in that, too, they were.

Soon, their eyes said. A promise both were committed to keeping.

Turning aside, they let their well-wishers claim them. Eventually, they were forced to part.

Dillon accepted the necessity, but before leaving Pris's side, he glanced up, and found her father waiting nearby to assume the duty of watching over her.

With a nod, he passed the baton to the earl, and allowed the crowd to come between him and Pris. The earl, the General, and Rus were all on hand, primed to ensure that whatever might happen, Pris remained safe, that regardless of any threat that might materialize, she would be neither a target nor able to involve herself in any willful, reckless way.

As for him . . . glancing around, he made his way to where Barnaby stood by the side of the room.

"Becoming inconspicuous was never so hard," Dillon grumbled as he joined Barnaby. He looked over the sea of guests. "Any action?"

"Not a hint that I can see." Barnaby grinned dourly. "I spotted the watchers outside. If Mr. X does make a move, he's going to get a surprise."

"We can only hope." Dillon noticed a number of Cynster scions heading their way, smiling and exchanging greetings as they unobtrusively—as unobtrusively as such men could—tacked through the crowd. Over the next several minutes, Demon and Vane, then Gabriel and Devil joined them.

"I take it your meeting with Tranter and company was fruitful?" Devil raised a brow. "I assume those were his men skulking outside."

Barnaby nodded. "His, or from one of the others. Mr. X's underworld enemies seem legion, and they've been as stumped as we in identifying him. Until we approached them, I hadn't realized how deeply they felt about him eluding them. He owes them a fortune, but it's his anonymity they view as a personal insult—a slap in the face, a matter of honor."

"Just so." Devil's lips curved cynically, also wryly. "Powerful men hate to find themselves helpless. Your Mr. X has miscalculated there."

"Hmm." Demon glanced around their circle. "If he does move against Dillon, and they nab him, what should we do—haul him free or leave him to their untender mercies?"

They all considered; eventually all looked to Devil, but he looked at Dillon and raised a brow. "You're the most involved"—his glance included others in the room, Pris, Rus, and those involved in the substitution switch—"on all counts. What say you?"

Dillon held Devil's pale green gaze; he considered the possibilities, how he felt—would feel . . . "I say it depends on his actions. If he strikes, but it's a token gesture, a jab at me before he goes slinking into the night, then we pull him out and hand him to Stokes. Tranter and crew won't like it, but handing him over to the authorities was part of our agreement—they'll accept it."

"They'll still benefit," Barnaby said. "They want him identified so they can pick over his financial bones in case there's anything they can salvage. And they're well aware they'll gain a modicum of status with the authorities for assisting in his capture. So yes, I agree, they'll go along with that."

"But what," Gabriel asked, "if his revenge is rather more than token?"

Dillon met his eyes. "Then we leave him to his fate. If he's that bent on revenge, handing him to the authorities will only create unnecessary difficulties."

Lips curved without a trace of humor. "Indeed." Devil nodded. "So that's what we'll do."

Vane looked at Dillon. "Planning aside, have you had any indication he's preparing an attack?"

Dillon shook his head. "This is all conjecture on our part—we've no evidence he'll try to take revenge at all."

Barnaby snorted. "If he doesn't, I'll eat my hat. The fact he's lain low and not acted precipitously only confirms that he's a cool, careful schemer."

"The most dangerous sort." Devil looked at Dillon. "Be careful."

Dillon met that direct, faintly disconcerting glance, and nodded. The group parted, donning their affably charming social masks and going their separate ways, but Devil's glance—and the injunction that lay behind it—remained in Dillon's mind.

Before Pris had come into his life and become such an essential part of it, he would have recognized Devil's look, and understood the implication, but not truly felt it, not as a threat. Now he did. He looked over the heads, and found Pris—the one thing he had to take greatest care of, as Devil had intimated. She was engaged with a bevy of guests, Rus by her elbow, her father nearby, fondly looking on.

Conscious that something within him eased, like a beast settling back to semislumber, Dillon smiled at Lady Folwell and stopped by her side to chat.

Pris was safe, the night would soon be over, and their wedding would be one day closer. Despite his impatience to have Mr. X act, be identified, and dealt with, he was equally impatient to dispense with town and head back home with Pris. If Mr. X didn't act soon, he would consign the substitution racket and its perpetrator to the past, and leave it behind. He and Pris had too much to do, too much to look forward to, to waste time on a ruined villain.

The ball was a certified crush, the evening declared a huge success. Horatia and Flick were both beaming. Dillon danced with them both, grateful but wary, too. Flick informed him that Pris intended to ask Prue to be a flower girl along with Pris's sisters; he asked if she didn't think it dangerous to be encouraging Prue to think of weddings—and set her laughing. He didn't think, faced with the same question, that Demon would even chuckle.

Twirling herself, Pris saw Dillon circling with a delighted Flick in his arms, and smiled.

"Mr. Caxton is indeed a lucky man."

The comment had her refocusing on her partner, Mr. Abercrombie-Wallace. Pris inclined her head and glanced over his shoulder as he steered her through the turn at the end of the room.

Rus's words returned to her mind; without looking back at Mr. Abercrombie-Wallace, she tested Rus's hypothesis that she didn't truly see men other than Dillon. Abercrombie-Wallace was a typical London gentleman, in age somewhere between Dillon and Demon. He was dark-haired, not quite so tall, a trifle heavier . . . her physical description wavered at that point. She supposed he had a typical English face, passable enough, with features that owed much to his aristocratic background. He was, she'd gathered, wellborn and well connected, from one of the older families of the haut ton; the quality of his clothes, the diamond in his cravat, smacked of wealth and affluence.

His address was polished, his character rather mild for her taste. He seemed, not shy, but reserved.

Her gaze sliding past his face, she inwardly shrugged. It was hardly a surprise he didn't impinge on her mind.

"Mr. Abercrombie-Wallace . . . I wonder, sir, what are your interests in the capital?" She quizzed him with her eyes. "Is it business or pleasure that claims you?" She'd noticed him at the balls they'd attended over the past days; her money was on pleasure.

He might not impinge on her mind, but she'd instantly and completely claimed his. His gaze—he had pale brown eyes—locked on hers. After a moment of rather disconcerting staring silence, he replied, "As it happens, it's a mixture of both."

His voice sounded faintly strained; it had been melodically smooth until then. Pris widened her eyes. "Indeed? How—oh!"

She stumbled and nearly fell. Abercrombie-Wallace caught her, steadied her, even while he apologized profusely for his clumsiness; he'd stepped on her skirt. Pris looked down at the lace trailing beneath her hem, and swallowed a curse. She'd have to pin it up.

"Forgive me, dear lady." Wallace had paled. "If I might suggest, if you have pins, there's a parlor across the corridor—just through that door." He nodded to a door in the paneling nearby. "You could repair the damage without having to fight your way up the ballroom first."

They were at the far end of the ballroom; Pris glanced at the door, then eyed the throng between her and the ballroom steps. "That would be best."

Abercrombie-Wallace opened the door for her, then followed her through. He closed the door, leaving the corridor dimly lit by a distant sconce. "Over there." He gestured to a door a little way along the corridor.

Holding her skirt with the damaged petticoat to one side, keeping the trailing lace clear of her feet, Pris headed that way. Wallace reached past her to open the door.

She walked in, one glance verifying that the room was a small parlor looking out on the side garden. The lace caught the toe of her shoe; she looked down, untangling it, then released her skirt and turned to thank Wallace and shut the door.

He was right there—almost face-to-face. The door was already shut.

She opened her lips to send him away—the words died in her throat as he drew something from his pocket and flicked; a long black scarf uncoiled from his fingers.

Hands rising defensively, she dragged in a breath, glanced at his face as she opened her mouth to scream.

He moved like lightning. He wound the material about her head and face, smothering her cry—smothering her. She was immediately short of breath, had to struggle to draw air through the fine-woven material.

"Indeed." The voice, steely and controlled, came from behind her, a cold whisper by her ear. "If you have any sense at all, you'll save your energies for breathing."

What? *Who?* Blind, dumb, and close to deaf, Pris couldn't get the words past her lips. But she could guess the answers.

He caught her hands, useless with her senses blocked and in turmoil; he swiftly secured them behind her back, then, holding her before him, guided her forward. He opened a door; faint, her head spinning, unable to do anything but follow his directions, she swayed, stepped out—and felt cool stone beneath her soles.

The waltz came to an end. Releasing Flick, Dillon escorted her back to the chaise where Horatia and Eugenia sat. He allowed them to twit him, then moved away. Instinctively, he scanned the room.

He couldn't see Pris.

He halted, scanned again, more carefully, telling himself that his suddenly screaming instincts couldn't possibly be correct . . . then he saw something that made his heart stop.

Rus—like him searching the guests, unlike him, openly perturbed.

By the time Dillon reached him, Rus was frowning. "Do you know where she is?" he asked without preamble.

"No." Dillon looked into Rus's eyes. "I don't think she's here, in the house. *Is she?*"

Rus blinked. His gaze grew distant, then, lips setting grimly, he shook his head. "I can't . . . sense her. But it's just a feeling. Perhaps—"

Fiercely, Dillon shook his head. "She's not here. I know it, too."

He glanced around. They stood near the steps and the main doors. None of the others were in sight. "Come on!"

They had to act now, seize the moment, take the risk.

He went up the steps two at a time. Rus at his heels, he strode through the foyer and hurried down the stairs.

Highthorpe was in the front hall.

"Have you seen Lady Priscilla?" Dillon asked.

"No, sir." Highthorpe glanced at his minion manning the doors; the footman shook his head. "She hasn't been this way."

Dillon hesitated, thinking, imagining, then he swore, and strode out of the doors, down the steps into the street. The nearer curb was lined with carriages; on the opposite side a little way back stood a lone black carriage, curtains drawn, the driver and a groom alert on the box. Turning in the other direction, Dillon saw a single hackney idly waiting for some gentleman to leave the ball; the hackney stood opposite the entrance to the lane that ran alongside the Cynsters' garden wall. He headed for the hackney.

Seeing him coming, Rus at his back, the driver stirred and sat up, gathering his reins. He touched his cap as Dillon reached him. "Where to, guv?"

"Did you see a carriage pick up someone in the lane?"

The driver blinked. "Aye—a friend o'mine picked up a fare there not two minutes since. He—m'friend—was in line ahead of me. A gent flagged him over into the lane. He had a woman with him, a lady—she looked poorly."

"Poorly how?" Rus asked.

The driver frowned. "Well, she had a veil thing over her head, and she seemed unsteady—the gent had hold of her. He helped her into the carriage."

"What color was her gown?" Dillon asked.

"Darkish—green, I think."

Rus swore. "What of the man?"

"Never mind that," Dillon cut in. "Did you hear the direction?"

The driver blinked. "Aye. Tothill Way. The gent said as how he'd direct Joe when they got there."

Dillon wrenched open the hackney door and waved Rus in. "Can you follow him?"

The driver's eyes lit. "Easy enough—I know the route he'll take."

"Ten sovereigns when you catch him." Dillon leapt into the carriage, slammed the door on the driver's cheery, "Right you are!" and slumped onto the seat as the hackney lurched into motion.

He and Rus clung to the straps as the driver set off to claim his reward. They rocked down the lane, clattered down a street, then turned into a more crowded thoroughfare—Piccadilly. They joined the slow river of carriages edging along. Rus swore, and looked out of the window.

The trap in the roof slid open; the driver called down, "I can see Joe ahead of us, sir, but I won't be able to get up to him 'til we're out of this crush."

"Just keep him in sight. As long as we catch him when he stops, the money's yours."

"Right!"

A moment later, the driver spoke again, his tone more careful. "Ah . . . I don't know as how I should mention this, sir, but there's a carriage following us. It's the one that was outside the house when you came out. I wouldn't mention it, but . . . I recognize the driver."

Dillon hesitated, then said, "I know who it is. They're supposed to be following us."

"Supposed to be?" The driver sounded intrigued, but relieved. After a moment, he called, "Right you are, sir." The trap dropped back into place.

Rus looked at Dillon. "Who's in the other carriage?"

"Most likely a man called Tranter, and some of his men. They won't bother us, and if we need help, they'll be there."

Rus studied him. After a moment, he said, "Who is he—the man who grabbed Pris?"

Across the carriage, Dillon met his eyes. "I don't know his name, but I'd wager my life he's Mr. X."

In the carriage ahead of them, Pris gave up trying to surreptitiously free her hands. He'd used silk to bind them, too; her efforts had only pulled the knots tighter. Relaxing as best she could against what she assumed was a hackney's seat, she forced herself to calm, to take stock.

She'd nearly fainted when he'd bundled her into the carriage. He'd loosened the silk wrapped about her head, but ruthlessly replaced it once she was breathing normally. The folds were now tight around her eyes, less tight about her lips, and not at all over her nose. She could breathe, but she couldn't cry out. The best she could do was mumble.

"Why?" She knew he sat opposite her. Was he who she thought he was? Could the Honorable Mr. Abercrombie-Wallace, tallish, dark-haired, slightly heavier in build and older than Barnaby, scion of a noble house, truly be Mr. X?

"I'm quite sure, my dear, that you're intelligent enough to work it out—your fiancé wouldn't have missed the chance to crow, to portray himself as a vanquishing defender of the turf."

His voice was cool, detached. No hint of humanity colored his tone.

"You're . . . ?" It was too difficult to manage whole sentences.

"Indeed. *I'm* the one he vanquished."

She could feel his eyes on her, cold, assessing. "So . . . ?"

"So now I'm *ruined*!" His façade cracked; emotion spilled through—fury, malevolence, naked hate. Suddenly, he was raging. "Completely and utterly! Like many of my peers, I've lived my life on tick, so the fact their bills haven't been paid hasn't immediately alerted my creditors. By the time they realize that this time is different, that this time they won't be paid at all, I'll be far away. *However,* I'm *not* delighted to be forced to leave my life here, so comfortable and accommodating, and disappear. Yet *that*—" His voice cracked as he spat the word, dripping with malice.

He paused; Pris heard him draw a deep breath, sensed him struggle to resume the mild, debonair mask he showed the world. "Yet that"—his voice was once again a smooth, melodic, well-conditioned drawl—"is what your fiancé has reduced me to. I'll have to scurry off to the Continent, and live hand to mouth until I can find some gullible soul to supply my needs. But that degrading scenario is not, in itself, why you're here. You see, now I haven't even the illusion of funds, I can't gamble."

Pris frowned.

"No—not the horses. Cards are my vice, and a very expensive mistress she's proved to be. But I could keep her, could feed and clothe her as long as I could tap funds from somewhere. And yes, that's where the horses came in. I care nought for the racetrack, but I found it, and those drawn to it, so useful. So easily twisted to my purpose. It was all working so well, until . . . until your fiancé, and if I have it correctly, your brother, intervened."

His voice had altered on that last phrase. Pris fought to

suppress a shiver. Was he taking her with him to the Continent?

She gathered enough breath, enough courage to mumble, "So me?"

A long silence ensued, then he said, "So you, my dear, are my revenge."

In the carriage behind, Dillon reached up and rapped on the trap door. When it opened, he asked, "How far ahead are they?"

" 'Bout a hundred yard, maybe more."

"Get as close as you can."

"Aye, sir. Joe always takes the route down Whitehall—I'll be able to close the gap then." The trap fell back into place.

They were rolling down Pall Mall, still slow as the hackney dodged the carriages of gentlemen out for a night in the hells.

"Tothill—that's the stews, isn't it?"

Dillon nodded. "One of the many."

"Why there?"

He hesitated, then answered truthfully, "I don't like to think."

The journey seemed interminable, but after heading down Cockspur Street, the hackney wheeled into Whitehall and picked up pace.

They rattled along at a good clip, then had to slow, with much cursing from the driver, as Westminster loomed on their left and the hackney had to negotiate the largely pedestrian traffic thronging the square before the Guild Hall.

At last they pulled free, but the cursing continued. Dillon risked standing, and pushed up the trap. "What is it?"

"Lost 'im!" the driver wailed. "I know he went up 'ere, but he's turned off somewheres."

Dillon swore and leaned out of the window to the right. "Slow down—we'll search."

Rus hung out of the other window as they rolled slowly along, but the bulk of Westminster Abbey blocked that side of the street. Then the abbey ended, and he peered into the night. A street opened ahead. As they neared, the driver called, "Should I head up to Tothill, then?"

"Wait!" Rus stared. "Down there—is that them?"

"That's him!" The driver swung his horse around, and they clattered down.

"Right two ahead," Dillon called.

"I see him." The driver took the turn too fast; he slowed, corrected, then swore volubly again. "Gone again."

"Search!" Dillon ordered.

They headed into a maze of narrow, cluttered lanes and fetid alleyways. It had always struck Dillon as one of fate's ironies that some of the worst stews in the capital existed in the shadow of the country's most venerated abbey. They quartered the area, the black carriage now directly behind them; they occasionally stopped to listen, and heard the clop of the other hackney's horse, but never spotted it. They reached one edge of the densely packed area; the driver slowed.

He leaned around the edge of the box to speak to Dillon. "We'll never find him this way, guv, but where he's gone in, he has to come out, and I know where he'll do that. Do y'want to try that way?"

Dillon hesitated, then nodded. "Yes."

Looking across the carriage, he met Rus's eyes. "Better to risk being a few minutes behind, than losing her trail altogether."

Grim-faced, Rus nodded.

The driver drove back to the first corner they'd turned down. He'd barely pulled to the side of the road, when he called, " 'Ere he comes now! Hey, Joe—pull up!" To make sure of it, the driver angled his horse across the street.

His mate drew up alongside the black carriage amid a welter of colorful curses. Dillon jumped down to the street. Rus hit the cobbles on the other side of the hackney.

" 'Ere." Joe eyed them warily. "What's up?" Belatedly, he touched his cap. "Gents?"

A smile was beyond Dillon. "You just carried a fare into the stews. A man and a lady—am I right?"

"Aye." Joe glanced at his friend.

"Just answer them. They're not after you."

"Was the lady struggling?" Rus asked.

Joe blinked. "No . . . well, not so's you'd notice. She had this thing over 'er head—she weren't fighting the gent, but then she couldn't, could she?"

"Where did you leave them?" Dillon rapped out, hideously conscious of the minutes ticking by.

"Where?" Joe stared at Dillon, then looked at his friend. "Ah . . ."

Suddenly, a shadow loomed at Dillon's shoulder. Dillon glanced at the newcomer, who'd approached on catlike feet. The man stood a head taller than Dillon, and was half again as broad, every inch of it muscle and bone. His hands were hams, his eyes small; he leaned close to tell Joe, "Mr. Tranter says as you should tell the gentl'man anything he wants to know."

Eyes like saucers, Joe just nodded.

The apparition waited, then inquired in the same innocuously dulcet tones, "What, then? Cat got your tongue?"

Joe nearly swallowed the appendage in question. He coughed, helplessly looked at Dillon. "Betsy Miller's place. That's where I set them down."

Dillon glanced at the giant. "Betsy Miller's?"

"It's a brothel," the giant helpfully supplied. "A high-class one. Caters for the likes o' the pair o'you." His nod indicated Dillon and Rus.

Over the back of Joe's horse, Dillon and Rus stared at each other.

The giant nudged Dillon. "Reckon you'll want to get on your way, like. Mr. Tranter, me, and the boys'll be right behind yer."

Dillon slammed the carriage door seconds later.

Twenty-three

Still blind and effectively dumb, Pris stumbled along what she assumed was a corridor at the top of a long flight of narrow stairs. Behind and to her side, Wallace paced, steering her, one hand wrapped about her arm.

"Here we are."

He halted her, reached across her to open a door, then pushed her through it.

She staggered over the threshold; instantly, the acrid smell she'd been aware of from the moment she'd been bundled into the building intensified. Sweat, men, and a peculiar mustiness. Starved of air, she thought she might swoon. Swaying, she held her breath, and fought the blackness back. This was not the time for sensitivity. She was going to need every ounce of wit, strength, and courage she could muster to escape whatever Wallace had planned.

She felt him tug at the knots securing the silk covering her face. An instant later, the folds loosened, then fell. While Wallace unraveled the long band, drawing it free, she licked her dry lips, then blinked and looked around.

At first glance, she thought she'd been mistaken in her impressions and Wallace had brought her up the back stairs of some mansion; the room looked like an opulently furnished bedchamber, with a large tester bed complete with red velvet hangings and crimson satin coverlet, with bloodred, embossed wallpaper on the walls. Then she blinked again, and her focus sharpened.

The velvet was thin, cheap, the satin tawdry and stained. The bed appeared solid enough, but was old and much scarred. The linen covering the pillows was worn and yellowed, the lace edgings spotted and torn.

All her impressions coalesced into one picture.

Wallace freed her hands.

She spun around, but he stood squarely between her and the door. "Where is this?"

Her voice, at least, was restored, her tone firm and sure.

Wallace was watching her closely. "This establishment is popularly known as Mrs. Miller's Sanctuary."

She arched a brow, openly suspicious.

Wallace smiled. "Indeed. Mrs. Miller is an abbess, and this is a sanctuary not for the girls who serve here, but for the gentlemen who visit to indulge their taste for females in various—shall we say esoteric?—ways. For instance, one of the specialties of the house is the deflowering of gently reared virgins. A surprising number fall on hard times, and find themselves here, selling their wares. You, of course, are hardly a pauper, but"—he shrugged—"you are here."

Pris quelled a shiver. She wasn't a virgin, but she couldn't see how that was going to help her. Stepping back, she folded her arms and glanced again at her surroundings. No door but the one beyond Wallace; no window at all.

Dillon would come after her; Rus, too. She knew it in her heart, *felt* it in her soul. She had to keep safe until they reached her.

She looked at Wallace. "Why here? Why this? As a means

of revenging yourself on Dillon and Rus, surely it lacks a certain something? Directness comes to mind."

Wallace's almost-smile chilled. "*Au contraire,* my dear. I flatter myself that the revenge I've planned will strike your fiancé and your brother where it will hurt the most—and they'll be helpless to protect themselves, or you." He shifted, viewing her, letting his gaze rove over her, not lasciviously but in cold calculation, with no more emotion than if he were assessing a side of beef.

"Consider, if you will"—his eyes rose to trap hers; his were pale, leached of recognizable feeling—"how much your fiancé has now invested in you. His love." Wallace softly snorted in derision. "His pride, too, the fool. Regardless, you've come to mean a great deal to him. As for your brother—he's not just your brother, he's your twin. More, you're his twin *sister*—his feelings for you have to run deep, have to be a part of how he sees himself. As with Caxton, you're a part of your brother."

Wallace's expression grew gloating. "What do you think it will do to them to know that because of their actions against me, they'll have brought about your ruination? More, your *defilement*?"

Pris stared at him and tried to block out his words. There was no point thinking about the pain that would cause Dillon and Rus; if she did, it would paralyze her . . . perhaps what Wallace was counting on?

Then again, she'd seen no indication that he saw her as anything other than an exceptionally beautiful but otherwise typical young lady. One who would swoon and collapse, rather than fight.

Wallace continued, his voice a smooth drawl; he was in control and knew it. "What I've planned for you, my dear, will be an excellent revenge on both Caxton and your brother. It will damage beyond bearing something they hold dear, in a way neither will ever be able to put right. It will haunt them all their days—they'll carry the guilt to their graves."

His eyes gleamed; he seemed to taste, to savor, the malice in his words. "Even with the backing of their powerful connections, they'll be helpless to repair what I've arranged to break." His gaze, cold and hard, fixed on her; his lips curved. "You."

She inwardly shook, but forced herself to ignore the room about her, to lift her chin defiantly. "What have you planned?"

He seemed amenable to explaining himself, and at some length. The longer he stood speaking with her . . .

With a wave, he indicated their surroundings. "As I mentioned, this establishment caters to a certain class of gentlemen. Those with money, and thus status. I've arranged for you to be the evening's entertainment for four young and exceedingly difficult to please bloods. Mrs. Miller was quite happy to help—she likes to keep her customers satisfied. And they'll be excellently well satisfied with the sport you'll provide them. All four, you see, are aristocrats, vicious young sods partial to the worst of perversions. They'll have seen you gracing tonnish dance floors, and will have lusted after your body from afar. All will have dreamed of having that luscious body to do with as they please . . . tonight, those dreams are going to come true."

His smile took on an edge; his eyes glittered. "Do fight them—they'll enjoy raping you all the more."

He turned and went to the door; pausing with his hand on the latch, he looked back. "If you survive the night, I'll make sure Caxton and your brother know where to find you. My only regret is that I dare not dally to witness their soul-tearing grief, but I'm sure you—and they—will understand."

A coldly triumphant glint in his eye, he swept her a mocking bow. "I'll bid you a good evening, Lady Priscilla."

Pris watched him leave; she was trying so hard not to imagine what he'd planned, her mind wouldn't function—she couldn't find any words, any more questions to delay him.

The latch clicked shut, and broke the spell. She dragged in a breath, and started toward the door—only to pull up, and step back as the door swung inward again.

Revealing one, then three more gentlemen. As Wallace had warned, they were of her class, with the telltale planes of cheeks, nose, and chin, the heavy-lidded eyes that immediately fixed on her, that roved freely over her figure as she backed; their every stalking movement screamed their self-confidence, their belief that they could seize and have whatever they wished.

All four were expensively but rakishly dressed. Their faces already bore the stamp of dissipation, along with lascivious sneers.

Their expressions openly and lecherously cruel, openly expectant, they moved into the room. She backed until her legs hit the end of the bed. She searched their faces and found no hope there; they'd been drinking but were very far from drunk. Then she looked into their eyes, and saw malice and a species of hate staring back at her.

She knew, then, that they fully intended the next hours to be worse than her worst nightmare.

The hackney driver hauled back on his reins; the carriage slowed.

Dillon was out of the door and on the cobbles before the horses came to a stamping halt. Rus tumbled out behind him.

The street was empty. "Which house?" Dillon looked up at the driver.

With his whip, the driver pointed to a narrow building on the opposite side of the street. "That's Betsy Miller's."

Dillon raced for the door, Rus on his heels.

The black carriage that had followed them from Mayfair passed; it pulled up a little way along. Dillon didn't spare it a glance. Reaching the door, he pounded on the panels.

Pleading wasn't going to work. Neither was screaming; as she watched them eyeing her, smiling with anticipation, Pris sensed that they'd like that, that sobbing and crying would only spur them on.

She'd backed as far as she could; there was nowhere she could run. No better place to stand; at least she had space to either side and some support at her back.

They'd closed the door; now they doffed their coats, tossing them onto a rickety chair in a corner. Two of them started to roll up their sleeves.

"Well, now, *Lady Priscilla.*"

The lout she instinctively knew was the leader—the dominant one, the one most important to distract—approached, weight balanced, ready to catch her should she try to bolt.

Years of wrestling with her brothers came back to her. She shifted her weight, her mind racing, assessing.

Four—at least two too many. But . . .

"*Lovely* Lady Priscilla," the leader sneered.

The others spread out, flanking him—and her. But it was the leader she watched.

He continued, his well-bred accent purring, "With that lovely mouth, and those luscious breasts, and those long, long legs, and that sweet little arse . . . my *how* you're going to entertain us tonight."

His voice changed over the last sentence, giving her a second's warning.

She braced as he and one other lunged and grabbed her arms; laughing at her attempts to resist, they effortlessly hoisted her up and back onto the bed.

Pris fought like a heathen, kicking and hitting—overconfident, they hadn't bothered to secure her limbs. The thin coverlet on which they held her down, the reek that came off it, engulfing her like a cloud, acted like a potion; a strength she hadn't known she possessed flooded her.

They cursed, exerted their strength. She bit one hand, kicked out on the other side—and felt the toe of her shoe sink into her target.

The leader howled, cupped himself, then collapsed. Her struggles shoved him off the bed; he landed with a thump.

The unexpected event transfixed the others for an instant. Pris took aim, and drove her fist up under the aristocratic nose of her second attacker.

He hadn't seen the blow coming; he took the full brunt, shrieked in pain as blood spurted. He clapped his hand to his face, but immediately pulled it away, stared in horror at his bloodied palm, then his face blanched and his eyes rolled back. He fell—across Pris, pinning her as she struggled to lever up onto her elbows.

The remaining two snarled. Aggression was suddenly thick in the air.

Pris could taste it, feel it choking her as the other two seized her arms—this time holding them down as they clambered up on their knees on the bed, using their weight to subdue her.

She threshed, but they were aided by the body of their insensate comrade. They trapped her arms, trapped her legs, leaning on her to immobilize her before they pushed their unconscious friend away and fell on her.

She gasped, and struggled for all she was worth—shut her ears to their swearing, their lewd promises of what they intended to do—but she was losing the battle, losing her air as they leaned heavily on her, grabbing her legs through her rucked gown, forcing them apart—

Something crashed.

They didn't hear. They pressed her more cruelly into the bed, their leering faces close—

Then they were gone. Flying through the air.

Pris turned her head in time to see one hit the wall. A similar thump from the opposite side of the room suggested the other had met a like fate.

She blinked, dragged much-needed air into her lungs, struggled up to her elbows, and managed to focus. On Rus, pummeling one of her attackers. She looked the other way, and found Dillon efficiently thrashing the other one.

Wriggling up, hauling her skirts out of the way, she got to her knees, and peered over the edge of the bed. The leader, still sobbing and wheezing, was writhing on the floor. She considered getting down and kicking him again. First, she clambered over to the other side and looked down. The one who'd fainted lay lifeless, still unconscious.

A condition now attained by the other two. Rus straightened as the man he'd been ministering to slid down the wall.

Pris glanced at Dillon; he'd already turned from his crumpled victim, his attention locked on her. His gaze raced over her. "Are you all right?"

She looked at him, saw the raw emotion in his face, in his eyes, and found she couldn't speak. She nodded.

Then he was there, relief sweeping through him as he swept her into his arms and crushed her to him.

She hugged him back, equally wildly, equally unrestrained. "You got here in time."

Not at any time had she doubted he would.

"I thought we wouldn't . . ." He mumbled the words against her hair.

She heard the fear, nay, terror, in them. "But you did." She hugged him again, then held out a hand to Rus, grabbed his fingers when they slid into hers. "You both got here in time."

Rus returned her squeeze, then released her hand and stepped back to look down at the unconscious man by the bed.

A heavy sigh filled the room.

It came from the door.

Rus looked, and froze. Without shifting from his position facing the bed, shielding Pris kneeling on it, Dillon turned his head.

Pris, her arms still wrapped around him, peeked around his arm, ignoring his surreptitious attempts to ease her away.

"It is so difficult to find intelligent help these days." Wallace stood in the doorway, his gaze burning with hatred, a pistol in one hand. "It appears, Lady Priscilla, that my revenge is to be commendably direct after all."

Smoothly, he raised the pistol—and leveled it at Dillon.

Dillon let Pris go. He turned.

Rus launched himself across the room.

"No!" Pris flung herself at Dillon.

The pistol discharged.

Bearing Dillon down, Pris heard a familiar whirr whizz past her ear as the pistol's report exploded through the room, loud as a cannon in the enclosed space. Dillon fell over the writhing man on the ground and hit the floor; in a tangle of arms, legs, bodies, and skirts, she landed on top of him.

Dillon caught her, lifted her—and saw Rus, hands locked on a second pistol, wrestling with Abercrombie-Wallace in the doorway. He swore, wedged Pris behind him, and fought to untangle his feet from the legs of the groaning man pinned beneath him.

He scrambled upright; over Rus's shoulder, Abercrombie-Wallace saw him.

Wallace let go of the pistol, shoving it with all his might at Rus, rocking Rus back on his heels. Wallace stepped back into the corridor; recovering his balance, Rus lunged at him.

Reaching to the side, Wallace hauled a large, shrieking female across and threw her at Rus.

The female and Rus went down, blocking the doorway.

Rus swore volubly. Dillon reached him as he pushed the woman from him and struggled to his feet.

Rus went to leap over the woman and race after Wallace.

Dillon caught his arm. "No."

The woman stopped shrieking. The clatter of Wallace's footsteps descending the stairs faded, then they heard a door slam.

Dillon exhaled, and released Rus's arm. "He's made his choice. Let him flee into the arms of his just reward."

Rus met his eyes, lowered his voice. "Those gentlemen in the black carriage?"

Dillon nodded. "Not that they're gentlemen, not by any stretch of the word."

Pris heard; she didn't understand, but she'd question them later. Now . . . now she felt shaky, so relieved to see them both hale and whole, to know she needn't fear the four "gentlemen" littering the floor.

Rising unsteadily to her knees, she put up a hand to push back the curls that had jarred loose to tumble about her face. She tucked them back; her hand brushed her ear—pain stabbed. Wincing, she felt dampness on her fingers. She looked at her hand.

At the blood streaking it.

Realized what that oddly familiar whirr had been.

She glanced up; both Dillon and Rus were helping the woman, wheezing, complaining, and protesting her innocence, to her feet. Quickly, Pris scrambled to hers, simultaneously fluffing her curls over her nicked ear. She surreptitiously wiped her hand on the crimson coverlet; at least the blood wouldn't show.

Suggesting she retreat to her parlor for a restorative, Dillon pushed the large woman out and closed the door.

Rus had already turned to survey their assorted victims. He nudged the one he'd rendered senseless with the toe of his shoe. "What should we do with these?"

A short discussion ensued. Eventually, instead of beating the four to a pulp, Rus's favored option, one with which Pris felt a certain amount of sympathy, they begged supplies from the madam, tied hands and hobbled legs, secured gags in place, and then, with all four roused if groggy, bullied them down the stairs and out into the street. There, they found the hackney Dillon and Rus had commandeered waiting, along with the one that had brought Pris to the brothel.

Joe tapped his cap. "Didn't seem right, once I thought on it. I came to see if there was anything I could do."

Pris smiled at him. "Thank you. If you could take these four scoundrels—they'll give you no trouble—and follow us?"

The black carriage had vanished. In procession, the two hackneys rattled back to Mayfair.

After their first stop, with the thrill of exacting a most suitable revenge glowing in her veins, Pris leaned against Dillon as the hackney swayed on its way to their next port of call.

She looked up at his face, caught his eyes, smiled. "You're rather good at designing devilish plans."

He looked into her eyes, then raised a hand and, gently, reverently, traced the side of her face. "When the spirit moves me."

His voice was low, a caress, a prayer. He glanced across the carriage to where Rus was studiously watching the passing façades, then bent his head, and kissed her.

Not a kiss of passion, but of thankfulness, of gratitude, of relief. She responded with the same emotions, her fingers clenching in his lapel, holding him to her.

The carriage slowed. Dillon lifted his head and looked out. "Next one."

Their vengeance was thorough, and shockingly apt. Dillon had recognized all four "gentlemen." They'd known who Pris was, had recognized her; they'd knowingly and with intent set out to ruin Lady Priscilla Dalloway, an earl's daughter. As the evening lengthened, Dillon, Pris, and Rus did the rounds of the major balls and parties, delivering each of the four, coatless, trussed, and sniveling, whence they'd come.

They delivered them to their mothers.

Four senior ladies of the ton had their evenings interrupted, disrupted, by having their errant sons thrust on their knees before them—in public. They had to sit and listen as their son's crimes were explained to them—in public, before their friends and acquaintances—by the much lionized and lauded, acknowledged ruler of the sport of kings, by his affianced wife, the fabulously beautiful earl's daughter who, kidnapped from her engagement ball and abandoned in a brothel, their vicious and dissolute sons had attempted to ruin rather than help, and by her brother, Viscount Rushworth, one of the most eligible young peers about town.

In one respect, their revenge was a reckless gamble, but all who witnessed the four spectacles were aghast. All righteously ranged themselves behind Pris in defense of gently bred ladies far and wide.

Each "gentleman," left to his mother's and the ton's mercy, found none.

It was late when they returned to Berkeley Square.

Buoyed by euphoria over having faced a terror and comprehensively triumphed, they walked into Horatia's front hall—straight into bedlam.

They'd left so precipitously no one had known where any of them had gone. Their reappearance, all a trifle less than their usual immaculate selves, brought on a spate of scoldings, along with wide-eyed demands to be told what had gone on.

Their tale, when everyone consented to sit and let them tell it, was the wonder of the night. In the hackney, they'd agreed to hold nothing back; the color and pace gave credence to their adventure, and in this case, there was no one they needed to protect.

The Honorable Hayden Abercrombie-Wallace no longer had any place in the ton. As he described their exit from the brothel onto a street with only two hackneys waiting, Dillon wasn't sure Wallace would still be among the living.

Everyone was predictably horrified, fired with indignation and righteous zeal, yet also glad to have been there to hear the tale, to have, however vicariously, shared in the downfall of the gentleman who had come worryingly close to holding the racing world to ransom.

Dillon, Rus, and Pris were hailed as heroes again; those who didn't know the full story of the substitution switch begged enlightenment from those who did. Barnaby, delighted even though he was miffed to have missed the action, left to take the word to Bow Street.

Meanwhile, Horatia's ball, which had been on the point of breaking up in confusion, took on new life. The musicians played softly in their alcove while the guests sat, talked, and marveled for what was left of the night.

Dillon glanced at Pris. She had a bright smile fixed on her face; beneath it, she was wilting. He was perfectly certain she wasn't truly listening to the *grande dame* bending her ear.

The instant the lady moved on, he touched Pris's arm, then closed his hand around hers as she turned his way. "Let's go home."

To Flick's house, where he could deal with the roiling, seething, unsettling emotions surging through him. He wasn't entirely sure what they were, or how to ease them.

Terror, fear, and relief had burgeoned, but then washed through him and subsided, leaving whatever this was behind. Exposed. Undeniable.

He'd hidden his emotions from everyone, even her, until now. Looking into her eyes as she searched his face, he let her see, and simply said, "I've had enough."

She hesitated for only a heartbeat, then nodded. "I'll tell Rus and Eugenia."

Dillon waited by the door. When she returned to his side, they found Horatia, who in the circumstances allowed them to slip quietly away. Taking Pris's hand, Dillon led her out of the ballroom, away from the glad furor of their victory, out into the cool of the night.

Jake, their driver, had elected to wait. He took them up and drove them the short distance to Half Moon Street. Dillon insisted on tipping him generously, even though Jake protested that the excitement had been gratuity enough; they parted with good wishes all around.

Dillon used his key to the front door. The house lay silent, sunk in peace; the servants had retired, and all the other above-stairs occupants were still at Horatia's. Quiet content wrapped about them as in the dark they climbed the stairs; reassurance that all was well had laid calming hands on him by the time they reached Pris's chamber and went in.

Pris crossed to the dressing table and set down her reticule; shrugging off her cloak, she let it fall over the stool. Dillon lit the candelabra on the dresser, shrugged out of his coat and waistcoat, then crossed to the hearth, where a fire was burning low. Crouching, he stirred it to life.

With a sigh, she turned, sank onto the stool, and watched him. Watched the flames rise, leap, and light his face.

She'd eagerly lent her aid with his plan to disgrace her four attackers; she'd stood beside him while they'd told Horatia's guests their tale. Now, however, she felt not just outwardly bedraggled, with her crumpled gown, her disarranged curls, and the bruises on her wrists, but rough and rather ragged inside, as if her very emotions had been abraded.

As for Dillon . . . she hadn't recognized or understood that look in his eyes, but she'd sensed, from the moment they'd taken stock in the brothel chamber, that he'd slammed a door on his reactions and had ruthlessly contained them through the following hours . . . none knew better than she that such control had its limits.

He reached for a log and laid it on the flames. She watched, savoring the play of muscles beneath the fine linen of his shirt, content that he was there, soothed by his presence. He was the only person she could have imagined being alone with in that moment. He'd spent most of the recent nights with her, in this room; she would have missed him had he not been there.

Soon he had a lovely fire blazing in the hearth, throwing light and welcome heat into the room. He rose, and stood staring down at the flames. She rose, too, and went to stand beside him.

His hand found hers; she twined her fingers with his.

After a moment, he shifted, and drew her into his arms.

She went readily, eagerly, lifting her face as he bent his head. His lips covered hers; she parted them, and welcomed him in.

Not the smooth, sophisticated, charming him but that other him, the passionate man that lurked behind the social mask. She tasted him, the untamed, not entirely safe, thrilling, exciting, wickedly sinful him.

She drew him to her. With her lips, with her body, she tempted and taunted, lured him with a wild and wicked promise of her own, offered her own passion, her heart and soul, in return for his.

The kiss turned greedy; her head started to spin.

One arm tightened, possessive and steely, about her

waist. His other hand rose, pushing aside her loosened curls to frame her face—

Pain stabbed, sharp, intense; she jerked, winced, before she remembered . . .

"What is it?" He'd lifted his head on the instant. He looked at his fingers, then pushed back her curls. "My God, you're bleeding!"

Pris fleetingly closed her eyes. *Damn!* "It's just a little nick." Opening her eyes, she tried to push back, but the arm about her waist gave not an inch.

"A nick? When . . ."

Dillon realized. He saw the faint powder burns around the ragged tear in the rim of her shell-like ear, the perfect alabaster curve desecrated beyond repair. She wouldn't die, the wound would heal, but that perfect curve would never be perfect again.

Remembered terror, he discovered, could be worse than the original fear. Could be deeper, broader, courtesy of time and the ability to think, to imagine, to fully comprehend what might have been.

An icy rage filled him, fueled by that stark terror. He blinked, and all he saw was the black well of despair that had so nearly claimed her—and him.

"You got this when you tried to save me." His voice was even—too even—his tone deathly cold.

Her head rose; his hand fell from her face as she angled her chin at him. "I didn't just try—I *saved* you. *You* were just standing there, letting him shoot at you!"

Everything male in him rose up and roared, *"Damn it! That's not the point!"*

She didn't so much as flinch. Instead, she leaned nearer and face-to-face clearly enunciated, "It is to me. You were about to get shot—what did you expect me to do? Sit safely shielded behind you and wring my hands?"

"Yes!" He forced his hands from her; it was that or shake her. "That's *precisely* what you should have done."

She pulled back and stared at him. "Don't be daft."

"Daft?" He clutched his hair and swung away from her. "Damn it, Pris, you were nearly *raped. Would* have been raped if Rus and I hadn't got there in time—and all because of *me*. Because of my wonderful plan to trap Mr. X, to protect us, to . . . to do what duty suggested."

Unyielding before the hearth, Pris frowned at him. "Yes, I know. But you *did* get there in time." She watched him pace before her, read the agitation in every wild and violent movement. What was this?

He shook his head. His face was set. "Yes, but . . . none of that was important. I thought it was, and at one level it is, but not at the level that matters most. *You* are important, and you—and what we have, you and I—all of that *I put at risk*." He halted, met her eyes, his gaze dark, turbulent, a little wild. "Bad enough. That's something I'll have to live with—something I'll never do again. Never risk again. *But*"—his hands fisted at his sides—"then *you*—you risked *yourself*! Trying to save me! Don't you ever do such a foolish thing again!"

She returned his furious glare, opened her mouth—

"Don't think I'm not grateful, but . . ." He dragged in a breath, spoke through clenched teeth. "You are going to promise me you'll never, *ever*, put yourself at risk again, not for anything. You promised me you never would—"

"Not unless you were with me! You were! That was the point—I had to save you."

"I don't *care*! You are going to promise me you'll never, ever, regardless of anything, risk yourself in any way whatever again!"

She narrowed her eyes on his. She let a telling moment tick by. "And if I won't?"

His nostrils flared, his chest swelled; his entire body went rigid. "If you won't, then I'll just have to make sure you never again have the chance . . ."

She listened, amazed, as he described in inventive detail

just how he would restrict her freedom, hem her in and restrict her ability to ever put herself in the way of any risk—no matter how infinitesimal.

How he would make it totally impossible for her to be her.

If it had been anyone but him, she would have screamed her defiance. Instead, she watched him pace, rant, and rave—watched his sophisticated carapace crack and shatter and fall away, leaving him exposed, vulnerable . . .

Blocking out his words, she concentrated on what he was really saying.

What emotion was riding him, driving him.

You are my life. You mean too much to me.

She saw, understood, and waited.

Eventually, he realized she wasn't reacting. He stopped and looked at her. Frowned. "What?"

She couldn't tell him what she'd seen in him, how it only made her love him more. She met his gaze, and quietly said, "Do you remember, when I asked how much you would surrender . . . for me, for my love? Do you recall what you replied?"

He studied her for a long moment. His lips thinned. " 'How much do you want.' "

She nodded. "You'll also recall I didn't reply." He stiffened; before he could speak she continued, *"This"*—she waved between them—"is part of the answer."

Stepping away from the fire so the flickering light reached his eyes, she held his gaze. "What I want from you in return for my hand is a partnership. A partnership of equals, each with our own strengths, our own weaknesses, maybe, and also our own wills and needs and wants."

Her gaze locked with his, she tilted her head. "We're alike in many ways—you understand how I feel. However you feel about me, I feel the same about you. So no, I won't sit meekly by when your life is at risk, any more than you would if mine were. I will always claim the right to act, to choose my path." She let her lips curve. "Just as I chose you—not just now, but in the summerhouse by the lake. That first time wasn't because of the register, although I allowed you to think so. That time, as with all subsequent times, was simply for you. Just you. You were all and everything I'd ever wanted, ever dreamed could be, so I gave and took, all those nights ago."

Drawing breath, she spread her hands; speaking truth at this level, this directly, was harder than she'd thought. "And what we have now—you, me, and what's between us—that's created by both of us, and if I lose you, I lose that, too. You can't expect me not to act to protect you, just as you would me. We're wild, we take risks, but we protect what's important to us—that's how we are, how we'll always be.

"I can't change, any more than you can. The price of my love is that you accept me as I am, not as you—or at least some part of you—might prefer me to be. My price is that you acknowledge what you know to be the truth—that I won't be your possession, yours to rule, that I'm as wild and reckless as you, that whatever danger you court, I'll be there, by your side, that whatever comes in the future to threaten us we'll meet it together, defend *us* together."

She paused. There was no sound in the room bar the crackling of the fire. She continued to hold his gaze, too dark for her to read, and slowly raised her hand—offered it to him. "I'm willing to accept you as you are—exactly as you are, *all* you are." His fingers closed, tight, about hers. She smiled. "I can't ask if you'll pay the price for my love when you already have it . . . but will you do the same for me? Will you accept me as me?"

For a long moment, he didn't answer, then he closed his eyes and sighed. "Not willingly." He opened his eyes; a flame lit the darkness. "But I'll do it. I'll do anything for you."

Dillon stared into her emerald eyes, and wondered where his violence and the terror behind it had gone. He could only marvel at her ability to cut through to the heart of him, to the soul of his needs, and soothe him. "Tonight . . ." He grimaced. "Just now—"

She came into his arms. "Tonight's behind us, past—and we have more than enough to deal with tomorrow." She held his gaze for a moment, then laid her hand on his cheek. "Let it go."

She was right. They were here, together, safe and free. Their future, joint and shared, beckoned. Their partnership for life.

He couldn't argue, didn't want to.

And she knew.

She took his hand and led him to her bed, and he let her. Let her take him in her arms, into her body, and lead him to paradise. To the wild and reckless place that together they could journey to, to the world that was wholly theirs, one of shared pleasures and joys created and embellished by one powerful, undeniable, irresistible force, their shared love.

They gave themselves up and it took them. Lifted them high, filled them with glory, fractured and claimed them, then, like warmed husks tossed on the wind, left them to drift slowly back to earth, to the soft sheets of her bed, to the warmth of each other's arms.

He settled her beside him, within the circle of his arms, felt the power drift like a benedictory hand over them.

She nuzzled his chest, then sighed.

Eyes closed, his arms around her, he murmured, just loud enough for her to hear, "Regardless, I'm not letting you near a pistol again."

She chuckled, then softly humphed.

He smiled, and slept.

Late the next morning, Dillon stretched beneath the covers, then glanced at Pris, slumped, sated, beside him.

He hadn't left before dawn; he much preferred waking up

beside her—he might as well start as he meant to go on.

"You should go," she mumbled, prodding his side.

The prods were weak; he grinned and remained where he was. From where he lay, all the world seemed rosy . . . except for one thing.

He glanced at the tumbled jumble of black curls poking above the covers. "This wedding of ours . . . does it really have to be so large? So involved?"

She stirred; one eye opened and regarded him, then she raised a brow.

"What I mean . . ." He sighed, shifted to face her, and confessed, "I'd much rather get a special license, do the deed, and whisk you away, back to Newmarket, so we can make a start on setting up our home together." He raised his brows back. "What do you think?"

The truth was he was feeling rather desperate, especially after the previous evening. Especially after all he'd felt, all he'd realized. Being married to Pris, getting her married to him, was his most urgent priority.

She studied his eyes, then smiled, raised a hand, and patted his cheek. "I think that's a pleasant dream, but it *is* a dream."

He managed not to frown, but disgruntlement wasn't far away. "So you really want a huge wedding?" He wouldn't have thought it of her—she was normally as impatient, if not more so, than he.

"Heavens, no! But they do."

He frowned then, but she shook her head at him. "You can't disappoint them, and, in truth, they're doing it for you."

"But . . ." He wheedled, he whined, he tried every argument he could think of, but, finally, he realized she was right; he didn't have it in him to disappoint Flick, Eugenia, Horatia, and all the rest. Especially not after all they'd done to help him.

He pulled a face at her, then inspiration struck. "Perhaps if you 'persuaded' me?"

She grinned, and did. She put her heart and soul into addling his brain sufficiently for him to smile and accept the inevitable.

A monstrous big wedding, complete with all the associated tortures.

In the blissful end, a quiet voice whispered that it was a small price to pay for this much love.

They were married in the church at Newmarket. The event, held just after the end of the racing season, was hailed as the highlight of the social year.

The other members of the Dalloway family and a host of connections traveled from Ireland to be present; still others journeyed from all over England to witness the nuptials of the Earl of Kentland's eldest daughter. The Cynsters and various other Caxton connections thronged the town; the gathering outside the church when the bride and groom emerged from the chapel was immense, swelled by hordes of local residents eager to see their hero wed.

Smiling proudly, Dillon refused to let go of Pris's hand as they stopped here and there on their way to the waiting carriage; they'd already weathered a veritable storm of rice. There were many among the crowd they owed a word, a greeting, an acknowledgment, but finally they reached the carriage, and amid rousing cheers, rolled away to the wedding breakfast.

Demon and Flick had insisted on holding the celebration at their home. By the time Dillon and Pris stepped out on the lawn beyond the drawing room, the wide expanse was already dotted with guests.

Dillon's two closest friends, Gerrard Debbington and Charlie Morwellan, had stood as his groomsmen. Gerrard was waiting just beyond the terrace with his wife, Jacqueline; Dillon and Pris joined them. As Gerrard and Jacqueline had wed only a few months before, the four had much in common.

"I'm still struggling to keep all the names and connections straight," Jacqueline confessed. "And the clan only keeps growing!"

Pris laughed. "And in more ways than one." She met Jacqueline's bright eyes; Jacqueline had whispered that she was increasing, something anyone seeing her beatific smile would surely guess.

Charlie came up as Gerrard and Jacqueline moved on. "Two down. I'm the last man left standing."

Dillon clapped him on the shoulder. "Your time will come."

Pris listened as Dillon and Charlie ribbed each other; when she and Dillon were about to venture on, she murmured, "Just remember—there's no escape."

Charlie stared at her. She smiled, patted his arm, and let a chuckling Dillon lead her away.

There were so many guests to speak with that her head was soon reeling, but it was a giddy, pleasurable feeling, one she embraced. While she hadn't specifically wished for it, she was now glad she'd listened to older and wiser heads, agreed to the large wedding, and persuaded Dillon to do the same. There was something so special in having everyone there to share the day; she would never forget these moments for as long as she lived—and that felt very right.

Barnaby was waiting amid the crowd. He apologized for broaching the subject before saying, "Stokes told me they pulled Abercrombie-Wallace's body from the Thames a week ago."

She frowned. "He drowned?"

Barnaby hesitated, but at a nod from Dillon said, "No. His throat was cut . . . eventually. From what Stokes said, Wallace's death wasn't peaceful."

All three of them exchanged glances, then, as one, closed the door on the past and turned their minds to thoughts more in keeping with the day.

Dillon was conscious of a heightened sensitivity, an awareness of people and their interactions, that he couldn't recall possessing before. He sensed a connectedness, warm and assured, intangible yet so powerful he felt he could almost touch it, as they chatted to Devil and Honoria, to Demon and Flick, to Gabriel and Alathea, and the other Cynster couples who had been a constant in his life over the last decade.

He felt the touch of that intangible force even more personally when he embraced his father, then watched the General beam at Pris, when he was the recipient of backslaps and warm handshakes from Rus and the earl, and when Pris laughed and wildly hugged them both.

He felt it when he saw Rus and Adelaide share a secret smile.

Pris's brother Albert, and her younger brother and sisters, were all present, Albert interested in all around him—in the stud and the town and Dillon's work—while the younger crew ran wild beneath the shade trees, laughing and playing with Nicholas and Prue and the small army of other children present. Dillon saw Pris, Flick, and a host of other ladies smile fondly, not just at their own siblings or offspring, but at others, too.

Inclusive, all-embracing.

As he strolled arm in arm with Pris through the throng, all in some way part of his extended family, he felt the strands of that familiar, warm and pleasurable power twining and sliding like ribbons linking them all.

Husband to wife, parent to child, sibling to sibling, twin to twin, between lovers, between uncles and aunts and nieces and nephews, the strands of that power reached and touched, linked and held, connected and supported.

Love.

It was in the air in so many guises, it was impossible not to feel it.

Dillon felt, saw, acknowledged, accepted, and let the power flow through him.

He glanced at Pris, on his arm, then looked around with eyes fully open. Soon, he hoped, another strand of love—the one that linked father to child—would find him. They moved through the crowd, and he drank in all he saw, and felt his heart swell with anticipation.

The majority of males, most of whom were married, congregated to one side of the lawn. Leaving Pris with the ladies sitting under the trees, Dillon joined the gentlemen, inwardly smiling at their glib comments, their habitual grumbling giving voice to their reluctance over attending such emotion-laden events.

He now had a deeper understanding of that reluctance. In this arena, it was exceedingly difficult not to wear their hearts on their sleeves, not to openly acknowledge that power that claimed them all so thoroughly. And that always left them feeling exposed and vulnerable, a reality they never appreciated acknowledging, even if for only a short time.

Regardless, they would always attend as commanded by their mothers, their wives, their daughters or sisters.

Because, as he now understood, when all was considered and weighed in the balance, feeling vulnerable and exposed was a very small price to pay . . . for this much love.

The following is a preview of

The Taste of Innocence

the newest Cynster novel from

New York Times bestselling author

STEPHANIE LAURENS

On sale in hardcover March 2007

February 1833
Northwest of Combe Florey, Somerset

He had to marry, so he would.

But on his terms.

The latter words resonated through Charlie Morwellan's mind, repeating to the thud of his horse's hooves as he cantered steadily north. The winter air was crisp and clear. About him the lush green foothills of the western face of the Quantocks rippled and rolled. He'd been born to this country, at Morwellan Park, his home, now a mile behind him, yet he paid the arcadian views scant heed, his mind relentlessly focused on other vistas.

He was lord and master of the fields about him, filling the valley between the Quantocks to the east and the western end of the Brendon Hills. His lands stretched south well beyond the Park itself to where they abutted those managed by his brother-in-law, Gabriel Cynster. The northern boundary lay ahead, following a rise; as his dappled gray gelding, Storm, crested it, Charlie drew rein and paused, looking ahead, yet not really seeing.

Cold air caressed his cheeks. Jaw set, expression impassive, he let the reasons behind his present direction run through his mind—one last time.

He'd inherited the earldom of Meredith on his father's death three years previously. Both before and since he'd ducked and dodged the inevitable attempts to trap him into matrimony. Although the prospect of a wealthy, now-over-thirty-years-old-as-yet-unwed earl kept the matchmakers perennially salivating, after a decade in the ton he was awake to all their tricks; time and again he slipped free of their nets, taking a cynical male delight in so doing.

Yet for Lord Charles Morwellan, 8th Earl of Meredith, matrimony itself was inescapable.

That, however, wasn't the spur that had finally pricked him into action.

Nearly two years ago his closest friends, Gerrard Debbington and Dillon Caxton, had both married. Neither had been looking for a wife, neither had needed to marry, yet fate had set her snares, and each had happily walked to the altar; he'd stood beside them there and known they'd been right to seize the moment.

Both Gerrard and Dillon were now fathers.

Storm shifted, restless; absentmindedly, Charlie patted his neck.

Connected via their links to the powerful Cynster clan, he, Gerrard, and Dillon, and their wives Jacqueline and Priscilla, had met as they always did after Christmas at Somersham Place, principal residence of the Dukes of St. Ives and ancestral home of the Cynsters. The large family and its multifarious connections gathered biannually there, at the so-called Summer Celebration in August and again over the festive season, the connections joining the family after spending Christmas itself with their own families.

He'd always enjoyed the boisterous warmth of those gatherings, yet this time . . . it hadn't been Gerrard's and Dillon's children per se that had fed his restlessness but rather what they represented. Of the three or them, friends for over a decade, *he* was the one with a recognized duty to wed and produce an heir. While theoretically he could leave his brother Jeremy, now twenty-three, to father the next generation of Morwellans, when it came to family duty he'd long ago accepted that he was constitutionally incapable of ducking. Letting one of the major responsibilities attached to the position of earl devolve onto Jeremy's shoulders was not something his conscience or his nature, his sense of self, would allow.

Which was why he was heading for Conningham Manor.

Continuing to tempt fate, courting the risk of that dangerous deity stepping in and organizing his life, and his wife, for him, as she had with Gerrard and Dillon, would be beyond foolish; *ergo* it was time for him to choose his bride. Now, before the start of the coming season, so he could exercise his prerogative, choose the lady who would suit *him* best, and have the deed done, final and complete, before society even got wind of it.

Before fate had any further chance to throw love across his path.

He needed to act now to retain complete and absolute control over his own destiny, something he considered a necessity, not an option.

Storm pranced, infected with his underlying impatience. Subduing the powerful gelding, he focused on the landscape ahead. A mile away, comfortably nestled in a dip, the slate roofs of Conningham Manor rose above the naked branches of its orchard. Weak morning sunlight glinted off diamond-paned windows; a chill breeze caught the smoke drifting from the tall Elizabethan chimney pots and whisked it away. There'd been Conninghams at the manor for nearly as long as there'd been Morwellans at the park.

Charlie stared at the manor for a minute more, then stirred, eased Storm's reins, and cantered down the rise.

* * *

"*Regardless,* Sarah, Clary and I *firmly* believe that you have to marry first."

Seated facing the bow window in the back parlor of Conningham Manor, the undisputed domain of the daughters of the house, Sarah Conningham glanced at her sixteen-year-old sister, Gloria, who stared pugnaciously at her from her perch on the window seat.

"*Before* us." The clarification came in determined tones from seventeen-year-old Clara—Clary—seated beside Gloria and likewise focused on Sarah and their relentless pursuit to urge her into matrimony.

Stifling a sigh, Sarah looked down at the ribbon trim she was unpicking from the neckline of her new spencer, and with unimpaired calm set about reiterating her well-trod arguments. "You know that's not true. I've told you so, Twitters has told you so, and Mama has told you so. Whether I marry or not will have no effect whatever on your come-outs." Freeing the last stitch, she tugged the ribbon away, then shook out the spencer. "Clary will have her first season next year, and you, Gloria, will follow the year after."

"Yes, *but* that's not the point." Clary fixed Sarah with a frown. "It's the . . . the *way* of things."

When Sarah cocked a questioning brow at her, Clary blushed and rushed on, "It's the unfulfilled expectations. Mama and Papa will be taking you to London in a few weeks for your *fourth* season. It's obvious they still hope you'll attract the notice of a suitable gentleman. Both Maria and Angela accepted offers in their second season, after all."

Maria and Angela were their older sisters, twenty-eight and twenty-six years old, each married and living with their husbands and children on said husbands' distant estates. Unlike Sarah, both Maria and Angela had been perfectly content to marry gentlemen of their station with whom they were merely comfortable, given those men were blessed with fortunes and estates of appropriate degree.

Both marriages were the conventional norm; neither Maria nor Angela had ever considered any other prospect, let alone dreamed of it.

As far as Sarah knew, neither had Clary or Gloria. At least, not yet.

She suppressed another sigh. "I assure you I will happily accept should an offer eventuate from a gentleman I can countenance being married to. However, as that happy occurrence seems increasingly unlikely"—she gave passing thanks that neither Clary nor Gloria had any notion of the number of offers she'd received and declined over the past three years—"I assure you I'm resigned to a spinster's life."

A massive overstatement, but . . . Sarah flicked a glance at the fourth occupant of the room, her erstwhile governess, Miss Twitterton, fondly known as Twitters, seated in an armchair to one side of the wide window. Now in middle age, Twitters's gray head was bent over a piece of darning; she gave no sign of following the familar discussion.

If she couldn't imagine being happy with a life like Maria's or Angela's, Sarah could equally not imagine being content with a life like Twitters's.

Gloria made a rude sound. Clary looked disgusted. The pair exchanged glances, then embarked on a verbal catalog of what they considered the most pertinent criteria for defining a "suitable gentleman," one to whom Sarah would countenance being wed.

Folding her new spencer with the too-garish scarlet ribbon now removed, Sarah smiled distantly and let them ramble. She was sincerely fond of her younger sisters, yet the gap between her twenty-three years and their ages was, in terms of the present discussion, a significant gulf.

They naïvely considered marriage a simple matter easily decided on a list of definable attributes, while she had seen enough to appreciate how unsatisfactory such an approach often was. Most marriages in their circle were indeed contracted on the basis of such criteria—and the vast majority, underpinned by nothing stronger than mild affection, degenerated into hollow relationships in which both partners turned elsewhere for comfort.

For love.

Such as love, in such circumstances, could be. Somehow less, somehow tawdry.

For herself, she'd approached the question of marriage with an open mind and open eyes. No one had ever deemed her rebellious, yet she'd never been one to blindly follow others' dictates, especially on topics of personal importance. So she'd looked and studied.

She now believed that when it came to marriage there was something better than the conventional norm. Something finer, an ideal, a commitment, that compelled one to grasp it, a state glorious enough to fill the heart with yearning and need, and ultimately with satisfaction, a construct in which love existed *within* the bonds of matrimony rather than outside them.

And she'd seen it. Not in her parents' marriage, for that was a conventional if successful union, one without passion but based instead on affection, duty and common cause. But to the south lay Morwellan Park, and beyond that Casleigh, the home of Lord Martin and Lady Celia Cynster, and now also home to their elder son, Gabriel, and his wife, Lady Alathea née Morwellan.

Sarah had known Alathea, Gabriel, and his parents for all of her life. Alathea and Gabriel had married for love; Alathea had waited until she was twenty-nine before Gabriel had come to his senses and claimed her as his bride. As for Martin and Celia, they had eloped long ago in a statement of passion impossible to mistake.

Sarah met both couples frequently. Her conviction that a love match, for want of a better title, was a goal worthy of her aspiration derived from what she'd observed between

Gabriel and Alathea and, once her wits had been sharpened and her eyes had grown accustomed, from the older and somehow deeper and stronger interaction between Martin and Celia.

She freely admitted she didn't know what love was, had no concept of what the emotion would feel like within a marriage. Yet she'd seen evidence of its existence in the quality of a smile, in the subtle meeting of eyes, the gentle touch of a hand. A caress outwardly innocent yet laden with meaning.

When it was there, love colored such moments. When it wasn't . . .

But how did one define that love?

And did it mysteriously appear, or did one need to work for it? How did it come about?

She had no answers, not even a glimmer, hence her unwed state. Despite her sisters' trenchant beliefs, there was no reason she needed to marry. And if the emotion that infused the Cynsters' marriages was not part of an offer made to her, then she doubted any man, no matter how wealthy, how handsome or charming, could tempt her to surrender her hand.

To her, marriage without love held no attraction. She had no need of a union devoid of that finer glory, devoid of passion, yearning, need, and satisfaction. She had no reason to accept a lesser union.

"You will promise to look, won't you?"

Sarah glanced up to find Gloria leaning forward, brown brows beetling at her.

"*Properly*, I mean."

"*And* that you'll seriously consider and *encourage* any likely gentleman," Clary added.

Sarah blinked, then laughed and sat up to lay aside her spencer. "No, I will not. You two are far too impertinent—I'm sure Twitters agrees."

She glanced at Twitters to find the governess, whose ears

were uncommonly sharp, peering myopically out of the window in the direction of the front drive.

"Now who is that, I wonder?" Twitters squinted past Clary, who swiveled to look out, as did Gloria. "No doubt some gentleman come to call on your papa."

Sarah looked past Gloria. Blessed with excellent eyesight, she instantly recognized the horseman trotting up the drive, but surprise and a frisson of unnerving reaction—something she felt whenever she saw him—stilled her tongue.

"It's Charlie Morwellan," Gloria said. "I wonder what he's doing here."

Clary shrugged. "Probably to see Papa about the hunting."

"But he's never here for the hunting," Gloria pointed out. "These days he spends almost all his time in London. Augusta said she hardly ever sees him."

"Maybe he's staying in the country this year," Clary said. "I heard Lady Castleton tell Mama that he's going to be hunted without quarter this season from the absolute instant he returns to town."

Sarah had heard the same thing, but she knew Charlie well enough to predict that he would be no easy quarry. She watched as he drew rein at the edge of the forecourt and swung lithely down from the back of his gray hunter.

The breeze ruffled elegantly cropped golden locks. His morning coat of brown Bath superfine was the apogee of some London tailor's art, stretching over broad shoulders before tapering to hug his lean waist and narrow hips. His linen was pristine and precise; his waistcoat, glimpsed as he moved, was a subtle medley of browns and black. Buckskin breeches molded to long powerful legs before disappearing into glossy black Hessians, completing a picture that might have been titled *Fashionable Peer in the Country.*

Irritation stirring, Sarah drank in the vision; his appearance—and its ridiculous effect on her—really wasn't fair. He knew she existed, but beyond that . . . From this distance, she couldn't see his features clearly, yet her besotted memory filled in the details—the classic lines of brow, nose, and chin, the aristocratic angles and planes, the patriarchal cast of high cheekbones, the large heavy-lidded, lushly lashed blue eyes, and the distracting, frankly sensual mouth and mobile lips that allowed his expression to change from delightfully charming to ruthlessly dominating in the blink of an eye.

She'd studied that face—and him—for years. She'd never known him to appear other than he was, a wealthy aristocrat descended from Norman lords with a streak of Viking thrown in. Despite his aura of ineffable control, of being born to rule without question, a hint of the unpredictable warrior remained, lurking beneath his smooth surface.

A stable boy came running. Charlie handed over his reins, spoke to the lad, then turned for the front door. As he passed out of their sight around the central wing, Clary and Gloria uttered identical sighs and turned back to face the room.

"He's really top of the trees, isn't he?"

Sarah doubted Clary required an answer.

"Gertrude Riordan said that in town he drives the most *fabulous* pair of matched grays." Gloria bounced, eyes alight. "I wonder if he drove them home? He would have, don't you think?"

While her sisters discussed various means of ascertaining whether Charlie's vaunted matched pair were at Morwellan Park, Sarah watched the stable boy lead Charlie's hunter off to the stables rather than walk the horse in the forecourt. Whatever Charlie's reasons for calling, he expected to be there for some little while.

Her sisters' voices filled her ears; recollections of their earlier comments whirled kaleidoscopically—to settle, abruptly, into an unexpected pattern. Leading to a startling thought.

Another frisson, different, more intense, slithered down Sarah's spine.

"Well, m'boy—" Lord Conningham broke off and laughingly grimaced at Charlie. "Daresay I shouldn't call you that anymore, but it's hard to forget how long I've known you."

Seated in the chair before the desk in his lordship's study, Charlie smiled and waved the comment aside. Lord Conningham was a bluff, good-natured man, one with whom Charlie felt entirely comfortable.

"For myself and her ladyship," Lord Conningham continued, "I can say without reservation that we're both honored and delighted by your offer. However, as a man with five daughters, two already wed, I have to tell you that their decisions are their own. It's Sarah herself whose approval you'll have to win, but on that score I know of nothing whatever that stands between you and your goal."

After a fractional hesitation, Charlie clarified, "She has no interest in any other gentleman?"

"No." Lord Conningham grinned. "And I would know if she had. Sarah's never been one to play her cards close to her chest. If any gentleman had captured her attention, her ladyship and I would know of it."

The door opened; Lord Conningham looked up. "Ah, there you are, m'dear. I hardly need to introduce you to Charlie. He has something to tell us."

With a smile, Charlie rose to greet Lady Conningham, a sensible, well-bred female he could with nothing more than the mildest of qualms imagine as his mother-in-law.

Ten minutes later, her wits in a whirl, Sarah left her bedchamber and hurried to the main stairs. A footman had brought a summons to join her mother in the front hall.

She'd detoured via her dressing table, dallying just long enough to reassure herself that her gown of fine periwinkle blue wool wasn't rumpled, that the lace edging the neckline hadn't crinkled, that her browny-blond hair was neat in its knot at the back of her head and not too many strands had escaped.

Quite a few had, but she didn't have time to let her hair down and redo it. Besides, she only needed to be neat enough to pass muster in case Charlie saw her in passing; it was too early for him to be staying for luncheon and there was no reason to imagine that her mother's summons was in any way connected with his visit . . . other than the ridiculous suspicion that had flared in her mind and set her heart racing. Reaching the head of the stairs, she started down, her stomach a hard knot, her nerves jangling.

All for nothing, she chided herself. It was a nonsensical supposition.

Her slippers pattered on the treads; her mother appeared from the corridor beside the stairs. Sarah's gaze flew to her face, willing her mother to speak and explain and ease her nerves.

Instead, her mother's countenance, already wreathed in a glorious smile, brightened even more. "Good. You've tidied." Her mother scanned her comprehensively from her forehead to her toes, then beamed and took her arm.

Entirely at sea, her questions in her eyes, Sarah let her mother draw her a few yards down the corridor to where an alcove nestled under the stairs.

Releasing her arm, her mother clasped her hand and squeezed her fingers. "Well, my dear, the long and short of this is that Charlie Morwellan wishes to offer for your hand."

Sarah blinked; for one instant, her mind literally reeled.

Her mother smiled, not unsympathetically. "Indeed, it's a surprise, quite out of the blue, but heaven knows you've dealt with offers enough—you know the ropes. As always the decision is yours, and your father and I will stand by you regardless of what that decision might be." Her mother paused. "However, in this case both your father and I would ask that you consider very carefully. An offer from any earl would command extra attention, but an offer from the eighth Earl of Meredith warrants even deeper consideration."

Sarah looked into her mother's dark eyes. Quite aside from her pleasure over Charlie's offer, in advising her in this, her mother was very serious.

"My dear, you already have sufficient comprehension of Charlie's wealth. You know his home, his standing—you know *of* him, although I accept that you do not know him, himself, well. But you do know his family."

Taking both her hands, her mother lightly squeezed, her excitement returning. "With no other gentleman have you had, nor will you have, such a close prior connection, such a known foundation on which you might build. It's an unlooked-for, entirely unexpected opportunity, yes, but a very good one."

Her mother searched her eyes, trying to read her reaction. Sarah knew all she would see was confusion.

"Well." Her mother's lips set just a little; her tone became more brisk. "You must hear him out. Listen carefully to what he has to say, then you must make your decision."

Releasing her hands, her mother stepped back, reached up and tweaked Sarah's neckline, then nodded. "Very well. You must go in—he's waiting in the drawing room. As I said, your father and I will accept whatever decision you make. But please, do think very carefully about Charlie."

Sarah nodded, feeling numb. She could barely breathe. Turning from her mother, she walked, slowly, toward the drawing room door.

Charlie heard a light footstep beyond the door. He turned from the window as the knob turned, watched as the door opened and the lady he'd chosen to be his wife entered.

She was of average height, subtly but sensuously curved; her slenderness made her appear taller than she was. Her face was heart-shaped, framed by the soft fullness of her lustrous hair, an eye-catching shade of gilded light brown. Her features were delicate, her complexion flawless—including, to his mind, the row of tiny freckles across the bridge of her nose. A wide brow, that straight nose, arched brown brows and long lashes combined with rose-tinted lips and a sweetly curved chin to complete a picture of restful loveliness.

Her gaze was unusually direct; he waited for her to move, knowing that when she did it would be with innate grace.

Her hand on the door knob, she paused, scanning the room.

His eyes narrowed slightly. Even across the distance he sensed her uncertainty, yet when her gaze found him she hesitated for only a second before, without looking away, she closed the door and came toward him.

Calmly, serenely, but with her hands clasping, fingers twining.

She couldn't have expected this; he'd given her no indication that marrying her had ever entered his head. The last time they'd met socially, at the Hunt Ball last November, he'd waltzed with her once, remained by her side for fifteen minutes or so, exchanging the usual pleasantries, and that had been all.

Deliberately on his part. He'd known—for years if he stopped to consider it—that she . . . regarded him differently. That it would be very easy, with just a smile and a few words, for him to awaken an infatuation in her, a fascination with him. Not that she'd ever been so gauche as to give the slightest sign, yet he was too attuned to women, certainly, it seemed, to her, not to know what quivered just beneath her cool, clear surface, the sensible serenity she showed to the world. He'd made a decision, not once, but many times over the years, that it wouldn't do to stir that pool, to ripple her surface. She was, after all, sweet Sarah, a neighbor's daughter he'd known all her life.

So he'd been careful not to do what his instincts had so frequently prompted. He'd studiously treated her as just another young lady of his local acquaintance.

Yet when he'd finally decided to select a wife, one face had leapt to his mind. He hadn't even had to think—he'd simply known that she was his choice.

And then, of course, he had thought and visited all the arguments, the numerous criteria a man like him needed to evaluate in selecting a wife. The exercise had only confirmed that Sarah Conningham was the perfect candidate.

She halted before him, confidently facing him with less than two feet between them. Confusion shadowed her eyes, a delicate blue the color of a pale cornflower, as she searched his face.

"Charlie." She inclined her head. To his surprise, her voice was even, steady if a trifle breathless. "Mama said you wished to speak with me."

Head high so she could continue to meet his gaze—the top of her head barely reached his chin—she waited.

He felt his lips curve, entirely spontaneously. No fuss, no fluster, and no "Lord Charles," either. They'd never stood on formality, not in any circumstances, and for that he was grateful.

Despite her outward calm, he sensed the brittle, expectant tension that held her, that kept her breathing shallow. Respect stirred, unexpected but definite, yet was he really surprised that she had more backbone than the norm?

No; that, in part, was why he was there.

The urge to reach out and run his fingertips across her collarbone—just to see how smooth the fine alabaster skin was—struck unexpectedly; he toyed with the notion for a heartbeat, but rejected it. Such an action wasn't appropriate, given the nature of what he had to say, the tone he wished to maintain.

"As I daresay your mother mentioned, I've asked your father's permission to address you. I would like to ask you to do me the honor of becoming my wife."

He could have dressed up the bare words in any amount of platitudes, but to what end? They knew each other well, perhaps not in a private sense, but his sisters and hers were close; he doubted there was much in his general life of which she was unaware.

And there was nothing in her response to suggest he'd gauged that wrongly, even though, after the briefest of moments, she frowned.

"Why?"

It was his turn to feel confused.

Her lips tightened and she clarified, "Why me?"

Why now? Why after all these years have you finally deigned to do more than smile at me? Sarah kept the words from her tongue, but looking up into Charlie's impassive face, she felt an almost overpowering urge to sink her hands into her hair, pull loose the neatly arranged tresses, and run her fingers through them while she paced. And thought. And tried to understand.

She couldn't remember a time when she hadn't had to, every time she first set eyes on him, pause, just for a second, to let her senses breathe. To let them catch their breath after it had been stolen away simply by his presence. Once the moment passed, as it always did, then all she had to do was battle to ensure she did nothing foolish, nothing to give away her secret obsession—infatuation—with him.

It was nonsense and brought her nothing but aggravation, but no amount of lecturing over its inanity had ever done an ounce of good. She'd decided it was simply the way she reacted to him, Viking-Norman Adonis that he was. She'd reluctantly concluded that her reaction wasn't her fault. Or his. It just *was*; she'd been born this way, and she simply had to deal with it.

And now here he was, without so much as a proper smile in warning, asking for her hand.

Wanting to *marry her.*

It didn't seem possible. She pinched her thumb, just to make sure, but he remained before her, solid and real, the heat of him, the strength of him wrapping about her in pure masculine temptation, even if now he was frowning, too.

His lips firmed, losing the intoxicating curve that had softened them. "Because I believe we'll deal exceptionally well together." He hesitated, then went on, "I could give you chapter and verse about our stations, our families, our backgrounds, but you already know every aspect as well as I. And"—his gaze sharpened—"as I'm sure you understand, I need a countess."

He paused, then his lips quirked. "Will you be mine?"

Nicely ambiguous. Sarah stared into his gray-blue eyes, a paler shade of blue than her own, and heard again in her mind her mother's words: *Think very carefully about Charlie.*

She searched his eyes, and accepted that she'd have to, that this time her answer wasn't so clear. She'd lost count of the times she'd faced a gentleman like this and framed an answer to that question, couched though it had been in many different ways. Never before had she even had to think of the crux of her reply, only the words in which to deliver it.

This time, facing Charlie . . .

Still holding his gaze, she compressed her lips fleetingly, drew in a breath and let it out with, "If you want my honest answer, then that honest answer is that I can't answer you, not yet."

His dark gold lashes, impossibly thick, screened his eyes for an instant; when he again met her gaze his frown was back. "What do you mean? When will you be able to answer?"

Aggression reached her, reined but definitely there. Unsurprised—she knew his charm was nothing more than a veneer, that under that glossy surface he was stubborn, even ruthless—she studied his eyes, and unexpectedly found answers to two of the many questions crowding her mind. He did indeed want her—specifically *her*—as his wife. And he wanted her soon.

Quite what she was to make of that last, she wasn't sure. Nor did she know how much trust she could place in the former.

She was aware that he expected her to back away from his veiled challenge, to temporize, to in one way or another back down. She smiled tightly and lifted her chin. "In answer to your first question, you know perfectly well that I had no warning of your offer. I had no idea you were even thinking of such a thing. Your proposal has come entirely out of the blue, and the simple fact is I don't know you well enough"—she held up a hand—"regardless of our long acquaintance—and don't pretend you don't know what I mean—to be able to answer you yeah or nay."

She paused, waiting to see if he would argue. When he simply waited, lips even thinner, his gaze razor sharp and locked on her eyes, she continued, "As for your second question, I'll be able to answer you once I know you well enough to know which answer to give."

His eyes bored into hers for a long moment, then he stated, "You want me to woo you."

His tone was resigned; she'd gained that much at least.

"Not precisely. It's more that I need to spend time with you so I can get to know you better." She paused, her eyes on his. "And so you can get to know me."

That last surprised him; he held her gaze, then his lips quirked and he inclined his head.

"Agreed." His voice had lowered. Now he was talking to her, with her, no longer on any formal plane but on an increasingly personal one, his tone had deepened, becoming more private. More intimate.

She quelled a tiny shiver; at that lower note his voice reverberated through her. She'd wanted to increase the space between them for several minutes, but there was something in the way he looked at her, the way his gaze held her, that made her hesitate, as if to edge back would be tantamount to admitting weakness.

Like fleeing from a predator. An invitation to . . . her mouth was dry.

He'd tilted his head, studying her face. "So how long do you think getting to know each other better—well enough—will take?"

There was not a glint so much as a carefully veiled idea lurking in the depths of his eyes that made her inwardly frown. She was tempted to state that she had no intention of being swayed by his undoubted, unquestioned, utterly obvious sexual expertise, but that, like fleeing, might be seriously unwise. He'd all too likely interpret such a comment as an outright challenge.

And that was, she was certain, one challenge she couldn't meet.

She hadn't, not for one moment, been able to—felt able to—shift her gaze from his. "A month or two should be sufficient."

His face hardened. "A week."

She narrowed her eyes. "That's impossible. Four weeks."

He narrowed his back. "Two."

The word held a ring of finality she wished she could challenge—wished she thought she *could* challenge. Lips set, she nodded. Curtly. "Very well. Two weeks—and then I'll answer you yeah or nay."

His eyes held hers. Although he didn't move, she felt as if he leaned closer.

"I have a caveat." His gaze, at last, shifted from her eyes, drifting mesmerically lower. His voice deepened, becoming even more hypnotic. "In return for me agreeing to a two-week courtship, you will agree that once you answer and accept my offer"—his gaze rose to her eyes—"we'll be married by special license no more than a week later."

She licked her dry lips, started to form the word why.

He stepped nearer. "Do you agree?"

Trapped—in his gaze, by his nearness—she just managed to draw in a breath. "Very well. *If* I agree to marry you, then we can be married by special license."

He smiled—and she suddenly decided that no matter how he took it, fleeing was an excellent idea. She tensed to step back.

Just as his arm swept around her, and tightened.

His eyes held hers as he drew her, gently but inexorably, into his arms. "Our two-week courtship . . . remember?"

She leaned back, keeping her eyes on his, her hands on his upper arms. His strength surrounded her. She felt giddy. "What of it?"

His lips curved in a wholly masculine smile. "It starts now."

Then he bent his head and covered her lips with his.